A Retelling of

Bayard Taylor's

Joseph and His Friend: A Pennsylvania Story

By Wayne Goodman

First paperback printing, July 2017

Copyright © 2017 by Wayne Goodman

Joseph and His Friend: A Pennsylvania Story by Bayard Taylor is in the Public Domain and not subject to Copyright protection.

All rights reserved. No part of this book may be reproduced, scanned, or distributed in any printed or electronic form without permission. Please do not participate in or encourage piracy of copyrighted materials in violation of the author's rights. Purchase only authorized editions.

Version 1.00

21 June 2017

ISBN: 978-0-9989007-4-2

Library of Congress Control Number: 2017907687

waynegoodman**books**

waynegoodmanbooks@gmail.com
Twitter: @Wgoodmanbooks

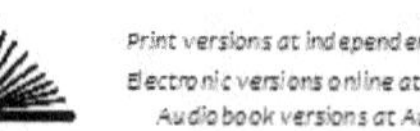
Print versions at independent booksellers
Electronic versions online at Amazon.com
Audiobook versions at Audible.com

Table of Contents

Acknowledgments

FIRST OF ALL, I must thank Anthony Marra, author of *A Constellation of Vital Phenomena* and *The Tsar of Love and Techno: Stories*. At a reading of Russian-American writing in February 2016, I read from my book *Vanya Says, "Go!": A Retelling of Mikhail Kuzmin's "Wings"* and Anthony read from his *Tsar of Love and Techno*. We spoke afterwards; I told him I had really enjoyed his writing and reading. In our discussion, he suggested I had developed a new genre: Retelling of historically-significant books mostly forgotten. Having taken a book nearly lost to obscurity, I had resurrected it and given it new life. That got me thinking about what other books might be out there waiting to be rediscovered.

A search of LGBTQ Literature provided a few potential works, but it was Bayard Taylor's *Joseph and His Friend: A Pennsylvania Story* that captured my attention because it was touted as "the first American Gay novel." With a bit of sleuth searching, I found a downloadable copy and my work began.

I must also thank Bayard Taylor for writing this ground-breaking story, as well as the eminent 19th Century poet Fitz-Greene Halleck, on whom the book was based.

Dr. Ajuan Mance, instructor of English Literature at Mills College in Oakland, California, provided guidance regarding the nomenclature and history of African-Americans of the 19th Century.

Also, special mentions for my Readers: Vincent Meis, Kevin Killian, Dr. Ajuan Mance, Edmund Zagorin, and Carlye Knight.

As always, I conclude with my gratitude to my partner, Richard May, without whose support I would never have begun nor finished this work. Thank you, my love.

Bayard Taylor

ORN IN 1825 TO A QUAKER COUPLE living in Chester County, Pennsylvania, Bayard Taylor began writing poetry in his late teens. With money he earned from his writing, he traipsed throughout Europe, sending travel articles home that got published in *The New York Tribune*, *The Saturday Evening Post*, and *The United States Gazette*.

In 1848, Horace Greeley hired Taylor to cover the California Gold Rush for *The Tribune*. His travelogues sold thousands of copies.

He married Mary Agnew in 1849, but she died within a year from tuberculosis. During his time in California, Taylor entered a contest sponsored by P. T. Barnum to write a set of lyrics for Jenny Lind. His *Greetings to America* won the prize, and the "Swedish Nightingale" sang the song all across the country.

In 1851, he met the renowned writer Fitz-Greene Halleck in New York at Bixby's Hotel, a notorious hang-out for "bachelors" and "poets." The two men maintained a life-long friendship and correspondence.

Taylor traveled abroad once again, writing of his experiences along the way, and he ended up accompanying Commodore Perry to Japan in 1852.

After a successful lecture tour along the East Coast, Taylor went to Germany in 1856, where he met and interviewed the prominent scientist and explorer Alexander von Humboldt (a bachelor and most likely homosexual).

He married Maria Hensen in 1857 and the couple moved to San Francisco, where Taylor continued to lecture. His first novel, *Hannah Thurston*, published in 1863, received critical acclaim, and his career as a novelist took off. In 1866, the Taylors relocated to Denver, where Bayard became the editor of *The Rocky Mountain News*.

When Fitz-Greene Halleck died in 1869, Taylor returned to

the East Coast to deliver an address at the unveiling of a memorial in Halleck's home town of Guilford, Connecticut. With his friend gone, Taylor was finally able to write the story he had been longing to tell.

Joseph and His Friend: A Pennsylvania Story, his fourth and final novel, appeared in 1870, first serialized in *The Atlantic*. It was not well-received. People felt the plot contrived and the characters distasteful. He continued to write until the time of his death, mainly poetry, travelogues, and an English translation of Goethe's *Faust*.

Taylor accepted an appointment as Minister to Prussia in 1878. Unfortunately, he died in Berlin six months after his arrival.

While Taylor never openly professed his attraction to men in public, his homage to Halleck (and his association with other known homosexuals) suggests he struggled with his own feelings, leading him to marry as insurance against accusations. *Joseph and His Friend: A Pennsylvania Story* paved the way for a new generation of authors to write more openly about same-sex relationships.

The Story Behind the Story

FITZ-GREENE HALLECK WAS BORN in the Puritanical town of Guilford, Connecticut, in 1790. He realized fairly early on that he had different desires from other boys. While his classmates went out for sports and chased girls, Fitz-Greene wrote frilly poetry and dreamed of courting other boys.

His first romantic encounter arrived from Cuba in the person of Carlos Menie. Sent by his father to learn English, Menie somehow ended up in the same village as 19-year-old Halleck. The two spent much time together, and following Menie's return to Havana a year later, Halleck penned scores of poems inspired by his pining for the dark-skinned boy he greatly missed.

At the first opportunity, Halleck ran off to New York, where he had heard he would meet men with similar inclinations. His poetry brought him to national attention early on, and he became known as one of this country's best writers. However, it was not the public's adoration he desired. Halleck wanted more than anything to be in a loving relationship with another man.

In confessional letters to his sister Maria, Fitz-Greene described the attributes (and pitfalls) of the men he knew through his work or at a series of Greenwich Village boarding houses. They all fell short of his high standards for matrimony.

Through a friend of Maria, Halleck finally met the man of his dreams, Doctor Joseph Rodman Drake, in 1813. Halleck and Drake quickly began a life together than included writing poetry collaboratively and entertaining other bachelor friends.

Bowing to family pressure, Drake married Sarah Eckford, a woman from a wealthy family, in 1816. Halleck refused to be part of the wedding ceremony, and the two hardly communicated for months.

In 1817, the two finally reconnected, at Drake's insistence. They worked together until Drake's early death in 1820.

Halleck quickly assumed the role of widow, with grief unbounded. The love of his life had perished much too soon. He wrote an elegy for Drake, and a few of the stanzas are carved into the headstone.

> *Green be the turf above thee,*
> *Friend of my better days!*
> *None knew thee but to love thee*
> *Nor named thee but to praise.*

Throughout the rest of his life, Halleck mourned Drake. His creative output diminished, and, starting in 1832, he worked for John Jacob Astor as an account manager, hardly ever writing poetry during that time.

After the death of Astor in 1848, Halleck could no longer afford living in New York, and he returned to his native Guilford. He spent the rest of his days lecturing and writing infrequently. Although he had received offers of marriage from women, some of whom were wealthy devotees, Halleck turned them all down, determined to live the life of a "gay bachelor."

Many compared his work (and life) to that of Lord Byron, for whom he compiled a complete edition entitled *Works of Lord Byron*.

Following the death of Halleck, Bayard Taylor decided to write a novel loosely based on his friend, the famous bachelor poet. There are many comparisons, parallels, and allusions to the relationship between Halleck and Drake woven into *Joseph and His Friend*. Due to the culture of the time, Taylor could not openly discuss the true nature of the friendship, and he had to resort to subtle phrases, coded language, and euphemisms. However, careful reading evokes the same-sex nature of the characters.

Homosexuality in the United States

MUCH OF THE HISTORY OF SAME-SEX CULTURE in America has been erased, forgotten, or whitewashed. There are tales of Native Americans having Two-Spirit or *berdache* tribe members who were highly regarded as spiritually-advanced. Some adopted the clothes and ways of the opposite sex, but their behavior was accepted and not considered improper.

The Judeo-Christian culture of the European explorers/ invaders did not accept same-sex relationships, and they attempted to squelch such behavior. The French tended to be more tolerant of homosexuality (France decriminalized same-sex activity in 1791), but the Protestant British accused those French Catholics of favoring a Mortal Sin.

Early Colonial laws regarding "Sodomy" and "Buggery" advocated capital punishment; however, over time, each state dropped its death sentence, with New York being one of the first, and Halleck's Connecticut being one of the last.

Due to its more relaxed and cosmopolitan nature, New York City became the center for homosexual culture in the early 19th Century. The Bowery was the hub for "like-minded" gentlemen, with such establishments as the Paresis Club, Little Bucks, Manilla Hall, the Palm Club, the Black Rabbit, Samuel Bickard's Artistic Club, the Slide, and Pfaff's.

Over time, the more conservative religious civic officials made it more difficult for same-sex couples to congregate in public, and raids on LGBTQ bars and establishments became fairly routine up until the 1969 Stonewall riots.

During the mid-19th Century, most people with homosexual feelings tended to move to larger population centers (New York, Philadelphia, Chicago, San Francisco) where they could be judged more on the quality of their work than by whom they wanted to be intimate with.

Most Judeo-Christian religions had harsh words for homosexuals, but Unitarians and the Quakers were more open to differences, as long as the differences did not compete with their core Christian values. Taylor, being brought up Quaker (and most likely homosexual himself), might have had more compassion and understanding than other writers of his time.

The word "homosexual" did not enter our common vocabulary until very late in the 19th Century. Until generally-accepted terms for people in non-heteronormative relationships emerged in the mid-20th Century, some of the derogatory words used were: sodomite, pederast, calamite, bugger, bender, poofter/poof, fairy, fey, invert, and Uranian. Some of these terms made same-sex activity sound illegal, immoral, or other-worldly. Over time, as society in general has become more tolerant and accepting, the LGBTQ communities have chosen their own labels and symbols to describe themselves.

In *Joseph and His Friend*, Taylor attempted to relate a tale of two men who found love with each other. However, due to the stringent restraints placed on mentioning such delicate subjects in literature at the time, he was not able to portray the story openly and had to use suggestive ways to describe his characters' motivations. Even so, the book has been labelled, "the first American Gay novel." *Better Angels* is my attempt to update his 1870 work, relating and retelling the tale frankly and more naturally.

Two loves I have of comfort and despair,
Which like two spirits do suggest me still;
The better angel is a man right fair,
The worser spirit a woman colour'd ill.
To win me soon to hell, my female evil
Tempteth my better angel from my side,
And would corrupt my saint to be a devil,
Wooing his purity with her foul pride.
And whether that my angel be turn'd fiend
Suspect I may, but not directly tell;
But being both from me, both to each friend,
I guess one angel in another's hell:
Yet this shall I ne'er know, but live in doubt,
Till my bad angel fire my good one out.

WILLIAM SHAKESPEARE, *Sonnet 144*

The shadows of our own desires stand
between us and our better angels, and thus
their brightness is eclipsed.

CHARLES DICKENS, *Barnaby Rudge*

The mystic chords of memory, stretching from
every battlefield and patriot grave to every
living heart and hearthstone all over this
broad land, will yet swell the chorus of the
Union, when again touched, as surely they
will be, by the better angels of our nature.

ABRAHAM LINCOLN, *First Inaugural Address*

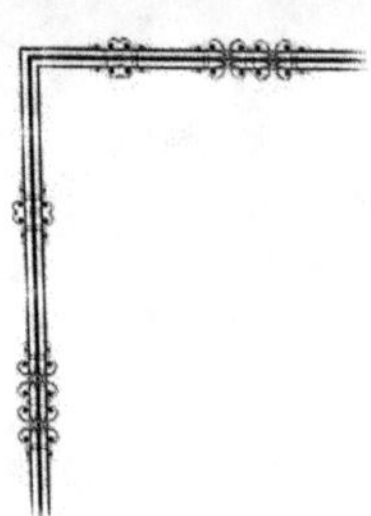

Chapter 1: Joseph and his Friend

Allegheny River Valley,
March 1867, Late Afternoon

JOSEPH AND ELWOOD LAY ON THEIR BACKS, panting for air, legs still intertwined. Sweaty and festooned with hay from the loft, they looked up at the roof.

"You got yerself a hole up there," Elwood pointed to a spot where the late afternoon sunlight busted through the thatching, illuminating the lackadaisical dust as it sifted down in no particular hurry.

Joseph smiled at his childhood friend. It had been their habit to climb up into the barn loft at least once a week to enjoy themselves for the last eight years or so. "Practicing," they called it. Preparing themselves for eventual marital conjugation.

He turned his innocent blue eyes upward. "Yes, I'll have to get Dennis on it before the rains start. Thank you, Elwood." He turned and kissed his friend lightly on the cheek.

Elwood flushed slightly. "Oh, Joseph. Don't go gettin' all romantic on me now!" He laughed loudly, an uninhibited, bucolic bray. With one hand he tousled some of his chestnut curls in a mock-feminine fashion.

Joseph winked at Elwood.

"Oh, come on, Joseph." Elwood sat up. "We're soon gonna hafta start thinkin' about gittin' married an' all. If we don't, there's sure to be talk in this little town. You know how Puritanical they can be around here. I once heard they locked up a man for kissin' his own wife on a Sunday."

"Nobody wants us, Elwood Withers," he smiled. "Nobody at all..."

"You are givin' me the guff, Joseph Asten! You are *the* most eligible bachelor I know for miles around." He poked his friend's chest, knocking some of the hay from the bare skin. "You got a farm and a wonderful little house here. So don't you go tellin' me nobody wants *you*." He poked again, and Joseph squirmed.

"Name one," he said as he sat up and poked Elwood just below the ribcage.

"Yow! Any of the Henderson sisters would gladly give themselves to you."

Joseph stared up at the hole in his barn's roof. "That Miss Lucy Henderson does stand out a bit to me, now that you mention it."

"An' I might just take a shine to her sister, Elizabeth, I might."

The two looked at each other and grinned. "Imagine us as married men, Elwood. I cannot see what benefit marriage would bring that we don't already enjoy. You and I could just remain happy bachelors together the rest of our lives."

Elwood busted out laughing. "It would be mighty difficult to raise children with just the two of us, you know. An' I'm right sure your Aunt Rachel is lookin' to have someone take the chores offa her hands."

Joseph smiled at his friend, "That could be you, Elwood."

Another round of laughter erupted. "Oh, Joseph, you go on so..." He pawed at the air as if he were waving a dainty handkerchief.

The two sat, half-naked in the hay, just staring at each other.

"Master Joseph!" came the call from just outside the barn. "Master Joseph!" Dennis, the hired man searched for his boss.

"Up here." Joseph stuck his head out the small window. "I'm

in the loft... just tidying up." Elwood had to suppress a laugh. Joseph turned back and put a finger to his lips in hopes of keeping his friend quiet. "I'll be down in a few minutes."

Elwood pointed up at the hole.

"Miss Rachel wanted me to let you know supper will be ready in an hour." He began walking back to the house.

"Thank you, Dennis. Oh, I will need my mount this evening after supper, and when we get a chance, there's a hole in the roof that will need fixing before the rains come," he shouted out the window and then turned back to his friend. "Now, you, Elwood Withers," he pointed a finger, "You go home and get yourself ready for this evening. I'll meet you at the gate at eight o'clock."

"The gate at eight," Elwood intoned. "Got it, boss. Anythin' else?"

"Not that I can think of. Just dress nice, especially if you want to impress your Miss Elizabeth Henderson."

"I believe I clean up right nice, I do." Elwood stood, put on his overalls, brushed off a few stray pieces of straw and started for the ladder down.

"And one more thing, Elwood."

"Yes?" He stopped with one foot on the top rung.

Joseph took in the lanky form of his friend, reminiscing about the activity that had occurred just a few minutes ago, "Next time we come up here, it's *my* turn."

"Oh, yes, sir," Elwood giggled and his hazel eyes flashed as he began to climb down. "Your turn, indeed." His head disappeared from view.

Joseph Asten sat for a few minutes in contemplation, his arms clasped about his bent knees. He had recently celebrated his 23rd birthday, and there would soon be new social expectations foisted upon him. Most men his age already had wives and babies. Girls did not interest him in the same way his other male friends talked about, and he would be very hesitant to give up his happy bachelor life. Sooner or later, there would be pressure to marry and father children.

He had no memory of his own father, who died when Joseph was but a few months old. His mother raised him with the best of intentions, shielding her boy as best she could from what she believed were the evils of the world. A rigidly-pious Quaker woman, she had nothing but tenderness for him. Wanting him to stay a little boy as long as possible, she steered him away from severe studies and lusty sports.

Joseph's mother died soon after he turned 12, and he went to live with her unmarried sister, Rachel Miller. His aunt wanted to continue the same tender treatment, but her habit of expression had become more restrained, possibly due to her barren life. Young Joseph saw her behavior as though she were guided by the strictest sense of duty, and from his perspective she seemed cold, severe, and unsympathetic. He either had to allow her absolute control of all his actions, or he wounded her to the heart by asserting a moderate amount of independence.

As he walked back to the 100-year-old farmhouse nestled atop a gentle knoll, he looked over the 200-acre farm, with excellent soil and plentiful stock, and Joseph felt fortunate in that moment. Yes, everything was in good order, and he would be the sole owner, but he frequently felt more of a slave to the farm than its proprietor. The physical requirements and the mechanical exhaustion of maintaining the crops and animals had begun to occupy his body and mind, yet he plowed on with the vague hope that some richer development of life might be his reward. But there were times when the fields looked very dreary to him. The solidly-rooted trees, growing under conditions they were powerless to choose or change, resembled tiresome types of himself. Even the beckoning heights far down the valley failed to touch his fancy with the hint of a broader world. *You must be perfectly contented in your place!* his own sense of duty called to him, but there was still the miserable, ungrateful, inexplicable fact of discontent.

His fields followed the soft undulation of the hills, with a view of a large stream to the south. It had been a region of peace and repose for as long as he and his neighbors could remember. Quiet, drowsy, and resplendent with natural beauty, the herd-speckled meadows belonged to the same families for generations. The bountiful soil had provided regular crops, and some of the farmers became notably rich; however, others lived in poverty.

Order and morality, as well as intermarriage and intercourse, maintained the constant stability, and any variation needed to be suppressed. Any hint of a different view or unusual taste excited the suspicion of the community, and most folks seemed incapable of abiding independent thought on moral and social questions. At times, a political excitement swept over the neighborhood, but in a mitigated form. The discussions that took place between those of opposite faiths generally repeated the arguments furnished by their respective county newspapers.

Joseph, with his two-fold nature, had begun to confront the common mold. As a boy, the probable map of his life had been drawn: young man, husband, father, and comfortable old man. But his nature reached beyond the ordinary necessities, and he hungered for the taste of higher things. He couldn't be content accepting the mechanical faith of passive minds, and in his own spiritual and mental growth he dared to challenge this long struggle of the human race.

The house's alternating pattern of red and black bricks had nearly surrendered to the proliferation of ivy vines. Gables terminated in broad double chimneys that straddled a railed walkway that hardly anyone ever used. He stepped up onto the stone-paved porch that ran along the front, shaded by two enormous sycamores older than the house itself. As he pulled the door open, he gazed back at the manicured garden, with its clambering grapevines and small, ornamental shrubs reminiscent of the taste from another generation. In the center of the turfy lawn stood a superb weeping willow that created a living wall separating the house from the barn.

Joseph entered and passed through the uninhabited dining room. The table appeared to be partially set for three people, and he ignored the noise emanating from the kitchen, which was most likely his aunt. As he grabbed the handrail for the stairway up to his room, it shuddered and shivered in his grasp. He shook his head slightly, making a mental note to add this to the growing list of chores for him and Dennis to get around to.

Thirty minutes later, he descended the same stairs, careful not to press too hard on the rail. Joseph had dressed in his Sunday finest, anticipating the evening's social. Aunt Rachel stood near the dining table, placing flatware for the imminent meal. She glanced up at her nephew with a shocked look, and her grayed head jerked backward.

"Joseph! You startled me! I expected you to come in from the barn, not the back stairs." Her nose wrinkled as he approached the table. "Is that pomatum I smell?" She wiped her hands on an off-white apron covering the front of a plain, brown floor-length dress.

"Yes, Aunt Rachel. I wanted to look my best for this evening." He ran a hand along his slicked-back, lemon-and-clove-scented hair for effect, then pulled out his usual chair and sat.

Rachel shook her head and asked, "What in the world does this mean?" After a few seconds, when Joseph had not responded, she poured the tea in eloquent silence, a hundred interrogation marks hanging in the air.

Dennis, still in his work clothes, entered and halted immediately. Because of his wall-eyed vision, he could see both of the others simultaneously. The room reeked of palpable tension, like the time he had killed Rachel's favorite speckled hen by mistake.

After a short period of furtive side glances, Rachel and Dennis sat. The three ate in wordless silence. Each, in turn, took awkward looks at the others, but no one spoke, thus, elevating the level of unease gradually. At one point, the hired man looked as if he were about to laugh, whether due to his own nervousness or the complete silliness of the situation.

Having completed his meal, Joseph stood and walked to the window, repeatedly drumming his fingers upon the pane. Rachel stood and began to clear the plates and cups together, delaying their removal, as was her wont.

Dennis leapt up, donned his coat and went to the door. With one hand on the knob, he asked, "Shall I saddle the horse right off?"

Joseph did not respond directly. After a moment's hesitation he responded, "I guess so," and Dennis exited quickly.

Rachel stood holding two silver spoons in one hand, and Joseph still drummed on the window, but with a more irregular rhythm.

"Well," his aunt spoke with her usual calmness, "a body is not bound to dress particularly fine for a death watching, though I would grant him all respect as with anyone else. Don't forget to ask Maria if there's anything I can do for her."

Joseph turned round with a surprised look, "Why, Aunt Rachel, what are you talking about?"

"You're headed over to the Penn's place, aren't you? They do have nearer neighbors, but when a good man dies, everybody is free to offer their services. He was always strong in the faith." She continued to assemble the used settings.

"Why no!" he exclaimed, face reddening up to the roots of his dark-blond hair. "I am spending the evening at the Warriners. There's to be a little company there—a neighborly gathering. It might have been talked of for a long while, but I was only invited today. I saw Bob, in the road-field." He pointed.

Rachel's face muscles began to tighten but quickly a small smile formed, and Joseph relaxed a bit. "Isn't it rather a strange time of year for evening parties?" The tone of her voice seemed a bit harsh and judgmental.

"They meant to have it in cherry-time, Bob said, when Anna's visitor had come from town." Joseph studied his aunt's expression for clues.

"That, indeed! I see!" She began fussing at the table again. "It's a sort of celebration for–oh, what's her name?– Blessing, I know... but the other.... ohhhh... Anna Warriner was there last Christmas, and I don't suppose the high notions are out of her head yet. Well, I hope it'll be some time before they take root here!" The clattering of china accompanied her prattle. "Peace and quiet–peace and quiet–that's been the token of the neighborhood, but city ways are the reverse." She clanked a teacup on top of the stack.

"All the young people are going," Joseph suggested. He referred to the men his age or younger, as so many of the slightly older ones had been lost in The War. "And so –"

"O! I don't say you shouldn't go... *this* time," she interrupted, "for you ought to be able to judge for yourself what's fit and proper... and what is not." She began placing her hands under the stack of dishes. "I should be sorry, to be sure, to see you doing anything and going anywhere that would make your mother uneasy if she were still with us. It's so hard to be conscientious, and to mind a body's bounden duty, without seeming to interfere." She sighed and lowered the pile back to the table, picked up a corner of her apron and touched it to the corner of her eye. Perhaps mentioning Joseph's dear, departed mother would soften the headstrong nephew.

"But, remember, Aunt Rachel," Joseph replied after a few contemplative moments, "I was not yet old enough to go into society. I am certain she would want me to have some independence... when the time came." His aunt's eyes appeared to be tearing up, but Joseph had some familiarity with this ruse of hers. "Besides, I am doing no more than all the young men of the neighborhood."

Rachel sniffled slightly, adding to the melancholy, "Ah, yes, I know. But they've got used to it by degrees–and mostly in their own homes–and with sisters to caution them, whereas, you're younger according to your years and innocent of the ways and wiles of men and... and girls." She turned her head away in a dramatic sweep.

Joseph knew his aunt's accusation to be quite correct, and he wanted to shout out: *Why am I younger 'according to my years' and why am I so much more 'innocent'–or do you mean ignorant–than others*? However, he blurted out instead, "Well, how am I ever to learn?"

His aunt faced him once again, eyes still moist from tears. "By patience... and taking care of yourself, Joseph. There's always safety in patience."

He bent his neck back, so that he looked up at the ceiling, and gritted his teeth.

"I don't mean you shouldn't go this evening," Rachel uttered, and Joseph's gaze returned to her, "since you've promised it and made yourself smart." She smiled tightly at his choice of attire. "But mark my words, this is only the beginning. The season makes no difference. City people never seem to know that there's such things as hay-harvest and corn to be worked. They come out for merry-makings in the busy time, and they want us country folks to give up everything for their pleasures. We've got to gear up the tired plough horses for 'em, and the cows'll have to wait an hour or two longer to be milked, the chickens killed half-grown, and the washing and baking put off when it comes to *their* way." She reached under the pile of plates again. "They're mighty nice and friendly while it lasts, but go back to 'em in town a week, a month, six months afterwards, and see whether they'll so much as ask you to take a meal's victuals!" Rachel lifted the stack as if it were a newborn hog and started toward the kitchen.

"It's not likely that I shall ever be asked to the Blessings for a meal," he chuckled to himself at the preposterous idea, "or that this Miss Julia–as they call her–would ever interfere with our harvesting or milking." He followed his aunt into the next room.

"The airs they put on!" She gently lowered the plates on the sideboard. "She'll very likely think that she's doing you a favor by so much as simply speaking to you." She held her hands up by the side of her head and then flapped her wrists smartly. "They may be very well in their own place, but–for my part–I should like them to stay there!"

Rachel began to place the dishes in the washing tub as the sound of horse hooves approaching grew louder.

"There, comes the horse," Joseph responded, "I must be on my way. I expect to meet Elwood Withers at the lane-end." He turned to go, paused and turned back. "But–about waiting, Aunt Rachel–you hardly need –"

"O, yes! I'll wait for you, of course. Ten o'clock is not so very late for me." She smiled as she began to work the squeaky pump.

Joseph's face crinkled. "It might be a little after." He craned his neck.

"Not much, I hope, but if it should be daybreak, wait I will!" She pointed a soapy finger in the air. "Your mother couldn't expect less of me."

He gave his aunt one more skeptical glance before dashing out the door to find Dennis with the horse.

Chapter 2: City Folk at a Country Gathering

"CAN YOU TELL ME WHERE MISTER JOSEPH ASTEN LIVES?" asked a dapper young gentleman in a checked, tweed coat and squat-crowned Melon hat. "He's an old man, very much bowed and bent." Elwood Withers hooted his garish bray, shaking the very ground from atop his horse.

Joseph blushed a bit, coughed a laugh, and gave a quick look at his friend's attire. "There's plenty of time," he said as he leaned over his horse's neck to lift the gate latch.

"Oh, all right, but you must now wake up. You're spruce enough to make a figure to-night!" Elwood whistled as his friend rode through the gate.

"Oh, no doubt!" Joseph responded gravely, "but what kind of a figure?" He reached down and fixed the latch behind him. The two started up the road side-by-side.

"Some people—I've heard say—may look into the lookin'-glass every day and never know how they look. You wouldn't be askin' such a question as that if you appeared to yourself as you appear to me." Elwood winked.

Joseph smiled, but just barely. "If I could not only think of myself at all, Elwood. If I could be as unconcerned as you are..."

"But I'm not, Joseph, my boy!" Elwood exclaimed as he pulled his horse closer and laid a hand on his friend's shoulder. "I tell you, it weakens my very marrow to walk into a room full o' girls, even though I know every one of 'em. They know it, too, and—shy and quiet as they all seem—they're unmerciful." Joseph's eyes widened. "There they sit, all lookin' so different, somehow—even a feller's own sisters and cousins—fillin' up all sides o' the room, rustlin' a little and whisperin' a little, but you feel that every one of 'em has her eyes on you, and would be so glad to see you flustered." He clapped his hand on Joseph's shoulder twice. "There's no help for it, though. We've gotta grow case-hardened to that much, or how ever could a man get himself married?"

"Well, get a look at your dandy self, Mr. Withers," Joseph chided. "Your fancy suit and your very fancy hat, there."

Elwood straightened his spine. "I'm no Quaker boy, like yourself." He brushed his suit with the back of the hand holding the reins. "I saved up for months to get this beauty." Elwood smiled, revealing his large teeth. "I'm fixin' to catch me one of those Henderson girls, and I'll need all the help I can get!" Once again, his bray ricocheted off the hills.

Joseph looked over at his friend, "Were you ever in love, Elwood?"

"Well"–he jerked on the rein, pulling up the horse–"you *do* come out plump. You take the very breath out of my body." He exhaled loudly. "Have I been in love?" Elwood glanced up at the waxing half-moon in the sky. "Have I committed murder? One's about as deadly a secret as the other!"

The two looked each other in the face. Joseph searched for the answer to his question in Elwood's eyes, but innocence prevented him from perceiving the message.

"It's easy to see *you've* never been," Elwood blurted but then dropped his voice to a grave gentleness, "If I should say, 'yes,' what then?"

Joseph looked away. "Then, how do you know it–I mean–how did you first begin to find it out?" He looked back at Elwood. "What is the difference between that and the feeling you have toward any pleasant person whom you like to be with?"

"All the difference in the world!" Elwood exclaimed energetically. He knit his brow, seemingly perplexed in thought. "But I'll be shot if I know exactly what else to say. I never thought of it before." He looked off into the darkening sky. "How do I know that I am, in fact, Elwood Withers? It seems just as plain as that–and yet–for one thing, she's always in your mind, and you think and dream o' just nothin' but her, and you'd rather have the hem of her dress touch you than kiss anybody else. You just want to be near her, and have her all to yourself. And it's hard to speak a sensible word to her when you come together–but what's the use? A feller must feel it himself, as they say of experiencin' religion. You must get converted or you'll never know." He glanced over at Joseph. "Did you even understand a word of what I've said?"

"Yes," Joseph acknowledged as his head dropped a bit. "I think so." He turned to Elwood, "It's only an increase of what we all feel toward some persons." A small glimmer of a smile appeared. "I have been hoping, latterly, that it might come to me, but... but..."

Elwood clapped his hand again. "But your time will come, like every man's." He smiled. "Maybe sooner than you think. When it does, you won't need ask anybody, though I think you're bound to tell me of it, after pumpin' my own secret outta me."

Joseph looked away.

"Oh, never mind. I wasn't obliged to let you have it. I know you're close-mouthed and honest-hearted, Joseph, but I'll never ask your confidence unless you can give it freely as I give mine to you."

Joseph turned and smiled at his friend. "And have it you shall, Elwood, if my time ever comes. You know how lonely it gets on the farm, and yet it's not always easy for me to run off into company. Aunt Rachel stands in mother's place to me, and maybe it's only natural that she should be over-concerned. Anyway... seeing what she has done for my sake, I am hindered from opposing her wishes too stubbornly." He smiled. "Now, to-night, my going to this gathering didn't seem right to her, and I shall not get it out of my mind that she is waiting up, fretting, on my account."

One corner of Elwood's mouth curled up. "Young feller, your age mustn't be so tender." He looked directly at Joseph. "If you had your own father and mother, they'd allow you more of a range. Look at me, with mine!" Elwood bobbled his head from side to side. "Why, I never as much as say 'by your leave.' Quite the contrary—so long as the work isn't slighted—they're rather glad than not to have me go out. And the house is twice as lively since I bring so much fresh gossip into it. But then," he looked down at himself, "I've had a rougher bringin' up."

"I wish I had such a rough upbringing!" Joseph cried out. "Aunt Rachel doesn't tolerate gossip, but, then, I really don't hear much myself." He smiled a bit.

Elwood glanced over slyly. "Are you tellin' me that Quakers aren't given to gossip?" His brows arched.

"Yet, no, when I think of mother, it is wrong to say just that about her. What I mean is, I wish I could take things as easily as you—make my way boldly in the world, without being held back by trifles, or getting so confused with all sorts of doubts. The more anxious I am to do right, the more embarrassed I am to know what is the right thing. I don't believe you have any such troubles."

They reached a fork in the road and took the path toward the Warriners' place.

"Well, for my part, I do about as other fellers. No worse, I guess, and likely no better." Elwood glanced up at the stars just beginning to appear. "You must consider, also, that I'm a bit rougher made, besides the bringin' up, and that makes a deal o' difference. I don't try to make the scales balance to a grain. If there's a handful under or over, I think it's near enough. However, you'll be all right in a while. When you find the right girl and marry her, it'll put a new face on to you."

Joseph's expression tightened into a grimace. The thought of having to marry a woman troubled him. He could have been just as content with Elwood's companionship for the rest of his days.

"There's nothin' like a sharp, wide-awake wife, so they say," Elwood prattled on, "to set a man straight." He poked a finger upward. "Don't make a mountain of anxiety out of a little molehill of inexperience. I'd take all your doubts and more,

I'm sure, if I could get such a two-hundred-acre farm along with 'em." He laughed out loud.

"Hush!" cautioned Joseph, "I know you don't mean others to hear you. Here come two down the branch road."

Elwood removed his hand from Joseph's shoulder and shifted his horse a bit farther away. A few horsemen, sons of the neighboring farmers, joined them, and they rode together up the knoll toward the Warriner mansion. Lights from the house glimmered through the trees. The gate stood open, and a dozen vehicles sat parked in the enclosure between the barn and the house. Bright, gliding forms could be seen on the portico.

"Just see," Elwood whispered to Joseph, "what a lot of posy-colors! You can be sure that every one o' them is watchin' us. No flinchin', mind. Straight to the charge! Let's walk up together, and it won't be half as hard for you."

They dismounted and tied their horses. As Elwood suggested, they walked side-by-side up to the house. Bob Warriner, in his Sunday best as well, met them at the gate and ushered them and the other party-goers into the parlor.

The Warriner home had high ceilings with dark green and scarlet brocade wallpaper above the hip-high wainscoting. Windows were narrow, but tall, surrounded by heavy, richly-colored fabric draperies. Even though they were Quakers, they used part of their accumulated wealth to embellish their home, including the addition of a ballroom, something no other house in the county had.

Around the parlor stood a flock of young ladies, silent and cool in their gingham and muslin dresses, who watched the men arrive. Elwood looked for Elizabeth Henderson and saw her standing in a corner near the hallway arch by the stairs.

Only one of the young women sat, Miss Blessing, who occupied the rocking chair in front of the mantel-piece. With the fire behind her, she cut a distinct silhouette in the brightness, with occasional half-shadows appearing when she turned her head just so. The lamplight of the room touched some rosebuds in her hair.

Bob Warriner presented Joseph and Elwood in turn. Miss Blessing lifted her face and smiled upon each, graciously offering her slender hand. Joseph, not knowing the proper protocol, took her hand with the slightest touch, his own trembling with fear of the unfamiliar situation. Elwood, who at least had some previous experience, gently lifted the offered hand to his lips and delivered a feathery kiss.

Miss Blessing differed from the neighborhood girls in many aspects. In contrast to the plump, ruddy, self-conscious girls standing along the walls, her slender, fair-skinned form and brilliant eyes exuded confidence. The lids drooped slightly, as if kindly veiling their beams, and her thin lips fashioned a delicate, sweet curve. Dark, raven hair fell about her neck in long, shining ringlets, resting lightly on the shoulders of her cloud-like dress, white and foamy. A cluster of rosebuds lay upon her bosom as if someone had casually tossed them there.

Joseph looked at Elwood, concerned that their attire might suddenly be too coarse and ill-fitting. The girls whom they knew seemed less airy and charming compared to former occasions. The appearance of this woman from the city had descended to them out of an unknown higher sphere, and their individual deficiencies became unwelcomely evident.

Without saying a word, her amiable nature could be sensed. Miss Blessing looked about with a pleasant expression and half-smiled—but deprecatingly—as if to say: *Pray, don't be offended!* She broke the awkward silence with her clear, modulated voice, "It is beautiful to arrive at twilight, but how charming it must be to ride home in the moonlight. So different from our lamps!"

The neighborhood residents looked at each other, as she had addressed no one in particular. All hesitated, and no one replied.

Miss Blessing turned her attention to Elizabeth Henderson across the room. "But is it not awful—tell me, dear—when you get into the shadows of the forests? We are all so apt to associate all sorts of unknown dangers with forests, you know."

Elizabeth, seemingly nervous to be singled-out so, blurted, "Oh, no! I rather like it, when I have company."

"To be sure!" Elwood exclaimed with a bit of his laugh, "the shade is fulla opportunities." He left his eyes on Miss Henderson a bit longer than he should, and she turned her head abruptly.

Giggles and shrieks filled the room, with some blushing and accelerated fanning.

Miss Blessing shook her closed fan warningly at Elwood. "How wicked in you! I hope you ride home alone to-night, after that speech." She glanced at the others, "But you are all so courageous—compared with *us*." The fan now pointed at her bosom. "We are really so restricted in the city that it's a wonder we have any independence at all." Her head turned back to the fire. "In many ways, we are like children."

"O, Julia, dear!" Anna Warriner stepped forward in protest. The rich sepia color of her dress nearly matched that of the window dressings. "And *such* advantages as you have! I shall never forget the day Mrs. Rockaway called—her husband is the cashier of the Commercial Bank—and brought you all the news direct from head-quarters—as she said."

"Oh, yes," Miss Blessing cast her eyes down and answered slowly, "there must be two sides to everything, of course. How much we miss until we know the country! Really, I quite envy you."

Without realizing it, Joseph had ended up standing next to Lucy Henderson, the one he liked most of all the girls present. He looked briefly into the straightforward glance of her large, brown eyes. It was as if she could reach right in, below the troubled surface, and this unwelcomed invasion proved to be too uncomfortable. Even though their previous interactions involved free and frank conversation, with mutual interests, the current situation proved slightly different. He admired that Lucy had never dropped one of those amused side-glances or uttered one of those pert, satirical remarks, the recollections of which in other girls stung him to the quick.

Elwood's earlier discussion upon the phenomenon of love lingered in Joseph's mind, and he began—involuntarily—to examine the nature of his feeling for Miss Lucy Henderson. He realized he had attended this gathering more on the hope of meeting her than upon any curiosity concerning Miss Blessing. He glanced down at the edge of Lucy's pale pink frock and wondered if he would rather touch that than kiss anybody else. He had only kissed Elwood up to that point (aside from his relations, that is), and his attention turned to her lips, fresh and sweet as never before. It shocked his heart to feel the blood rush to his own cheeks as he thought, once more, about touching the edge of her dress.

Their eyes met again—a moment only, but an unmeasured time of delight and fear to him—and then Lucy turned her head away. He felt a lovely and bold desire to speak with her, and he fancied her face a brightened color, but when he looked again, it was gone. Lucy appeared as calm and composed as before.

During this time, a few other people had arrived, and Lucy moved aside to make room for some ladies from a neighboring town. The parlor seemed swollen with more reserved guests, and the sounds of merry chat on the portico invaded the stately constraint of the room.

Miss Blessing stood and addressed Anna Warriner, "O, *do* let us go outside! I think we are well enough acquainted now to sit on the steps together." Her hand made a slight, but irresistibly inviting, gesture, and all began funneling toward the grand entrance.

As the throng pressed cheerfully out, Julia seized Anna's arm and drew her back into the dusky nook under the staircase.

"Quick, Anna! Who is the roguish one they call Elwood?" she whispered. "*What* is he?"

Miss Warriner smiled knowingly. "A farmer. He works his

father's place on shares."

"Ah!" came Miss Blessing's response in a peculiar tone. "And the blue-eyed, handsome one, who came in with him?" Her head swiveled to look at Joseph as he exited. "He looks almost like a boy."

Anna followed Julia's gaze. "Joseph Asten? Why, he's twenty-two or three. He has one of the finest properties in the neighborhood—and money besides—they say. Lives alone with an old dragon of an aunt as housekeeper." She looked back at her guest. "Now, Julia dear, there's a chance for you!"

"Pshaw, you silly Anna!" Miss Blessing whispered, playfully pinching her ear. "You know I prefer intellect to wealth."

"As for that –" Anna began, but before she could say anything more, Julia danced down the hall toward the front door, her gossamer skirts puffing and floating out until they brushed the wainscoting on either side.

Miss Blessing hummed a tune—"O Night! O Lovely Night!"–skimmed over the doorstep and descended into an ethereal heap against one of the pillars of the portico. Her pupils, clear and brilliant in the moonlight, showed fully from beneath the now fully-opened eyelids.

"Now, Mr. Elwood—Oh, excuse me—I mean Mr. Withers," she batted her eyes as she spoke. "You must repeat your joke for my benefit. I missed it, and I feel so foolish when I can't laugh with the rest."

Anna stood wide-eyed in the doorway observing her guest's commencement of a flirtation, but before Elwood could fulfill the request, Mrs. Warriner summoned her from the kitchen to supervise the preparation of the refreshments.

In the absence of her chaperone-hostess, Miss Blessing ingratiated herself among the guests, accommodating herself to their speech and ways. In the passing of a half-hour, one would have thought they had always known her. She laughed with their merriment and flattered their sentiment with a tender ballad or two. Her voice sounded veiled but not un-pleasant. She would frequently say, "Pray, don't mind me at all. I'm like a child let out of school!" Miss Blessing tapped one girl on the shoulder, the neck of another she tickled stealthily with a grass-blade. She took the rosebuds from her hair and stuck them in the buttonholes of the young men.

Anna Warriner appeared from the house, observed the proceedings and whispered to her friends nearby, "Just see Julia! Didn't I tell you she was the life of society?"

Joseph stood off to the side, amused by Elwood's growing uneasiness at being watched and criticized, seeming like he wished nothing more than to escape from the lively circle around Miss Blessing. As the evening progressed, Joseph found himself, once again, close to the pale pink dress he knew.

Lucy Henderson observed his attention and moved nearer. Joseph took a step and they were side-by-side.

Following a few brief, discomfited moments she asked, "Do you enjoy these meetings, Joseph?"

"I think I should enjoy everything," he answered abruptly, "if I were a little older, or... or..."

"Or more accustomed to society?" Lucy smiled. "Is not that what you meant? It is only another kind of schooling, which me must all have. You and I are in the lowest class, as we once were. Do you remember?"

"I don't know why," Joseph responded slowly, "but I must be a poor scholar. See Elwood, for instance!" He pointed at his close friend just as another bray of laughter erupted.

"Elwood?!" Lucy repeated in bewilderment. "He is another kind of nature altogether."

The two gazed at each other without speaking. Just as Joseph opened his mouth to voice his opinion, he felt something wonderfully soft touch his cheek, and a delicate, violet-like aroma swept upon his senses. He heard a low musical laugh at his very ear.

"There! Did I frighten you?" Miss Blessing had stolen behind him and, standing on tiptoe, reached a light arm over his shoulders to fasten her last rosebud in the upper buttonhole of his coat.

"I quite overlooked *you*, Mr. Asten," Julia continued, "Please turn a little toward me. Now! Has it not a charming effect? I do like to see some kind of ornament about the gentlemen, Lucy. And since they can't wear anything in their hair–but tell me–wouldn't a wreath of flowers look well on Mr. Asten's head?"

Joseph and Lucy passed an uncertain glance between them. "I can't very well imagine such a thing," Lucy said after a moment.

"No? Well, perhaps I am foolish, but when one has escaped from the tiresome conventionalities of city life and comes back to nature, and delightful natural society, one feels so free to talk and think! Ah, you don't know what a luxury it is, just to be one's true self!"

Joseph swallowed nervously and turned to look at Miss Blessing fully, wondering if she had sensed *his* true nature. Wishing to place a wreath of flowers upon his head as if he were a girl and saying quite plainly how it is a luxury to be one's true self made it seem as though she could see deeply into him and appreciate his hidden feelings.

"Lucy," Elwood said as he approached, "you came with the McNaughtons, didn't you?"

This interruption broke the spell, and she turned away from the interaction between her friend and the visitor from the city. "Yes. Are they going?"

"They are talkin' of it now, but the hour is early, and if you don't mind ridin' on a pillion, you know my horse is gentle and strong..."

"That's right, Mr. Withers!" Miss Blessing interrupted. "I depend upon you to keep Lucy with us. The night is at its loveliest, and we are all just fairly enjoying each other's society."

She turned back to Joseph. "As I was saying, Mr. Asten, you cannot conceive what a new world this is to *me*. Oh, I begin to breathe at last!"

In demonstration, she drew in a long, soft inspiration, held it for a mere moment, and gently exhaled it again, ending with a slight flutter, sounding more like a sigh. A short giggle followed.

"Even though I cannot see your face, I know you are smiling at me, Mr. Asten." She turned her head in his direction then away again. "But you have never experienced what it is to be shy and uneasy in company, feeling that you are expected to converse, and knowing not what to say. And when you finally say something, you are startled at the very sound of your own voice." Miss Blessing touched a finger to the side of her mouth. "To stand, to walk, or sit, and imagine that everybody is watching you. To be introduced to strangers and be awkward as if each of you spoke a different language, unable to exchange a single thought." She turned back to Joseph. "But here in the country, you experience nothing of this at all."

Joseph turned to face Julia, "Indeed, Miss Blessing, it is just the same to us—to me, that is—as city society is to you."

A smile consumed her pale face. "How glad I am!" she exclaimed, clasping her hands. "Perhaps it is selfish for me to say this, but I can't help being sincere toward sincere folk. I shall now feel ever so much more freedom in speaking with you, Mr. Asten, since we share *one* particular experience." Her voice shifted to a low, penetrating tone, "Don't you think, if we all knew each other's natures truly, we should be a great deal more at ease—and consequently happier?" She lifted her inquisitive face to meet his gaze a moment. Now fully opened, the large, clear eyes appeared more appealing in their expression. Her lips parted like those of a child. Before Joseph could respond, Julia darted away, crying, "Yes, Anna, dear!"

Anna Warriner, who had been observing from near the front door, answered, "What is it, Julia?"

Miss Blessing halted. "Oh, didn't you call me?" Anna shook her head. "Somebody surely called 'Julia,' and I'm the only one, am I not?" She looked about, but no one responded. "I've just arranged Mr. Asten's rosebud so prettily, and now all the gentlemen are decorated. I'm afraid they think I take great liberties for a stranger, but then, you all make me forget that I am strange." A girlish titter sprung forth. "Why is it that everybody is so good to me?"

With a radiant expression, she turned her face upon the others. Some of the young women nearby gave her impulsive hugs, which she returned with kisses. A few of the young men tutted their earnest protests.

Elwood had been sitting beside Elizabeth Henderson on the steps of the portico. "Why, we owe it to you that we're here to-night, Miss Blessing!" he exclaimed. "We don't come together half often enough as it is, and what better could we do than meet again, somewhere else, while you are still in the country?"

"O, how delightful! How kind!" Julia chirped while fluttering the layers of her gossamer gown. "And while the lovely moonlight lasts! Shall I really have another evening like this?"

A few of the partygoers immediately offered their invitations to host such an event. Miss Blessing accepted each of the propositions in turn. Before this evening, these young country folks had never been so free, so cheerfully excited. The introduction of someone from the city with ease of manner, grace and sweetness–and a quick, bright sympathy with country ways–had so warmed and fused them, that they lost the remembrance of their stubborn selves and yielded to the magnetism of the hour. Their collective manners had improved greatly, simply by forgetting that they were expected to have any.

One of the happiest in the throng, Joseph eagerly gave his word to be present at the entertainments to come. His heart beat with delight at the prospect of other such evenings. The opportunity to speak with Miss Lucy Henderson, and the charm of Miss Blessing's winning frankness, took equal possession of his thoughts.

It was only when he went to retrieve his horse that he thought of Elwood, who stood next to his own horse, fixing the makeshift seat behind his saddle so that Lucy Henderson would have a place to sit. Once Elwood mounted, Joseph assisted Lucy up onto the pillion behind.

"Is it ten o'clock, do you think?" Joseph asked as he climbed on his steed.

Elwood chuckled, "Ten? It's nigher mornin' than evenin'!"

"Well, a good-night, you two," Joseph said with his eyes firmly fixed on the young lady. Lucy looked over and smiled back. "Take good care of her, Elwood Withers," he shouted as the other horse drove off into the dusty darkness.

The imp on the crupper struck his claws deep into Joseph's sides. As he was riding alone, he could go at his own pace, urging his horse into a gallop, crossing the long rise in the road, dashing along the valley-level, with the cool, dewy night air whistling in his locks.

As he drove on, two memories from the evening haunted him. No two girls could be more unlike than Lucy Henderson and Julia Blessing. He had known Lucy most of his life, but had just made Julia's acquaintance. If he thought of Lucy's eyes, Julia's hand stole over his shoulder. When he recalled Julia's glossy brunet ringlets of hair, Lucy's faint, flushed cheeks and her pure, sweet mouth recaptured his imagination.

Once through the gate of his own lane, he dropped the reins and allowed the panting horse to choose his own gait. As he approached the house, he thought of Lucy sitting quietly by the window and Julia skipping lightly along the hallway. One lifted a fallen rose-branch and the other snatched the reddest blossom from it. One leaned against the trunk of the old hemlock tree while the other fluttered in and out among the clumps of shrubbery. It fascinated Joseph that he could summon the phantoms of these two girls more willingly than that of his closest friend, Elwood.

Hints of starlight sparkled through the locust trees, piercing him with the sting of an unwelcome external conscience, in which he had no part, yet which he could not escape. As he secured his steed in the stable, he could see the lamplights in the farmhouse.

As he opened the door, Rachel Miller looked wearily up from her knitting. She made a feeble attempt to smile, but the expression of her face suggested imminent tears.

"Aunt, why did you wait?" She stared at him as if he had just slapped her across the face. "I forgot to look at my watch, and I really thought it was no more than ten…"

He observed her gaze move to the tall, old-fashioned clock. He turned to see the hands indicating half-past twelve, and every cluck of the ponderous pendulum distinctly taunted, "Late! Late! Late!"

Instead of risking further admonishments, he lit a candle, said, "Good night, Aunt!" and carefully climbed the stairs to his room.

"Good night, Joseph!" she responded solemnly.

Just as Joseph closed his door, he heard a deep, hollow sigh from below.

Chapter 3: Aunt Rachel Receives Unexpected Visitors

RACHEL MILLER STOOD WATCHING HER NEPHEW work the fields. In the days since the gathering at the Warriners, Joseph had redoubled his efforts with the farm, working briskly and cheerfully. Even his attitude with her had brightened, and she scrutinized his actions with a watchful eye.

Joseph waved to her as he approached the farmhouse. "Aunt Rachel, what are you doing out here?"

She blinked a few times before responding, "I finished my knitting for today, and my thoughts have gotten the best of me, I'm afraid."

"Your thoughts?" he inquired as he removed the leather work gloves. "What has so eclipsed your thinking?"

She swallowed noticeably and said, "I have the strongest sense that another gathering is impending, and that you are planning to attend. Am I correct?" Her buzzard stare glared at him.

Joseph dropped his head. "How did you know, Aunt Rachel? Did one of the neighbors tell you?"

"I don't need neighbors to tell me of a change in the winds, Joseph." She raised her chin slightly. "Ever since you went to that social, you have acted differently, but that was to be expected."

He looked directly at his aunt. "However do you mean? I have been doing nothing but working this farm. I felt badly that you waited up for me that night–for no particular reason–but I have naught else to apologize for."

"No, I suppose not." Rachel turned her gaze away. "When you told me about that city girl–Miss Blessing–visiting the Warriners and having a gathering at this time of year, I thought to myself: 'I'm very much mistaken if *that's* the end.'" She looked at Joseph. "Get a-going once, and there's no telling where you'll fetch up. I suppose that city girl won't stay much longer–the farmwork of the neighborhood couldn't stand it–and so she means to have all she can while her visit lasts."

"Indeed," Joseph replied, "there is to be another gathering this evening. I meant to tell you about it sooner, but I have been so busy lately." His aunt glared at him. "And it was Elwood Withers who first proposed it, and the others all agreed."

"Elwood," she snorted with a shake of her head. "And ready enough they were, I'll be bound."

"Why, yes, they were," Joseph asserted, "all of them. And there was no respectable family in the neighborhood that wasn't represented."

"I see," Rachel muttered before walking back into the house.

•▼•

After a mostly-silent meal, Rachel Miller asked calmly, "And where are the festivities this evening?"

Joseph stood and went to the window. "The Frosts." He turned to his aunt. "And please do not wait up for me. I know not how late I shall be."

She stood and began collecting the dishes slowly and meticulously without responding.

Dennis jumped up and moved to the door. "Shall I get your horse ready, Master Joseph?"

"Yes, please. Thank you, Dennis." Joseph stood at the window watching his aunt pile the plates and silverware until he heard the hoof steps outside. "A good evening to you, Aunt Rachel," he offered before leaving. She turned her head away and did not respond in kind.

At the end of the lane, Elwood Withers, once again in his fancy suit, waited.

"Do you want to borrow my pillion in case Miss Lucy wants

you to take her home this time?" Elwood asked.

Joseph shook his head as he locked the gate behind him. "No, but thank you, Elwood. I wouldn't want to give her the wrong impression."

"The wrong impression?" he asked with surprise. "You practically courted her at the last gatherin'. She'll probably be expectin' nothing less than a proposal of marriage tonight." Elwood smiled. "I've been thinkin' about Miss Elizabeth Henderson, and whether I should make my feelin's known to her."

Joseph looked over at his friend. "You mean to marry her, Elwood?"

"Well..." The normally brash farm boy blushed and turned away. "I'm not sayin' I wouldn't mind, now."

The two smiled at each other and rode on to the Frost residence without any further discussion.

When they arrived, they saw the same group of people as last time, except now, Miss Julia Blessing stood in the center of the crowd wearing a country-made, pale blue, gingham outfit with a sober linen collar. As they approached, Joseph heard her calling the people by their names, as if she had always known them. It was a bit of a surprise that she now wore a dress that conformed to country ways, yet the airy, graceful freedom of her manner gave it a character of elegance that sufficiently distinguished her from the other girls.

As they approached the group, Joseph could sense Miss Blessing looking at him, as by an innocent natural instinct. She worked her way through the mass of partygoers and approached Joseph directly. She began speaking to him in a lively manner, with sentence fragments and parenthetical expressions frequently dropped in. A quick glance at his face communicated the thought: *We have one feeling in common. I know that you understand me.*

This new and fascinating experience charmed and bewildered Joseph. Her seemingly random looks drew him in, and he found himself anticipating those moments. When they came, he shrunk timidly, feeling the desire to be in the quiet corner with Lucy Henderson, outside the merry circle of talkers.

Eventually, Miss Julia Blessing moved on to others, and Joseph managed to find Lucy. She stood stiffly, seeming grave and preoccupied. "Good evening, Lucy. Are you enjoying yourself?" he inquired.

Without turning to face him fully, she responded coolly, "Why, yes." He could see her eyes wandering over the company as if she were trying to listen to their conversations. "And you?"

Her manner had changed greatly since their last encounter at the Warriners. Gone were the pleasant directness and self-possession that had made her society so comfortable previously. Had he done something to upset her? Should he have volunteered to provide a ride home for her instead of letting Elwood do it?

Joseph stood searching the crowd for his friend, hoping that he might be able to provide some insight into Lucy's abrupt change of heart. Just as he caught sight of Elwood chatting with Miss Elizabeth Henderson, someone grabbed his wrist and held it up.

"I have it!" cried Julia Blessing, "it shall be *you*, Mr. Asten!"

"Yes!" Anna Warriner echoed as she approached, "if it could be. How delightful!"

"Hush, Anna, dear!" Julia whispered with a mysterious air, "Let us keep the matter secret. We shall slip away and consult, and–of course–Lucy must come with us."

Joseph and Lucy gazed at each with other quizzical looks as they were led to the Frosts' old-fashioned dining room. Julia began, "Now, we must, first of all, explain everything to Mr. Asten." Joseph looked at Lucy, who merely raised her eyebrows and shrugged. "The question is: Where shall we meet next week." Julia cocked her head and looked directly at

Joseph. "The McNaughtons are building an addition—I believe you call it—to their barn, and a child has the measles at another place, and something else is wrong somewhere else."

Joseph squinted and asked, "But what does this have to do with me?"

Julia smiled brightly. "We cannot interfere with the course of nature; however, neither should we give up these charming evenings without making an effort to continue them. Our sole hope and reliance is on you, Mr. Asten." She clasped her hands and looked at Joseph with her bright, eager, and laughing eyes.

He turned to Anna and then Lucy, but neither changed expression. After a hard swallow, he began, "If it depended on myself —"

"O, I know the difficulty, Mr. Asten!" Julia interrupted, "and, really, it's unpardonable in me to propose such a thing. But isn't it possible—just possible—that your Miss Miller might be persuaded by us?"

Anna turned to Miss Blessing, "Julia, dear! I believe there's nothing you'd be afraid to undertake."

As Joseph looked at each of the girls, he began to feel his face flush with color and ready to turn pale the next moment. The thought of his aunt receiving such an astounding proposition beguiled him. He had no idea how to respond.

"There is no reason why she should be asked," Lucy chimed in. "It would be a great annoyance to her."

Joseph silently thanked Miss Henderson for speaking with the voice of reason.

"Indeed?" Miss Blessing's tone rose. "Then I should be *so* sorry! But I caught a glimpse of your lovely place the other day as we were driving up the valley. It was a perfect picture, and I have such a desire to see it nearer!" Her excitement bubbled over.

"Why will you not come, then?" Joseph felt compelled to ask. Even though Lucy's words had been intended for his relief, he subsequently felt them to be blunt and unfriendly.

Julia batted her eyes. "It would be a great pleasure. Yet, if I thought your aunt would be annoyed…"

"I'm sure she will be glad to make your acquaintance," Joseph offered, with a reproachful side-glance at Lucy Henderson.

Miss Blessing's eyes followed the glance. "*I* am more sure that she will be very much amused at my ignorance and inexperience," she said playfully. "And I don't believe Lucy meant to frighten me. As for the party, we won't think of that now, but you will go with us, Lucy—won't you—with Anna and myself—to make a neighborly afternoon call?"

Lucy looked to Joseph, but he gave no clue. She silently nodded, acquiescing to the new situation.

Lucy and Joseph did not speak with each other the rest of the evening. Elwood spent the entire time with Elizabeth Henderson. Julia Blessing continued to float among the neighbors, listening to their stories and reacting with concern. At one point, Bob Warriner approached Joseph, and the forgettable conversation kept him occupied until he retrieved his horse and rode back to his farm shortly after ten o'clock.

As Joseph approached the darkened farmhouse, he had hoped that his aunt would still be awake so that he could inform her of the impending visit. However, it appeared she had retired early, and he climbed the stairs as quietly as possible. Only the clucking of the clock in the sitting-room broke the silence of the night.

•▼•

The following Saturday, Rachel Miller worked at her light task of sewing and darning. In her favorite chair in the sitting-room, she worked quietly, looking up every so often and gazing out the window.

The weather had turned fine and warm, and a brisk drying breeze for the hay on the hill-field rattled one of the panes once and again. As she looked down the valley, she could see the mowers swinging their way through the Hunters' grass and that the Cunninghams' corn sorely needed working.

She could be proud that their farm lacked for nothing. Between her nephew and the hired man, Dennis, everything had been done, and well done, up to the front of the season.

Joseph continued to work harder than ever, with a different spirit and renewed interest. He diligently looked here and there, even inspecting with his own eyes the minor duties that had formerly been entrusted to Dennis.

Rachel's peaceable mood swiftly changed when she spied the top of a carriage through the bushes fringing the lane. When the vehicle came into view, she could see Anna Warriner driving with two other ladies on the back seat. As they drew up to the hitching-post on the green, Lucy Henderson stepped down, assisting an airy stranger—a girl with dark, falling ringlets. She wore the same pale blue, gingham dress from the recent gathering at the Frosts, but now she carried a work-bag as well.

Setting her sewing down, Rachel went to meet her visitors. As she approached, Anna Warriner began, "We thought we could come for an hour this afternoon without disturbing you." She smiled at Joseph's Aunt but was met with only stern countenance. "Mother has lost your receipt for pickling cherries, and Bob said you were already through with the hay-harvest, and so we brought Julia along." She presented her guest. "This is Julia Blessing."

"How do you do?" Julia said timidly, extending her hand and slightly dropping her eyes. When Rachel did not take the offered hand, she fell behind Anna and Lucy.

Rachel turned and walked into the sitting-room, and the three young women followed. "How do you like the country by this time?" she asked while indicating seats for the others.

"So well that I think I shall never like the city again." Julia glanced about at the furnishings in the cozy farmhouse. "This quiet, peaceful life is such a rest, and I really never before knew what order was, and industry, and economy…" The sight of the barn through the eastern window caught her attention.

"Yes, your ways in town are very different," Rachel replied as she sat in her chair.

"It seems to me, *now*, that they are entirely artificial. I find myself so ignorant of the proper way of living that I should be embarrassed among you, if you were not all so very kind. But I am trying to learn a little," and she smiled in her child-like way.

"O, we don't expect too much of city folks," Rachel said as she sized-up her guest. "We're always glad to see them willing to put up with our ways. But not many are."

Miss Blessing stood, dropping the work-bag to the floor. "Please don't count *me* among those!" she exclaimed, hand to bosom.

"No, indeed, Miss Rachel!" Anna Warriner upheld. "You'd be surprised to know how Julia gets along with everything. Don't she, Lucy?"

Lucy had been gazing out the windows, not paying much attention to the conversation. The glare of Anna's eyes brought her back into focus. "Oh, yes, she's very quick," she offered.

Julia sat down again, her eyes downcast, shaking her head.

Rachel turned to Anna, "Please tell me a bit of what has been going on in our neighborhood. I have not had the chance to get out much lately."

The request opened the sluices of Miss Warriner's gossip, and she began to share the ways and doings of various local individuals.

At times, Miss Blessing remarked on the news, displaying a complete familiarity. Her manner appeared grave and attentive as Rachel snuck a glance or two.

When Anna had run out of steam, Julia stood and asked, "May I look at your trees and flowers?"

They all rose and went out on the lawn. Rose, woodbine, phlox, and verbena delighted Miss Blessing, but it was the long, rounded walls of boxwood that attracted her attention. As it was Rachel's own hand that had planted the shrubs, she led the way through the garden.

Anna Warriner touched Lucy's hand, and the two lagged behind. "Let us go down to the spring-house. We can get back again before Julia has half finished her raptures."

Lucy hesitated and glanced at Julia just as she was saying, "O, don't mind me!" to Rachel. The two dashed off without saying a word.

At the end of the long avenue of boxwood, walls curved outward, forming three-fourths of a circle, spacious enough to contain several seats. The verdant valley opened up before them.

"The loveliest place I ever saw!" Julia exclaimed, taking one of the rustic chairs. "How pleasant it must be, when you have all your neighbors here together!"

Rachel Miller looked at her guest with a cocked head. Before she could reply, Julia began speaking again.

"There is such a difference between a company of young people here in the country, and what is called 'a party' in the city. There it is all dress and flirtation and vanity, but here it is only neighborly visiting on a grander scale." She surveyed the vista. "I have enjoyed the quiet company of all your folks *so* much the more because I felt that it was so very innocent. Indeed, I don't see how anybody *could* be led into harmful ways here."

"I don't know," Rachel responded, "We must learn to mistrust our own hearts."

"You are right!" Julia stood. "The best are weak–of themselves–but there is more safety where all have been brought up unacquainted with temptation."

At the word "temptation," Rachel's gaze fixed squarely on Julia.

"Now, you will perhaps wonder at me when I say that I could trust the young men—for instance, Mr. Asten, your nephew—as if they were my brothers." She turned to see Rachel's hardened expression. "That is, I feel a positive certainty of their excellent character. What they say they mean—it is otherwise in the city. How delightful to see them all together, like members of one family." Julia turned her gaze as to give a side-glance. "You must enjoy it, I should think, when they meet here."

Rachel's eyes went wide, her face pulled a puzzling and searching expression. Miss Blessing looked back at her with almost infantile simplicity, her lips slightly parted, seemingly unaffected by the other woman's scrutiny, accepting it with a quiet cheerfulness in perfect candor.

"The truth is," Rachel spoke at last, and at a slower pace, "this is a new thing. I hope the merry-makings are as innocent as you think, but I'm afraid they unsettle the young people, after all."

"Do you really?" squeaked Miss Blessing. "What have you seen in them which leads you to think so? But no—never mind my question—you may have reasons which I have no right to ask." She turned to look at the view then turned back. "Now, I remember Mr. Asten telling Anna and Lucy and myself how much he should like to invite his friends here, if it were not for a duty which prevented it. A duty, he said, was more important to him than a pleasure." Julia's bright eyes studied Rachel Miller's face.

"Did Joseph say that?"

"O, perhaps I oughtn't to have told it," Miss Blessing said, casting down her eyes and blushing. "In that case, *please* don't say anything about it! Perhaps it was a duty toward you, for he told me that he looked upon you as a second mother." Her gaze rose to take in Rachel's reaction.

A few seconds passed, and the older woman's expression softened. "I've tried to do my duty to him, but it sometimes seems an unthankful business, and I can't always tell how he takes it." Rachel addressed Julia directly, "And so he wanted to have a company here?"

"I am so sorry I said it!" Miss Blessing exclaimed, tears welling in her eyes. "I never thought you were opposed to company–on principle." A dainty sniffle emanated from her pale nose. "Miss Chaffinch–the minister's daughter, you know–was there the last time, and, really, if you could see it… But it is presumptuous in me to say anything." She wiped at the moisture on her face. "Indeed, I am not a fair judge because these little gatherings have enabled me to make such pleasant acquaintances." She leaned a bit forward. "And the young men tell me that they work all the better after them."

Rachel looked out into the fields where her nephew stood tending the hay. "It's only on *his* account."

"Nay, I'm sure that the last thing Mr. Asten would wish would be your giving up a principle for his sake! I know from his face that his own character is founded on principle. And, besides, here in the country you don't keep count of hospitality, as they do in the city, and feel obliged to return as much as you receive." She stepped around to face Rachel directly. "So, if you will try to forget what I have said…"

"No, I meant something different." Rachel turned to face Julia. "Joseph knows why I objected to parties. He must not feel under obligations which I stand in the way of his repaying. If he tells me that he should like to invite his friends to this place, I will help him to entertain them."

Miss Blessing's mouth formed a half-smile. "You *are* his second mother, indeed." Her eyes began to sparkle. "And now I can hope that you will forgive my thoughtlessness. I should feel humiliated in his presence if he knew that I had repeated his words. But he will not ask you, and this is the end of any harm I may have done."

"No, I suppose he won't ask," Rachel mused. "But won't I be

an offense in his mind?"

Julia placed both her hands on Rachel's broad shoulders. "I can understand how you feel. Only a woman can judge another woman's heart. Would you think me too forward if I tell you what might be done—just this once?" Her delicate eyebrows raised slightly.

Rachel did not respond. She merely turned her head away.

Julia moved one of her hands down to the other woman's wrist. "Perhaps I am wrong, but if *you* were the first to suggest to your nephew that if he wished to make some return for the hospitality of his neighbors—or put it in whatever form you think best—would not that remove the 'offense'—although he surely cannot look at it in that light—and make him grateful and happy?" Her eyelids closed slightly, dimming the bright light just a bit.

"Well," Rachel said after a moment's reflection, "if anything is done, that would be as good a way as any."

Julia patted the back of the other woman's hand. "And, of course, you won't mention me?"

"There is no call to do it—as I can see." Rachel looked off again.

Anna approached from the lane, "Julia, dear! Come and see the last load of hay hauled into the barn!" Lucy Henderson walked a few paces behind.

"I should like to see it," Julia murmured to Rachel, who nodded. "I have taken quite an interest in farming," she beamed. "If you will excuse me..."

As they walked past the porch, Rachel took the first step and asked of Anna, "You'll bide and get your suppers?"

"Oh, I don't know," Anna said ruefully, "we didn't mean to, but we stayed longer than we intended..."

Rachel smiled. "Then you can easily stay longer still."

Anna looked to Rachel Miller for a hint of her sincerity and then laughed. She took Julia's arm and started for the barn.

Lucy quietly followed Rachel into the farmhouse, and the two set out arranging the dining table.

Julia and Anna paused on the green to watch a huge, fragrant load of hay approach. The freshly-mowed grass overhung and concealed the wheels of the cart, as well as the hind quarters of the oxen. At the summit of the pile stood Joseph in rolled-up shirt-sleeves, leaning on a pitch-fork. Sweat trickled down his face and neck, and he removed his hat to fan himself with it.

"Hallo!" cried Anna.

Joseph heard his friend's voice and bent forward with a surprised look. "Well, hallo yourself!" He waved the hat in greeting as the cart trundled toward the barn.

"O, take care! Take care!" Julia exclaimed as the load approached the big, open doors. Joseph dropped to his knees and bent his shoulders as he passed through to avoid being knocked off by the large cross-bar.

Once inside, Joseph sprang lightly to a beam, stepped to the loft, and descended the upright ladder. The two women had followed him into the barn and greeted him upon his arrival on the ground.

"We have kept our promise, you see," Julia stated with joyful eyes.

Joseph's own eyes went wide at the thought of Miss Blessing conversing with his aunt, whom he had negligently forgotten to warn of this impending visit. "Have you been in the house yet?"

Anna responded, "Oh, for an hour past, and we are going to take supper with you. Lucy Henderson is helping your aunt with the preparations."

A surprised and shocked look overtook Joseph's face. "Dennis!" he called out, "Dennis!" When the hired man appeared from behind the cart, Joseph commanded, "We shall let the load stand to-night," and Dennis nodded before walking off.

Julia grabbed Anna's arm "How much better a man looks in shirt-sleeves than in a dress-coat!" Joseph pretended not to hear such girl talk.

"Why, Julia," Anna responded, "you are perfectly countrified! I never saw anything like it!"

When Joseph turned to them again, he caught Miss Blessing's eyes, full of admiration before the lids fell modestly over them. A bright flush rose on his face.

As the three walked slowly toward the farmhouse, Joseph inquired, "So you've seen my home already?"

"O, not the half yet!" Julia answered in a low, earnest tone. "A place so lovely and quiet as this cannot be appreciated at once. I almost wish I had not seen it. What shall I do when I must go back to the hot pavements, and the glaring bricks, and the dust, and the hollow, artificial life?" Her attempt at a sigh failed after she had inhaled some bits of hay kicked up by their walking. Instead, she laughed lightly then went on, "I wonder if everybody doesn't long for something else?" She turned to the other young woman, "Now, Anna here would think it heavenly to change places with me."

"Such privileges as you have!" protested Anna.

"Privileges?" echoed Julia. "The privilege of hearing scandal, of being judged by your dress, of learning the forms and manners, instead of the good qualities of men and women?" She raised a hand to her chin. "No! Give me an independent life."

"Alone?" Anna queried.

Joseph turned to look at Miss Blessing, who made no reply. She had shifted her gaze away. Perhaps Anna's indelicacy had offended her. They spoke no more along the rest of the walk.

Meanwhile, Aunt Rachel and Lucy Henderson had been preparing the evening meal. When Joseph entered, he caught Lucy's look and sensed her temporary astonishment. Perhaps his aunt had said something inadvertently offensive, as was her wont.

"I must help, too!" cried Miss Blessing as she skipped into the kitchen after Rachel. At the arch, she turned back and said, "That is one thing, at least, which we can learn in the city. Indeed, if it wasn't for housekeeping, I should feel terribly useless."

Joseph excused himself so as to dress properly for the meal. As he ascended the stairs, he could hear his aunt protesting the offer and Julia's laughter answering in a manner which conveyed the impression she sincerely wanted to help.

When he descended a few minutes later in fresh attire, he could scarcely believe his eyes. Miss Blessing appeared to be assisting his aunt without opposition. It almost seemed as though she enjoyed the company.

Lucy Henderson had moved to the chair by the window, sullen and withdrawn. It might have been Aunt Rachel's confrontational manner that had put her off. However, Joseph felt so happy, so free, so delighted to assume the character of a host that Lucy's silence threw no shadow upon his cheerfulness.

Rachel had to constantly prompt Joseph to do his duty as a host in maintaining the usual decorum. He was unaccustomed to this role, and her directions did not offend him.

Miss Blessing tasted the cream and butter and marmalade, cooing and uttering "Mmmmm, mmmm!" with enthusiasm. Rachel Miller cracked a smile at these appreciations of her handiwork. Her nephew hardly ever spoke words of praise.

As Rachel stood and began to collect the plates, Anna Warriner announced, "We are going to take Lucy on her way as far as the cross-roads so there will not be more time to get home by sunset."

"Thank you for the lovely meal, Miss Miller," Julia smiled, "and the tour of your blessed garden." Anna and Lucy nodded in agreement. Rachel continued to pile the dishes without responding.

Joseph rose and escorted the three young ladies to their carriage. Just as they reached the vehicle, Elwood Withers drove up with a horse-cart. He jumped down and hugged Joseph heartily before greeting the three others.

"Lucy," he spoke directly to Miss Henderson, "I was goin' to a township-meeting at the Corner, but Bob Warriner told me you were here with Anna, so I thought I could save her a roundabout drive by taking you myself." He smiled broadly.

Joseph looked at Lucy, who stared back at him blankly. He could not decipher her mood.

"Thank you," Lucy said at last, "but I'm sorry you should go so far out of your road." Her face had gone pale, and her smile appeared forced.

"Oh, he'd go twice as far for company," Anna Warriner remarked. "You know I'd take you—and welcome—but Elwood has a good claim on you now."

"I have no *claim*, Miss Lucy," barked Elwood. "No claim at all."

"Let us go, then," Lucy responded coolly.

Elwood assisted her into his rig, and Joseph gave his hand to Miss Warriner and Miss Blessing. The two vehicles drove off as the sun began to touch the hills. He observed one pair chatting and laughing merrily while the other drove in grave silence.

Chapter 4: A Change in the Winds

UPON ENTERING THE FARMHOUSE, Joseph felt trapped and restless. Following the gaiety of the evening, he had no desire to sit alone with his maiden aunt and listen to her go on about the disagreeable deportment of his friends. The thought of remaining at home after having spent an enjoyable society seemed unbearable. He grabbed his riding gear and went to the kitchen, where his aunt stood washing plates.

"Where are you going at this time of day?" she inquired.

"Aunt Rachel, I realized that I must find something I need in the village." He donned the overcoat. "I should not be gone long."

As he walked away, Rachel muttered—mostly to herself— "Find something...? That village store closed hours ago..."

Joseph saddled his horse and set out on the road leading away from the village. An empty path like this one meant he would probably not encounter any other person along the way, and he wanted to be alone with his feelings and his thoughts.

The regular movements of the animal relieved him by giving the unquiet motions of his mind a wider sweep and a more definite form. He realized that he had utilized his strong body to uphold the weight of the world, like Atlas; however, he sensed a clog upon all his thoughts, an ever-present sense of restriction and impotence. But when lifted above the soil, with the air under his foot-soles, swiftly moving without effort, his mind seemed to soar on winged heels, like Hermes.

Riding toward the setting sun liberated him, bestowing new and nimble powers. His inner vision opened to wider horizons where obstacles could be measured or overlooked. The brute strength under him charged his whole nature with a more vigorous electricity.

Joseph felt the hum from the multitudinous spirits of life in every nerve and vein, marching triumphantly in a procession through secret passages and summoning the phantoms of sense to their completed chambers. He imagined his mind and soul balanced above a strong pinion as he rode farther and farther from his home.

At once, the great joy of human life filled and thrilled him. All possibilities of action and pleasure and emotion swam before his eyes. He envisioned many of the individual careers he had ever read about in all ages, climates, and conditions of humanity—dazzling pictures of the myriad-sided Earth. All this could be his if he but dared to seize the freedom waiting for his grasp.

He finally accepted that he did feel love for his longtime friend, Elwood Withers, as he himself had described it on their ride to the first gathering at the Warriners. Joseph would rather touch Elwood's hand, or shirt, more than kissing anyone else. Miss Blessing and Lucy Henderson may have stirred a mild passion in him, but nothing like his constant craving for male companionship. Even with all the buffoonery and loud talk, Elwood had captured Joseph's heart. Elwood embodied all the things Joseph aspired to be—outgoing, confident, worldly—and it made his brain run to his heels whenever Elwood came into view.

However, Elwood professed to be interested in the young women, particularly Miss Elizabeth Henderson. Joseph understood his feelings could not be reciprocated, and he had to accept that his feelings differed from the others. His love for another man made him feel like a lone stalk of corn in a field of waving wheat.

He slowed the horse and turned back. Back to the farmhouse on the knoll where he felt trapped by duty and responsibility.

As the last bit of the sun disk sank below the distant hills, Joseph broke free of his self-imposed prison. A very fair and saintly-visaged jailer of thought had kept strict guard over every outward movement of his mind. *No! No farther! It is prohibited!* the jailer kept telling him whenever his hopes, desires, and conjectures reached a certain line. With one strong, involuntary throb, he found himself beyond that line, with all the ranges ever trodden by man stretching forward to a limitless horizon. Rising, standing tall in the stirrups, he threw out his arms, baring his naked soul, lifted his face toward the darkening sky and cried, "God! I see what I am!"

As he approached his farm, Joseph noticed a horse and cart coming up the other way. At the road-end he saw it was Elwood, and his face flushed for having such thoughts as he did about his friend.

"Joseph!" Elwood cried out, "I must speak with you!"

The two pulled up side-by-side, and Joseph asked, "What is it that is so important, Elwood? You startled me."

"I am so sorry, Joseph, but Miss Lucy Henderson imparted some information to me that I thought you should know straightaway!" His normally-curly hair stuck flat to his sweaty scalp.

"What is it that has you worked up so?"

Elwood took a few breaths to calm himself. "Miss Lucy was pretty quiet and sullen at first. It almost made me sorry I went outta my way to help her. But then she started sayin' things..." He looked away.

"What kind of things, Elwood?" Joseph wanted to reach over and hug his friend, but he knew that would now be improper.

"Well... I do believe that Lucy Henderson has some feelin's for you–to be sure–but what they are I cannot tell."

Joseph thought back to previous interactions with her. Lucy could be warm and open, but then she could be cold and clam-like. Her behavior confused him.

"But the important thing is what she said about Miss Blessing!"

"Miss Blessing?" Joseph echoed, eager to hear the news. "What of her?"

Elwood looked straight-on at his friend, "As it turns out, this whole afternoon and the plan for a gatherin' on your farm has been a dodge o' Miss Blessing."

"A dodge? How so?"

"It was Miss Blessing who suggested the visit to your farm, and it was her who manipulated your aunt into offerin' to host the gatherin'. But Lucy said she objected because such an undertakin' would be a burden on your aunt."

Joseph looked into the darkening distance. "I see…"

"Lucy had not many good things to say about this city girl, I tell you. She said Miss Blessing is willful in her ways, but her manner is very amiable."

"She did wear that ridiculous dress at the Warriners—so ruffled and puckered, stuck all over with ribbons and things, that you can't rightly tell what that stuff was."

"To be sure!" Elwood agreed. "However, it is Miss Lucy's belief that Miss Blessing has her eye to *you*, Joseph."

"To *me*?"

"'First and foremost,' she said. Oh, and Miss Henderson thinks you're as innocent as a year-old baby who had a bringin' up fitter for a girl than a boy, and you haven't cut your eye-teeth yet, but *she* certainly has."

Joseph listened with a blank expression.

"I don't think she meant any harm by that. It seemed to me that she felt protective of you and she couldn't quite express her true feelin's. But she does think Miss Blessing has it out for you, and I just thought you deserve to know."

"Thank you, Elwood," Joseph nodded, "you are a true friend." He wanted to touch Elwood more than anything, and a kiss would have meant the world to him.

"Well, it's gettin' late and I imagine your aunt is sittin' up waitin' for you." He began to turn the horse cart.

"Good-night," Joseph managed to say without revealing his true feelings, as much as he dreamed to express his love. He watched with remorse as Elwood drove off.

This new development sparked his hope. As much as he wanted to share his life with Elwood, it was not to be. However, the news of Miss Blessing's interest in him presented an avenue he had not considered. She, herself, had been able to look into his true nature and not been frightened by what she saw. She fascinated him–outgoing, confident, worldly–the same traits he admired in Elwood. If others expected him to marry, and Miss Blessing had detected his secret desires, perhaps a bargain could be struck. Yes, Miss Julia Blessing might just be the answer to his prayers.

Upon entering the farmhouse, he saw Aunt Rachel sitting in her chair fretting over some darning work. She looked up at her nephew, appraising the unfamiliar, self-satisfied expression on his face.

"Aunt," Joseph declared, "do you know that I have never really felt until now that I am the owner of this property? It will be more of a home to me after I have received the neighborhood as my guests." He removed his riding gear. "It has always controlled me, but now it must serve me." The spontaneous laugh expressed his good-humor.

Rachel Miller turned to look at the chair recently occupied by Miss Julia Blessing. When she turned back to Joseph, her face displayed a smug smile. "Did you find what you needed?"

Joseph smiled, patted his chest over his heart, and responded, "Yes, aunt, I believe I did."

•❧•

Over the next few days, as Joseph continued to work the farm with excitement and satisfaction, Aunt Rachel prepared for the impending gathering.

Two days before the event, she stood near the hitching-post handing Dennis a list of goods to procure from the village store just as a fine buggy pulled up to the garden. It was Mrs. Warriner, Anna's mother. Her dark-brown braided hair hung in a black snood.

"Miss Miller! Miss Miller!" she shouted as she pulled up. Rachel walked over to meet her uninvited guest, the first one in many months.

"Mrs. Warriner. Always a pleasure. What brings you all the way out here?"

"Well, I heard from my children that you are to be holding a gathering soon, and I just wanted to make myself available, should you need my assistance."

"That's mighty kind and neighborly of you, Mrs. Warriner, but I think Joseph and I have things pretty much under control now. Thank you." She started back toward the farmhouse.

"I see." Mrs. Warriner glanced over the garden. "What a beautiful garden you have, Miss Miller. Do you think your house will be large enough for such a neighborhood gathering?"

Rachel paused and walked back to the buggy. "We'll be fine, Mrs. Warriner, just fine. Thank you."

"Perhaps I could share with you *my* plan of entertaining company from our very successful gathering."

Rachel Miller stared up at Mrs. Warriner with the skeptical eye she used on the traveling dry goods salesmen who dared approach her. "I don't believe I shall be requiring any assistance from you, Mrs. Warriner. The good Reverend Mr. Chaffinch has already stated he is willing to be present. I am certain he will maintain the strictest orthodoxy as far as the entertainment is concerned. This is a Quaker household, and I am determined to keep the faith. Good day, Mrs. Warriner." She turned and walked back to the farmhouse.

"But..."

"Good day, Mrs. Warriner," Rachel shouted without turning round.

The visitor drove off as quickly as she had arrived.

Before Rachel reached the door, Joseph approached from the barn. "Who was that, Aunt Rachel? Were you expecting a visitor?"

"Oh, it was just Mrs. Warriner trying to meddle her way into our entertainment plans. As if I needed *her* help. Them and their fancy ballroom…"

"But we could use some help, aunt. This has been quite taxing on you, I know."

"If I was better acquainted with Miss Blessing, she might help me a good deal in fixing everything just as it should be. There are times, it seems, when it's an advantage to know something of the world."

"I'll ask her!" Joseph proclaimed.

"You!" she almost choked. "And a mess you'd make of it, very likely. Men think they've only to agree to invite a company, and that's all!" She wagged a finger at her nephew. "There's a hundred things to be thought of that women must look to. You couldn't understand 'em. As for speaking to her, *she's* one of the *invites*, and it would never do in the world."

Rachel walked into the farmhouse, leaving Joseph standing outside. He figured he could just ask Miss Blessing when she arrived, if there were time. It might be just the thing to get her in better standing with Aunt Rachel, adding to the influence she had already acquired.

The next day, after Joseph had completed his farm chores, he decided to ride over to the Warriners in the hope of catching a moment's conference with Miss Blessing in advance of the occasion.

Anna answered the door, "Well, hello, *Mr. Asten*! What a pleasure to see you again, *Mr. Asten*!"

Joseph heard rapid footsteps on the stairs. "Yes, well, hello Anna, I've come to –"

"I'm sorry, *Mr. Asten*!, I can't speak with you right now as I am very busy with my household duties, but you are welcome to visit with my guest, Miss Julia Blessing, with whom you are already acquainted." Anna opened the door fully, and Julia appeared, brushing down her gingham dress as if she had just risen from lounging.

"Why, Mr. Asten, how nice of you to come a-calling. Please, do come in." Miss Blessing led the way to the sitting parlor.

"Thank you, Anna," Joseph called to his friend before she disappeared into the kitchen with a nod.

Joseph and Julia sat not looking at each other for a minute or two. Finally, Miss Blessing opened the conversation, "Now, Mr. Asten, I see by your face that you have something particular to say. It's about to-morrow night, isn't it?" He nodded slightly. "You must let me help you, if I can, because I am afraid I have been—without exactly intending it—the cause of so much trouble to you and your aunt."

Joseph looked at Miss Blessing fully, the first time since his horseback epiphany, and opened his heart. "Why, yes, Miss Blessing, if you could help me and my aunt I would be forever grateful to you. I have little understanding of the ways of your world, and Aunt Rachel, well, I can't expect her to do all the work." He averted his eyes for fear that she might reject his entreaty.

"Oh, Mr. Asten, I know this sounds like vanity in me, but I really hope it is not. You must remember that in the city we are obliged to know all the little social arts—and artifices—I am afraid. It is not always to our credit, but then, the heart *may* be kept fresh and uncorrupted." She looked at him with smiling eyes, partially lidded, and a slight bounce of her eyebrows.

As Joseph returned the gaze, she cast her eyes down. He knew that if he were to proceed with his plan, he must be able to speak freely with her. "Tell me, Miss Julia, did you not suggest this party to Aunt Rachel?"

Julia looked up with a momentary expression of surprise at the implication, but it quickly shifted to her usual girlish smile. "Don't give me too much credit!" she chuckled. "It was talked about, and I couldn't help saying 'Aye.' I longed so much to see you—all—again before I depart."

He pressed on, "And Lucy Henderson objected to it?"

"Lucy," she glanced up as if trying to remember something forgotten, "I think, wanted to save your aunt the trouble. Perhaps she did not guess that the real objection was inexperience, and not want of will to entertain company. And very likely she helped to bring it about, by seeming to oppose it. So, you must not be angry with Lucy. Promise me?" A few bats of her eyes lured Joseph toward her. She extended her hand, as if to draw him closer.

Joseph grabbed the offered hand but with manly pressure. After a moment's silence, Julia glanced down at their conjoined hands and returned the pressure with a knowing smile.

Anna Warriner entered from the kitchen, catching her two guests hand-in-hand. "Well, I am so glad to see the two of you finally getting along!"

Chapter 5: The Gathering

ON THE DAY OF THE GATHERING, Joseph worked in the fields until he stopped for his midday meal. After that, he left the rest of the work to Dennis and began to clean himself up for the evening ahead.

From his room, he heard voices below, some male, some female. Perhaps Aunt Rachel had invited a few people to assist her with the preparations. He descended the stairs, once again in his Sunday best.

In the sitting-room, Aunt Rachel occupied her favorite chair. Around her sat the Reverend Mr. Chaffinch and his daughter, Miss Julia Blessing, as well as Bob and Anna Warriner.

"Mr. Asten, do come join us!" chirped Miss Blessing, as if it were her own home, and she had assumed the role of hostess. She patted an empty space on the settee next to her.

Joseph looked at his aunt with a quizzical air. "It's all right, Joseph. I invited a few people to help us with the festivities. I hope you don't mind."

It boggled Joseph that his aunt had sought assistance after all. Initially, she had protested such thoughts, not wanting to have the *invites*, as she called them, assist with the party they were to subsequently attend. He sat next to Miss Blessing, leaving a few inches of space between them.

"My, don't you look handsome in that suit?" Julia exclaimed. She turned to Aunt Rachel. "He seems almost god-like in those togs." She smiled at each of the other guests in turn.

Rachel stood and walked toward the dining room. "Let's eat these victuals before they get any colder. Mr. Chaffinch, would you please supply the blessing."

The dining table had disappeared beneath a feast of chickens stewed in cream, roasted corn, garden greens, and country bread. After all had been seated, the Reverend mumbled for a few seconds, and then pronounced, "Amen!" very clearly. The remaining company echoed his sentiment, and Rachel served the meal.

With so many wonderful things to eat, the only words spoken were requests to pass dishes. Joseph looked upon his aunt's face, and it appeared to him that it might have been the first time he remembered her looking truly happy.

"You have entertained us almost too sumptuously, Miss Miller," the Reverend imparted as he began to rise from the table. "And, now, let us go out on the portico to welcome the young people as they arrive."

The expression on Rachel's face turned to one of alarm. "I need hardly ask you, then, Mr. Chaffinch, whether you think it right for them to come together in this way."

"Decidedly!" He walked toward the door, and Aunt Rachel followed, leaving the plates on the table in an uncharacteristic manner. "That is, so long as their conversation is modest and becoming. It is easy for the vanities of the world to slip in, but we must watch. We must watch!" He pointed a cautionary finger heavenward.

As the Reverend and Aunt Rachel sat on the steps of the portico, Anna Warriner put her arm around Miss Chaffinch's waist and drew her toward the mown field beyond the barn, her brother following close behind.

Joseph and Miss Blessing walked to the bottom of the lawn. To the west, a cool, broad shadow covered the hills. The treetops flushed with a rich orange to the east and brightened as the sky above them deepened into the violet-gray of coming dusk. Moist, delicious freshness from the valley below slowly crept up the branching glen, tempering the air about them. Birds chirped happily from a nearby bush, and the cattle lowed in the pasture-fields beyond.

"Ah!" sighed Miss Blessing, "this is too sweet to last. I must learn to do without it." She looked at him swiftly, with tiny tears in her eyes, then glanced away.

Joseph opened his mouth to speak, but she turned back and laid a hand on his arm.

"Hush! Let us wait until the light has faded."

He beheld Julia, the most captivating thing to him amidst all the beauty of his farm.

Behind them, the glow moved to the summits of the distant hills, fringing them with a thin, wonderful radiance. The next moment it broke on the irregular topmost boughs and then vanished, as if blown out by a breeze from the sudden lifting of the sky.

Julia tugged Joseph's arm, and they walked slowly together toward the house. As they neared the garden, she exclaimed, "That superb avenue of boxwood! I must see it again, if only to say farewell."

Once they entered the garden, Joseph could smell the seductive odor of the dense green wall hiding them from the sight of the other guests. Looking down through the southern opening of the avenue, it appeared they were totally alone in the evening valley.

Miss Blessing kept her hand on Joseph's arm, and his heart beat fast and strong. Wild fear interfused with pleasure filled his head. When she clasped her hand a bit harder, he realized he had been trembling.

"If life were as beautiful and peaceful as this," she whispered, "we should not need to seek for truth and... and... sympathy. We should find them everywhere."

He gazed down at her. "Do you not think they are to be found?"

"O, in how few hearts! I can say it to *you*, and you will not misunderstand me." She cast her eyes down once more. "Until lately I was satisfied with life as I found it. I thought it meant diversion and dress and gossip and common daily duties, but now..."–she looked again on his face–"now I see that it is the union of kindred souls!"

She clasped both of her hands over his arm and leaned slightly toward him–closer to a life of country beauty and farther from the dreary, homeless world.

It took Joseph a few seconds to explore the action expressed and attempt an interpretation. He answered unsteadily, "And yet–with a nature like yours–you must surely find them."

Julia shook her head in disappointment, "Ah, as a woman, I cannot seek. I never thought I should be able to say–to any human being–that I have sought, or waited for, recognition. I do not know why I should say it now. I try to be myself–my true self–with all persons, but it seems impossible. My nature shrinks from some and is drawn toward others." She looked directly at him. "Why is this? What is the mystery that surrounds us?"

Joseph considered the proposition for a few moments, then countered, "Do you believe that two souls may be so united that they shall dare to surrender all knowledge of themselves to each other, as we do, helplessly, before our God?"

"O, it is my dream!" she murmured with a bright face. "I thought I was alone in cherishing it!" She tightened her grip. "Can it ever be realized?"

His brain grew hot. The resolution he had invoked during his sprint on the horse sprang to life and urged him forward. Words flew from his lips with little thought, "If it is my dream and yours–if we both have come to the faith and the hope we find in no others–and which alone will satisfy our lives–is it not a sign that the dream is over and the reality has begun?"

Miss Blessing withdrew her grip and covered her face. "Do not tempt me with what I had given up, unless you can teach me to believe again!" she cried.

"I do not tempt you," he reassured her breathlessly, "I tempt myself." He paused before adding, "I also believe."

Laying a hand upon his shoulder, Julia lifted her face and looked into Joseph's eyes with an expression of passionate eagerness and joy. Her pale-brown eyes–dark and deep–almost tearful, drew him with irresistible force. His previous shy, reticent self disappeared, dissolved in the strong instinct that possessed him body and soul. After a dizzying moment, he lowered his head to her bosom as she placed her other hand on the side of his head.

"I should like to die now," she whispered into his ear, "I never can be so happy again."

"No, no!" Joseph pulled back and stared directly into Julia's eyes. "Live for me!"

They gazed upon each other for what felt an eternity, and then she raised herself to kiss him again and again. Joseph surrendered to the passion of the moment and returned the caresses with equal warmth. The twilight deepened around them as they stood, still half-embracing.

Miss Blessing licked her lips daintily, looked up into his innocent blue eyes and asked, "Can I make you happy, Joseph?"

This conjugation fulfilled his desire to join with Miss Julia Blessing, a person whom he believed knew of his secret desires but still desired him. He smiled and responded, "Julia, I am already happier than I ever thought it possible to be."

She returned the smile then drew away impulsively. "Joseph!" she whispered, "will you always bear in mind what a cold, selfish, worldly life mine has been?" her eyes full of interrogation marks. "You do not know me. You cannot understand the school in which I have been taught. I tell you, now, that I have had to learn cunning and artifice and equivocation." Julia studied Joseph, as if waiting for a change in expression, but none came. "I am dark beside a nature so pure and good as yours!" she continued, her head resting on his chest, "If you must ever learn to hate me, begin now!" His smile only grew at her rambling words. "Take back your love. I have lived so long without the love of a noble human heart that I can live so to the end!"

With a dramatic flourish, she stepped back and moved her hands to cover her face again. Her frame shrank, as if dreading a mortal blow. Joseph reached behind and guided her back to his breast, touched, and even humiliated, by such sharp self-accusation.

When she looked up at him, her eyes appeared moist. She smiled pitifully and murmured, "I believe you *do* love me."

Joseph nodded, grinned, and said, "And I will not give you up, though you should be full of evil—as I am myself." He nodded slightly.

Julia laughed lightly and patted his cheek. She appeared to have returned to her frank, bright, winning manner at once.

Then commenced those reciprocal expressions of bliss, which are so inexhaustibly fresh to lovers, so endlessly monotonous to everybody else. Lost to time, place, and circumstance, Joseph would have prolonged them far into the night but for Miss Blessing's returning self-possession.

"I hear wheels," she warned. "The evening guests are coming, and they will expect you to receive them, Joseph." She placed one hand on his arm. "Your dear, good, old aunt will be looking for me to assist with clearing the table, to be sure." She pulled her hand back and turned away, "O, the world, the world! We must give ourselves up to it, and be as if we had never found each other. I shall be wild unless you set me an example of self-control." Joseph gently turned her head toward him with a single finger. "Yes. Let me look at you once—one full, precious, perfect look—to carry in my heart through the evening!"

They looked deeply into each other's faces, but looking was not enough, and their lips fashioned their temporary farewell without the use of words.

Joseph hurried across the bottom of the lawn to meet the stream of approaching guests, which filled the lane. Julia lingered at the top of the garden. She plucked amaranth leaves for a wreath that would look well upon her dark hair. As she skipped to the farmhouse, she sang in a voice loud enough to be heard from the portico, "Ever be happy, light as thou art, Pride of the pirate's heart!"

The partygoers began to arrive, and there were plenty—

including some who had not received a direct invitation. The easy habits of country society allowed for such transgressions, and no one got turned away. Joseph played the role of host with courage and cordiality, greeting each new arrival with his sparkling blue eyes and animated face, wishing them well.

After the dinner dishes had been put up–with the assistance of Miss Blessing–Aunt Rachel stood with the Reverend Mr. Chaffinch observing the gaiety of the company. His presence seemed to maintain the young people's behavior within decorous bounds. This allowed Rachel Miller to just stand and observe the goings-on without having to act the part of a moral detective.

Throughout the evening, Joseph continued playing at the new and uncomfortable role of host. He meandered through the garden, greeting his guests–whether invited or not–making polite conversations. It amazed him as to the number of people who attended the gathering, and it made him wonder how many were actually there to see him, his farm, or–perhaps–just Miss Blessing.

Such cordiality with his guests kept Joseph from conversing with Julia, the one person with whom he truly wished to speak. When people began to leave, he kept his eye on the Warriners' carriage, as that would be the one she would ride away in.

The air had begun to chill, and Joseph returned to the house to retrieve his gloves. In the hall, he met up with Miss Lucy Henderson. He detected a grave change in her face. Her manner not so quietly attractive, as usual. He felt the absurd blood rush to his cheeks and brow. His tongue hesitated and stammered.

He wanted to ask Lucy about her day, how she enjoyed the gathering, if she needed anything. Her uncomfortable silence squelched his ability to speak.

Without saying anything, Joseph turned and walked away. Upon looking back, he observed Lucy regarding him with an expression of surprise, not one of pain, as he had expected.

When he caught sight of Bob and Anna Warriner heading toward their rig, Joseph went out to meet them. As Miss Julia Blessing stepped up, she took his hand under her shawl, pulled him close, and whispered, "Come *soon*!" After a squeeze, she let him go and climbed aboard.

Joseph stood and watched the carriage pull away toward the main road. "Great party, Mr. Asten!" Elwood Withers pronounced from out of sight.

Joseph turned to see his friend standing behind him. His heart melted at seeing Elwood, conscious of a tenderer feeling of friendship than he had ever before felt. "Please stay the night, Elwood. I crave your company."

"Do you really mean it?"

"Yes. I feel the need to converse with you." Instead of replying, Elwood stood staring at Joseph with a cocked head. "I don't understand you, Elwood," Joseph said after a brief pause.

"Perhaps I don't understand myself." A bit of his usual laughter broke the calm. "Never mind. I'll stay."

"Thank you. Let's get your rig in the stable."

Joseph's room had two beds. As Elwood had been such a frequent visitor, Aunt Rachel saw no wrong in having a spare for her nephew's friend, just in case. Sometimes they slept in the same bed, but tonight the two men had their own.

"Did you enjoy yourself tonight?" Joseph asked.

"Oh, boy, oh, boy, I'll say I did indeed!" A smile beamed from Elwood's face. "I'm sorry that I did not get to spend much time with you, as you were playin' at bein' a host, an' all... But I made up for it by courtin' Miss Elizabeth Henderson." He looked over at Joseph, who seemed absorbed in his own thoughts. "Your Aunt Rachel put up some mighty nice refreshments. I might have gotten a bit farther with Miss Elizabeth, but with the Reverend standin' and watchin' I had to right behave myself." As Joseph had not changed his expression, Elwood inquired, "Did you spend some time with Miss Lucy Henderson?"

"Hmmm?" Joseph heard Lucy's name and it broke his concentration. "Lucy? Oh, yes."

Elwood continued to observe his friend, waiting for him to say something. When he could stand it no longer, he posed, "Do you know anything more about love, by this time?"

Joseph continued his internal debate as to whether he should confide his wonderful secret. After another awkward silence, Elwood rose up in his bed, leaned forward, and whispered, "I see. You need not answer." Still no response. "But tell me this one thing: Is it Miss Lucy Henderson?"

Joseph startled at Lucy's name. "No! Oh, no!"

"Does she know of it? Your face told some sort of a tale when you met her tonight."

"Not to her. Surely, not to her."

"Well… I'm guessin' this won't come as much of a surprise to you, but I believe I am in love with Miss Elizabeth."

"Elwood!" Joseph exclaimed as he bounded out of his bed and across the room. He sat next to his friend and hugged him. Joseph could smell the combination of Elwood's own natural perspiration combined with that of Acqua Colonia lime-and-nutmeg toilet water he had purchased at the village store a few months back. "You are happy too!" He released the hug. "O, now I can tell you all. It is Miss Julia Blessing!" Joseph smiled like a schoolboy who just learned the school had burnt down.

"Ha! Ha!" Elwood laughed. Not his usual bray, but a short, bitter, laugh that suggested disappointment. "Forgive me, Joseph, but there's a deal o' difference between a mitten an' a ring." He pulled back slightly. "You will have one an' I the other. But we won't talk o' this any more. There's many a roundabout road that comes out into the straight one at last." He smiled at Joseph. "But you! I can't understand the thing at all. How did she... Did you come to love her?"

"I don't know. I hardly guessed it myself until this evening." Joseph did not want to disclose—even to his closest friend—that he had resolved himself to hope for Miss Blessing's affection.

"Then, Joseph,"—Elwood took his friend's hand—"go slowly, and feel your way. I'm not the one to advise, after what has happened to me, but maybe I know a little more of womankind than you." He tightened his grasp a bit. "It's best to have a longer acquaintance than yours has been. A feller can't always tell a sudden fancy from a love that has the grip o' death."

They both giggled at Elwood's turn of phrase.

"Now, I might turn your own words against you, Elwood, for you tried to tell me what love is."

"I did,"—he nodded once—"and before I knew the half. But come, Joseph, promise me that you won't let Miss Blessing know how much you feel until –"

"Dearest Elwood," Joseph breathlessly interrupted, "she knows it now! We were together this evening."

Elwood fell back on the pillow with a groan. "I'm a poor friend to you. I want to wish you joy, but I can't. Not to-night. The way things are fixed in this world stumps me, out an' out. Nothin' fits as it ought, an' if I didn't take my head in my own hands an' hold it towards the light by main force, I'd only see backwards... and death... and hell..." He rolled onto his side, facing the wall.

Joseph stole back to his own bed and lay there silently. He had entertained the thought of one last tousle with Elwood before they went on to pursue their respective young ladies, but there seemed no hope for that. Recalling the glow of the tender scene in the garden with Julia could not thaw the subtle chill that had just fallen over the heart of his happiness.

Chapter 6: A Visit to the City

THE NEXT MORNING, Joseph woke to the sight of Elwood sitting on the bed beside him. A kind smile and a warm hug from his friend signified the chill of the past night had been forgotten. The betrothal, which had almost seemed like a fetter upon his future, now gave him a sense of freedom and strength.

"Thank you, Elwood," Joseph muttered. "Your friendship means the world to me." He kissed his friend gently on the cheek, believing this may be the last time he would enjoy such intimacy.

Once Elwood had left, Joseph turned to the business of tidying up from the previous evening's gathering. Dennis helped him and Aunt Rachel sort things and collect the various dishes, plates, cups, and glasses left about the property.

Joseph's thoughts strayed to Miss Julia, and he wanted to go directly to the Warriners, but his sense of duty kept him at his own farm. Besides, calling upon his intended so soon might have betrayed his secret. Miss Blessing wasn't supposed to return to the city for three days, which left him some time to plan a proper farewell visit. He continued on with his regular duties and chores, allowing another taxing day to intervene.

Joseph waited yet another intolerable day before announcing to his aunt that he wished to call on Miss Blessing before her imminent departure. Aunt Rachel nodded her ascent, seemingly unaware of what had transpired within her row of prized boxwood.

Anna Warriner met him at the door. She led Joseph to the parlor, where Miss Blessing sat waiting for her visitor. Anna smiled, nodded, and left the room quietly.

Joseph and Julia looked at each other. He hoped she had not had a change of heart during the intervening days. The bland smile upon her pale face gave no clue.

"Please sit, Mr. Asten," Julia began.

Joseph moved to the chair nearest him, directly across the room from Julia.

She laughed in her girlish way. "No, not there, silly." She pointed to the chair next to hers. "Here."

At that, he presumed her feelings had not changed since the evening of the gathering at his farm, and his chest felt warm and expansive over the prospect. Before sitting in the requested seat, he bowed, gently took Julia's hand and kissed it lightly, similar to what he remembered Elwood doing the night they had been first introduced.

"Oh, Mr. Asten,"–she flushed–"I guess there's no need to inquire into whether our little agreement is still in effect." She averted her eyes.

"No, I should say not," Joseph responded as he sat. "My feelings are much the same–if not stronger." He looked at Julia and asked, "And you?" She merely nodded. "Then I must ask–because, after all, you have more experience in such matters–what is our next step?"

Julia smiled and dropped her gaze to the floor. "I think it best that nothing should be said–by either one of us–until I have had an opportunity to acquaint my parents with our engagement." She then looked at her intended. "There might be some natural differences to overcome. This will be so unexpected, you know, and the idea of losing their daughter might be... unwelcome... at first."

Joseph nodded, agreeing to her wise words of caution.

"Once I return home, I shall wait a few days before broaching the subject with them. Then I will write of their reaction, and then you must come to make the acquaintance of my family."

"That sounds eminently reasonable," Joseph concurred.

"*Then*, I shall have no fear. When they have once seen you, all difficulties will vanish. There will be no trouble with ma and my sister Clementina, but pa is sometimes a little peculiar, on account of his connections." Joseph sighed and looked away. "There! Don't look so serious all at once. It is *my* duty, you know, to secure you a loving reception. You must try to feel already that you have two homes, as I do." She smiled.

"Miss Blessing, I fear that while I am marginally familiar with city ways—having gone there to negotiate sales of animals and grains—it is my sincerest hope that my country ways will not insult your parents or shed a light of contempt upon you."

Julia burst out with unexpected laughter. "My dear Mr. Asten! If only you knew—and you shall in a short time. City people may take notice of your different behavior, but they would never shame you for it. In fact, you might find my own father exhibiting some shameful behavior of his own."

Over the next half-hour or so, they spoke of trivial things just to keep company and delay their inevitable parting. Upon Anna Warriner's entrance, they both stood.

"Mr. Asten will be leaving now," Julia announced.

"Very good, Miss Blessing," Anna responded, as if she were a servant. "I shall show him to the door."

Joseph and Julia looked at each other one last time. "I shall write soon," she stated.

"I await your letter," Joseph replied before following Anna out.

•▼•

If it hadn't been for the farmwork, Joseph might have given in to insanity while waiting to hear from his betrothed. Every evening after supper, he rode his horse out the road to be alone with his thoughts, revisiting his decision to court Miss Blessing. He believed she truly understood him—and the internal struggle with his feelings toward other men—and he did not want to pass by this opportunity to bond with such a sympathetic person, city-bred or otherwise.

On the tenth day following her departure, the promised letter arrived:

> Would you believe it, dear Joseph, pa makes no dif-
> ficulty! He only requires some assurances which
> you can very easily furnish. Ma, on the other hand,
> don't like the idea of giving me up. It really went to
> my heart when ma met me at the door, and cried
> out, "Now I shall have a little rest!" I can hardly say
> it without seeming to praise myself, but
> Clementina never took very kindly to housekeeping
> and managing, and even if I were only indifferent
> in those branches, I should be missed."

> You may imagine how hard it was to tell her the
> news of our situation. But she is a dear, good
> mother, and I know she will be so happy to find a
> son in you—as she certainly will. Come, soon—soon!
> They are all anxious to know you.

Joseph had to manufacture a believable reason for Aunt
Rachel to explain his seemingly unnecessary excursion to the
city. She accepted his explanation with the usual skepticism.
However, Joseph imagined that as long as all the work had
been done, and Dennis would be able to help with whatever
his aunt might require, he should be granted a few days
respite.

Dennis transported him the next day—at a very early hour—
to the Oakland Station, where he boarded the train. The
tracks meandered through the Allegheny Valley and headed
eastward toward the city, a day's journey. By the time they
arrived at the station, the sun just touched the hills to the
west.

Joseph showed the Blessings' address to a nearby railroad
agent and received directions. He commenced the miles of
hot, dusty, rattling pavements seeking the brick nest which
sheltered his love within.

As he walked along the broad city streets lined with tall, brick
and marble buildings, he contemplated his circumstances. If
the consciousness of loving and being loved were not quite
the same in experience as it had seemed to his ignorant

fancy, it was yet a positive happiness. Wedlock should, therefore, be its unbroken continuance. Julia stated she had prepared for his introduction into her family. He must learn to accept her parents and sister as his own.

However, as he continued toward the Blessings' residence, a physical pressure began to build upon his breast. This mysterious force resisted his progress, and he considered turning back. His heart felt as if it were attempting to bound from its vault. Perhaps this impractical endeavor would prove more anomalous and stressful than he could handle.

He reached the cross-roads where he needed to turn northward, as the Blessing home lay several squares farther. Ahead of him lay the broad river, bristling in the late afternoon sunlight playing on its surface. Instead of heading directly to his destination, he proceeded forward. The sight of a large body of water attracted him like a siren. His home in the Allegheny River Valley had a few small lakes but nothing as large and grand.

The street ended at the riverbank, and there he caught sight of gliding sails, the lusty life and labor along the piers. Men tramped up and down the gangways of the clipper-ships, derricks slowly swung bales and boxes over the sides. Drays clattered to and fro. Everywhere he looked, he saw a picture of strength, courage, reality, and solid work. These men took life simply as a succession of facts, and if these did not fit smoothly into each other, they either gave themselves no trouble about the rough edges, or drove them out of sight with a few sturdy blows.

He observed the laborers, glistening in the last yellow glimmering of day, wondering if any of those strapping forms could comprehend the disturbance of his mind? Did any of these robust, physical men have the same strong emotional affection toward other men? Could some of them be struggling with the same conflicting desires?

The thought of Lucy Henderson's notion about going to school crossed his mind. Directly before Joseph, this riparian activity presented a class where he would be apt to stand at the foot for many days.

Joseph noticed that some of the fellows had very dark skin. He had never seen anyone of African descent until that very moment. It had only been a few years since the end of the War of the Rebellion, but he imagined that people from all over the globe found work on sailing vessels. He regarded the sable warmth, the brawny muscles, the gleam of their sweat.

He mused that should he ask any one of these workers, they would probably advise him to go to the nearest apothecary-shop and purchase a few blue-pills. As he continued to observe the goings-on at the riverside, the more he felt the contagion of their unimaginative, face-to-face grapple with life. Suddenly refreshed, Joseph reacted to the manly element within him—checked for so long—and he began to push a vigorous shoot toward the light.

It is only the old cowardice, after all, he thought to himself, *I am shrinking from the encounter with new faces!* A satisfied smile appeared on his face. *A lover, soon to be a husband, and still so much of a green youth! It will never do. I must learn to handle my duty—my duties—much the way that stevedore handles those barrels. Take hold with both hands, push and trundle and guide until the weight becomes a mere plaything.* He let free a short laugh. *There! He starts a fresh one. Now for mine!*

Joseph spun himself about and walked sternly back to the cross-street and turned without pausing at the corner. He still had many blocks to walk, and the street—its uniform brick houses with white shutters, green interior blinds and white marble steps—grew more silent and monotonous.

Various odors reached his nose: salt-fish, molasses, and decaying oranges at every corner. Dark wenches lowered the nozzles of their jetting hose as he passed, and girls in draggled calico frocks looked at him from the entrance of gloomy tunnels that led, presumably, to the back yards. A man with undistinguishable wares in a cart uttered from time to time a piercing unintelligible cry. Barefooted children played at marbles on the sidewalk, swearing unrepeatable phrases as they won or lost. Once and again, a marvelous moving fabric of silks and colors and glosses floated by him. He paused for none of them. His heart beat faster and faster, the strange resistance seemed to intensify with the increasing number of houses, now rapidly approaching The One. Then it appeared!

The entire block contained narrow, three-storied dwellings with crowded windows and flat rooves. As Joseph had little understanding of the city, he had been unable to recognize the air of cheap gentility that exhaled from them. Someone might as well have posted a sign reading, "Here we keep up appearances on a very small capital."

All the marble steps and front doors seemed alike until he came upon a brass plate inscribed "B. Blessing." For no particular reason, he looked up and saw a mass of dark curls vanish with a start from a window above. The door opened suddenly–before he could touch the bell-pull–and two hands upon his own drew him into the diminutive hall.

Behind him, the door closed instantly, then two arms flew around his neck, and his willing lips received a subdued kiss.

"Hush," she said, "It is delightful that you have arrived, though we didn't expect you so immediately. Come into the drawing-room and let us have a minute together before I call ma."

Julia tripped lightly in front of him along the narrow, rather plain, passage, and they ended up sitting side-by-side on a sofa.

"What could have brought me to the window just at that moment?" she whispered. "It must have been presentiment."

Joseph smiled at the thought his intended had sensed his arrival and watched him appear. He now felt foolish about his niggling fears, setting them aside for now. "And I was long on the way. What will you think of me, Julia? I was a little afraid."

"I know you were, Joseph," she nodded, "It is only the cold, insensible hearts that are never agitated."

Their eyes smiled as one, and, for the first time, he noticed their peculiar pale-brown, almost tawny, clearness, similar to the color of the shipmen who had fascinated him a short time before. The next instant, her long lashes slowly fell and half-concealed the beauty of her eyes.

"I should like to be beautiful for your sake. I never cared about it before." Without giving him any time to reply, she rose and moved toward the door, looked back, smiled, and disappeared.

He stood and walked softly up and down the room. In his eyes, it seemed an elegant, if rather chilly, apartment. Long and narrow, it had a small, delusive white marble fireplace in the middle of the side wall, a carpet of many glaring colors, and a paper brilliant with lilac-bunches on the walls. He stopped near a center-table that had some lukewarm literature cooling itself on the marble top. Behind him stood an *étagère* with a few nondescript cups and flagons. To the side sat a cottage piano, on which lay several sheets of music by Verdi and Balfe. What furniture there was had been upholstered in a nankeen summer dress.

On the opposite wall hung two portraits, a gentleman and a lady. The fixed stare of their lusterless eyes made it difficult to turn away. Vestiges of imperfect daylight through the bowed window shutters revealed a florid, puffy-faced young man whose head appeared to sit upon a high black satin stock. He leaned against a fluted pillar, apparently constructed of putty, behind which fell a superb crimson curtain, lifted up at one corner to disclose a patch of stormy sky. His long locks, tucked in at the temples, the carefully-delineated whiskers, and the huge signet-ring on the second finger of the one exposed hand indicated the subject of this portrait possessed or claimed of right a certain "position" in society. Joseph imagined it represented "B. Blessing" as he appeared twenty or thirty years before.

The other portrait, a slender lady, meant to be graceful, her head inclined so that the curls on the left side rolled in studied disorder upon her shoulder. Her thin, long face, while not unpleasant, had been well-marked. The bloom on her cheek seemed too positive, and the fixed smile on the narrow mouth scarcely harmonized with the hard, serious stare of her eyes. One plump, bare arm hung with a listless grace from under a royal purple gown.

Joseph looked from one portrait to the other with a curious interest, and the painted eyes appeared to follow his gaze. Strangers out of a different sphere of life, yet they must become—nay, they were already—a part of his own! The lady scrutinized him closely, despite her clever smile, but the gentleman remained indifferent, blandly satisfied with himself, giving little assurance to his prospects.

The sound of footsteps from the hall interrupted his reverie, and he had barely time to slip into the seat when the door opened. Julia entered, followed by the original of one of the portraits. Joseph recognized her easily, although the curls had disappeared, some gray had infiltrated the dark hair. Deep lines about the mouth and eyes suggested an expression of care and discontent. His own aunt displayed similar signs of aging. However, this woman's eyes were gray, the one apparent distinguishing difference between mother and daughter here.

As Joseph rose to meet Julia's mother, she bent her head with a stately air, walked past her daughter, and extended her hand with the words, "Mr. Asten, I am glad to see you. Pray be seated." The three of them sat, Julia and her mother occupied a pale-colored, padded settee. "Excuse me if I begin by asking a question," she continued, "You must consider that I have only known you through Julia, and her description could not—under the circumstances—be very clear." Her gray eyes, like the representation in the portrait, seized his attention. "What is your age?"

"I recently attained my twenty-third year," Joseph replied.

"Indeed! I am happy to hear it. You do not look more than

nineteen. I have reason to dread *very* youthful attachments"–she rolled her eyes–"and am therefore reassured to know that you are fully a man and competent to test your feelings. I trust that you *have* so tested them. Again I say, excuse me if the question seems to imply a want of confidence. A mother's anxiety, you know..."

Julia clasped her hands and bent down her head.

"I am quite sure of myself," Joseph responded, "and would try to make you as sure, if I knew how to do it."

The mother studied him with renewed vigilance. "If you were one of us–of the city, I mean–I should be able to judge more promptly. It is many years since I have been outside of our own select circle, and I am, therefore, not so competent as once to judge of men in general. While I will never–without the most sufficient reason–influence my daughters in their choice, it is my duty to tell you that Julia is exceedingly susceptible on the side of her affections. A wound *there* would be incurable to her." She shifted her gaze to Julia. "We are alike in that. I know her nature through my own."

Julia leaned toward her mother and hid her face upon the ample shoulder. Joseph swallowed with some difficulty upon seeing the display of tenderness between the two, racking his brain for some form of assurance that might remove the maternal anxiety.

"There," Mrs. Blessing announced, "we will say no more about it now. Go and bring your sister!"

At the command from her mother, Julia stood, smiled at Joseph and left the airless room.

"There are some other points, Mr. Asten," the mother continued after the daughter had left, "which have no doubt already occurred to your mind. Mr. Blessing will consult with you in relation to them. I make it a rule never to trespass upon his field of duty. As you were not positively expected to-day, he went to the Custom House as usual, but it will soon be time for him to return. Official labors–you understand–cannot be postponed. If you have ever served in a government capacity, you will appreciate his position. I have sometimes wished that we had not become identified with political life, but–on the other hand–there are compensations."

Mrs. Blessing's important manners impressed Joseph more than the words she uttered. He offered, "I beg that my visit may not interfere in any way with Mr. Blessing's duties."

"Unfortunately, they cannot be postponed." Her nose shifted up slightly. "His advice is more required by the Collector than his special official services. But–as I said–he will confer with you in regard to the future of our little girl." She smiled tightly and turned to look at the spot Julia had recently occupied. "I call her so, Mr. Asten, because she is the youngest, and I can hardly yet realize that she is old enough to leave me." Mrs. Blessing returned her attention to Joseph. "Yes, the youngest, and the first to go. Had it been Clementina, I should have been better prepared for the change, but a mother should always be ready to sacrifice herself where the happiness of a child is at stake." She gently pressed a small handkerchief to the corner of each steely eye then heaved a breathy sigh.

At this point, Joseph reconsidered a story from the Bible. Jacob had agreed to work on Laban's farm for seven years in the expectation of Rachel's hand in marriage. He did not know there was an older daughter whom the father believed should marry first, and he substituted Leah on the wedding day. Jacob agreed to work yet another seven years to wed Rachel. Joseph hoped that Mr. Blessing's attitude differed from that of Laban because did not want to be 37 years old when he would finally be able to marry Julia.

The door opened presently, and Julia re-entered, followed by her sister.

"This is Miss Blessing," the mother introduced.

Julia's older sister bowed very formally, and would have

completed her greeting, but Joseph had already risen and extended his hand. She presented the tips of four limp fingers, which he attempted to grasp and then let go.

Clementina appeared somewhat taller than her younger sister, perhaps as much as a head, and her frame reflected ample proportions. Her mouth looked small and petulant, her undersized gray eyes sat beneath a low, narrow forehead. Light brown hair framed a face as puffy as on her father's portrait, yet her beautiful complexion suggested a bloom of brilliance.

On her first glance at Joseph, a faint expression of curiosity passed over her face, but she uttered no word of welcome.

Joseph turned to Julia, who had become suddenly subdued, and he perceived a rivalry between the two sisters. The stolidity of Clementina's countenance indicated that sort of indifference more offensive than enmity. As much as Joseph would have preferred to like her straightaway, this first impression fostered aversion.

"Pleased to make your acquaintance, Miss Blessing," Joseph attempted to break the chilled air.

Clementina merely nodded and uttered, "Sure."

Joseph turned to Julia, but she kept modestly silent. Mrs. Blessing spoke up, "Dear, why don't you tell Mr. Asten that you are happy to meet him?"

"Yes," came the terse answer with a silver sweetness that seemed at variance with her face and manner.

"Mr. Asten has a very large farm in the Allegheny River Valley," announced Mrs. Blessing. "Two hundred acres, I believe."

"Mmmm," responded Clementina with a cryptic smile and slight tilt of her head.

"Come along, Clementina," the mother began to stand. "Of course you will stay for our family dinner, Mr. Asten," she turned to Joseph. "I will order it to be earlier served, as you are probably not accustomed to our city hours." With her eldest daughter in tow, she left the room and closed the door behind her.

Julia immediately perked up. "Now! When ma says *that*, you may be satisfied. Her housekeeping is like the laws of the Medes and Persians. She probably seemed rather formal to you, and it is true that a certain amount of form has become natural to her, but it always gives way when she is strongly moved. Pa is to come yet, but I am sure you will get on very well with him. Men always grow acquainted in a little while. I'm afraid that Clementina did not impress you very... very genially. She is—I may confess it to you—a little peculiar."

Not wanting to say anything negative about his prospective sister-in-law, Joseph said, "She is very quiet... and very unlike you." He smiled at Julia.

"Everyone notices that. And we seem to be unlike in character. So much so as if there were no relationship between us. But I must say for Clementina, that she is above personal likings and dislikings. She looks at people abstractly. You are only a future brother-in-law to her, and I don't believe she can tell whether your hair is black or the beautiful golden brown that it is."

Joseph smiled and blushed slightly due to Julia's delicate flattery. "I am all the more delighted that you are different. I should not like you, Julia, to consider me an abstraction."

She chuckled. "You are very real, Joseph Asten, and very individual," she answered with one of her loveliest smiles.

"You make me supremely happy, Julia Blessing—soon to be Asten—to receive such a positive assessment." He returned the smile. Joseph enjoyed her gay, unrestrained talk.

The sound of a latch-key from beyond the door interrupted their conversation. Julia sprang up, laid a forefinger on her lips, gave Joseph a swift, significant glance, and darted into the hall. He could hear whispering and the deep, hoarse murmur of an older man's voice.

The door opened, and in stepped Mr. Blessing, without the

fluted pillar and the crimson curtain. The years had added to his body and taken away from his hair. As high stocks around the neck were no longer in fashion, his face had lost its rigid lift, and it expressed the chronic cordiality of a popular politician. Beneath the full lids, the rims of his eyes showed a redness, which could also have denoted political habits. However, despite wrinkles, redness, and a general roughening and coarsening of the features, he still strongly resembled the portrait. Overall, a less formidable man than Joseph had anticipated. He stood and offered his hand as soon as Mr. Blessing entered the room.

"Very happy to see you, Mr. Asten," Julia's father affirmed. "An unexpected pleasure, sir." He then attended to his own clothing, first removing the glove from his left hand. After that, he pulled down his coat and vest, felt the tie of his cravat, twitched at his pantaloons, ran his fingers through his straggling gray locks, and finally threw himself into a chair exclaiming, "After business–pleasure, sir!"

Julia offered Joseph a sly smile, but his attention focused on the act of disassembling just carried out before him.

"My duties are over for the day," Mr. Blessing continued. "Mrs. Blessing probably informed you of my official capacity, but you can have no conception of the vigilance required to prevent evasion of the revenue laws." He squinted and then smiled. "We are the country's watch-dogs, sir."

Joseph sat. "I can understand that an official position carries with it much responsibility."

"Quite right, sir, quite right, and without adequate remuneration." He poked a finger in the air pointedly. "Figuratively speaking, we handle millions, and we are paid by dimes. Were it not for the consciousness of serving and saving for the nation–but I will not pursue the subject." He held up an open palm as if to halt the conversation. "When we have become better acquainted, you can judge for yourself whether preferment always follows capacity. Our present business is to establish a platform–and I think you will agree with me that the circumstances of the case require frank dealing, as between man and man." By the end of his soliloquy, Mr. Blessing's attention focused squarely on Joseph.

"Certainly!" Joseph answered. "I only ask that–although I am a stranger to you–you will accept my word until you have the means of verifying it." He observed the older man for a sign of concurrence.

"I may safely do that with you, sir. My associations–duties, I may say–compel me to know many persons with whom it would *not* be safe. We will forget the disparity of age and experience between us. I can hardly ask you to imagine yourself placed in my situation, but perhaps we can make the case quite as clear if I state to you–without reserve–what *I* should be ready to do–if our present positions were reversed." He coughed into a fist and then turned to his daughter, "Julia, will you look after the dinner?"

"Yes, pa," she responded and slipped out of the drawing-room.

Mr. Blessing turned his attention to Joseph once more. "If I were a young man from the country, and had won the affections of a young lady of... well–I may say it to you–of an old family, whose parents were ignorant of my descent, means, and future prospects in life, I should consider it my first duty to enlighten those parents upon all these points." He jabbed a stubby finger at Joseph. "I should reflect that the lady must be removed from their sphere to mine, that while the attachment was–in itself–vitally important to her and to me, those parents would naturally desire to compare the two spheres, and assure themselves that their daughter would lose no material advantages by the transfer." His eyes widened suddenly. "You catch my meaning?"

Despite the intense scrutiny imposed by his future father-in-law, Joseph responded calmly. "I came here with the single intention of satisfying you–at least, I came hoping that I shall be able to do so–in regard to myself." He stared back. "It will be easy for you to test my statements."

Mr. Blessing nodded. "Very well. We will begin, then, with

the subject of Family. Understand me, I mention this solely because, in our old communities, Family is the stamp of Character." He assumed a pose similar to the one in the old portrait. "An established name represents personal qualities and virtues. It is indifferent to me whether my original ancestor was a De Belsain–though beauty and health have always been family characteristics–but it *is* important that he transmitted certain traits which... which others, perhaps, can better describe." Mr. Blessing turned a probing eye toward Joseph. "The name of Asten is not usual. It has, in fact, rather a distinguished sound, but I am not acquainted with its derivation."

Joseph took a deep breath before continuing. "My great-grandfather came from England more than a hundred years ago. That is all I positively know. I have heard it said that the family was originally Danish."

Once again, Mr. Blessing scrutinized Joseph's face. "You must look into the matter, sir. A good pedigree is a bond for good behavior. The Danes–I have been told–were of the same blood as the Normans." A small cough emanated from his throat. "But we will let that pass. Julia informs me you are the owner of a handsome farm, yet I am so ignorant of values in the country, and my official duties oblige me to measure property by such a different standard that, really, unless you could make the farm evident to me in figures I –"

"I have two hundred acres"–he interrupted, having prepared himself to deliver the desired intelligence–"and a moderate valuation of the place would be a hundred and thirty dollars an acre. There is a mortgage of five thousand dollars on the place, the term of which has not yet expired, but I have nearly an equal amount invested so that the farm fairly represents what I own." He wanted to smile with satisfaction at his recitation, but fought to keep his pride within.

"Hmmmmm," Mr. Blessing mused, thrusting his thumbs into the arm-holes of his waistcoat. "That is not a great deal here in the city, but I dare say it is a handsome competence in the country. It doubtless represents a certain annual income!"

"It is a very comfortable home, in the first place." Joseph felt uncomfortable being challenged on the quality of his family's fine property. "The farm ought to yield–after supplying nearly all the wants of a family–an annual return of a thousand to fifteen hundred dollars, according to the season."

"Twenty-six thousand dollars! And five percent!" Mr. Blessing exclaimed. "If you had the farm in money, and knew how to operate with it, you might pocket ten, fifteen, twenty per cent. Many a man with less than that to set him afloat has become a millionaire in five years' time, but it takes pluck and experience, sir!"

"More of both than I can lay claim to," Joseph remarked, "but what there is of my income is certain. If Julia were not so fond of the country–and already so familiar with our ways–I might hesitate to offer her such a plain, quiet home, but –"

"O, I know!" Mr. Blessing interrupted. "We have heard of nothing but cows and spring-houses and willow-trees since she came back. I hope, for your sake, it may last for I see that you are determined to suit each other. I have no inclination to act the obdurate parent. You have met me like a man, sir. Here's my hand." He stood and moved to Joseph. "I feel sure that–as my son-in-law–you will keep up the reputation of the family!"

Following a hearty handshake, Mr. Blessing led the way to a small dining-room at the rear of the home. Upon seeing Mrs. Blessing, her husband performed a queer gesture–touching the tip of his right ear with the index finger of his left hand. She nodded. Mrs. Blessing then caught Clementina's attention and performed an exaggerated nod of her head. It seemed that the family had a secret communication system Joseph had yet to decipher.

They all sat at a table very unlike what Joseph would have seen at home. Instead of large bowls and platters heaping with food, the Blessing table contained diminutive dishes containing slices so delicate as to mock, rather than excite, the appetite.

When offered tea, Joseph took the little cup, the thin tea, five drops of milk, and a fragment of sugar without asking himself about the palatability of the beverage. He divided a leaf-like piece of flesh and consumed several wafers of bread, blissfully unaware whether it satisfied his stomach.

He knew the Blessings had accepted him as one of their own when Clementina asked, in her most silvery tone, "May I offer you the butter, Mr. Asten?" The furtive signals passed along earlier must have conveyed Mr. Blessing's blessing.

While Joseph saw his future father-in-law as bland, his wife seemed maternally interested, and they had appeared to acquiesce to his presence. Clementina recognized his existence, and Julia—he needed but one look at her sparkling eyes, her softly flushed cheeks, her bewitching excitement of manner, to guess the relief of her heart. Once he realized Julia's happiness, he forgot the vague distress that had preceded his arrival and the embarrassment of his first reception.

"Joseph," Mrs. Blessing declared, "if I may call you that now that we are properly acquainted"—Joseph nodded his acceptance—"as I cannot yet entitle you 'son' until after the happy day." She smiled brightly with a slight tilt of her head. "You shall remain with us tonight." He began to hold up a hand in dismissal. "No, I will not take 'no' for an answer, young man. I insist." Joseph cast his eyes down. "I want you to consider this house as your home as well."

"Thank you, Mrs. Blessing. I appreciate your hospitality." He began to feel more comfortable about her as a mother figure, perhaps even closer than his own Aunt Rachel back home.

"Let us retire to the drawing-room," Mr. Blessing suggested as he stood. The family trundled back down the hall. Clementina played the old piano and Julia sang in her bird-like voice. The parents continued to observe Joseph as he watched the performance. A clock struck the hour.

"Oh, my, how late it has gotten," Mrs. Blessing commented. "Perhaps you should show Mr. Asten to his room, Mr. Blessing. He has had a long day's journey, and we may have already passed over his accustomed hour for retiring. If so, I know he will excuse us. We shall soon become familiar with each other's habits."

Joseph said good-night to each of the ladies, saving Julia for the last. He followed Mr. Blessing to the stairs and up to the second floor.

"You shall stay here for the night, Mr. Asten," the older man commanded, showing Joseph into a small, sparsely-furnished bedroom.

"Thank you, sir, and a good-night to you."

"Yes," Mr. Blessing huffed, "a good-night to you." He closed the door behind him.

As the walls and floors of the house had been fashioned with the thinnest possible materials, Joseph could hear Mr. Blessing descending the staircase and returning to the parlor below. While he could not discern every word, he could tell who spoke as the family continued to converse. The smell of stale tobacco permeated the room, suggesting that Julia's father took to cigars.

Even with all the day's events, Joseph felt no inclination to sleep. He sat in the small chair by the open window–the very one Julia must have espied him from earlier–and looked down into the dim, melancholy street. Every so often, a forlorn pedestrian approached through gloom and lamplight, the shrinking and lengthening shadows intrigued him.

The new acquaintances he had just made remained all the more vividly in his thoughts from their nearness. He remained within their atmosphere. He had never known any people like the Blessings, and he worried that he might do them injustice by a hasty estimate of their character.

While the parents had received him with as much consideration as a total stranger could expect, her sister, Clementina did not behave as charitably. Whatever they might all be, Julia appeared the same here, in her own home, as when a visitor in the country.

He began to consider whether her present life in the city might not be congenial to her playful, winning, and natural character. If so, her happiness would be all the more assured by her departure.

This thought led him into a pictured labyrinth of anticipation, in which his mind wandered with delight. In his thoughts he began to plan his new household, how he could make accommodations for Julia that would ease her transition to country life. He felt that living away from the complications and struggles of the city would be the best thing for her.

Presently, he heard the two sisters at the top of the stairs entering the rear room on the same floor.

"White satin!" Clementina's distinctively brusque voice pronounced. "Of course, I shall have the same. It will become *me* better than you."

"I should think you might be satisfied with a light silk," Julia countered. "The expenses will be very heavy. It will be an autumn wedding, and the weather will remain pleasant."

"We'll see," Clementina answered shortly. Pacing up and down the room could be heard.

Julia spoke after a pause, "Never mind. I shall soon be out of your way."

The pacing stopped abruptly. "I wonder how much he knows about you!" It appeared the women had no idea that Joseph remained awake and that their conversation carried down the hall. "Your arts were new there, and you played an easy game." Clementina's voice diminished, and Joseph could only distinguish a detached word now and then.

He rose from the chair, indignant at this unsisterly assault, thinking, at first, that he wished to hear no more, but, instead, he crept to the door and placed one ear upon it just in time to hear Julia say, "complexion."

"You are fortunate that ma and pa have accepted your choice," Clementina's voice rang clearly again. "At least pa approves of his *worth!*"

"Sister!" Julia exclaimed. "How indelicate! If my marriage to Joseph can keep our family from having to pawn the cherished contents of our home–as well as ma's diamonds, my rubies and your precious pearls–you should be happy for me–if not for yourself."

"Oh, Julia, if you can't have white, you turn around and say there's no other color than black."

"Dear sister, we must maintain our place in the circle, you know," Julia responded. "Save face. We must save face."

"Well, there is one thing," Clementina taunted, "one thing you will keep very secret, and that is your birthday, dear sister. Are you going to tell him that you are –"

The door must not have closed all the way because as Joseph leaned a bit harder to hear, the latch made a loud "clack!" Concerned that his subterfuge might be discovered, he quickly walked across to the window and closed it, not wanting the frequent noises from the street to interrupt his sleep.

Joseph slipped into the bed and could still hear the two sisters talking, but he could not make out the words used. Before drifting off to sleep, he came to the conclusion that he would be more than a lover to Julia; he would be her deliverer. This welcome idea gave a new value and significance to his life.

Chapter 7: Joseph and his New Friend

JOSEPH NEEDED TO GET BACK TO THE STATION quite early the next morning in order to catch the train home. In the hall outside the room where he had slept, he met Julia and Clementina emerging from their rooms.

"Good morning, Mr. Asten," Julia warbled with a pert smile, "I hope you slept well."

"Yes. Yes, I did, and thank you for asking," he responded. "I trust that you both had a pleasant night as well. I would have liked to speak with you more; however, I must leave fairly soon to catch my train."

"That is too bad. We wanted to discuss our future plans. Can you not stay another day?" Julia entreated with rueful eyes.

Joseph shook his head. "No. I must return immediately. I am not sure Aunt Rachel can manage with me gone for more than two days."

"Yes. I understand," Julia replied. "Well"–she shot a glance at her sister–"we have decided the wedding should be in October. Does that date bode well for you?"

He thought of the coming harvest and his other duties about the farm. "I believe October bodes well for us. Most of the important chores should be finished or near-finished by then."

"It is settled!" Julia proclaimed. "October it is! I shall hope to see you before then."

"Oh, yes. We must meet again before too long, but at this moment, I need to meet a train." He walked toward the top of the stairway. Clementina stood partially blocking the way. "Miss Blessing?" Joseph requested politely. Clementina merely nodded and stepped aside barely enough for him to pass.

"Good-bye, my love," Julia waved from the landing. "Safe travels to you."

Joseph stopped at the bottom of the stairs to take one last look at his wife-to-be before he departed. Out on the busy street, he encountered many of the same sounds and smells as the day before. When he reached the street that led to the docks, he momentarily thought of taking a few minutes to observe the working men once more but then realized he might miss his appointment at the rail station.

He arrived with a few minutes to spare. It did not take long to find an empty seat next to a window. As the train moved slowly through the straggling and shabby suburbs, it increased in speed as the city melted gradually into the country.

Because he began to approach the usual destiny of men, they had a new interest for him. He used to look upon strange faces very much as on strange languages, without the thought of interpreting them. He gave new attention to the hieroglyphics upon the masks of others and attempted to decipher the meaning they suggested.

He leaned back in his seat and took note of his fellow-travelers. The figures about him told so many sitting, silent histories, so many locked-up records of struggle, loss, gain, and all the other forces that give shape and color to human life. Most of them had no knowledge of the others as well and as reticent in their railway conventionality as himself. He reflected on how the whole range of passion, pleasure, and suffering could be illustrated in this collection of existences. His own troublesome individuality grew fainter, so much of it seemed merged into the common experience of men.

Joseph observed the portly gentleman of fifty, still ruddy and full of unwasted force. The keenness and coolness of his eyes, the few firmly marked lines on his face, and the color and hardness of his lips proclaimed to everybody, "I am bold, shrewd, successful in business, scrupulous in the performance of my religious duties (on the Sabbath), sitting well with my party, and not likely to be fooled by any kind of sentimental nonsense."

Beside that fellow sat a thin, not very-well-dressed man with irregular features and an uncertain expression. His general appearance seemed to say, "I am weak, like others, but I never consciously did any harm. I just manage to get along in the world, but if I only had a chance, I might make something better of myself."

Across the way sat a man with an ample mouth, large nostrils, and the hands of a mechanic. His story might have been, "On the whole, I find life a comfortable thing. I don't know much about it, but I take it as it comes and never worry over what I can't understand."

The faces of younger men, however, proved more difficult to interpret. On them, life had only begun its plastic task, and it required an older eye to detect the delicate touches of awakening passions and hopes. He spied a fresh, healthy fellow holding a sleeping child in his lap while his wife nursed a younger one. What secrets they must have that he could not unmask due to their youth.

Joseph consoled himself with the thought that his own secrets lay as undiscoverable by other strangers. If they were still ignorant of the sweet experiences of love, he felt superior to them. Should they have been sharers in it–though strangers–he felt nearer to them. Had he not left the foot of the class after all?

All at once, a new face, three or four seats from his own, attracted his eye. The stranger had shifted his position so that Joseph could see him full-on, rather than from behind. The man appeared to be a few years older than Joseph, but it might have been difficult to tell because he had dark, sable skin similar to the men working on the docks by the river. His eyes–deep green, like a polished jadestone–still shown bright with the charm of early manhood. Joseph observed his hands, which appeared graceful without being effeminate, as belonging to someone familiar with manual work, not those of the idle gentleman. Atop his head sat a squat, round-crowned, short-brimmed black hat covering his closely-cropped and oiled black hair. A mustache concealed his upper lip, but the lower one appeared firm and full.

Joseph sensed an immediate attraction to him, not just because of his moderate good looks, but because he sensed a more developed character and a richer past history expressed in those features than in any other face there. He felt sure—and smiled at himself for the impression—that at least some of his own doubts and difficulties had found their solution in this stranger's nature. As a Colored person, he must have to deal with the fact of his being different every day, if not every minute. The more Joseph studied the face, the more he became conscious of its attraction. His instinct of reliance—though utterly without grounds—justified itself to his mind in some mysterious way.

It didn't take long before the unknown felt Joseph's gaze. He turned slowly in his seat and answered it. Joseph dropped his eyes in some confusion, but not until he had caught the other's full, warm, intense expression. From that momentary flash, he fancied that he read what he had never before found in the eyes of strangers: a simple, human interest, above curiosity and above mistrust. One would usually reply to such a gaze with unconscious defiance, the unknown nature on its guard. However, the look which might convey, *We are men, let us know each other!* is, alas, too rare in this world.

While Joseph fought the irresistible temptation to look again, a sudden thud of the car-wheels threw many of the passengers from their seats, only to be thrown into them again by a quick succession of violent jolts. Joseph caught sight of the stranger springing toward the bell-rope. The next moment, he and all others seemed to be whirling over each other. He heard a crash, a horrible grinding and splintering sound, and, at the end of it all, a shock. He lost consciousness before he could guess the intensity of its violence.

●▼●

After a while—out of some blank—haunted by a single lost, wandering sense of existence, he began to awaken slowly to life. Flames danced in his eyeballs while waters and whirlwinds roared in his ears. He felt himself partially lifted and his head supported. The cacophony of noises all about overwhelmed him. A soft warmth fell upon the region of his heart, and his effort to regain consciousness fixed itself on that point alone, and he grew stronger as the warmth on his chest calmed the confusion of his nerves.

"Dip this in water!" someone said as the warmth–which might have been a hand–lifted from his heart. Something cold came over his forehead, and at the same time warm drops fell upon his cheek.

"Look out for yourself. Your head is cut!" exclaimed another voice.

"Only a scratch," the person nearest to him said calmly. "Take the handkerchief out of my pocket and tie it up. But first, ask that gentleman for his flask." This voice resounded like Gabriel's golden horn, but much deeper in tone. It filled Joseph with reassurance and hope.

When Joseph opened his eyes, they could barely make out the face that bent over his, and he closed them again. Gentle and strong hands raised him, someone set a flask to his lips, and he drank mechanically. A full sense of life followed the draught. He looked up wistfully into the stranger's face and attempted to reach out to touch it.

"Wait a moment!" the dark, blurry face ordered. "I must feel your bones before you try to move." Joseph could feel powerful, firm hands on his body testing the fitness of his skeleton. "Arms and legs all right... impossible to tell about the ribs... There! Now put your arm around my neck–and lean on me as much as you like–while I lift you."

Joseph did as bidden, but he still felt weak and giddy. After a few steps, they both sat down together upon a bank. It had been the Colored fellow who rescued him. The handsome stranger from the passenger car who sat a few rows away, he remembered. His face arranged itself into a smile instinctively.

The splintered car lay near them upside down. The passengers had been extricated from it and others busily aided the few who had been injured. Some seemed worried about their own health, or the health of others. Many voiced their concerns about the delay.

Joseph could now see the rest of the train cars sitting on the track above, still and waiting. He turned to the obliging stranger. "How did it happen?" A blood-stained gray handkerchief circled the fellow's head. "Where was I, and how did you find me?"

"The usual story: a broken rail," the gentleman said in his deep, golden voice. "I had just caught the rope when the car went over, and was swung off my feet so luckily that I somehow escaped the hardest shock. I don't think I lost my senses for a moment." The deep green eyes peered into Joseph's. "When we came to the bottom, you were lying just before me. I thought you dead until I felt your heart. It is a severe shock, but I hope nothing more."

"But you? Are you badly hurt?" Joseph pointed to the handkerchief.

"It must have been one of the splinters." The fellow pushed up the handkerchief that someone had tied around his head and felt his temple. "I know nothing about it. But there is no harm in a little blood-letting"–he chuckled and then looked at Joseph–"except the spots on your face." He removed the cloth from his head, revealing a small gash along the temple. Then he dabbed at Joseph's face and tucked the handkerchief back into its pocket.

The whistle sounded two short bursts, a warning of departure. All around, people began climbing the hillside, with the injured carried by other passengers or rail staff.

"I think we can get up the embankment now," said the stranger. "You must let me take care of you still. I am traveling alone." The gentleman picked up his hat and placed it on his head, covering the dried wound.

Joseph nodded and they ascended together, slowly, with

Joseph leaning on his care-taker's arm for added support. Just as they neared the top, Joseph looked behind at the wrecked car below. "Are they just going to leave that there?"

"I guess so." The other fellow turned and looked down. "These people seem quite determined to get to wherever it is they're going."

"Is this a frequent occurrence?"

"I should hope not," the stranger said with raised eyebrows as he climbed onboard and then assisted in raising Joseph onto the car.

They sat side-by-side, and Joseph leaned his head back on the supporting arm. After two long whistle toots, the train began to move again, and he felt a new power, a new support, had come to his life.

The face upon which he looked no longer seemed strange. The hand that had rested on his heart had been warm with kindred blood. Involuntarily, he extended his own. The other fellow took it and held it, the green, courageous eyes turned to Joseph with a silent assurance that needed no words.

After a brief silence, the stranger said, "It is a rough introduction. My name is Philip Held. I was on my way to Oakland Station, but if you are going farther –"

"Why, that is my station also!" Joseph exclaimed. "I live nearby. My name is Joseph Asten."

"Then we should have probably met–sooner or later–in any case." He smiled warmly. "I am bound for the forge and furnace at Coventry, which is for sale. If the company who employs me decides to buy it–according to the report I shall make–the works will be placed in my charge."

"It is but six miles from my farm," Joseph announced, "and the road up the valley is the most beautiful in our neighborhood. I hope you can make a favorable report."

The two men gazed into each other's eyes for an indeterminable amount of time. Their hands grew warm, and beads of sweat began to form on their foreheads.

"It is only too much to my own interest to do so." Philip let go of Joseph's hand, picked up the handkerchief and wiped his brow. "I have been mining and geologizing in Nevada and the Rocky Mountains for three or four years, and I long for a quiet, ordered life." He returned the cloth to his pocket. "It is a good omen that I have found a neighbor in advance of my settlement. I have often ridden fifty miles to meet a friend who cared for something else than horse-racing or *monte*. Your six miles"–he pointed at Joseph–"it is but a step!"

Joseph studied his new friend for a moment. He had never spoken to another man with such dark skin before. Rumors abounded–of course–how disorderly some people of the Negro Race behaved, especially after President Lincoln ordered their freedom from enslavement in the Southern states. He had heard stories of wild abandon, looting, riots, and chaos, all retribution for the way they and their ancestors had been treated. Philip exhibited none of those disagreeable qualities and so many of the ones Joseph admired.

"How much you have seen!" said Joseph. "I know very little of the world. It must be easy for you to take your own place in life."

Philip's face shifted, as if a cloud passed over it. "It is only easy to a certain class of men," he said guardedly. "A class to which I should not care to belong." He faced Joseph directly. "I begin to think that nothing is very valuable, the right to which a man don't earn–except human love, and that seems to come by the grace of our Lord."

Joseph smiled at this sentiment. He then felt compelled to pose a question. "Philip, I don't mean to be insensitive, but I've never met someone like you–someone of your Race–before. If I may ask, do prefer to be called a Negro, Black, or some other –"

"I would prefer it if you called me Philip," he interjected.

Joseph laughed nervously. "Of course. Forgive me. I am younger than you are–just twenty-three. You will find that I am very ignorant."

"And I am twenty-eight, just beginning to get my eyes open, like a nine-days' kitten. If I had been frank enough to confess my ignorance five years ago—as you do now—it would have been better for me." He smiled at Joseph. "But don't let us measure ourselves or our experience against each other. That is one good thing we learn in Rocky Mountain life: There is no high or low, knowledge or ignorance, except what applies to the needs of men who come together." Philip became serious suddenly. "So there are needs which most men have—and go all their lives hungering for—because they expect them to be supplied in a particular form. There is something deeper than that in human nature."

Joseph longed to open his heart to this man, every one of whose words struck home to something within himself. He had never heard another man speak so eloquently and expressively in a way that cut right to his essential being.

The effects left behind by the shock began to take hold, and a lassitude gradually overcame him. Joseph suffered his head to be drawn upon Philip Held's shoulder, and there he slept until the train reached Oakland Station.

Dennis stood waiting on the platform, the farm's light country cart off to the side. News of the accident had reached the station, and the hired man displayed dismay upon seeing the two bloody faces. Dr. Worrall, the village physician, had been summoned, and he gave them an examination. For Joseph, he prescribed quiet and bromide. The doctor then went on to treat other passengers. Once he had finished with all the familiar faces, he then turned his attention to Philip and applied a plaster on his abraded temple.

"Would you please accompany us back to my farm, Mr. Held?" Joseph asked his new friend.

Philip smiled at the request. "It would be my pleasure, Mr. Asten. However, please keep in mind that I have an appointment in the morning."

"Yes, of course. Dennis?"

The three men walked to the vehicle and boarded. Along the way, Joseph pointed out various landmarks to Philip.

Upon arrival at home, Aunt Rachel stood outside the farmhouse door, her agitation clearly discernable at the sight of her nephew's condition. She ran up to the approaching cart but abruptly halted a few steps away. Her face quickly angled to the unfamiliar Black man sitting with Dennis and her nephew. After a few scrutinizing glances, she shouted, "Joseph! Joseph! What has happened to you?"

He hugged his aunt gently. "Aunt Rachel, this is Mr. Philip Held. We met on the ill-fated train, and if it were not for the assistance of this gentleman, I might not be here now to tell the story." He turned to Philip. "And this is my Aunt, Rachel Miller."

Rachel might have had previous encounters with men of Philip's Race in the past, but she gave no indication of favor or distaste. She extended her hand in welcome as she might to any unfamiliar person.

"Miss Miller, a pleasure to meet you, ma'am," Philip grasped the offered hand lightly.

Rachel grabbed Philip's hand with both hands and squeezed tightly. "Mr. Held, thank you for bringing my boy back to me. Will you please stay for dinner?"

Philip looked at Joseph—who merely smiled in delight at seeing his aunt take to a stranger so quickly—then back at Rachel. "I would be delighted, ma'am, but I will need to leave before sunset as I must get to Coventry before nightfall. The proprietor of the forge there is expecting me in the morning."

She led them into the house, Joseph in her right hand, Philip in her left. "You mean you won't stay the night? I insist."

"We do have an extra bed..." Joseph added.

"No, no, I cannot accept your gracious hospitality, I'm afraid, but a meal would do much to erase some of the day's unhappy memories."

Over dinner, Joseph and Philip described the train accident.

Philip had to narrate the part after the crash as Joseph had been unconscious. Rachel looked from one to the other as the events unfolded across her table.

"Mr. Held, I cannot say enough to express my appreciation of your good deeds today. While I understand you are unable to remain with us for the night, will you at least allow Dennis to convey you to Coventry?"

Philip glanced at Joseph, who nodded, and then turned to Rachel. "Miss Miller, I thank you for your kind consideration and this wonderful meal. Yes, I would gladly accept a ride to my destination."

"I'll go with you!" Joseph exclaimed.

Both Rachel and Philip looked at him with concern. "As much as I would cherish further conversation with you, my friend, I believe that Dr. Worrall ordered you to rest, and it might be better if you remained here with your aunt."

"Yes, of course. You're right," Joseph lowered his head.

"But Mr. Held will return to visit with you soon, I'm sure," Aunt Rachel beamed. "And, if it's not too much to ask, could you assist my nephew with getting up to his bed?"

"Of course," Philip answered promptly. "It would be my pleasure.

The two started up the stairs as Dennis exited and Rachel began clearing the table. Philip assisted Joseph into his bed.

"Thank you for everything. I do believe I might have died today without your care, Philip. When will you return?" he asked with pleading eyes.

"Sooner than you might expect," Philip replied with a quick wink. He bent down over Joseph, hugged him and then kissed him on the cheek.

Chapter 8: Approaching Fate

ELWOOD WITHERS CAME TO VISIT THE NEXT AFTERNOON, once he completed all of his farm chores. Aunt Rachel sent him upstairs to Joseph's room.

"Joseph!" he shouted as he saw his friend resting in bed.

"Elwood!" Joseph responded. "Come on in. Sit down." As Elwood moved to the other bed, Joseph noticed something seemed different about his best friend. He appeared to have grown older in the short time that had elapsed since they had last seen each other, just a few days ago. Was that a gray hair? A wrinkle near his eye?

"I hear you had quite the tumble yesterday, an' I see you are recoverin' nicely," Elwood observed.

"Aunt Rachel won't hardly let me lift a finger. For once, I'm the one being attended to."

"And you hate it?" Elwood posed.

Joseph smiled at his friend, "Yes. I absolutely hate it. I'm the one who is supposed to be doing the chores and taking care of everybody. That's what the man of the farm does."

"Perhaps she'll let you take a walk with me. You do need some exercise for healin'."

"Yes, I believe you are correct in that, my friend." Joseph shifted to a sitting position and placed his feet on the floor. His first attempt at standing failed due to his weakened state.

Elwood stood and moved to Joseph. On the second attempt, Joseph achieved a wobbly vertical position with his friend's assistance. "Looks like you need to get yourself some practice there."

They negotiated the stairs together and Aunt Rachel met them at the bottom. "Where do you think you're going, young man?"

"Elwood believes I should get some exercise, and I agree with him."

Rachel's stern glance nearly froze the two young men on the spot. "Well, I guess it'd be okay with you, Elwood. I wouldn't trust my boy to anyone else... 'ceptin' that Mr. Held fellow."

"Mr. Held?" Elwood queried, looking at Joseph.

"He's the gentleman who rescued me yesterday and accompanied me back here. Fine, fine fellow. He spent a good bit of time working the Rocky Mountains as a geologist, and now he's looking to hire on at the new forge over in Coventry."

The two young men walked a bit around the garden until Joseph felt his strength return. Then they strolled up the long hill behind the house and sat beneath a noble pin-oak on the height, where they had a lovely view of the valley for many miles to the southward.

"Feelin' better?" Elwood asked after they had both reached the ground. Joseph merely nodded. "Your crops are lookin' good. Mighty good, indeed." Joseph nodded again. "Not much for talkin' right now, are ya?"

Joseph smiled and looked at his friend. "I'm sorry, Elwood. It's just that I have so much on my mind."

Elwood dropped his head. "Your fate is settled by this time, I s'pose?"

"It is arranged at least, but I can't yet make clear to myself that I shall be a married man a few months from now."

"Does the time seem long to you?" Elwood studied Joseph's face.

"No, it is very short."

Elwood turned away to conceal a melancholy smile. "Joseph," he said after a brief silence, "are you sure–quite sure–you love her?"

"I am to marry her."

"I meant nothin' unfriendly," Elwood spoke in a gentle tone.

"My thought was this: If you should ever find a still stronger love growin' upon you–somethin' that would make the warmth you feel now seem like ice compared to it–how would you be able to fight it?" Joseph's head snapped to Elwood. "I asked the question o' myself for you. I don't think I'm much different from most soft-hearted men– 'ceptin' I keep the softness so well stowed away that few persons know of it–but if I were in your place, within two months of marriage to the girl I love, I should be miserable!"

"Miserable?" Joseph spat out.

"Miserable from hope and fear," Elwood responded. "I should be afraid o' fever, fire, murder–thunderbolt! Every hour of the day I should dread lest somethin' might come between us. I should prowl around her house day after day to be sure that she was still alive! I should lengthen out the time into years, an' all because I'm a great, disappointed, soft-hearted fool!" He hung his head.

"Elwood, I see that it is not in my power to comfort you," Joseph stated with some remorse. "If I give you pain unknowingly, tell me how to avoid it!" He looked directly at his friend. "I meant to ask you to stand beside me when I am married, but now you must consider your own feelings in answering, not mine. The Hendersons are not likely to be there."

"That would make no difference," Elwood declaimed, and he turned to face Joseph. "Force of will is o' no use. As to faithfulness–why, what it's worth can't be shown unless somethin' turns up to try it. But you had better not ask me to be your groomsman. Neither Miss Blessing nor her family would be overly pleased."

"Why so? Julia and you are quite acquainted, and she was always friendly toward you."

Elwood turned his face away, but not before Joseph could catch a glimpse of the color rising. "I've got the notion in my head. Maybe it's foolish, but there it is. I talked a good deal with Miss Blessing, it's true, an' yet I don't feel the least bit acquainted." He turned back to Joseph. "Her manner to me was very friendly, an' yet I don't think she likes me."

Joseph forced a little laugh, even though Elwood's confession annoyed him somewhat. "Well! I never gave you credit for such a lively imagination. Why not be candid and admit that the dislike is on your side? I am sorry for it, since Julia will so soon be in the house there as my wife. There is no one else whom I can ask, unless it were Philip Held..."

"Held!" Elwood pointed at Joseph. "To be sure. He took care of you, which I reckon it as a piece of good luck for you. If I can't stand with you, there's no better person for it." He nodded. "I've found that there are men, all, maybe, as honest and outspoken as they need to be, yet two of 'em will talk at different marks an' never fully understand each other, an' other two will naturally talk right straight at the same mark an' never miss." He looked away. "It sounds like your Mr. Held is the sort that can hit the thing in the mind of the man they're talkin' to. It's a gift that comes o' bein' knocked about the world among all classes of people. What we learn here, always among the same folks, isn't a circumstance."

"You seem to know quite a bit of him without even having met him." Joseph studied his friend's face but did not comprehend the subtle message in Elwood's expression. "Then you think I might ask him?"

"He sounds like the type of man that you're safe in askin' to do anythin'. Make him spokesman of a committee to wait on the President, arbitrator in a crooked lawsuit, overseer of a railroad gang, leader in a prayer-meetin' (if he'd consent, that is), or whatever else you choose, an' he'll do the business as if he was used to it!" Elwood started to stand. "It's enough for you that I don't know the city ways an' he does. It's considered worse, I've heard, to make a blunder in society than to commit a real sin."

Joseph stood and followed Elwood back down the hill as the sun began to set. "I'm not sure how you could surmise all of that about Mr. Held without knowing him, but I'd bet you'd be right on all accounts."

Elwood turned to Joseph as they walked. "I don't know whether you meant to have the news of your engagement circulated, but I guess Anna Warriner has heard, an' that amounts to –"

"To telling it to the whole neighborhood, doesn't it?" Joseph interrupted. "Then the mischief is already done, if it is a mischief. It is well, therefore, that the day is set. The neighborhood will have little time for gossip." He smiled with satisfaction.

"Don't remember anythin' against me, Joseph." Elwood halted with tears in his eyes and seized Joseph by the arms. "I've always been honestly your friend, an' mean to stay so."

Joseph nodded in agreement and they walked the rest of the way without talking.

After dinner, Joseph went to the sitting-room while Aunt Rachel cleared the table. As he positioned himself on the settee and gazed out the window, he thought about his chat with Elwood and realized his thoughts dwelt much more on Philip Held than on Julia Blessing. He had only known Philip briefly, but the man had saved his life and also appeared to be like-minded in many ways. Joseph ran through a swift, involuntary chain of reasoning, to account to himself for his feeling toward Julia, and her inevitable share in his future. However, toward Philip, his heart sprang with an instinct beyond his control. He could not help but imagine that Philip would be entwined, like a bright thread, through the web of his coming days.

He had not heard the approach of a carriage, and a rapping broke his meditation. He went to the door to find the Reverend Mr. Chaffinch. "Come in. Please, come in."

From the kitchen Aunt Rachel roared, "Who is it, Joseph?"

"It's the Reverend Chaffinch!"

"Offer him some tea!"

"Would you like some tea, Reverend," Joseph asked.

"No, thank you," Mr. Chaffinch demurred.

"He doesn't want any tea, Aunt Rachel!" Joseph yelled to the back of the house.

"How is your health? I hear you had quite the brush yesterday," the Reverend inquired.

"Healing nicely, I suppose. Thank you for asking. Shall we sit?" Joseph returned to the settee and indicated Aunt Rachel's favorite chair for the Reverend.

Joseph attempted to guess the reason for the unexpected and unannounced call. The Reverend's face seemed melancholy, the eyes, so long uplifted above the concerns of this world, had ceased to vary their expression materially for the sake of any human interest. He had fulfilled his duties as expected, and, perhaps, this visit fell under that category.

"It was a merciful preservation," Mr. Chaffinch offered. "I hope you feel that it is a solemn thing to look Death in the face."

The sudden mention of such a horrid subject surprised Joseph. "I am not afraid of death," he stated.

Mr. Chaffinch's faced shifted to a kindly smile. "You mean the physical pang, but Death includes what comes after it: Judgment. That is a very awful thought." The smile subsided.

"It may be to evil men, but I have done nothing to make me fear it."

The Reverend considered Joseph. "You have never made an open profession of faith, yet it may be that grace has reached you." He stared intently. "Have you found your Savior?"

"I believe in him with all my soul!" Joseph cried. "But do you mean something else by 'finding' him? I will be candid with you, Mr. Chaffinch. The last sermon I heard you preach, a month ago, was upon the nullity of all good works, all Christian deeds. You called them 'rags, dust, and ashes,' and declared that man is saved by faith alone." He took a deep breath. "I *have* faith, but I can't accept a doctrine which denies merit to works. And you, unless I accept it, will you admit that I have 'found' Christ?"

"There is but One Truth!" exclaimed the Reverend, very severely, with one finger pointed up.

"Yes," Joseph answered reverently, "and that is only perfectly known to God."

Joseph could see the annoyed look on Mr. Chaffinch's face. He worried that if his steadfast belief did not match that of the Reverend exactly, Joseph's continued participation in the church might be discouraged.

Aunt Rachel arrived as the Reverend stood.

"We will talk again when you are stronger. It is my duty to give spiritual help to those who seek it." With a lift of his saggy chin, he turned to Rachel Miller. "I cannot say that he is dark. His mind is cloudy, but we find that the vanities of youth often obscure the true light for a time."

Rachel saw the Reverend out and then sat in the recently-occupied chair. She looked upon her nephew with the usual cloud of interrogation marks.

"Aunt," Joseph began after a few moments of silence, "why do you suppose I went to the city?"

"I suppose to see about the fall prices for grain and cattle."

"No, aunt," he said with determination, turning to face her directly as foolish blood ran rosily over his face, "I went to get a wife!"

The color drained from Rachel's face, and she sat staring at the rosy sign on Joseph's cheeks and temples. "Miss Blessing?" she asked, almost in a whisper. He nodded, and she took three long, deep breaths. "Well, fancy that!" she exclaimed in an undecipherable tone.

"I knew you would be surprised because it is almost a surprise to myself." He smiled at his aunt. "But you and she seemed to fall so easily into each other's ways that I hope –"

"Why, you're hardly acquainted with her!" Aunt Rachel shouted. "It is so hasty! And you are so young!"

"No younger than father was when he married mother, and

I have learned to know her well in a short time. Isn't it so with you, too, aunt? You certainly liked her."

"I'll not deny that, nor say the reverse now"–her face hardened–"but a farmer's wife should be a farmer's daughter."

"But suppose, aunt, that the farmer doesn't have an interest in any farmer's daughter, and *does* have an interest in a bright, amiable, very intelligent girl who is delighted with country life, eager and willing to learn, and very fond of the farmer's aunt–who would be able to teach her everything."

"Still, it seems to me a risk," Rachel responded cautiously.

"There is none to you," Joseph said, "and I am not afraid of mine. You will be with us, for Julia couldn't do without you, if she wished." He smiled, hoping to convince his aunt of the positive consequences. "If she were a farmer's daughter, with different ideas of housekeeping, it might bring trouble to both of us. But now you will have the management in your own hands until you have taught Julia, and afterward she will carry it on in your way."

Rachel did not reply directly. However, Joseph could see a change in her expression. After a minute or so, she stood, walked across the room, leaned over and kissed him upon the forehead. Then she just walked away.

•❦•

A note from Philip Held arrived the following day. It was but a few lines, and he disclosed that his assessment of the forge and furnace proved satisfactory, and the sale would doubtless be consummated in a short time. However, it might be months before he would take charge of the works, and that he planned to return to the city directly. Philip included the address so that Joseph could either visit or write to him.

It gave Joseph great pleasure to hear from Philip; however, the news of his imminent departure left him feeling a bit hollow. He had hoped to have developed a friendship with Mr.

Held, one that might take the place of the dwindling one he had with Elwood.

With each new day, Joseph regained strength and began to take on more and more of his regular chores. Thankfully, Dennis had been able to maintain the farmstead on his own during this time, and Joseph was quite sure he felt relieved to share the work with his boss once again.

A few days later, a letter from the city arrived for Joseph. He took it up to his room for fear that his nosy aunt might espy the communications with his intended. When he was alone, he opened the letter and read:

> Dearest Joseph,
>
> What a fright and anxiety we have had! When pa brought the paper home, last night, and I read the report of the accident, where it said, 'J. Asten, severe contusions,' my heart stopped beating for a minute, and I can only write now (as you see) with a trembling hand. My first thought was to go directly to you, but ma said we had better wait for intelligence. Unless our engagement were generally known, it would give rise to remarks—in short, I need not repeat to you all the worldly reasons with which she opposed me, but, oh, how I longed for the right to be at your side, and assure myself that the dreadful, dreadful danger has passed! Pa was quite shaken with the news. He felt hardly able to go to the Custom-House this morning. But he sides with ma about my going, and now, when my time as a daughter with them is growing so short, I dare not disobey. I know you will understand my position, yet, dear and true as you are, you cannot guess the anxiety with which I await a line from your hand, the hand that was so nearly taken from me forever!

He read the letter twice, and was about to read it again when he heard his aunt shouting from below, "Joseph! Elwood is here to see you!"

Joseph tucked the letter under his mattress and went down

to the sitting-room, where Elwood stood, waiting. They shook hands cordially.

"Elwood! What brings you here?"

"Well, Joseph"–Elwood appeared to be on the verge of a blushing attack–"I was headed over to a homestead in the village, an' I thought I might see if you were well enough to go."

Joseph looked at his aunt's stern face. "Aunt, I have been laboring in the fields for a few days now. I believe I have earned the right for a bit of celebration."

She shook a finger at him. "I don't want you staying out late, and I don't want you riding your horse all alone!"

"Not to worry, Miss Miller," Elwood crooned, "I brought our buggy. I'll bring him back by eleven o'clock for sure!"

"Ten! And not a second later!"

"Yes, Miss Miller! Ten it is!" Elwood turned to Joseph. "Shall we?"

"But I'm not dressed for a social occasion, Elwood. Let me change into something more proper."

"Aw, shucks, Joseph, you look just fine. If people saw you in your Sunday best one more time, they might just get to thinkin' those were the only threads you got!" He laughed quietly.

Joseph grabbed his coat from the peg. "I shall see you before ten o'clock, Aunt Rachel."

"Hmmmmph. We shall see about that!"

"Have you heard from your intended?" Elwood asked once they were underway.

"Yes. I received a letter today. She said she wanted to come visit straightaway, but her mother thought it best not to so as not to raise suspicions about our arrangement."

"Sounds like her mama has some smarts. I just hope she passed 'em along." Now that he was outdoors, he let his laugh fly.

When they reached the homestead, Lucy Henderson stood outside gazing up at the dusky sky. She looked pale and fatigued. Joseph began to think this might have been the reason Elwood brought him along.

"Evenin', Miss Henderson," Elwood greeted Lucy. "Is your sister Elizabeth about?" Lucy nodded with her head to indicate her sister's presence inside the house. "If you two will excuse me," he said as he disappeared through the door.

Joseph and Lucy stood silently in contemplation for a few minutes. "I take it you have heard the news?" Joseph asked, and Lucy nodded. "I'm sorry I did not have the opportunity to tell you myself, but I have been recuperating these last few days."

Lucy looked at Joseph with concern. "I heard the awful news of the train wreck, and I feared you might be dead. Your friendship has always been dear to me."

Joseph smiled. "I am glad to hear you say that, Lucy. I was afraid you might feel differently after hearing about Miss Blessing and me." He searched her face for a reaction, but her expression remained unchanged. "I hope you can be happy for us."

She smiled faintly. "Some say that people are attracted by mutual unlikeness. This seems to me to be a case of the kind, but you are free choosers of your own fates."

Joseph sighed and felt relieved.

At quarter to ten, Elwood approached Joseph and told him it was time to go home. Joseph felt quite certain that after Elwood dropped him off, he returned to the homestead to visit with Miss Elizabeth Henderson some more.

Even though the hour was late, Joseph did not feel tired. He sat at his desk and wrote a letter.

  My Dearest Philip:

I was so happy to receive the news of your satisfaction with the equipment in Coventry, but at the same time dismayed that you returned to the city before we could visit.

There is also another matter I wish to present. Our short time together did not permit me to announce to you that I am to be married in October, to a Miss Julia Blessing, and I want you to consider taking the part of the nearest friend, if there are no other private reasons to prevent you from doing so. I realize we haven't known each other for very long, but you did save my life once, and perhaps I could implore you to do so again by standing with me at the altar.

I apologize if this is very sudden or uncomfortable, asking for such a mark of confidence on so short an acquaintance, but it would mean the world to me to see you again in any capacity.

Your friend,

Joseph Asten

•▼•

A few days later came the response:

My dear Asten,

Do you remember that curious whirling sensation, when the car pitched over the edge of the embankment? I felt a return of it on reading your letter, for you have surprised me beyond measure. Not by your request, for that is just what I should have expected of you, and as well now, as if we had known each other for twenty years, so the apology is the only thing objectionable. But—I fear I am tangling my sentences—I want to say how heartily I return the feeling which prompted you to ask me, and yet how embarrassed I am that I cannot unconditionally say, 'Yes, with all my heart!'

My great, astounding surprise is to find you about to be married to Miss Julia Blessing, a young lady whom I once knew. And the embarrassment is this: I knew her under circumstances (in which she was not personally concerned, however) which might possibly render my presence now, as your groomsman, unwelcome to the family. At least it is my duty—and yours, if you still desire me to stand beside you—to let Miss Blessing and her family decide the question. The circumstances to which I refer concern them rather than myself. I think your best plan will be simply to inform them of your request and my reply, and add that I am entirely ready to accept whatever course they may prefer.

Pray don't consider that I have treated your first letter to me ungraciously. I am more grieved than you can imagine that it happens so. You will probably come to the city a day before the wedding, and I insist that you shall share my bachelor quarters, in any case.

Always your friend,

Philip Held

Philip, a former acquaintance of the Blessings! How perplexing. Formerly, but not now. And what could those mysterious "circumstances" have been that had so seriously interrupted their intercourse? Even though Joseph knew it quite useless to conjecture, he could not resist the feeling that another shadow hung over the aspects of his future. Did he exaggerate Elwood's unaccountable dislike to Julia? It had only been implied, not spoken.

Here was a positive estrangement on the part of the man who was so suddenly near and dear to Joseph. The candor and cheery warmth of the letter rejoiced his heart. The thought of suspecting Philip Held of any kind of blame felt abhorrent.

It appeared the best course, as suggested by Philip, would be to inform the Blessings of the situation and leave the decision to Julia and her parents. He read Philip's letter once more before starting one to the Blessings.

Chapter 9: An October Wedding

NEARLY A WEEK PASSED WITH NO RESPONSE FROM JULIA. With no word from the Blessing household to direct his ambitions, Joseph tormented himself by imagining the wildest reasons for their silence. At least he had the farm chores to keep himself busy. As summer progressed, the amount of necessary work increased, and he spent most of his waking hours in the fields.

Elwood paid the occasional visit, but the two never returned to the hayloft, as Joseph had suspected. An unseen barrier had begun to sprout between them, one that allowed continued acquaintance but diminished their emotional relationship.

When the letter at last arrived, Joseph had to read it a few times before comprehending its import.

> Dearest Joseph,
>
> You must really forgive me this long trial of your patience. Your letter was so unexpected–I mean its contents–and it seems as if ma and pa and Clementina would never agree what was best to be done. For that matter, I cannot say that they agree now. We had no idea that you were an intimate friend of Mr. Held (I can't think how ever you should have become acquainted!) and it seems to break open old wounds–none of mine, fortunately, for I have none. As Mr. Held leaves the question in our hands, there is, you will understand, all the more necessity that we should be careful. Ma thinks he has said nothing to you about the unfortunate occurrence, or you would have expressed an opinion. You never can know how happy your fidelity makes me, but I felt that the first moment we met.
>
> Ma says that at very private (what pa calls informal) weddings there need not be bridesmaids or groomsmen. Miss Morrisey was married that way not long ago. It is true that she is not of our circle,

nor strictly a first family (this is ma's view, not mine, for I understand the hollowness of society), but we could do very well the same. Pa would be satisfied with a reception afterwards. He wants to ask the Collector, and the Surveyor, and the Appraiser.

Clementina won't say anything now, but I know what she thinks, and so does ma; however, Mr. Held has so dropped out of city life that it is not important. I suppose everything must be dim in his memory now. You do not write to me much that he related. How strange that he should be your friend, a person of that Race.

They say my dress is lovely, but I am sure I should like a plain muslin just as well. I shall only breath freely when I get back to the quiet of the country (and your–soon to be our–charming home, and dear, good Aunt Rachel!) and away from all these conventional forms. Ma says if there is one grooms-man there ought to be two. Either is very simple, or according to custom.

In a matter so delicate, perhaps, Mr. Held would be as competent to decide as we are. At least I am quite willing to leave it to his judgment. But how trifling is all this discussion, compared with the importance of the day to us! It is now drawing very near, but I have no misgivings, for I confide in you wholly and forever!

Joseph inferred three things from the letter: (1) His acquaintance with Philip Held was not entirely disagreeable to the Blessing Family; (2) They would prefer the simplest style of a wedding (which was in consonance with his own tastes; although, he wondered if it might be a scheme of frugality on their part after what he had overheard that night at their home); and (3) Julia still clung to him as a deliverer from conditions with which her nature had little sympathy.

He surmised her incoherent writing arose from an agitation he easily understood. His return letter would be composed with an intent to soothe and encourage her. However, informing Philip Held that his services would not be required would prove more challenging. He did not wish to imply the existence of an unfriendly feeling toward him; therefore, he would readily accept the invitation to stay the night before the wedding. The mysterious difficulty did not seem to concern Julia, and he could welcome Philip's friendship.

•❖•

September, the Ninth Month (as Quakers called it), sped by. Elwood Withers had said something about a lingering, passionate uncertainty, but the days passed almost too swiftly. Joseph scarcely had time in the hurry of preparation to look beyond the coming event and estimate its consequences. His pure and perfect conscience made him oblivious to doubt, and he had no thought of admitting that changing the course of his destiny was possible.

The neighbors might have been spinning their gossip outside of his presence, but what little he heard of it did not disagree with him. Joseph's immediate concern remained his aunt. He would be bringing another woman into the home she alone had ruled for over ten years. No doubt, with time, her authority would diminish as control of the farmhouse became the obligation of the new Mrs. Asten.

In his mind, two shadows loomed, raised by the two men he loved best. Would he accidentally throw them from clouds beyond the horizon of his life? Joseph clung to this thought, in spite of a vague, utterly formless apprehension that he felt lurking somewhere in the very bottom of his heart.

•❖•

The intervening weeks seemed like a blur to Joseph, and the day for travel to the city quickly arrived. Dennis drove him to the Oakland Station very early in the morning, and he did not have a chance to say farewell to his sleeping aunt.

This time, the train arrived safely, and Philip met him at the platform. After a short carriage ride, they arrived at his house, which overlooked one of the leafy squares and proved to be quite pleasant. Broad floor-boards lay beneath welcoming windows that provided a view as far as the taller buildings a few blocks away.

Once he had brought his traveling satchel inside, Joseph headed to the Blessing mansion, not that distant. A flutter of preparations greeted him, and although they cordially welcomed him, he felt that—with the exception of Julia—he was subordinate in interest to the men who came every quarter of an hour, bringing bouquets, silver spoons with cards attached, and pasteboard boxes containing frosted cakes. Even the enjoyment of Julia's society occurred in scanty installments, as her mother or Clementina perpetually summoned her to consult about some indescribable figment of dress.

Mr. Blessing arrived in the drawing-room, after occupying his time inspecting various hampers in the basement. He greeted Joseph with both hands and rambling phrases.

Fortunately, Julia interposed, "You must not forget, pa, that the man is waiting. Joseph will excuse you, I know." The two of them descended to the basement, leaving Joseph alone in the now-familiar room.

In the evening, Julia cheered Joseph on by saying, "We can't complain of all this confusion when it's for our sakes, but we'll be happier when it's over. Won't we?" She saw him to the door, and he gave her an affirmative kiss before withdrawing.

Upon returning to Mr. Held's home, he found Philip comfortably disposed in an arm-chair reading. "Ah! You find that a house is more agreeable any evening than that before the wedding?"

"There is one compensation," responded Joseph. "It gives me two or three hours with you." He smiled at his handsome new friend.

"Then take that other arm-chair and tell me how this came to pass. You see, I have the curiosity of a neighbor already."

Joseph explained the circumstances leading up to the morrow's nuptials. He left out much of his internal philosophical debate for fear that Philip might not fully understand the vulnerability of his position in the community. Even though Philip occasionally asked a pertinent question or made a suggestive remark, Joseph did not want to risk the fragility of his new association.

At the end of the tale, Joseph rose and commenced walking up and down the comfortable room. He longed to ask his host for an explanation of the circumstances regarding the Blessing family, but doubt checked his tongue.

As if reading Joseph's thoughts, Philip stood and said, "I owe you my story, and you shall have it after a while when I can tell you more. Please sit down." He indicated the arm-chair, and both men sat. "I was a young fellow of twenty when I knew the Blessings, and I don't attach the slightest importance now to anything that happened. Even if I did, Miss Julia had no share in it." He paused and glanced up. "I remember her distinctly. She was then about the same age, perhaps a year or two older, but hers is a face that would not change in a long while."

Joseph stared wide-eyed at his friend. Philip had originally stated he was 28 years old, and the shocking, unexpected, and unwelcome revelation that Julia must be the same age or slightly more–revealed by involuntary mathematics– startled him.

"Her father had been lucky in some of his 'operations,'" Philip continued, "but I don't think he kept it long. I hardly wonder that she should come to prefer a quiet country life to such ups and downs as the family has known." He looked directly at Joseph. "Generally, a woman don't adapt herself so readily to a change of surroundings as a man. Where there is love, however, everything is possible."

"There is!" Joseph exclaimed, "There is!" hoping to certify

the fact to himself as much as to his friend. He rose and stood beside him.

Philip stood as well, facing Joseph with a grave, tender expression. "What can I do?"

Joseph felt lost in the deep jade of Philip's eyes. "What should you do?" he asked without realizing it.

"This!" Philip proclaimed, laying his hands on Joseph's shoulders. "This, Joseph! I can be nearer than a brother. I know that I am in your heart as you are in mine. There is no faith between us that need be limited. There is no truth too secret to be veiled. A man's perfect friendship is rarer than a woman's love, and most hearts are content with one or the other. Not so with yours and mine!" He leaned forward and kissed Joseph on the lips and then resumed a vertical position. "I read it in your eyes when you opened them on my knee. I see it in your face now. Don't speak. Let us clasp hands."

Joseph could not speak. They stood just holding hands for a while before Philip led them to a comfortable bed, where they spent the rest of the night before the wedding.

•▼•

"There!" Philip proclaimed, "Now study the general effect. I think nothing more is wanting." Morning sunlight played off the polished wooden flooring.

"It hardly looks like myself," Joseph remarked, looking into the mirror. His face did not appear that of the happy bridegroom, and he seemed to have aged several years overnight. The boyish softness and sweetness had become hard and sour.

Philip assisted him in dressing due to his preoccupation. Joseph could only manage in an abstracted, mechanical air, and Philip lent a hand to his friend.

"In all the weddings I have seen," Philip went on, "the bride-grooms were pale and grave, the brides flushed and trembling. You will not make an exception to the rule, but it is a solemn thing, and I–don't misunderstand me, Joseph–I almost wish you were not to be married to-day."

"Philip!" Joseph exclaimed. "Let me think, now, at least–now, at the last moment–that it is best for me! If you knew how cramped, restricted, and fettered, my life has been, and how much emancipation has already come with this–this love!" He turned back and gazed at Philip. "Perhaps my marriage is a venture, but it is one which must be made, and no consequence of it shall ever come between us!" He hugged his friend then stepped back.

"No, and I ought not to have spoken a word that might imply a doubt. It may be that your emancipation–as you rightly term it–can only come in this way. My life has been so different that I am unconsciously putting myself in your place instead of trying to look with your eyes." Philip took a step away. "When I next go to Coventry Forge, I shall drive over and dine with you, and I hope your Julia will be as ready to receive me as a friend as I am to find one in her." He glanced out the window. "There is the carriage at the door, and you had better arrive a little before the appointed hour. Take only my good wishes and my prayers for your happiness along with you." He stepped back to hug Joseph and planted a long kiss beside his quivering lips.

The air in the carriage felt hot and stifling. He pulled up the curtains and lowered the window to let the air blow upon his heated cheeks. However, Joseph soon became painfully conscious of the curious glances that fell upon him, and he pulled down the curtains. The ride to the Blessing mansion did not take very long, and a festive hired waiter admitted him entrance. Curious eyes in the windows all around watched him during the few seconds it took to get from the carriage into the home.

Mrs. Blessing, resplendent in purple–and so bedight that she seemed almost as young as her portrait–swept into the drawing-room. She inspected him rapidly, apparently with approval, advanced to him and favored his cheek with a thin, dry kiss.

"It lacks half an hour," she bemoaned, "but you have the usual impatience of a bridegroom. *I* am accustomed to it. Mr. Blessing is still in his room. He has only just commenced arranging his cambric cravat, which is a work of time. He cannot forget that he was distinguished for an elegant tie in his youth." Clementina entered as her mother spoke. "Dear daughter, is the bride completely attired?"

"All but her gloves," replied the sister, offering three-fourths of her hand to Joseph. "And she don't know what ear-rings to wear."

"I think we might venture," Mrs. Blessing remarked, "as there seems to be no rule applicable to the case, to allow Mr. Asten a sight of his bride." She looked at Joseph with a slightly cocked head and one eyebrow raised. "Perhaps his taste might assist her in the choice."

The three ascended the stairs, Joseph behind, and after some whispering at the door, they admitted him. He blanched at the sight of Julia, younger, brighter, rounder, fresher, and with the loveliest pink flush on her cheeks. The gloss of her hair rivaled that of the white satin that draped her form and gave grace to its outlines. The neck and shoulders appeared slight, but no one could have justly called them lean. Even the thinness of her lips disappeared beneath the vivid coral color. At that moment, in all her certain beauty, a stranger would have supposed her to be young.

Joseph observed his bride looking upon his face, and he worried that she saw him as older, paler, with a grave and serious bearing. However, she smiled with maiden shyness. It might have been just the thing for Joseph to say *How lovely you are!* but no words came to him. Instead, he experienced a feeling of relief, but he knew not why, and could not for his life have put it into words. She seemed satisfied to have his eyes follow and dwell upon her as a form of recognition.

Mrs. Blessing inspected the dress with a severe critical eye, pulling out a fold here and smoothing a bit of lace there, until nothing further could be detected. Once she had completed her last duty, she sat down and wept moderately.

"Oh, ma, try to bear up!" Julia chided with the very slightest touch of impatience. "It is all to come yet."

A bell sounded below.

"That must be your aunt," Mrs. Blessing announced, drying her eyes. "My sister," she added, turning to Joseph. "Mrs. Woollish, with Mr. Woollish and their two sons and one daughter. He's in the... the leather trade, so to speak, which has thrown her into a very different circle, but, as we have no nearer relations in the city, they will be present at the ceremony. He is said to be wealthy. I have no means of knowing, but one would scarcely think so, to judge from his wedding-gift to Julia."

"Ma, why should you mention it?"

She turned to Julia, "I wish to enlighten Mr. Asten." Mrs. Blessing threw her gloved hands into the air. "Six pairs of shoes! All of the same pattern, of course. And the fashion may change in another year!"

"In the country we have no fashions in shoes," Joseph suggested. "What about those ear-rings?" He pointed to a simple pearl arrangement among those displayed on the dresser.

"Certainly!" Julia agreed. She handed the ear-rings to Clementina who installed them. "Ma, *I* find Uncle Woollish's present very practical indeed."

Mrs. Blessing looked at her daughter and said nothing.

The sound of footsteps on the landing preceded Mr. Blessing's arrival. The triumphant cambric about his throat looked like a pedestal for his very red face. He struggled with getting his fat hands into a pair of No. 9 gloves. Joseph could smell a strong aroma of turpentine or benzine.

"Eliza, you must find me some *eau de cologne*," he ordered.

"The odor left from my... my rheumatic remedy is still perceptible. Indeed, patchouli would be better if it were not the scent peculiar to *parvenus*."

Clementina picked up a bottle of No. 7411 from the dresser and handed it to her father. Just as he pulled his handkerchief from the pocket, the hired waiter announced the clergyman's carriage had reached the door. Mr. Blessing hurried downstairs, mopping his gloves and the collar of his coat with liquid fragrance by the way. Mrs. Blessing and Clementina followed.

Once the others had left, Joseph asked, "Julia, have you thought that this is for life?"

She looked up with a tender smile, but when she gazed upon Joseph's face, the smile froze.

"I have lived ignorantly until now," he continued, "innocently and ignorantly. From this time on I shall change more than you, and there may be—years hence—a very different Joseph Asten from the one whose name you will take today." He took her hand but cast down his eyes. "If you can accept me, as I accept you, through all new knowledge and experience, there will be no discord in our lives." He looked directly at her. "We must both be liberal and considerate towards each other. It has been but a short time since we met, and we have still much to learn."

"O, Joseph!" she murmured in a tone of gentle reproach, "I knew your nature at first sight."

"I hope you did," he answered gravely, "for then you will be able to see its needs." Joseph dropped her hand and turned away. "But Julia, there must not be the shadow of concealment come between us. Nothing must be reserved. I understand no marriage that does not include perfect trust." He turned back. "I must draw nearer, and be drawn nearer to you, constantly, or..." Joseph decided to wait until another time to utter the further sentence that weighed in his mind.

Julia glided to him, clasped her arms about his waist, and laid her head against his shoulder. The two stood like that until they heard a rustle on the stairs.

Clementina entered with a young woman. "Mr. Bogue has arrived, and ma thinks you should come down soon." She surveyed the couple. "Are you entirely ready? I don't think you need the salts, Julia, but you might carry the bottle in your left hand. Brides are expected to be nervous." Her laughter–much like the purl and bubble of a brook–caused Joseph to shrink with an inward chill.

"So! Shall we go? Fanny and I–Oh, I beg pardon for not introducing–Mr. Asten, Miss Woollish–will lead the way. We will stand a little in the rear, not beside you, as there are no groomsmen." Clementina began to push Miss Woollish out into the hall. "Remember, the farther end of the room!"

The two attendants rustled slowly downward, in advance, and the bridal pair followed. Mr. Bogue, the clergyman stood in the center of the room.

"… praise for such lovely weather on this blessed –"

The crowd around Mr. Bogue parted and the guests took their seats.

For the next few minutes, Joseph's mind entered a dream-like state. He could see the clergyman's lips moving but his speech sounded far-away and muffled. When Mr. Bogue stared directly at him–and he felt Julia's dainty elbow in his side–his lips opened mechanically, and a voice that did not exactly seem to be his own uttered, "I will!" His mind went blank without any thought or memory until Mr. Blessing shook his hand violently.

Later he would recall happy faces with tears and beams of congratulations. Miss Fanny Woollish put her arms around the couple's shoulders and whispered, "I have never seen a *sweeter* wedding!"

Her mother, a stout, homely little body, nodded and added, "Yes, you both did beautifully!"

Mr. Bogue produced the marriage certificate for them to sign. The company then partook of wine and refreshments.

Mrs. Blessing moved about restlessly, her eyes wandered to the front window. Suddenly, three or four carriages came rattling together up the street. She turned to her husband and whispered loudly, "There they are! It will be a success!"

A few minutes later, the little room became uncomfortably crowded. The Blessings presented Joseph to many new people so rapidly that he had no memory of the faces or names. Julia, however, knew and welcomed every one with the most bewitching grace. She received kisses from the gorgeous young ladies and compliments from the young men with weak mouths and retreating chins.

Amidst the confusion, Mr. Blessing introduced—with a wave and flourish—Mr. Collector Twining, Mr. Surveyor Knob, and Mr. Appraiser Gerrish. The three greeted Joseph with bland, almost affectionate, cordiality.

The door of the dining-room flew open, and the three dignitaries accompanied the bridal pair to the table. Two servants rapidly whisked the champagne bottles from a cooling-tub in the adjoining closet. Mr. Blessing commenced stirring and testing a huge bowl of punch.

Speeches followed, and each of the titled men gave neat, little toasts to the health of the bride and bridegroom. Mr. Blessing dabbed himself with the handkerchief smelling equally of benzine and *eau de cologne*. He stepped forward and began his own peroration.

"On this happy occasion, the elements of national power and prosperity are represented. My son-in-law, Mr. Asten, is a noble specimen of the agricultural population, the free American yeomanry. My daughter—if I may be allowed to say it in the presence of so many bright eyes and blooming cheeks—is a representative child of the city, which is the embodiment of the nation's action and enterprise. The union of the two is the movement of our life. The city gives to the country as the ocean gives the cloud to the mountain-springs. The country gives to the city as the streams flow back to the ocean." A few people clapped politely. "Then we have, as our highest honor, the representatives of the political system under which city and country flourish alike. The wings of our eagle must be extended over this fortunate house to-day, for here are the strong claws which seize and guard its treasures! To their health." He raised his arm holding the punch-glass.

The three dignitaries held their glasses high. Mr. Collector Twining exclaimed, "Admirable! Very, very admirable, sir!" The four men touched their glasses, and every touch required the contents be replenished, so that the bottom of the punch-bowl nearly emerged.

A short while later, after all the hugging, kissing, congratulating and hand-shaking had ceased, the guests slowly filed out of the Blessing home. Mr. and Mrs. Blessing smiled at each other and then at the new couple.

When Joseph returned to the drawing-room after changing into his traveling-dress, the crowd had departed. Strewn about the carpet he could see leaves, withered flowers, crumbs of cake, and crumpled cards. He found Mr. Blessing in the dining-room with his cravat loosened, smoking a cigar at the open window.

"Come in, son-in-law! Take another glass of punch before you start."

"No, thank you," Joseph demurred. "I am not accustomed to the beverage."

"Nothing could have gone off better!" proclaimed Mr. Blessing. "The Collector was delighted. By the by, you're to go to the St. Jerome this evening. He called and had the bridal-chamber reserved for you. Tell Julia. She won't forget it. That girl has a deuced sharp intellect. If you'll be guided by her in your operations –"

"Pa, what are you saying about me?" Julia interrupted as she hastily entered the room in her plain clothes.

"Only that you have a deuced sharp intellect, and to-day proves it. Asten is one of us now, and I may tell him of his luck." He winked and laughed stupidly. "Don't forget the St.

Jerome. The bridal-chamber is ordered for you. I will see to it that Mumm writes a good account for the *Evening Mercury*."

Julia glanced at Joseph and indicated with a hand, "I believe that mother is waiting to speak with you in the drawing-room."

Mrs. Blessing sat, handkerchief to eye, as Joseph entered. "Ah, son-in-law, as I may now call you. Should you choose, you may refer to me in kind, or simply as 'mother,' as you see fit." She barely smiled, as if something preoccupied her thoughts. "We have provided for you the best beginning possible for a long and happy marriage with our daughter. Mr. Blessing and myself now expect you to uphold your end of the bargain and provide a happy life for our little Julia."

Before Joseph could respond, the father and daughter entered, followed by Clementina. All hugged–except for Joseph and Clementina–and the newlyweds stepped outside.

As they rolled through the streets toward the hotel, Julia laid her head upon her husband's shoulder, drew a long, deep breath, and said, "Now all our obligations to society are fulfilled and we can rest a while. For the first time in my life I am a free woman–and you have liberated me!"

Joseph nodded with a smile. As the carriage moved on, the memory of Philip's earnest, deep green eyes, warm with more than brotherly love, haunted Joseph's memory, and he knew that Philip's faithful thoughts followed him.

Chapter 10: Clouds of Presentiment

FORTUNATELY FOR JOSEPH, he had "practiced" sufficiently with Elwood, and his first night with Julia went as well as could have been expected. Even so, he had to envisage Philip Held and hold the image in his mind in order to complete his husbandly duties. Memories of his night at Philip's home bounced through his head.

"What are you smiling about, Mr. Asten?" Julia looked up from the pastel pink silk sheets of the hotel bed. "I sure do hope it was me." She smiled in anticipation of his affirmative answer.

"Of course, Mrs. Asten. Of course," Joseph replied absent-mindedly. The first deception of their marriage had been his. He could hardly sleep, given the circumstances of sharing a bed with a person he barely knew and the guilt of betrayal in his mind.

In the morning, hotel waiters brought breakfast to their room so that they did not have to leave. Joseph sat and listened to his wife recount the details of the ceremony she felt most compelling or poignant. Every so often he would nod his head, which seemed more full of Philip than Julia.

They returned to the Blessing home later in the day to have dinner with the family. A depressing atmosphere seemed to fill the house. Mrs. Blessing looked pinched and care-worn. Clementina appeared more discontented than usual, and Mr. Blessing—more melancholy plebeian than buoyant politician—seemed dour.

"What's the matter?" Julia asked her mother in an undertone. "I hope he hasn't lost his place."

"Lost my place!" Mr. Blessing exclaimed. "I'd like to see how the collection of customs would go on without me. But a man may keep his place and yet lose his house and home."

Clementina dashed off and Mrs. Blessing followed, handkerchief to eye. "If you'll excuse me," Julia said and hastened after them. "Ma! Dear ma!"

Mr. Blessing held up an accusing finger. "It's only on *their* account." He spoke with Joseph as if he were a peer. "A plucky man never desponds, sir, but women—you will find—are upset by every reverse."

Joseph looked at his new father-in-law. "May I ask what has happened?"

"A delicate regard for you would counsel me to conceal it," Mr. Blessing began, "but my duty as your father-in-law leaves me no alternative." He took a seat. "I am but one out of the many millions of victims of mistaken judgment. The case is simply this: I will omit certain legal technicalities touching the disposition of property, which may not be familiar to you, and state the facts in the most intelligible form. Securities which I placed as collaterals for the loan of a sum—not a very large amount—have been very unexpectedly depreciated, but only temporarily so, as all the market knows. If I am forced to sell them at such an untoward crisis, I lose the largest part of my limited means. If I retain them, they will ultimately recover their full value."

Joseph waited until he felt certain his father-in-law had stopped speaking. "Then why not retain them?"

"The sum advanced upon them must be repaid, and it so happens—the market being very tight—that every one of my friends is short. Of course, where their own paper is on the street, I can't ask them to float mine for three months longer, which is all that is necessary. A good indorsement is the extent of my necessity. For anyone who is familiar with the aspects of the market can see that there must be a great rebound before three months."

While Joseph had no understanding of the stock market mechanics Mr. Blessing referred to, he did have experience with the up-and-down movement of crop prices. "If it were not a very large amount..." he offered.

"Only a thousand!" Mr. Blessing proclaimed. "I know what you were going to say. It is perfectly natural. I appreciate it because if our positions were reversed, I should have done the same thing." He turned his head. "It might be said that I had availed myself of your entrance into my family to beguile you into pecuniary entanglements." He faced Joseph again. "No, no! Let me make the sacrifice like a man! I'm no longer young, it is true, but the feeling that I stand on principle will give me strength to work."

"On the other hand, Mr. Blessing, very unpleasant things might be said of me if I should permit you to suffer so serious a loss."

"I don't deny it. You have made a two-horned dilemma out of a one-sided embarrassment. I confess, the temptation is strong. The mere use of your name for a few months is all I should require. Either the securities will rise to their legitimate value or some of the capitalists with whom I have dealings will be in a position to accommodate me. I have frequently tided over similar snags and sand-bars in the financial current, and this is an instance where an additional inch of water will lift me from wreck to flood-tide." He turned his eyes upward.

"But your family –"

"I know! I know!" Mr. Blessing cried, leaning his head upon his hands. "There is my vulnerable point–my heel of Achilles! There would be no alternative. Better to sell this house than have my paper dishonored. You see the considerations that sway me." He looked up at Joseph. "Unless you withdraw your most generous offer, what can I do but yield and accept it?"

"I have no intention of withdrawing it," Joseph answered, taking his father-in-law's words literally. "I made the offer freely and willingly. If my indorsement is all that is necessary now, I can give it at once."

Mr. Blessing grasped him by the hand, winked hard three times, and turned his head away without speaking. From his breast pocket, he drew a large leather pocket-book, opened it, and produced a printed promissory note.

"We will make it payable at your county bank because your name is known there." Mr. Blessing went on. "Upon acceptance—which can be procured in two days—the money will be drawn here. Perhaps we had better say four months, in order to cover all contingencies." He smiled at Joseph with a politician's glow, stood, went to a small writing-desk at the farther end of the room, and filled the blanks in the note.

Joseph walked to where his father-in-law stood, looked over the form, picked up the pen and endorsed it.

Mr. Blessing smiled again, picked up the note, folded it neatly and lodged it safely in his breast-pocket. "We will keep this entirely to ourselves. My wife—let me whisper to you—is very proud and sensitive. Although the De l'Hotels—now the Doolittles—were never quite the equals of the De Belsains, but women see matters in a different light. They can't understand the accommodation of a name, but fancy that it implies a kind of humiliation, as if one were soliciting charity." He shook his head in incredulity, laughed then looked directly at Joseph and rubbed his hands. "I shall soon be in a position to render you a favor in return." He gazed out the window. "My long experience, and—I may add, my intimate knowledge of the financial field—enables me to foresee many splendid opportunities. There are, just now, some movements which are not yet perceptible on the surface." He faced Joseph again. "Mark my words! We shall shortly have a new excitement, and a cool, well-seasoned head is a fortune at such times."

Joseph studied the older man, taking in the words, and attempting to make sense of their intent. "In the country, we only learn enough to pay off our debts and invest our earnings. We are in the habit of moving slowly and cautiously. Perhaps we miss opportunities, but if we don't see them, we are just as contented as if they had not been there." He took a step forward. "I have enough for comfort and try to be satisfied."

Mr. Blessing spread his coat and parked his thumbs in the waistcoat again. "Inherited ideas! They belong to the community in which you live. Are you satisfied with your neighbors' ways of living and thinking?" He held up an open hand. "I do not mean to disparage them, but have you no desire to rise above their level? Money—as I once said at a dinner given to a distinguished railroad man—money is the engine which draws individuals up the steepest grades of society; it is the lubricating oil which makes the trucks of life run easy; it is the safety-brake which renders collision and wreck impossible!" A brief pause and a brief smile. "I have long been accustomed to consider it in the light of power, not of property, and I classify men according as they take one or the other view. The latter are misers, but the former, sir, are philosophers!"

Joseph had little experience listening to men of a political nature. At election time, he had always attended the town-house meetings for the congressional candidates, but country politicians speak more of livestock and crop yields, not ethereal wisps of philosophical flummery.

The three Blessing women entered before Joseph had a chance to muster a response. Each swiftly scrutinized the two gentlemen. Mrs. Blessing seemed to have lost her woe-worn expression, but Clementina wore a malicious gleam of satisfaction.

"Dinner is served," Julia announced, and the five of them retired to the dining-room.

•⋎•

Early the next morning, the coachman busied himself with the travelling-trunks, many satchels and little packages—an astonishing number. Final farewells came from all around, and the newlyweds climbed into the carriage.

They reached the station with a few minutes to spare. Onboard the train the Astens found their private room. Once they had passed through the meandering suburbs, Julia turned to Joseph and said abruptly, "I am sure, Joseph, that pa made use of your generosity. Pray, don't deny it!"

A faint trace of hardness in her voice led Joseph to interpret this as an indication of dissatisfaction with his failure to confide the matter to her. "I have no intention of denying anything, Julia," he responded. "I was not called upon to exercise generosity. It was simply what your father would term as 'accommodation.'"

Her face grew tight. "I understand. How much?"

"An endorsement of his note for a thousand dollars—which is little, when it will prevent him from losing valuable securities."

Julia turned to the window and watched the passing scenery for ten minutes without speaking. When she turned back to face her new husband, her expression suggested a sternness vainly concealed under a wreathed smile. "In future, Joseph," she began, "I hope you will always consult me in any pecuniary venture. I may not know much about such matters, but it is my duty to learn. I have been obliged to hear a great deal of financial talk from pa and his friends, and could not help guessing some things which I think I can apply for your benefit. We are to have no secrets from each other, you know."

His own words! Even though he had overheard Julia and her sister discussing the family's dire financial situation, as well as Julia's true age being more than she let on, what she said was just and right. Why should it be unwelcome that he had tried to help her family? Joseph could not explain to himself why he felt annoyed. He wanted to banish the feeling, hide it under self-reproach and shame, but it clung to him most uncomfortably.

The rest of the journey passed with little conversation. Julia sat looking out the window, and Joseph sat thinking of Philip.

At Oakland Station, Dennis waited with the cart. He piled their traveling cases, as well as the gift boxes and satchels, into the back and assisted the newlyweds into the seat.

As they moved through the village and out into the farm-lands, Joseph observed the sadness of late autumn upon the fields. He heard spring saying, *I am coming!* in the young wheat. The houses looked warm and cozy behind their sheltering fir-trees. Cattle still grazed on the meadows, and corn awaited husking. The impending sunset gave a bright edge to those somber colors of the landscape, and to Joseph's eyes, he had never seen such beauty before.

"Is it always this windy here in the fall?" Julia complained as she leaned back.

"There!" Joseph cried out as a view of his valley opened below them. The stream flashed like steel between the leafless sycamores. "There is our home-land. Do you know where to look for our house?"

Julia leaned forward, smiled, and pointed silently across the shoulder of a hill to the eastward. "You surely didn't suppose I *could* forget," she murmured.

Rachel Miller awaited them at the gate. Julia had no sooner alighted than she flung herself into the older woman's arms. "Dear Aunt Rachel! You must now take my mother's place. I have *so* much to learn from you! It is doubly a home since you are here. I feel that we shall all be happy together!" She looked from Joseph to Rachel as Dennis took the cart to the stable.

Rachel shot Julia a skeptical glance before turning to her nephew. She kissed him first, clasping both his hands and looking at a face that appeared to have grown a few years older in the time of a few days absence. "I wish I could have gone with you and shared in the happy moments, but somebody had to stay home and take care of things." Then she turned to Julia, giving her a light peck on the cheek. "Welcome, my dear, to your new home. I am certain we can learn from each other as we share the womanly duties."

The three walked into the house, and Joseph led Julia up the stairs to the room they would both occupy. Before he had left for the city, he and Dennis had moved the two beds together.

Joseph smiled at his handiwork, but Julia scowled at the room, which had half the floor space of her bedchamber at home.

Aunt Rachel requested Julia's assistance with preparing the dinner. As they ate together, Joseph and Julia described the wedding proceedings to the delight of Rachel and Dennis. Following the meal, the two women cleared the table in record time, and after they set the dishes to dry, joined Joseph in the sitting-room. The wind roared through the dusky trees.

Joseph watched his new bride as she sifted through the pile of gift boxes and bags. Every so often she giggled at some trifling object she held up for Joseph to see. Rachel brought him up-to-date on the farm. He only answered in short utterances, attempting to appear attentive.

However, under his current state ran a graver thought process. He had wanted independence and a chance of growth for his life. Marriage seemed to have been the answer. He considered how this hour began the new life of his dreams. Whether the decision proved wise or rash, nothing could change. He felt limited as before, but within a different circle. Joseph realized he could pace his schooling to its fullest extent, but all the lessons he had yet learned required him to be satisfied within it.

•▼•

Over the next few weeks, neighbors started to pay friendly visits to the Asten farm, followed by return visits and invitations, which Julia willingly accepted. Joseph observed how very amiably she conducted herself and how she took pains to confirm the favorable impression she had made earlier in the year. Everybody remarked how she had improved in appearance, how round and soft her neck and shoulders, how bright and fresh her complexion. To the surprise of many people, she thanked them with numerous grateful expressions for their friendly reception of her into their society.

However, at home, she indulged in criticisms of their manner and habits, frequently in an unfriendly manner. Although she delivered these judgments in a light, playful tone, Aunt Rachel and Joseph seemed uncomfortable upon hearing them.

Autumn lapsed into winter, and the farm household began to share the isolation of the season. During the quiet, lonely days, Julia undertook to master the details of the housekeeping. She proceeded from garret to cellar, inspecting every article in closet and pantry, censuring occasionally. When it appeared Aunt Rachel grew tired and irritable, Julia would offer a spoonful of praise.

At first, Julia made no material changes, even though her stubborn views upon many points appeared obvious. She possessed a marked, tightfisted tendency for what the country people called "nearness." Little by little, she diminished the bountiful, free-handed manner of provisions that had been the habit of the house.

In some directions, Julia seemed the reverse of "near," as Joseph saw it. She persuaded him into expenditures that other people might have considered extravagant.

When the snow came, the old, open, wooden cart would no longer do, and the Astens purchased an elegant sleigh with a silver mounted harness, silver-sounding bells, and a wolf-skin robe. It became the envy of all the young men and an abomination to the old. Joseph did not want to begrudge his wife's pleasure, and they had sufficient funds to afford such luxury easily. However, after some of the neighbors began to hint about their feelings toward the flashy buggy, Joseph started to change his relation to them. He would have had difficulty explaining why they should resent this or any other slight departure from their fashions, but such had always been their custom.

The snow soon vanished, and a tiresome season of rain and thaw succeeded. South-eastern winds blew from the Atlantic across the intervening lowlands and rolled interminable gray masses of fog over the hills, blurring the scenery of the valley.

Dripping trees, soaked meadows, and sodden leaves detached themselves from the general void, becoming visible to those who traveled the deep, quaking roads. Social intercourse in the neighborhood ceased perforce, though the need of it had never been great. From time-to-time, Julia would stand in the front window, looking at what little of the main highway down to the valley she could see. It forever appeared empty and deserted.

Having exhausted her understanding of the house resources, she insisted on acquainting herself with the barn and everything in it. She laughingly asserted that her education as a farmer's wife had only begun, and she must know the amount of crops, the price of grain, the value of the stock, the manner of work, and whatever else seemed necessary to her position.

Even with all her pretty blunders, Joseph appreciated her unusually-quick apprehension. Whatever she acquired became fixed in her mind as if for some possible future use. Trivial details did not seem to weary her, and, at times, Joseph would have willingly shortened his lessons. It made him uncomfortable and singularly disturbed that he felt trapped between his desire to be gratified by Julia's curiosity and her eager, persistent character.

Joseph began to suspect a misplaced confidence but stubbornly admitted that he might have been too innocent, too unsophisticated, too revealing. He eagerly clung to every look and word and action that confirmed his sliding faith in his wife's sweet and simple character. He fiercely asserted to his own heart that he had every reason to be happy; however, he became consumed with a secret fever of unrest, doubt, and dread.

Chapter 11: Visitors from the City

THE HORNS OF THE GROWING MOON still turned downwards, and cold, dreary rains poured upon the land. Even though Julia's patience in such straits had proved wonderful, Joseph felt she exhibited subtle signs indicating a change might be welcome.

It came as no surprise when she proposed a visit from her sister. Joseph found the request natural enough, as he had anticipated such an occurrence. However, he thought it intriguing that she wanted to invite Clementina out to the country rather than go back to the city herself. She had not seen her family during the intervening months, and he had suspected her longing for a familiar face.

Julia wrote to her sister directly to arrange the travel. On the appointed day, Joseph rode to the station to meet the westward train from the city.

At first, he did not recognize his sister-in-law on the platform, as she wore a cloak and hood. The deliberate grace of her movements gave her identity away, and he approached the shrouded figure. She extended her hand, giving his a cordial pressure.

"I will wait in the ladies' room," Clementina said as she handed Joseph a few brass baggage-checks. Apparently, she expected her brother-in-law to pay the ransom for her luggage.

Just as he turned to go into the station, someone grasped Joseph's arm.

"What a lucky chance!" exclaimed the deep, resonant voice of Philip Held. He suddenly paused his greeting, lifted his hat and bowed to Clementina, who nodded slightly as she passed into the room. "Let me look at you!" Philip resumed, laying his hands on Joseph's shoulders. Their eyes met and lingered.

Joseph felt blood rise to his face as Philip's gaze sank more deeply into his heart and seemed to fathom its hidden trouble. He smiled broadly.

"I scarcely knew, until this very moment, that I had missed you so much, Joseph Asten!"

"Have you come to stay?"

"I think so. The branch railway down the valley, which you know was projected, is to be built immediately, but there are other reasons why the furnaces should be in blast." Philip's eyes roamed the form of the man before him. "If it is possible, the work—and my settlement with it—will begin without any further delay." He pointed toward the ladies' room. "Is she your first family visit?"

Joseph took a second to respond as he had been daydreaming about the man before him, recalling the night before his wedding. "Oh, yes. She will be with us a fortnight, but you will come, Philip?"

"To be sure!" Philip exclaimed. "I only saw her face indistinctly through the veil, but her nod said to me, 'A nearer approach is not objectionable.' Certainly, Miss Blessing, but with all the conventional forms, if you please!" He laughed with what sounded like scorn or bitterness, and Joseph looked upon him with a puzzled air. "You may as well know," Philip whispered, "that when I was a spoony youth of twenty, I very nearly imagined myself in love with Miss Clementina Blessing, and she encouraged my greenness until it spread as fast as a bamboo or a gourd-vine. Of course, I've long since congratulated myself that she cut me up, root and branch, when our family fortune was lost. The awkwardness of our intercourse is all on her side. Can she still have faith in her charms and my youth, I wonder? Ye gods! That would be a lovely conclusion of the comedy!"

They laughed raucously, but Joseph turned serious a moment later. "Please pardon my insensitivities, Philip, but is it possible... I mean legally possible... for a person of... of your Race to... uh... to..."

Philip spoke to end his friend's sufferings. "To wed a person of your Race? Was that the question?" Joseph nodded with relief. "Yes, my friend. There are other states—mostly to the South from here—where our two Races are legally prohibited from marrying. 'Miscegenation' they call it. However, in this part of the country, there are no barriers for two people who truly love one another." He pierced Joseph's eyes with his penetrating stare.

They both smiled and parted with a great hug. The news of Philip's involvement with Clementina aroused Joseph's interest.

He paid for the checks and loaded the luggage into the cart. As they drove toward the farm, Clementina broke the icy silence. "I am surprised to see Mr. Held."

"I expect a visit from him soon," Joseph responded, but Clementina said nothing. "You have no objection to meeting with him, I suppose?"

"Mr. Held is still a gentleman, I believe," she answered curtly. "Fine weather you have."

Julia flew at her sister with open arms and showered on her a profusion of kisses, all of which she received with perfect serenity. When she could finally get a breath, Clementina announced, "Dear me, Julia, I scarcely recognize you! You are already so countrified!"

Aunt Rachel stood off to the side, observing Clementina's slow, deliberate movements, and her even-toned musical utterances. If someone else had used the same words, they might have expressed malice or heartlessness. Julia's expression indicated one of annoyance and puzzlement.

Over dinner, Clementina asked Joseph, "Aren't you having another birthday soon? I seem to remember my dear sister telling me that she met you soon after you had just turned 23." Her raised eyebrows suggested she sought information other than the direct answer to her question.

"Why, yes. You are quite correct in that." Joseph looked at his wife. "My 24th year is quickly approaching."

"Oh, yes," Julia chimed in. "We will have to devise a special celebration for you. Another gathering!" She looked at Joseph with a smile and then at Clementina with a scowl. Aunt Rachel observed this behavior without comment.

"By the way, Mr. Asten"–Clementina used her most silvery tone–"has Julia told you her age?"

Aunt Rachel choked on a bit of meat, and Julia gave a little start, but presently looked up with an artless expression.

Joseph jumped in before his wife had a chance to respond, "I knew it before we were married."

Clementina bit her lip. Julia flashed a triumphant glance at her sister. She turned to Joseph and said tenderly, "We will both let the old birthdays go, and we shall have one and the same anniversary from this time on!" A satisfied smile occupied her face.

Without facing her directly, Joseph could sense–through some natural magnetism–how Clementina sharply and curiously watched the relationship between himself and her sister. Although he had no fear of her detecting misgivings that were not yet acknowledged to himself, he instinctively knew to be on his guard in her presence.

•∀•

A few days later, Mr. Philip Held paid a visit to the Asten farm. Julia received him cordially, as the friend of her husband. Clementina bowed while remaining seated, an impassive look upon her face.

Philip crossed the room and gave her his hand, saying cheerfully, "We used to be old friends, Miss Blessing. You have not forgotten me?"

Clementina turned her face in Philip's direction but did not meet him head-on. "We cannot forget when we have been asked to do so," she warbled and picked up an album from the side table.

As he sat, Philip studied the two sisters. "Eight years! I am the only one who has changed in that time."

Julia looked to her sister, but Clementina appeared lost in comparing some zephyr tints.

"The whirligig of time!" Philip exclaimed. "Who can foresee anything? Back then, I was but an ignorant, petted young aristocrat, an expectant heir. Now, behold me—working among miners and puddlers and forgemen. It's a rough but wholesome change." He turned to Julia. "Would you believe it, Mrs. Asten, I've forgotten the mazurka!"

"I wish to forget it," Julia replied. "The spring-house is as important to me as the furnace to you."

Clementina abruptly slammed the book closed with a report. "Have you seen the Hopetons lately?" she asked of Philip but faced no one in particular.

Joseph observed a shade pass over Philip's face. He hesitated before answering. "I hear they will be neighbors of mine in summer. Mr. Hopeton is interested in the new branch down the valley and has purchased the old Calvert property for a country residence." He looked at Joseph with a downturned mouth.

"Indeed? Then you will often see them." Clementina appeared to enjoy making Mr. Held uncomfortable.

"I hope so. They are very agreeable people. But I shall also have my own little household." He glanced toward Clementina but not directly at her. "My sister will probably join me."

"Not Madeline!" exclaimed Julia.

Philip smiled and faced Julia. "Madeline. It has long been her wish, as well as mine." He then turned to his friend. "You know the little cottage on the knoll at Coventry, Joseph? I have taken it for a year."

Clementina raised her chin and proclaimed in her sweetest tones, "There will be quite a city society. You will need no commiseration, Julia." She looked at her sister. "Unless, indeed, the country people succeed in changing you all into their own likeness. Mrs. Hopeton will certainly create a sensation. I am told that she is very extravagant. Mr. Held?"

Philip coughed then said dryly, "I have never seen her husband's bank account." He rose. "If you will all excuse me, I must be on my way." He strode to the door.

Joseph accompanied him to the lane. Philip picked up the bridle-rein and rested it over his arm. With mechanical speech—the type that always absurdly comes to the lips when graver interests have possession of the heart—he said, "Joseph, something is coming over both of us—not between us. I thought I should tell you a little more, but perhaps it is too soon. If I guess rightly, neither of us is ready." He then looked directly into Joseph's eyes. "Only this: let us each think of the other as a help and support!"

"I do, Philip!" Joseph answered quickly, even though he felt—rather than saw—some unknown matter troubled his friend. "I can tell there is some influence at work which I do not understand, but I am not impatient to know what it is. As for myself, I seem to know nothing at all, but you can judge. You see all there is." After he said these words, Joseph felt their insincerity, and he almost expected to find an expression of reproof in Philip's eyes.

As the two men stood gazing upon each other's face, Joseph observed Philip softening to a pitying tenderness. He then knew that Philip clearly perceived the doubts he had resisted with all the force of his nature.

Once they had shaken hands, Philip mounted his horse and rode off. Joseph stood watching his friend depart, and when he could no longer see the trail dust rising in the golden light of late afternoon, he looked up to the gray blank of heaven and asked himself, "Is this all? Has my life already taken the permanent imprint of its future?"

When the time came for Clementina to return to the city, she spoke to her brother-in-law with more conventional tenderness. "Dearest Joseph, I thank you and your wonderful aunt for the hospitality. You and my sister have provided me with all the comforts I could have wished for outside our city home. It is my fondest wish and hope that you will allow me to return and renew my visit a few months hence."

It startled Joseph somewhat that the usually stand-offish Clementina spoke so eloquently with him. It could have been that she had been unsuccessful in her mission to discover problems and negative outcomes at the Asten farm. Perhaps the sight of Philip Held awoke old feelings, or maybe it could have been spending some time outside the malcontent influence of city society that allowed her to relax her usual rigidity. Whatever the cause, Joseph had enjoyed the restoration of the early harmony to his household. Julia's manner had been so gentle and amiable that—upon looking back—he believed that only the loneliness of her new life had been responsible for any change.

However, Julia's hard, watchful expression returned soon after her sister's departure. The eyelids no longer gave a fictitious depth to her shallow, tawny pupils, the soft roundness of her voice took on a frequent harshness, and she resumed asserting her own will in all things.

Joseph's doubts reawakened in a more threatening form. He could not guess the terrible chafing of a smiling mask. It confounded him that the gentleness—which had nearly revived his faith in her—would so suddenly disappear, like a glimpse of the sun through winter fog.

In the early spring, when the roads began to improve, Julia insisted in driving to the village alone. She had utilized the winter to make herself acquainted with all the details of the farm business. Joseph's friends informed him that on these unaccompanied journeys, Julia extended her knowledge of the social and pecuniary standing of all the neighboring families. She talked with farmers, mechanics, and drovers. Her education included the fluctuations in the prices of grain and cattle, and she learned–to the penny–the wages paid for every form of service. As the weeks passed, Joseph sensed the ground growing more secure under his wife's feet.

It came as no surprise that his aunt's participation in the direction of the household gradually diminished. He observed her increasing silence and troubled expression. According to what Joseph heard from the neighbors, his farm maintained the veneer of domestic harmony. The shift in management had progressed quite gradually.

Aunt Rachel surprised Joseph with a request. "Nephew, can you take or send me to Magnolia to-morrow?"

"Certainly, Aunt! I suppose you want to visit Cousin Phoebe. You have not seen her since last summer."

She wrung her hands. "It was that... and something more." When she paused, Joseph looked at her face for an indication. "She has always wished that I should make my home with her, but I couldn't think of any change so long as I was needed here." Rachel Miller waved her hand to indicate the farm. "However, it seems to me that I am not really needed now."

"Why, Aunt Rachel!" Joseph exclaimed. "I meant this to be your home always, as much as mine!" He moved to her and put an arm around her shoulder. "Of course you are needed, not to do all that you have done heretofore, but as a part of the family. It is your right." He squeezed gently.

"I understand all that, Joseph," she said as she maneuvered away. "But I've heard it said that a young wife should learn to see to everything herself, and Julia, I'm sure, doesn't need either my help or my advice."

"Has she…"–Joseph looked at his aunt with a grave expression–"has she…?"

"No," Rachel interjected. "She has not said it… in words. Different persons have different ways. She is quick–O, very quick!–and capable. You know I could never sit idly by and look on. It's hard to be directed. I seem to belong to the place and everything connected with it, yet there's times when what a body ought to do is plain." She looked off over the valley.

"Aunt Rachel," Joseph spoke feeling a bit confused and troubled, "I know that Julia is very anxious to learn everything which she thinks belongs to her place–perhaps a little more than is really necessary." He winked at his aunt. "She's an enthusiastic nature, you know. Maybe you are not fully acquainted yet. Maybe you have misunderstood her in some things. I would like to think so." His expression changed to one of woe.

"It is true that we are different, Joseph–*very* different. I don't say, therefore, that I am always right. It's likely, indeed, that any young wife and any old housekeeper like myself would have their various notions. But where there can be only one head, it's the wife's place to be that head." She held her chin up proudly. "Julia has not asked it of me, but she has the right. I can't say, also, that I don't need a little rest and change, and there seems to be some call on me to oblige Phoebe." Joseph looked away, toward the hills. "Look at the matter in the true light and you must feel that it's only natural."

After a long pause he responded, "I hope so. All things are changing."

That evening after dinner, when the Astens had retired to their small room upstairs, Julia put her hand on Joseph's shoulder and spoke sweetly, "You have been very quiet. Is something wrong that I should know about?"

Joseph turned toward his wife with a bit of a tear in one eye. "Aunt Rachel has announced her desire to relocate to

Magnolia to live with Cousin Phoebe."

"What can we do?" Julia asked, sounding half-genuine. "It would be so delightful if she would stay, and yet I have had a presentiment that she would leave us, if only for a little while." She moved to the window. "Dear, good Aunt Rachel! I couldn't help seeing how hard it was for her to allow the least change in the order of housekeeping. No two women have exactly the same ways and habits. She would be perfectly happy if I would sit still all day and let her tire herself to death. I know she manages to see the least that I do and secretly worries about it in the very kindness of her heart. I suppose we are too peculiar–perhaps I am just as much so as Aunt Rachel." Julia faced her husband. "Why can't women carry on partnerships in housekeeping as men do in business?" She shook her head gently. "If she *will* go, Joseph, she must at least leave us with the feeling that our home is always hers, whenever she chooses to accept it."

She bent over Joseph, who sat in the chair, and gave him a rapid kiss. Julia then went down to the kitchen to speak with Aunt Rachel, leaving Joseph alone in the bedroom.

Once again, the introduction of Julia into his life had led to the departure of another cherished person. Elwood Withers, Lucy Henderson, and, perhaps, Philip Held. How many more people would turn away due to his queer marriage? He had hoped that such a union would bring more friends, but all he had gained were in-laws.

Within a week, Rachel Miler had gathered her belongings into a large box and left the farm to reside with her widowed niece in Magnolia.

The day following her departure, another surprise came to Joseph in the person of his father-in-law. Mr. Blessing arrived in a hired vehicle from the station. The March winds had rendered his face red and radiant. Joseph could not be certain whether this sudden arrival should be interpreted as happenstance or an omen of ill-fortune.

Mr. Blessing shook hands with the Irish groom who had

driven him from the station, and he gave the fellow a few dollar coins as a gratuity. The driver pulled an elegant traveling-satchel from under the seat and handed it to Mr. Blessing and then departed.

"God bless you, son-in-law!" Mr. Blessing began with a breezy burst of feeling. "It does my heart good to see you again! And then, at last, the pleasure of beholding your ancestral seat." He glanced about. "Really, this is quite... quite manorial!"

Julia rushed from the house crying, "O pa!"

"Bless me, how wild and fresh the child looks!" Mr. Blessing proclaimed after the embrace. "Only see the country roses on her cheeks! Almost too young and sparkling for Lady Asten... of Asten Hall, eh?" He smiled at his suggestion. "As Dryden says, 'Happy, happy, happy pair!'" He turned to Joseph. "It takes me back to the days when *I* was a gay, young lark, but I must have a care and not make an old fool of myself." Mr. Blessing handed his satchel to Joseph and put his arms around the Astens' shoulders. "Let us go in and subside into soberness. I am ready both to laugh and cry."

After dinner, they retired to the sitting-room, a blaze in the fireplace. Mr. Blessing took Aunt Rachel's favorite chair, cigar in mouth, slippers on feet. He pulled a leather-covered flask from his robe.

"I am still plagued by cramps. Physiologists, you know, have discovered that stimulants diminish the wear and tear of life, and I find their theories correct." He held up the flask. "A little water, if you please, Julia."

His daughter smiled as she shook her head, went to the kitchen and returned with a glass half-filled. Mr. Blessing took it and poured a measured dose.

"You, in your pastoral isolation and pecuniary security, can form no conception of the tension under which we men of office and of the world live." He held up the glass. "*Beatus ille*, and so forth," he toasted and downed the liquid. "Strange that the only fragment of Latin which I remember should be so appropriate!" He smiled at his own amusement.

Mr. Blessing handed the empty glass to his daughter, who returned it to the kitchen. "Have you been dipping into oil?"

Joseph had no idea what his father-in-law had asked. He found it odd that he waited until Julia had left the room to pose his curious question. "Dipping into oil"? What could that mean?

When Julia returned, Joseph stated, "Your father has just asked if we have been dipped in oil."

Mr. Blessing chuckled. "No, not quite, my boy. The phrase was, 'dipping *into* oil.' Perhaps you have not heard of the rush over in Titusville, Oil City, and Pithole. It was Colonel Drake who made the first discovery of rock oil a while back, and investors have been making quite a fortune from the black, gooey stuff!"

"Not yet," Julia responded, "but almost everybody in the neighborhood is ready to do so now that Clemson has realized fifty thousand in a single year. They are talking of nothing else in the village. I heard, yesterday, that Old Bishop has taken three thousand dollars' worth of stock in a new company."

"Take my advice and don't touch 'em!" Mr. Blessing opined.

Joseph realized that his wife knew more about the people in his village than he did. While he had been busy working the farm, she had been getting to know the neighborhood. Old Bishop did not seem like the kind of man who would risk his old money on new ideas.

"I had not intended to," Joseph said while taking a fresh look at his wife.

"There is this thing about these excitements," Mr. Blessing went on. "They never reach the rural districts until the first sure harvest is over. The sharp, intelligent operators in the large cities—the men who are ready to take up soap, thimbles, hand-organs, electricity, or hymn-books at a moment's notice—always cut into a new thing before its value is guessed by the multitude." He shifted his focus to Joseph. "Then the smaller fry follow and secure their second crop, while your quiet men in the country are shaking their heads and crying, 'humbug!' Finally, when it really gets to be a speculative humbug, they just begin to believe in it and become fair game for the bummers and camp-followers of the financial army." He turned to his daughter. "I respect Clemson, though I never heard of him before. As for Old Bishop, he may be a very worthy man, but he'll never see the color of his three thousand dollars again."

"Pa!" cried Julia. "How clear you do make everything. And to think that I was wishing—Oh, wishing *so* much!—that Joseph would go into oil." She stood by her husband and put a hand on his shoulder.

A quick gleam of satisfaction passed over her father's face. He smiled to himself, puffed rapidly at his cigar for a minute, and then resumed. "In such a field of speculation, everything depends on being initiated. There are men in the city—friends of mine—who know every foot of ground in the Allegheny Valley. The can smell oil, even if it's a thousand feet deep. They never touch a thing that isn't safe, but, then, they know *what's* safe." He grinned in self-satisfaction. "In spite of the swindling that's going on, it takes years to exhaust the good points. Just as I am so sure that your honest neighbors here will lose, I am just so sure these friends of mine will gain." Mr. Blessing looked at his son-in-law. "There are millions in what they have underway, at this moment."

Julia's face brightened. "What is it?" She stepped away and looked at her husband's face, as if expecting some sign of interest.

Mr. Blessing unlocked the satchel and took from it a roll of paper. He unfolded the map upon his knees. "Here"—he pointed—"you can see this bend of the river, just about the center of the oil region, which is represented by the yellow color." He glanced up to look at both his daughter and son-in-law. "These little dots above the bend are the celebrated

Fluke Wells, the other dots below are the equally celebrated Chowder Wells. The distance between the two is nearly three miles." He pointed at a spot on the map. "Here is an untouched portion of the treasure, a pocket of Pactolus waiting to be rifled. A few of us have acquired the land and shall commence boring immediately." A grand smile traversed his face.

Something occurred to Joseph. "Wait! It seems to me that either the attempt must have been made already or that the land must command such an enormous price as to lessen the profits."

"Wisely spoken!" Mr. Blessing nodded. "It is the first question which would occur to any prudent mind." He looked from one to the other. "But what if I say that neither is the case?" He then looked directly at his son-in-law. "The owner of the land was one of your ignorant, stubborn men who took such a dislike to the prospectors and speculators that he refused to let them come near. Both the Fluke and the Chowder Companies tried their best to buy him out, but he just let them make ridiculous offers and then refused to sell." He turned to his daughter. "Well, a few months ago he died, and his heirs were willing enough to let the land go. Oddly enough, around the same time, the Fluke and Chowder Wells decreased in flow, and their shares fell from 270 to 95. Once the sale price of the land dropped, we purchased it at a modest sum."

Both Julia and Joseph stared at the older man with interrogatories unspoken.

"I see the question in your mind," Mr. Blessing went on. "Why should we wish to buy when the other wells were giving out?" He took a few short, quick puffs from the cigar. "There comes in the secret, which is our veritable success. Consider it whispered in your ears and locked in your bosoms." He glanced at Julia then at Joseph. "Torpedoes!" He pointed sharply downward with a bounce. "We bought at the low figure, in the very nick of time! Within a week, the Fluke and Chowder Wells were torpedoed and came back to more than their former capacity. The shares rose as rapidly as they had fallen." A waggle of his eyebrows gave him a look of smug satisfaction. "If you take them as the two arms, we hold the central body, which could now be sold for ten times what it cost us!" He pointed to the map with a grand smile and a light of merited triumph in his eyes.

Julia clapped her hands and bounced on her feet. "Trumps at last!" she proclaimed.

"Yes, my dear Julia, trumps at last. Wealth, repose for my old days. Wealth for us all!" He yawned. "My goodness. It has been a long day for me. Perhaps if you will show me to my room, I can get some rest, and we can continue this discussion over breakfast." Mr. Blessing stood and followed his daughter to the room that used to belong to Aunt Rachel.

"Good-night, dear father," Joseph heard Julia say as visions of gushing oil wells and stacks of money filled his head.

Chapter 12: Taking Stock

JOSEPH COULD HARDLY SLEEP THAT NIGHT in anticipation of further discussion with his father-in-law. Perhaps this was the reward for assisting him a few months back. Mr. Blessing had said he knew of many opportunities, and this might be just the thing.

Over breakfast, Mr. Blessing announced, "You know, son-in-law, why the endorsement you gave me was of such vital importance. The note–as I am sure you are aware–will mature in another week. Why should you not charge yourself with the payment, in consideration of the transfer to you of shares of the original stock, already so immensely appreciated in value?" Joseph, not sure of how to respond, merely stared at his father-in-law. "I have delayed making any provision, for the sake of offering you the chance."

Joseph glanced at his wife, who looked as if she wanted to speak, but then appeared to restrain herself with an obvious effort.

"I should like to know," he asked, "who are associated with you in the undertaking?"

"Well done again!" Mr. Blessing charged with a forkful of egg. "Where did you get your practical shrewdness?" He turned to his daughter. "The best men in the city! Not only the Collector and the Surveyor, but Congressman Whaley, E. D. Stokes–of Stokes, Pirricutt and Company–and even the Reverend Doctor Lellifant. If I had not been an old friend of Kanuck, the agent who negotiated the purchase, my chance would have been impalpably small." He patted a pocket in his robe. "I have all the documents with me. There has been no more splendid opportunity since oil became a power!" A smile mutated into a serious expression. "I hesitate to advise even one so near to me in such matters, but if you knew the certainties as I know them, you would go in with all your available capital." The smile returned. "The excitement, as you say, has reached the country communities, which are slow to rise and equally slow to subside. All oil stock is in demand, but the Amaranth–'The Blessing' they wished to call it, but I was obliged to decline, for official reasons–the Amaranth shares will be the golden apex of the market!"

Joseph observed his wife's eager, hungry eyes. The scheme's prospect of easy profit warmed and tempted him as well. Only the habit of his nature resisted, but with diminishing force. "I... might venture the thousand," he announced.

"It is no venture!" Julia cried. "In all the speculations I have heard discussed by pa and his friends, there was nothing so admirably managed as this. Such a certainty of profit may never come again. If you will be advised by me, Joseph, you will take shares to the amount of five... or maybe ten thousand."

Mr. Blessing narrowed his eyes slyly. "Ten thousand is exactly the amount I hold open. That, however, does not represent the necessary payment which can hardly amount to more than twenty-five percent before we begin to realize." He turned to Joseph. "Only ten percent has yet been called, so that your thousand at present will secure you an investment of ten thousand. Really"–he glanced at his daughter–"it seems like a fortunate coincidence."

Joseph looked at Julia, who merely nodded her head eagerly.

"I will make no precise estimate of the profits because it is not prudent to fix our hopes on a positive sum," Mr. Blessing began. He continued to speak in dazzling and bewildering language, only some of which Joseph could comprehend.

As the father-in-law spoke, the son-in-law went into a mental haze. Joseph considered some of the risks involved. The mortgage upon his farm would expire in a year, but he had invested the sums for the purpose of meeting it when due. However, Julia's father laid out an almost-certain investment, which, if he chose to accept, could bring back immense wealth for them. He had already lent Mr. Blessing a thousand dollars, and Joseph had to believe that most of that money went into purchasing shares of the oil property. As he watched Mr. Blessing through blurry vision, a pencil scribbled down figures that excited Julia, and when his focus finally returned, he looked at the bottom line, and it almost took his breath away.

With a glance at Julia, he said, slowly and deliberately, "It is settled that I take as much as the thousand will cover, but I would rather think over the matter quietly for a day or two before venturing further."

"You must," replied Mr. Blessing, patting him on the shoulder. "These things are so new to your experience that they disturb and—I might almost say—alarm you. It is like bringing an increase of oxygen into your mental atmosphere, but you are a healthy organization, and, therefore, you are certain to see clearly. I can wait with confidence."

The next morning, Joseph arose early, and without disturbing his sleeping wife or father-in-law, drove to Coventry Forge to consult Philip Held, who might have some insight into the potential value of the proposed investment. As he passed up the valley in the mild March weather, he sped by the crimson and gold of flowering spice-bushes and maple-trees. However, all of that beauty could not prevent his thoughts from dwelling on the delights of wealth—society, books, travel, and all the mellow, fortunate expansion of life. He hoped Philip's counsel might coincide with his father-in-law's offer.

The Held cottage on the knoll proved empty. It had been re-painted and redecorated in various ways. Joseph found the sign-spiritual of his friend in numerous little touches and changes. It seemed to him that a new soul had entered into the scenery of the place.

He rode on, a mile or two farther up the valley, to the Calvert mansion. A company of mechanics and laborers worked at tearing the inside out. House, barn, garden, and lawn underwent a complete transformation. Joseph paused at the entrance of the private lane, surveying the operation.

Mr. Clemson rode down from the house to meet him. "Hello,

Joseph. Is there something I can assist you with?"

"Oh, no. I recently heard that a family from the city had purchased this place, and as I happened to be nearby, I thought I would come take a bit of a look." He smiled over at Mr. Clemson.

"The city folk–the Hopetons–will be migrating early in May. Work on the new railway has already commenced, and in another year, a different life will come upon this whole neighborhood."

"I thank you for the intelligence, Mr. Clemson. May I trouble you for a few moments more?"

"Why, of course, young Mr. Asten. Of course!"

Joseph took a moment to assemble his thoughts so that he could phrase the question to the best of his advantage. "Have you had any news of the recently formed oil companies over near Titusville?"

Mr. Clemson licked his parched lips. "Frankly, I had invested a tidy sum of money, but I have withdrawn from further speculation. Once I satisfied my fortune, I knew it was the correct time to remove my interest."

"I see." Joseph felt secure enough to pursue the matter a bit further. "Have you heard of the Fluke and Chowder Wells?"

"Oh, yes!" Mr. Clemson smiled. "They have become old, well-known and profitable. The new application of torpedoes has restored their failing flow, and their stock has recovered from its temporary depreciation. However, my own venture went into another part of the region. I am certain there is still money to be made, if prudently placed."

"Thank you, Mr. Clemson." Joseph warbled as he continued to envision showers of bank notes falling from the sky and into his waiting hands.

The ride home flew by. His wife and father-in-law sat at the kitchen table upon his arrival at home.

"And where have you been?" Julia quizzed. "From the sweat

on your forehead, I would guess that you've been out riding."

"Yes," Joseph answered. "I drove over to look at the old Calvert mansion, and, by luck, met with Mr. Clemson. He told me about the work on the house for the... uh... Hopetons."

Julia studied his face before continuing. "Did he say anything about his investments in the oil?"

"As a matter of fact"–Joseph said as he sat down and poured himself a mug of coffee–"he told me that he pulled his funds once he had satisfied his fortune."

"Good for you, my boy," Mr. Blessing commended. "It is in your own best interests to inquire into the fortunes of others when such uncertain speculation is first considered." He focused on Joseph. "Have you made your decision?"

A smile slowly crept across Joseph's face, and he nodded. His wife and father-in-law beamed with joy.

•▼•

A few weeks after he returned home, Mr. Blessing sent a notice that a second assessment of ten percent on the Amaranth stock had been made. The news hit Joseph as both unexpected and disquieting. The accompanying letter described that not only the necessity but the admirable wisdom of a greater present outlay had been anticipated.

The first of the Fourth Month, April–the neighborhood's usual business anniversary–passed by smoothly. The Asten credit had always been sound, Joseph had plenty of money, and for the first time, he tasted a pleasant sense of power in so easily receiving and transferring considerable sums. He now had the clearest evidence of the difference between a man who knew the world and valuable to it, and their slow, dull-headed country neighbors.

However, Julia's nature developed into a new phase. Not only did she accept the future profit as certain, she calculated

149

its exact amount and framed her plans accordingly. Her previous disparagement of the shams and exactions of "society" disappeared as suddenly and coolly as if she had never affected them.

Joseph saw—with a deadly chill in his heart—the change in her manner, a change so complete that another face confronted him at the table, even as another heart beat beside his on the dishallowed marriage-bed. He wondered if she supposed his fresh, unsuspicious nature had been so plastic that she had sufficiently impressed it in her custom.

The gentle droop from her eyelids vanished, leaving the cold, flinty pupils unshaded. A habitual rigid, almost cruel, compression seemed to have taken over the soft appeal of her half-opened lips. All the slight dependent gestures, the tender airs of reference to his will or pleasure, had rapidly transformed themselves into expressions of command or obstinate resistance.

Joseph decided to remain silent about the circumstances, even though his silence covered an ever-increasing sense of outrage.

One day at dinner, Julia launched into an unusually eloquent speech regarding "what pa is doing for us," and what use they should make of "pa's money," as she called it.

"You seem to forget, Julia," Joseph interrupted, "that without my money, not much could have been done."

An angry color came into her face. She bent her head and murmured in an offended tone, "It is very mean and ungenerous in you to refer to my family's temporary poverty of a few months back. You might forget, by this time, the help pa was compelled to ask of you."

"Yes. I did not think of that!" he exclaimed. "Besides, you did not seem entirely satisfied with my help at the time."

Julia's head snapped up and away. "O, how you misunderstand me!" she groaned. "I only wished to know the extent of his need. He is so generous, so considerate towards us"— Joseph could hear the tears in her voice—"that we only guess his misfortune at the last moment."

He thought back to his first visit to the Blessing home. Late-night chit-chat between the two sisters had led him to believe the family had overspent their money, and having that knowledge helped Joseph to decide in signing the endorsement. Julia had accused him of being unjust, unaware of his grasp of the subject. When he looked upon her again, the tears had risen to her eyes.

"What can have become of Elwood Withers?" He changed the subject unexpectedly. "I have not seen him for months."

"I don't think you need care to know," Julia remarked disdainfully. "He's a rough, vulgar fellow. It's just as well if he keeps away from us."

"Julia!" Joseph stood. "He is my friend and must always be welcome to *me*. You were friendly enough towards him, and towards all the neighborhood, last summer. How is it that you have not a good word to say now?"

She looked up at her husband with a calm, smiling face. "It is very simple. You will agree with me in another year. A guest, as I was, must try to see only the pleasant side of people. That's our duty. And I so enjoyed–as much as I could– the rusticity, the awkwardness, the ignorance, the–now, don't be vexed, dear!–the *vulgarity* of your friend." Joseph turned away. "As one of the society of the neighborhood, as a resident, I am not bound by any such delicacy. I take the same right to judge and select as I should take anywhere. How shall I ever get you to see the difference between yourself and these people unless I continually point it out? You are too modest and don't like to acknowledge your own superiority."

Tears turned to laugher as she rose from the table. She left the room humming a lively air.

•❦•

While surveying his fields the next day, Joseph noticed the work on the branch railway extended down the valley far enough that he could now see it. He rode over to inspect the operations and found a pleasant surprise. Elwood Withers had left his father's place and become a sub-contractor.

After a hearty hug, Elwood said, "I've been meanin' to come up, but this is a busy time for me. It's a chance I couldn't let slip, an' now that I've taken hold, I must hold on." He looked directly into his friend's eyes. "I begin to think this is the thing I was made for, Joseph."

Joseph took stock in his wiry friend. "I never thought of it before, and yet I'm sure you are right." He smiled. "How did you hit upon it?"

"*I* didn't. It was a Mr. Held. Colored feller."

"Philip?" asked Joseph with surprise. "He's the one who rescued me after the train accident."

"Him." Elwood nodded. "You know I've been haulin' for the Forge, an' so it turned up by degrees, as I may say. But how *are* you now, really?"

The question meant a great deal more than Joseph knew how to say. Suddenly, in a flash of memory, their talk of the previous year returned to his mind. He saw his friend's true instincts and his own blindness as never before. Unfortunately, he must dissemble, if possible, with that strong, rough, kindly face before him.

"Oh," he began, attempting a cheerful air, "I am one of the old folks now. You must come up..." The recollection of Julia's words cut short the invitation upon his lips. A sharp pang pierced his heart, and the treacherous blood crowded his face all the more that he tried to hold it back.

"Come, an' I'll show you where we're gonna make the cuttin'," Elwood said quietly, taking Joseph by the arm. The special kindness of Elwood's manner rankled a suspicion in Joseph's mind, as if he had been slighted by his friend.

As they walked, Elwood pointed out various parts of the engineering he had worked on. It impressed Joseph that his friend had found a career that galvanized him.

After a while, Joseph's curiosity got the best of him. "Elwood, when was the last time you encountered Mr. Held?"

"Oh, he was just here this mornin', but I don't expect to see him again until to-morrow. He's probably at home, and, I expect, lookin' for you."

•⊺•

Following the encounter with Elwood Withers, Joseph once again busied himself beyond all need with the work of his farm. Even though he knew Philip had returned from the city with his sister, he shrank with a painful dread from Philip's heart-deep, intimate eye.

The soft spring weather allowed Julia to further survey the social ground of the neighborhood. Joseph scarcely knew how extensive her operations had been until she announced an invitation to dine with the Hopetons, who now occupied the renovated Calvert place.

Julia spent all the day preparing for dinner at the Hopetons. She wore a rosy flowing silk dress. Her complexion shone bright and dazzling, with all her former grace of languid eyelids and parted lips. The void in Joseph's heart grew wider at the sight of her. He perceived, as never before, her consummate skill in assuming a false character.

Joseph chided himself for having been so deluded by her. For the first time, a feeling of repulsion–almost disgust– came over him as he listened to her prattle of delight in the soft weather and the fragrant woods and the blossoming orchards. He had to ask himself if her delight had been assumed. *False in one thing, false in all.* That fatal logic began to torment him.

Julia chattered on, enlarging–more than necessary–on the

distinguished city position of the Hopeton family and the importance of "cultivating" its country members. He had never met the Hopetons, and from his wife's description, he had little interest either. He had only accepted the invitation because it seemed so important to her.

As they pulled up to the Calvert place, Joseph noticed that so much had been achieved in such a short time. The house appeared brighter, surrounded by light, airy verandas. The lawn and garden merged together and given into the hands of a skillful gardener. He hardly recognized the old mansion. A broad, solid gravel-walk replaced the old tan-covered path. Thick beds of geraniums in flower studded the turf, and veritable thickets of rose-trees awaited June. A pretty fountain tinkled before the door.

Mr. Hopeton met them with the frank, offhand manner of a businessman. A short, solid-looking man in ripe middle age, he appeared thoroughly cosmopolitan, though not a remarkably intellectual stamp.

The rooms within appeared to have been thrown together, the walls richly—yet harmoniously—colored. Sumptuous furniture received a sparse, proper setting. The place had an air of joyous profusion, of a wealth that delighted in itself—in contrast with the homes of even the wealthiest farmers, which expressed a nicely reckoned sufficiency of comfort.

Mrs. Hopeton joined her husband. She wore a high-necked, crocus-colored dress, plainly trimmed. No artful makeup covered her natural pallor, and no ornamentation bedecked her gown. Joseph remarked the simple grace of her movement, her large, dark, inscrutable eyes, the smooth bands of her black hair, and the pure—though somewhat lengthened—oval of her face. Her gentle dignity of manner more than refreshed, it soothed him. At once he realized how much younger she appeared than her husband, and Joseph involuntarily wondered how they should have come together.

Just as Julia and Mrs. Hopeton touched hands, Philip and Madeline Held arrived. Joseph had thought he and his wife were to be the only guests, and this surprise entrance warmed his heart immensely.

Philip first introduced his sister to Julia, who kissed Madeline with the least little gush of tenderness. Upon presentation to Joseph, he noticed the family resemblance at once. She had the same wavy, dark hair, but her eyes shone a clear hazel, unlike her brother's deep jade color. Their faces contained the same frank firmness, but her woman's smile proved sweeter, as she had lovelier lips. Joseph seemed to clasp an instant friendship in her offered hand.

One other guest arrived soon after, Miss Lucy Henderson. Julia did not let on whatever she might have felt, and she made so much reference to their former meetings as might satisfy Lucy without conveying to Mrs. Hopeton the impression of any special intimacy. Lucy looked thin and worn. Her black silk dress might not have been as fashionable as the others, and she seemed like the poor relation of the company. She looked upon the Held siblings as if they were foreigners, people she might not have chosen to dine with even though they both wore suitable attire.

Although Joseph felt the presence of some new element of strength and self-reliance in her nature, her manner to him remained as simple and friendly as ever. "Good evening, Mr. Asten," she remarked in greeting. "I trust that all is well with you and Mrs. Asten." She took a side-glance at Julia.

The interview caught Joseph off-guard. "Yes. Why, yes. Thank you for asking. I hope you do not find it out-of-line for me to express some surprise at seeing you here this evening."

Lucy gave a half-smile and said, "Perhaps you had not heard that I have taken a position as a teacher at the schoolhouse nearby. Mrs. Hopeton invited me out of sheer neighborliness."

The party sat around a sturdy walnut dining-table, ladies across from their gentlemen, with Lucy the odd one out. Joseph sat next to Mrs. Hopeton with Lucy on the other side of the hostess. Servants brought a tureen of *Soupe à la Reine*, followed by Salmis of Duck with olives, and Larded Sweet-breads with green peas.

Philip and Mr. Hopeton monopolized the conversation, confining it too exclusively to the railroad and iron interests. Eventually, these topics languished and gave way to others in which all could take part. More than anything, Joseph wished to have a private conversation with Philip, but that appeared beyond his reach, for the time.

"Mr. Held or Mr. Asten," Mr. Hopeton began, "either of you know both—what are the principal points of difference between society in the city and the country?"

"Indeed, I know too little of the city," Joseph looked across at Philip.

"And I know too little of the country," Philip added, "here, at least. Of course, the same passions and prejudices come into play everywhere." He looked at each of the ladies in turn. "There are circles, there are jealousies, ups and downs, scandals, suppressions, and rehabilitations. It can't be otherwise."

"Are they not a little worse in the country?" asked Julia, and all heads turned to her. "I believe I may ask the question here, among *us*—because there is less refinement of manner."

Following a momentary silence, Philip continued, "If the external forms are ruder, it may be an advantage, in one sense. Hypocrisy cannot be developed into an art."

Julia bit her lip and remained silent.

Mrs. Hopeton spoke up. "But are the country people hereabouts so rough? I confess that they don't seem so to me." She turned to Lucy. "What do you say, Miss Henderson?"

Lucy appeared startled to have been asked a question directly. She gathered her thoughts and responded, "Perhaps I am not an impartial witness. We care less about what is called 'manners' than the city people. We have no fixed rules for dress and behavior. Only we don't like anyone to differ too much from the rest of us."

"That's it!" Mr. Hopeton pointed at her across the table. "The tyrannical leveling sentiment of an imperfectly developed community!" He smiled at his guests then looked down at his empty plate. "Fortunately, I am beyond its reach."

Julia's eyes sparkled. She peered across at her husband with a triumphant air.

"How would you correct it?" Philip posed, raising his head. "Simply by resistance?"

Mr. Hopeton laughed and turned at the questioner. "I should no doubt get myself into a hornet's nest. No... by indifference!"

Madeline Held raised a hand. "Excuse me, but is indifference possible, even if it were right? You seem to take the leveling spirit for granted without looking into its character and causes. There must be some natural sense of justice, no matter how imperfectly society is developed." She gazed across at her brother. "We are members of this community—at least Philip and I consider ourselves so—and I am determined not to judge it without knowledge—or to offend what may be only mechanical habits of thought—unless I can see a sure advantage in doing so."

Joseph turned to observe Lucy Henderson's expression change from one of disrespect for the speaker to a bright, grateful face. He faced forward and saw Julia, silent and watchful.

"But I have no time for such conscientious studies," Mr. Hopeton resumed. "One can be satisfied with half a dozen neighbors and let the mass go. Indifference, after all, is the best philosophy. What say you, Mr. Held?"

"Indifference!" Philip echoed. His face seemed to flush, and he remained silent a moment. "Yes, our hearts are inconvenient appendages. We suffer quite a deal from unnecessary sympathies and from imagining, I suppose, that others feel them as we do. These uneasy features of society are simply the effort of nature to find some occupations for brains otherwise idle—or empty. Teach the people to think, and they will disappear."

Joseph stared at Philip, sensing a secret bitterness hidden under his careless, mocking air.

As Mrs. Hopeton rose, the conversation halted and the company stood. Joseph noticed Madeline Held's troubled expression and a singular brightness in Julia's eyes.

"Emily, let us have coffee on the veranda," Mr. Hopeton suggested expressionlessly, leading the company out of the room.

Philip held Joseph's hand, drawing him aside. "Don't seriously remember my words against me," he whispered. "You were sorry to hear them, I know. All I meant was that an over-sensitive tenderness towards everybody is a fault. My people have had to endure much, much worse. Besides, I was provoked to answer him in his own vein."

"But, Philip," Joseph responded in a soft voice as well, "such words tempt me! What if they were true?"

Philip grasped his friend's arm with a painful force. "They never can be true to you, Joseph."

•▼•

On the ride home, Julia asked, "Well, what do you think of the Hopetons?"

"She is an interesting woman," Joseph answered flatly.

"But reserved, and she shows very little taste in dress. However, I suppose you hardly noticed anything of the kind. She kept Lucy Henderson beside her as a foil. Madeline Held would have been damaging."

Joseph could only partly guess her meaning. It seemed repugnant, and he determined to avoid its further discussion.

"Hopeton is a shrewd businessman," Julia continued, "but he cannot compare with his wife for shrewdness—either with her or Philip Held."

"What do you mean?" Joseph felt a sting in his chest at the suggestion that Philip might be other than genuine.

"Honestly, Joseph, did you notice nothing?"

"What should I notice beyond what was said?"

"That was the least!" she cried. "But, of course, I knew you couldn't. And perhaps you won't believe me when I tell you that Philip Held—your particular friend, your hero, for aught I know, your pattern of virtue and character, and all that is manly and noble—that Philip Held, I say, is furiously in love with Mrs. Hopeton!"

Joseph didn't know whether to laugh or pretend to act shocked. He decided the best course of action would be to keep his private relationship with Philip secret. "Julia! How dare you speak so of Philip!" he said with scorn.

She laughed. "Because I dare speak the truth when I see it. I thought I should surprise you. I remembered a certain rumor I had heard before she was married—while she was Emily Marrable—and I watched them closer than they guessed. I'm certain of Philip. As for her, she's a deep creature, and she was on her guard, but they are near neighbors."

Joseph had to continue the subterfuge even though the idea of Philip chasing Emily Hopeton amused him. "It is your own fancy! You hate Philip on account of that affair with Clementina, but you ought to have some respect for the woman whose hospitality you have accepted."

"Bless me!" Julia pronounced in rhythm. "I have any quality of respect both for her and her furniture." Her head turned away. "By the by, Joseph, our parlor would furnish better than hers. I have been thinking of a few changes we might make which would wonderfully improve the house." She faced her husband. "As for Philip, Clementina was a fool. She'd be glad enough to have him now, but in these matters, once gone is gone for good. Somehow, people who marry for love very often get rich afterwards—ourselves, for instance."

Just before they reached their home, Joseph said, "Julia, do not mention your fancy to another soul than me. It would reflect discredit on you."

"You *are* innocent," she reproved. "And you are not complimentary. If I have any remarkable quality, it is tact. Whenever I speak, I shall know the effect beforehand. Even pa, with all his official experience, is no match for me in this line. I see what the Hopetons are after, and I mean to show them that *we* were first in the field. Don't be concerned, you good, excitable creature. You are no match for such well-drilled people. Let me alone, and before the summer is over, *we* will give the law to the neighborhood!"

Chapter 13: Changes in the Landscape

ALTHOUGH JOSEPH WANTED TO VISIT PHILIP the following day, he gave himself some time to further observe his wife's behavior before returning to Coventry. To his dismay, she spoke no words of contrition regarding her outburst on the ride home after their dinner at the Hopetons.

He found Philip busy in forge and foundry. "This would be the life for you!" he said. "We deal only with physical forces, human and elemental. We direct and create power, yet still obey the command to put money in our purses." The gleam of Philip's smile heartened Joseph.

"Is that one secret of your strength?"

Philip's grin broadened, and his eyes sparkled. "Who told you that I had any?"

"I feel it." Even as he said this, Joseph remembered Julia's unworthy suspicion.

"Come up and see Madeline a moment and the home she has made for me. We get on very well, for brother and sister, especially since her will is about as stubborn as mine."

As they rode up the knoll together, Joseph hungered to speak with Philip regarding Julia's duplicities. Before he could find the words to begin, they arrived at the cottage.

Madeline sat busy with some task of needle-work, which she did not lay aside when the men arrived. She wore a very simple dress, and her bright, cheerful manner gave Joseph no indication of a stubborn will.

"You might pass already for a member of our community," he could not help saying upon observing her craft.

"I think your most democratic farmers will accept me," she answered with a dubious expression, "when they learn that I am Philip's housekeeper." She snorted. "The only dispute we have had, or are likely to have, is in relation to the salary." A tight smirk contorted her face.

"She is an incredible creature, Joseph." Philip placed a hand on his sister's shoulder. "I was obliged to offer her as much as she earned by her music-lessons before she would come at all, and now she can't find work enough to balance it."

She looked up at her brother. "How can I, Philip, when you tempt me every day with walks and rides, botany, geology, and sketching from nature?" Her tone suggested a sarcastic manner.

Joseph smiled at the playful gossip between the two. It communicated a sense of frank, affectionate confidence that both comforted and pained him.

"Come, let me show you about," Philip invited.

"If I had only had a sister," Joseph sighed as they walked down the knoll. "I wish I had such good interactions with Julia as you have with Madeline."

Philip halted. "Are things not well with you two? So soon?"

Joseph's sense of outrage, so strong and keen, burned upon his consciousness like a dull physical pain. *False in one thing, false in all,* he kept thinking to himself, the single, inevitable conclusion. "Oh, Philip, if you only knew..." Tears in his voice betrayed the stoic appearance he had intended to maintain for his friend.

They continued down the valley path without speaking. The stream had risen to its banks, crystal clear. Shoals of young fish passed like drifted leaves over the pebbly ground, and fragrant water-beetles skimmed the surface of the eddies. Above them, vaults of great elms and sycamores glowed with green, deliciously illuminated tender foliage.

"May I speak now?" Philip's tone conveyed infinite love and pity. He took Joseph's hand.

"Yes."

"It has come," Philip continued. "You cannot hide it from yourself any longer. My pain is that I did not dare to warn you, though at the risk of losing your friendship. There was so little time..."

"You *did* try to warn me, Philip!" Joseph tightened his grasp. "I have recalled your words, and the trouble in your face as you spoke, a thousand times. I was a fool, a blind, miserable fool, and such folly has ruined my life!" He wanted to pull his hand away to cover his quickly-blushing face, but Philip held fast.

"What has she done to you, my friend? Your essence has changed significantly from our first encounter."

Joseph thought back to the night he and Julia returned from dinner with the Hopetons. The bare, repulsive, inexorable truth oozed from her at last. All the joy, the trust, the hope faded from his life, and that fanciful delusion of a few months had fixed his fate forever.

"She never loved me," Joseph confessed. "All her coy maiden airs, her warm abandonment to feeling, her very tears and blushes–all artfully simulated. I believe she laughed in her heart at my credulous tenderness. There is no name for her crime and no punishment to reverse the secret justice of my soul."

"Strange," Philip mused after a pause, "that only a perfectly good and pure nature can fall into such a wretched snare. 'Virtue is its own reward'; how that phrase is dinned into our ears! You are in Hell for a single fault–oh, not even a fault– an innocent mistake! But let us see what can be done. Is there no common ground whereon your natures can stand to- gether?" He looked directly at Joseph. "If there should be a child..."

Joseph shuddered noticeably. "Once it seemed too great, too wonderful a hope, but now, I don't dare to wish for it. Philip, I am too sorely hurt to think clearly. There is nothing to do but to wait. It is a miserable kind of comfort to me to have your sympathy, but I fear you cannot help me."

Philip's face lost its color and his hand trembled. He led Joseph to the bank, sat down with him, and laid his arm about his neck.

This position brought back memories of their first meeting.

The silence and the caress soothed Joseph more than any words. After a while he calmed and remembered an important part of his errand: to acquaint Philip with the oil speculation and seek his advice.

"Philip, I wish to change the subject to something less painful now. I want to call upon your knowledge of geology. Have you had any experience with drilling for oil?"

"You want to ask me of geology and petroleum?" Philip seemed amused at the new topic. "If I can be of any help on any topic, my soul is replenished."

Joseph assembled the various facts in his head before speaking. "Julia's father has brought me into his oil scheme. A while back, he and some friends acquired—at a bargain price—the piece of land situated between the Fluke and Chowder Wells. Have you heard of them?" Philip nodded wide-eyed. "He has allowed me to purchase on a ten percent margin—I believe that is the correct term—shares in the project. The other participants are men of high regard, and I could not believe that such men would readily gamble their fortunes on a dry well."

"I have some knowledge of the situation. Word spread rapidly of the decline in production from Fluke and Chowder..."

"That was the time when the group managed to purchase the virgin property. Mr. Blessing believes in such providence."

Philip coughed. "As I have remarked before, Mr. Blessing seems to have some ethereal sense of a good deal; however, his presence in the undertaking does not inspire much confidence. He has been known to throw his speculation money away. How much have you already paid on the stock?"

"Three installments, which Mr. Blessing thinks is all that will be called for. However, I have the money for a fourth, should it be necessary. He writes to me that the stock has already risen one hundred percent in value."

Philip looked up and away. "If that is so, let me advise you to sell half of it at once. The sum received will cover your liabilities, and the half you retain, as a venture, will give you no further anxiety."

Joseph nodded in agreement. "I had thought of that, yet I am sure that my father-in-law will oppose such a step with all his might. You must know him, Philip. Tell me, frankly, your opinion of his character."

Before speaking, Philip turned to his friend and looked deep into his eyes. "Blessing belongs to a class familiar enough to me, yet I doubt whether you will comprehend it. He is a swaggering, amiable, magnificent adventurer, never purosely dishonest, I am sure, yet sometimes engaged in transactions that would not bear much scrutiny." Joseph nodded. "His life has been one of ups and downs. After a successful speculation, he is luxurious, open-handed, and absurdly self-confident. His success is too soon flung away. He then, good-humoredly, descends to poverty because he never believes it can last long. He is unreliable, from his over-sanguine temperament, and yet this very temperament gives him a certain power and influence. Some of our best men are on familiar terms with him. They are on their guard against his pecuniary approaches. They laugh at his extravagant schemes, but they now and then find him useful. I heard Gray, the editor, once speak of him as a man 'filled with available enthusiasm,' and I guess that phrase hits both his strength and his weakness."

While much of Philip's assessment provided grounds for dissatisfaction, Joseph felt rather relieved than disquieted. The two of them began walking back to the cottage.

As they approached the fence, Mrs. Hopeton stood at the gate holding a bunch of wild-flowers: pink azaleas, delicate sigillarias, valerian, and scarlet painted cup. With a flushed face, she called out, "Mr. Held, may I have a moment?"

"Joseph, will you excuse me?" Philip asked and began walking toward his home.

Joseph went to his horse. As he looked back at the cottage, he observed Philip and Mrs. Hopeton in a lively conversation, each speaking in turn, stepping back and forward, changing position. When the lady began to walk away, Philip called out, "Emily!" and she stopped. Mrs. Hopeton walked back to Philip, listened for a moment and then involuntarily dropped the bouquet to the ground. Philip knelt and collected the flowers as he continued to speak with her. Joseph could not make out the conversation, but he could hear the voices distinctly.

Philip handed the bouquet back to Mrs. Hopeton, but he also clasped her hand and they looked into each other's eyes. She withdrew her hand and covered her face. Philip began walking back to Joseph as Mrs. Hopeton retreated down the hill.

"I am sorry to keep you waiting, Joseph." He glanced back at Mrs. Hopeton. "It appears we had some unfinished business."

Joseph recalled Julia's accusation of an unspoken attraction between Mr. Held and Mrs. Hopeton. He had dismissed it at first, but perhaps there had been some accuracy in it after all.

"I need to return quickly to the Forge, and, as you will be riding in a different direction, I hope you do not mind if I leave you on your own now." Philip mounted his horse and drove off, not waiting to hear an answer.

As Joseph rode across the meadow, he spied the figure of Mrs. Hopeton once again. She had stopped by the little stone schoolhouse at the foot of the next hill. The merry whoops and calls of children echoed in the wind. Although the afternoon waned, the mellow, languid heat of the day had lifted, and the breeze winnowing down the valley brought with it the smell of blossoming vernal grass.

Joseph reined his horse and moved behind a bush where he could observe Mrs. Hopeton without her seeing him. While he knew it might not be proper to eavesdrop so, he had a strong desire to discover more about the younger woman who married the older Hopeton. Had they a child for whom she gathered the wild-flowers? No, she appeared too youthful to have a school-aged youngster.

Miss Lucy Henderson exited the schoolhouse. Joseph recalled from the recent dinner conversation that she had taken the teacher position there.

The two women approached each other magnetically—apparently unaware of Joseph's proximity or vantage. Mrs. Hopeton handed the bunch of flowers to Lucy, who blushed as she accepted them. Again, Joseph could not hear the conversation but knew who spoke. After a few bits of conversation, Mrs. Hopeton threw her arms around Lucy's neck and kissed her.

Lucy's head swiveled one way and then the other, presumably to check for lingering students. She then clasped her hands behind Mrs. Hopeton's back, still holding the gathered flowers. They began to kiss passionately and hug each other. Joseph had never seen two women in loving embrace before. How he envied them. No such tenderness existed between him and his wife. He felt a small twinge of resentment.

Such a turn of events! Perhaps it had been Lucy Henderson's plan all along to wed Joseph because she knew of their mutual feelings toward members of the same sex. That might have explained her swift change in manner when Joseph proclaimed his engagement to Julia. And Philip appeared to have social ties with Mrs. Hopeton as well. How complicated their slow, humdrum lives had become.

∙▼∙

"We received a letter from your dear Aunt Rachel today," Julia announced a few weeks later. "She has settled into your Cousin Phoebe's home quite nicely and looks forward to us visiting her soon." Joseph did not respond, his mind more focused on people and situations a few miles away. "I think you should write her soon and tell her how well we're doing. Don't you think? Joseph? Are you listening?"

"Yes, a letter to Aunt Rachel. Good idea."

Julia stood next to her husband. "I have a plan," she went on.

"Can you guess it? No, I think not, yet you *might!*" She ran her fingers through Joseph's curly hair. "O, how lovely the light falls on your locks. They are perfect satin!" One hand rested on his shoulder. Her face sparkled all over with a witching fondness. This current phase of an amiable mood had lasted three days.

"Is it that I shall wear my hair upon my shoulders or that we shall sow plaster on the clover-field, as Old Bishop advised you the other day?"

She laughed lightly. "Now you are making fun of my interest in farming, but wait another year. I am trying earnestly to understand it, but only so that ornament—beauty—what was the word in those lines you read last night?—may grow out of use. That's it! Beauty out of Use! I know I've bored you a little sometimes—just a little, now, confess it!—with all my questions, but this is something different. Can't you think of anything that would make our home, O, *so* much more beautiful?"

Joseph did not care to play at her guessing games, but he did want to maintain the good humor as long as possible. "A grove of palm-trees at the top of the garden? Or a lake in front, with marble steps leading down to the water?"

"You perverse Joseph!" she admonished playfully. "No! Something possible, something practicable, something handsome, something profitable! Or are you so old-fashioned that you think we must drudge for thirty years and only take our pleasure after we grow rheumatic?"

He looked at her with a puzzled, yet cheerful, face.

"You don't understand me yet!" she exclaimed. "And, indeed, indeed, I dread to tell you for one reason: You have such a tender regard for old associations—not that I'd have it otherwise if I could. I like it! I trust I have the same feeling, yet a little sentiment sometimes interferes practically with the improvement of our lives."

"What do you mean, Julia?" His patience grew thin.

"No! I will not tell you until I have read part of pa's letter, which came this afternoon. Take the arm-chair and don't interrupt me."

Joseph did not care to be ordered about by his pretentious wife, and he marched, albeit grudgingly, to the chair and sat. Julia seated herself on the window-sill and glanced over at her husband with a girlish smile.

"I saw how uneasy you felt when the call came for the fourth installment of ten percent on the Amaranth shares, especially after I had so much difficulty in persuading you not to sell the half. It surprised me, although I knew that, where pa is concerned, there's a good reason for everything. So I wrote him the other day, and this is what he says. You remember Kanuck is the company's agent on the spot." She opened the letter and read:

> Tell Joseph that in matters of finance there's often a wheel within a wheel. Blenkinsop, of the Chowder Company, managed to get a good grab of our shares through a third party, of whom we had not the slightest suspicion. I name no name at present, from motives of prudence. We only discovered the circumstance after the third party left for Europe. Looking upon the Chowder as a rival, it is our desire, of course, to extract this entering wedge before it has been thrust into our vitals, and we can only accomplish the end by still keeping secret the discovery of the torpedoes (an additional expense, I might remark) and calling for fresh installments from *all* the stockholders. Blenkinsop, not being within the inside ring–and no possibility of his getting in!–will naturally see only the blue of disappointment where we see the rose of realized expectations. Already, so Kanuck writes to me, negotiations are on foot which will relieve our Amaranth of this parasitic growth, and a few weeks–days–hours, in fact, may enable us to explode and triumph!
>
> I was offered yesterday, by one of our shrewdest operators, who has been silently watching us, ten shares of the Sinnemahoning Hematite for eight of

ours. Think of that—the Sinnemahoning Hematite! No better stock in the market, if you remember the quotations! Explain the significance of the figures to your husband and let him see that he has—but no, I will restrain myself and make no estimate. I will only mention, under the seal of the profoundest secrecy, that the number of shafts now sinking (or being sunk) will give an enormous flowing capacity when the electric spark fires the mine, and I should not wonder if our shares then soared high over the pinnacles of all previous speculation!

"No, nor I!" Julia exclaimed as she refolded the letter. "It is certain, positively certain! I have never known the Sinnemahoning Hematite to be less than 147." She smiled triumphantly. "What do you say, Joseph?"

At once he marveled how his wife could quote stock prices and discuss business dealings like a savvy capitalist. How her upbringing had prepared her to manipulate the innerworkings of finance—and marriage.

"I hope it may be true," Joseph answered. "I can't feel so certain, while an accident—the discovery of the torpedo-plan, for instance—might change the prospects of the Amaranth. It will be a great relief when the time comes to 'realize,' as your father says."

"You only feel so because it is your first experience, but for your sake, I will consent that it shall be your last. We shall scarcely need any more than this will bring us. For, as pa says, a mere competence in the city is a splendid fortune in the country. You need leisure for books and travel and society, and you shall have it." She stood and stepped to the center of the room. "Now, let us make a place for both!"

Joseph watched in awe as his wife paced off distances. "We could combine these two rooms and have alcoves for bookcases and space for a piano." She pointed at the various locations as she spoke. "We could add a new veranda to the western end of the house. The plastering might be renewed, with a showy cornice, giving an air of elegant luxury to the new apartment."

The design she proposed reminded him somewhat of the drawing-room in the Blessing home. A farm did not require a fancy cornice or a piano. These things belonged to the well-to-do, and the Astens could not afford to purchase such frivolous appointments. Perhaps a pang at changing the ancient order of things plucked at him, and a temptation to behold a more refined comfort took its place.

"The things you propose sound well and good, but might we delay any decisions until the assurance of a positive result is received? If the business dealings do not work out as expected, we may have to return these new purchases, and I do not wish you to go through such public humiliation."

Her expression hardened. "That is, oh, so considerate of you, dear husband, but I trust my father completely, and if he says something is certain, you may rely upon it. If he predicts rain in July, people would laugh until their heads became wet with precipitation. Let me take charge of this renovation, and I am certain you will be quite happy with the results." She batted her lovely eyes.

It appeared that Julia wished to engage in a competition with the Hopetons. The couple with the grandest home would take the advantage. Even though Joseph saw through her artfulness, he agreed to have a mechanic examine the house to determine whether the suggested changes would be possible and to make an estimate of the expense. After all, he thought upon the old adage: *The man who deliberates is lost.*

Chapter 14: On the Rails

TWO DAYS LATER, JULIA HIRED A MECHANIC to assess their house and provide an estimate for the renovations she had suggested. She presented the paperwork to Joseph for his implicit approval.

Three days after that, demolition began, and by the beginning of the next week, the state of extensive ruin made the restoration a matter of necessity.

Joseph cautiously observed Julia's manner with the workmen. She presented a lively, playful attitude in their presence, but a cold, inflexible obstinacy when it was just the two of them. Her original plan changed almost daily, with the addition of showy and expensive features, every one of which appeared devised to surpass the modifications made by the Hopetons in their new residence.

In private, Joseph remonstrated his concern for their financial condition, but no effect could be seen. He felt unable to speak his mind when in the presence of workmen because any practical interference might suggest domestic trouble.

Days dragged on, and the breach widened with no effort on either side to heal it. Observing Julia's temporary fondness positively disgusted Joseph. Every caress and loving glance in the company of others only reminded him of their selfish purpose. He endured such tenderness as it helped to mislead the neighbors as well as half-deceive himself.

Julia's popularity increased with her knowledge of the people, while their manner toward Joseph became a shade less frank and cordial. She would say of the needlessly extravagant changes in his home, "Joseph is making the old place so beautiful for me!" accompanied with a loving look.

Mr. Chaffinch visited more frequently, and Julia became more regular in her attendance at his church. Did she believe that a more religious veneer might diminish Joseph's suspicions? He considered her actions as either hostile or heartless. This behavior repelled him as it provided a clearer image of a nature so utterly foreign to his own. How near beyond all others it had once seemed!

It might have been his pure, guarded youth that never permitted him to suspect any human being. Had he more familiarity with the ways of men and women, he might have discovered some manner of controlling her nature, as even the very shrewdest and falsest have their vulnerable side. However, Joseph endured so much keen spiritual pain encountering her in her true character that such a course had become simply impossible.

•▼•

The sun rose, and the sun set on the ever-expanding Asten home. Expenses for labor and materials had already doubled from the original estimates made by the mechanics. The workers presented bills for payment, but no news of success came from the Amaranth. Their finances finally reached the point where Joseph accepted the dreadful fact that he had no alternative but to obtain a temporary loan at a county town, the center of transactions for all the debtors and creditors of the neighboring country.

What a disagreeable experience for Joseph to appear in the character of a borrower, which he adopted most reluctantly. However, the reality proved a greater trial than he had suspected. Somehow, preposterous stories of his extravagance floated about: He was transforming his house into a castle; He had made, lost, and made again a large fortune in petroleum; He had married a wealthy wife and squandered her money; He drove out in a carriage with six white horses; He was becoming irregular in his habits and heretical in his religious view; He intermingled with Colored People. It amazed him how such marvelous powers of invention exercised by the members of that quiet, sluggish community surpassed even that of Arab story-tellers.

The money-agents verbalized their suspicions, and it required Joseph to maintain all his self-control to convince them of the true state of his circumstances. He did, in the end, obtain the loan, but after such a wear and tear of flesh and spirit as made it seem a double burden.

Upon returning home, he made no effort to conceal his distress, and Julia must have detected some difficulties as she managed to be cheerful and careless when asking, "Have you brought my supplies, dear?"

"Yes." He handed her a sack.

"Here is a letter from pa," she said as she peered into the bag. "I opened it because I knew what the subject must be. But if you're tired, pray don't read it now, for then you may be impatient. There's a little more delay." She held out the folded letter.

"Then I'll not delay to know it." He took the papers from her hand. The first page, a printed slip, called upon the stockholders of the Amaranth to pay a *fifth* installment. Behind that, he found a hastily scribbled note from B. Blessing:

> Don't be alarmed, my dear son-in-law! Probably a mere form. Blenkinsop still holds on, but we think this will likely bring him at once. If it don't, we shall very likely have to go on with him, even if it obliges us to unite the Amaranth and Chowder. In any case, we shall ford or bridge this little Rubicon within a fortnight. Have the money ready, if convenient, but do not forward unless I give the word.
>
> We hear, through third parties, that Clementina (who is now at Long Branch) receives much attention from Mr. Spelter, a man of immense wealth, but, I regret to say, no refinement.

A grim smile crept across Joseph's face when he finished reading. "Is there never to be an end of humbug?" he exclaimed.

"There now!" cried Julia. "I knew you'd be impatient. You are so unaccustomed to great operations. Why the Muchacho Land Grant–I remember it because pa sold out just at the wrong time–hung on for seven years!"

"Damn! Curse the Muchacho Land Grant! And the Amaranth too!" Joseph had lost his self-discipline and yelled. He had already endured sufficient trauma that day.

"Aren't you ashamed!" taunted Julia, taking on a playful air of offense. "But you're tired and hungry, poor fellow!" She put her hands on his shoulders, raised herself on tiptoe, and attempted to kiss him.

Unable to control his sudden instinct, Joseph swiftly turned away his head.

"O! You wicked husband! You deserve to be punished!" she cried, slapping him on the cheek.

The sting roused Joseph's heated blood. He started back a step and looked at her with flaming eyes. "No more of that, Julia! I know—*now*—how much your arts are worth. I am getting a vile name in the neighborhood—losing my property, losing my own self-respect—because I have allowed you to lead me!" The intensity of his stare deepened. "Will you be content with what you have done, or must you go on until my ruin is complete?"

"Oh! Oh! Such words to me!" she groaned, hiding her face between her hands as if *he* had struck *her*. "I never thought *you* could be so cruel!" She stepped back. "I had *such* pleasure in seeing you rich and free, in trying to make your home beautiful, and now this little delay, which no businessman would think anything of, seems to change your very nature! But I will not think it's your true self. I know something has worried you to-day. You have heard some foolish story –"

"It is not the worry of to-day," he interrupted in haste to state his whole grievance before his weak heart had time to soften again. "It is the worry of months past!" Julia's face transformed into one of doubts. "It is because I thought you true and kind-hearted, and now I find you selfish and hypocritical!" He began to pace. "It is very well to lead me into serious expense while so much is at stake, and now likely to be lost. It is very well to make my home beautiful, especially when you can outshine Mrs. Hopeton!" He gestured toward

Coventry. "It is easy to adapt yourself to the neighbors and keep on the right side of them, no matter how much your husband's character may suffer in the process!"

"That will do!" she commanded, suddenly becoming rigid. "A little more and it would be too much for even *me*!" She lifted her head and wiped at some tears. "What do I care for 'the neighbors'? Persons whose ideas and tastes and habits of life are so different from mine? I have endeavored to be friendly with them for *your* sake. I have taken special pains to accommodate myself to their notions just because I intended they should justify *you* in choosing me!" She pointed to herself. "I believed–for you told me so–that there was no calculation in love, that money was dross in comparison, and how could I imagine that you would so soon put up a balance and begin to weigh the two?" A scowl consumed her face. "Am I your wife or your slave? Have I an equal share in what is yours, or am I here merely to increase it?" She took another step away. "If there is to be a question of dollars and cents between us, pray have my allowance fixed so that I may not overstep it and may save myself from such reproaches! I knew you would be disappointed in pa's letter. I have been anxious and uneasy since it came–through my sympathy with you–and was ready to make any sacrifice that might relieve your mind, and now you seem to be full of unkindness and injustice!" More tears slid down her nose. "What shall I do? O, what shall I do?" She threw herself upon a sofa, weeping hysterically.

Joseph took a deep breath before pressing on. "Julia! You purposely misunderstood me. Think how constantly I have yielded to you against my own better judgment! When have you considered *my* wishes?"

"When?" she repeated. "He asks, 'when?'" She addressed the cushion with a hopeless, melancholy air then turned to face her husband. "How could I misunderstand you? Your words were as plain as daggers. If you were not aware how sharp they were, call them back to your mind when these mad, unjust suspicions have left you! I trusted you so perfectly, I was looking forward to such a happy future. And now... now... all seems so dark! Like a flash of lightning. I am weak and giddy. Leave me!" She pointed toward the door. "I can bear no more!" With that, she covered her face and sobbed wretchedly.

Joseph observed Julia's behavior and then remarked, "It satisfies me that you are not as ignorant as you profess to be." He turned and left, confused by his wife's unexpected way of taking his charges in flank instead of meeting them in front, as a man would have done. Questions arose in his mind: *Could she be sincere? Was she really so ignorant of herself as to believe all that she had uttered?*

Her grief and indignation showed no shadow of hypocrisy. The tears appeared real. Then why not her smiles and caresses? Either she had been horribly, incredibly false–worse than he dared dream her to be–or so fatally unconscious of her nature that nothing short of a miracle could ever enlighten her.

One thing Joseph realized as certain: No confidence existed between them, and there might never be again.

He walked slowly forth from the house, seeing nothing and unconscious of what direction he strode. With head bent and a brain that vainly strove to work its way to clearness through the perplexities of his heart, Joseph moved on.

Without realizing it, he had headed toward Philip's forge. When he finally grew weary, though not consciously calmer, he paused and looked about, like waking from a dream. At once, he noticed the old road had been moved to accommodate the new branch railway.

The ring of hammers came up from the embankment above. He stood near Lucy's schoolhouse, and just as he looked, she appeared, accompanied by her scholars. They clambered up to watch the operation of laying track. Elwood Withers, hale, sunburnt, full of lusty life, walked along the sleepers directing the workmen.

Joseph said to himself, "He was right–only too right! Why could I not see with his eyes? 'It's the bringin' up,' he would say, but that is not all. I have been an innocent, confiding boy, and thought that years and acres had made me a man. Oh, *she* understood me—she understands me now, but in spite of her—God help me—I shall yet be a man."

As he stood watching, Elwood ran down the steep side of the embankment to greet Lucy and help her up to the top. The children whooped and cried.

"Would it have been different," Joseph continued his soliloquy, "if Lucy and I had loved and married? A year ago, I might have loved her." He clambered over the fence, crossed the narrow strip of meadow, and climbed the embankment.

Elwood stood with his back toward Joseph as he spoke to Lucy. "It all comes o' takin' an interest in what you're doin'. The practical part is easy enough, when you once have the principles. I can manage the theodolite already, but I need a little showin' when I come to the calculations. Somehow, I never cared much about study before, but here it's all applied as soon as you've learnt it, an' that fixes it, like, in your head." He pointed to his in illustration.

Lucy listened with an earnest, friendly interest on her face. She startled slightly when Joseph appeared. After the first surprise, her manner toward him seemed quiet and composed. Elwood's eyes brightened, and his appearance acquired a fresh intelligence. Perhaps the habit of command had already given him a certain dignity.

"How can *I* get knowledge which may be applied as soon as learned?" Joseph asked, endeavoring to remain calm, the manner furthest from his true feelings. "I'm still at the foot of the class, Lucy." He turned to her.

"How?" Elwood replied. "I should say by goin' around the world alone. That would be about the same for you as what these ten miles I'm overseein' are to me. A little goes a great way with me, for I can only pick up one thing at a time." He smiled a big, toothy grin.

"What kind of knowledge are you looking for, Joseph?" Lucy asked with grave concern.

Joseph answered with a darkening face, "Of myself."

"That's a true word!" Elwood exclaimed with a grin, then he caught Lucy's narrowed eye and added awkwardly, "It's about what we all want, I take it."

During that moment, Joseph recovered himself and forced a smile. "Shall we examine your work, Elwood?"

As the proud Mr. Withers gave an account of what had been done and what would be accomplished, the Hopeton carriage came up the highway near at hand. The passenger, Mrs. Hopeton, tapped to indicate she wanted to stop.

"I was looking for you Lucy—Miss Henderson," she called. "If you are going towards the cutting, I would like to join you."

Lucy and Elwood nodded. Mrs. Hopeton got out and sent the coachman home with the carriage, and the four of them proceeded to walk on the track. For some unknown reason, Mrs. Hopeton's presence brought Joseph some relief.

"It's rather a pity to cut into the hills an' bank up the meadows in this way, ain't it?" Elwood asked.

"And to disturb my school with so much hammering," Lucy rejoined. "When the trains come, I must retreat."

"None too soon," Mrs. Hopeton added. "You are not strong, Lucy, and the care of a school is too much for you."

Joseph, oblivious of the previous judgment, enquired in a sharp, cynical tone, "After all, why shouldn't nature be cut up? I suppose everything was given to us to use, and 'the more profit, the better the use' seems to be the rule of the world. 'Beauty grows out of Use,' you know."

Lucy shot him an irritated side-glance.

"I believe it is a rule of art," Mrs. Hopeton chimed in, "that mere ornament for ornament's sake is not allowed. It must always seem to answer some purpose, to have a necessity for its existence. But, on the other hand, what is necessary should also be beautiful"—she glanced at Lucy—"if possible."

"A loaf o' bread, for instance," suggested Elwood.

They all laughed at this suggestion, the temporary tension dispelled by this good nature. As they passed around a sharp curve of the track in a narrower part of the valley they had just entered, the group found themselves face-to-face with Philip and Madeline Held.

"Two inspecting committees at once!" cried Philip. "It is well for you, Withers, that you didn't locate the line. My sister and I have already found several unnecessary curves and culverts."

"And *we* have found a great deal of use and no beauty," Lucy answered.

"Beauty!" exclaimed Madeline. "What is more beautiful than to see one's groceries delivered at one's very door? The opera and the picture-gallery will soon be but two hours distant." She turned to her brother. "How far are we from a lemon, Philip?"

"You were a lemon, Mad, in your vegetable, pre-human state. You are still acid and agreeable." He smiled.

"Sweets to the sweet!" she gaily cried. "And what, pray, was Miss Henderson?"

"Don't spare me, Mr. Held," Lucy said as he looked at her with a little apprehension.

"An apple."

"And Mrs. Hopeton?" Lucy asked.

"A date-palm."

Mrs. Hopeton did not look up, but an uninterpretable expression just touched her lips and faded.

"Now it's your turn, Miss Held," Elwood suggested. "What were we men?"

"Oh... Philip a prickly pear, of course, and you... well... some kind of a nut, and Mr. Asten..."

"A cabbage," said Joseph quickly.

"What vanity!" Madeline chuckled. "Do you imagine that you

are all head? Or that your heart is in your head? Or that you keep the morning dew longer than the rest of us?"

"It might well be," Joseph muttered. He noticed Philip pinch his sister's arm gently from behind.

"My, look at the beautiful circle of hills..." Mrs. Hopeton remarked.

As the others studied the landscape, Philip took Joseph's arm and led him a little aside from the group.

"Philip, I want you!" Joseph whispered, "but no, not quite yet. There is no need of coming to you in a state of confusion. In a day or two more I shall have settled a little."

"You are right," Philip studied his friend. "There is no opiate like time, be there never so little of it." He bent forward and spoke softly into Joseph's ear. "I felt the fever of your head in your hand. Don't come to me until you feel that it is the one thing which must be done! I think you know why I say so." He stood straight again.

"I do!" Joseph exclaimed. "I am just now more of an ostrich than anything else. I should like to stick my head in the sand and imagine myself invisible. But, Philip, here are six of us together. One other, I know, has a secret wound, perhaps two others. Is it always so in life? I think I am selfish enough to be glad to know that I am not specially picked out for punishment."

A warm smile filled Philip's face. "Upon my soul, I believe Madeline is the only one of the six who is not busy with other thoughts than those we all seem to utter." He looked at Joseph. "'Specially picked out?' There is no such thing as special picking out in this world, Joseph! It may seem hard and schoolmaster-like in me again to say, 'wait!' yet that is the only word I can say."

"Good evenin', all!" cried Elwood. "I must go down to my men, but I'd be glad o' such an inspiration as this, a good deal oftener."

"I'll go that far with you," Joseph offered.

Mrs. Hopeton took Lucy's arm with a sudden, nervous movement. "If you are not too tired, let us walk over the hill together. I want to find the right point of view for sketching our home."

Joseph smiled to himself at this. He wondered how much walking and viewing they might accomplish between the hugging and kissing.

Philip and his sister walked off up the track.

"Elwood," said Joseph when they had walked a little distance in silence, "do you remember the night you spent with me a year ago?"

"I'm not likely to forget it."

"Let me ask you one question, then. Have you come nearer to Miss Lucy Henderson?"

"If no further off means nearer–an' it almost seems so in my case–yes!" Elwood smiled. "I have spent some time with Miss Elizabeth Henderson, an' Miss Lucy was present off-an'-on."

"And you see no difference in her–no new features of character–which you did not guess at first?"

"Indeed, I do!" Elwood emphatically answered. "To me, she grows less an' less like any other woman: so right, so straightforward, so honest in all her ways and thoughts! Perhaps it is *she* who I should be courtin' instead." He cocked his head in thought. "If I am ever tempted to do anything– well, not exactly mean, you know, but such as a man might as well leave undone–I have only to say to myself, 'If you're not thoroughly good, my boy, you'll lose her!' an' that does the business right away. Why, Joseph, I'm proud o' myself. I mean to deserve her."

"Ah!" a sigh, almost a groan, came from Joseph's lips. "What will you think of me? I was about to repeat your own words– to warn you to be cautious and take time. Test your feelings and not be too sure of *her* perfection! What can a young man know about women? He can only discover the truth after marriage, and then—they are indifferent how it affects them—*their* fortunes are made!"

"I know," answered Elwood, turning his head away slightly, "but there's a difference between the women you seek an' work to get… an' the women who seek an' work to get you."

Joseph nodded. "I understand you."

"Forgive me for sayin' it!" Elwood cried. "I couldn't help seein' and feelin' what you know now. But what man—leastways, what friend—coulda said it to you with any chance o' bein' believed? You were like a man alone in a boat above a waterfall. Only *you* could bring yourself to shore. If I stood on the bank an' called, an' you didn't believe me, what then? The Lord knows I'd give this right arm"—he patted his shoulder—"strong as it is, to put you back where you were a year ago."

"I've been longing for frankness, and I ought to bear it better." Joseph looked at his friend. "Put the whole subject out of your thoughts, and come to see me as of old. It is quite time I should learn to manage my own wife." He grasped Elwood's hand convulsively, sprang down the embankment, and pulled him into the deeper woods. "It's my turn this time, remember?" he whispered and Elwood smiled slyly.

Chapter 15: The Wharf-Rat

ON HIS WALK HOME, Joseph reviewed the quarrel with a little more calmness, and, while admitting his own rashness and want of tact, felt relieved that it had occurred. The time he had just spent with Elwood also helped to relieve some of his pent-up, repressed passions.

Julia had now heard, at least, how sorely he had been grieved by her selfishness. If she really loved him, she would have an opportunity to show whether her nature capable of change.

He determined to make no further reference to the dissension and to avoid what might lead to a new one. As he approached the house, he could see Julia standing, watching at the front window. She slipped back to the sofa and covered her head just before he reached the door.

For the next few days, renovation of the Asten home continued. Joseph and Julia maintained a silent distance except in the presence of the workmen, when she displayed her affectionate playfulness. Now and then, a sharp, indirect allusion showed that she had not forgotten, and Joseph closed his teeth firmly upon his tongue lest the potentially-explosive household atmosphere reignite.

A very brief note from Mr. Blessing announced the fifth installment would be needed and that he would explain everything by a later mail.

Joseph showed the note to Julia, merely saying to her, "This comes as no surprise; however, I have not the money, and if I had, he could scarcely expect me to pay it without knowing the necessity. My best plan will be to go to the city at once."

He observed a flash of a smile on his wife's face before she responded. "I think so too. You will be far better satisfied when you have seen pa, and he can also help you to raise the money temporarily, if it is really inevitable. He knows all the capitalists."

"Perhaps I should sell enough of the stock to pay for the installment," Joseph considered aloud. "Nay, I shall sell it all if I can do so without loss."

Julia's unnatural smile converted to a fiery furnace. "Are you –?" she began fiercely then checked herself, merely adding, "See pa first. That's all I stipulate."

Her behavior confirmed Joseph's suspicion that his wife would prefer him gone. In his absence, she could oversee the progress on the embellishments to their home single-handedly, without his intrusive meddling.

•▾•

The following afternoon, Joseph went to his in-laws' home only to find that Mr. Blessing had not yet returned from the Custom-House. Rather than sit in the dark parlor and wait for his father-in-law, Joseph took a carriage to the office. He plunged boldly into the labyrinth of clerks, porters, inspectors, and tide-waiters. Everybody knew Blessing, but nobody could tell where he might be found. Finally, someone more obliging than the rest suggested Joseph try the Wharf-Rat.

Nearly invisible, in a narrow alley behind the Custom-House, a time-worn sign for the Wharf-Rat Saloon hung over an indistinguishable door. Immediately inside, a Venetian screen prevented one from seeing the persons at the bar. However, Joseph recognized his father-in-law's voice at once, "Straight, if you please!"

Mr. Blessing leaned against one end of the bar, with a glass in hand, engaged in hushed conversation with an individual of not very prepossessing appearance. At first glance, he resembled a balding General Grant in a business suit and necktie.

"You understand," Mr. Blessing whispered to his companion, "the collector can't be seen every day. It takes time, and—more or less—capital. The doorkeeper and others expect to be fed."

Upon Joseph's approach, his father-in-law displayed a flash of uncomfortable surprise, an angry, suspicious look that did not change into one of welcome immediately. Joseph recognized this expression as one shared with another member of his family. Once the look of welcome arrived, it deepened and mellowed. It became so warm and rich that only a cold, contracted nature could have refused to bathe in its effulgence.

"Why!"–Mr. Blessing cried, with hands extended–"I should as soon have expected to see daisies growing in this sawdust, or to find these spittoons smelling like hyacinths!" He turned to the other fellow. "Mr. Tweed–one of our rising politicians–this is Mr. Asten, my son-in-law!" The two shook hands perfunctorily. "Asten, of Asten Hall, I might almost say, for I hear that your mansion is assuming quite a palatial aspect." He turned to the barman. "Another glass, if you please." To Joseph, he said, "Your throat must be full of dust–*pulvis faucibus hœsit*, if I might be allowed to change the classic phrase."

As much as Joseph tried to decline, he compromised on a moderate glass of ale. Mr. Blessing poured something from a black bottle into his own empty glass, nodded to Mr. Tweed saying, "Always straight!" and drank it off.

Joseph looked about the dark, cramped room full of dark men in dark suits drinking at dark tables from dark bottles. He wondered how many other public officials frequented this establishment or others like it.

"You would not suppose," Mr. Blessing resumed, "that this little room, murky as it is, and not agreeably fragrant, has often witnessed the arrangement of political manœevers which have decided the City, and through the City, the State. I have seen together at that table"–he pointed–"at midnight, Senator Slocum and the Honorables Whitstone, Hacks, and Larruper. Why, the First Auditor of the Treasury was here no later than last week! I frequently transact some of the confidential business of the Custom-House within these precincts, as at present!" He winked at Mr. Tweed, who smelled of stale whiskey.

"Shall I wait for you outside?" Joseph asked.

"I think it will not be necessary." He turned to the other fellow. "I have stated the facts, Mr. Tweed, and if you accept them, the figures can be arranged between us at any time. It is a simple case of algebra: By taking x, you work out the unknown quantity."

With a hearty laugh, he shook Mr. Tweed's hand and guided Joseph outside.

"We can talk here as well as in the woods. Nobody ever hears anything in this crowd," Mr. Blessing informed Joseph. "But perhaps we had better not mention the Amaranth by name, as the operation has been kept so very close. Shall we say 'Paraguay' instead or–still better–'Reading,' which is a very common stock? Well, then, I guess you have come to see me in relation to Paraguay–I mean, the Reading?"

"Mr. Blessing, I must confess my embarrassment. Due to the extensive costs of remodeling our home, much to my discontent, I had to take out a loan from the county bank. The call for the fifth installment has caught me unawares and unprepared. Also, I have been having doubts about the success of this speculation. So much time has elapsed with no fulfilling return."

Mr. Blessing had listened patiently, hearing him to the end. "I understand, most perfectly, your feeling in the matter. Further, I do not deny that in respect to the time or realization from the Am–Uruguay–uh, Reading, I should say–I have also been disappointed. It has cost me no little trouble to keep my own shares intact, and my stake is much greater than yours, for it is my *all*! I am ready to unite with the Chowder at once. Indeed, as one of the directors, I mentioned it at our last meeting, but the proposition, I regret to say, was not favorably entertained. We are dependent, in a great measure, on Kanuck, who is on the spot superintending the... Reading. He has been telegraphed to come on, and promises to do so as soon as the funds now called for are forthcoming. My faith, I hardly need intimate, is firm."

Joseph looked into the steely eyes of his father-in-law. All along, he had taken the counsel of this man, but doubt had begun to sprout in his mind. "My only resource, then, will be to sell a portion of my stock, I suppose?"

Joseph could almost hear the clockwork of Mr. Blessing's mind in action. "There is one drawback to that course, and I am afraid you may not quite understand my explanation. The Reading has not been introduced in the market, and its *real* value could not be demonstrated without betraying the secret level by which we intend hoisting it to a fancy height. We could only dispose of a portion of it to capitalists whom we choose to take into our confidence. The same reason would be valid against hypothecation."

"Have *you* paid this last installment?"

Mr. Blessing looked one way then the other. "N–no, not wholly, but I anticipate a temporary accommodation. If Mr. Spelter deprives me of Clementina, as I hear–through third parties–is daily becoming more probable, my family expenses will be so diminished that I shall have an ample margin. Indeed, I shall feel like a large paper copy, with my leaves uncut!" He rubbed his hands gleefully.

"Is that how you felt when I 'deprived' you of Julia last year?"

The joy on his father-in-law's face vanished, and a serious expression replaced it. "*This* might be done. It is not certain that all the stockholders have yet paid. I will look over the books, and if such be the case, your delay would not be a spo-radic delinquency. If otherwise, I will endeavor to gain the consent of my fellow-directors to the introduction of a new capitalist, to whom a small portion of your interest may be transferred. I trust you perceive the relevancy of this caution. We do not mean that our flower shall always blush unseen and waste its sweetness on the oleaginous air. We only wish to guard against its being 'untimely ripped'–as Shakespeare says–from its parent stalk." He looked upon his son-in-law tenderly. "I can well imagine how incomprehensible all this may appear to you. In all probability, much of *your* conversation at home, relative to crops and the like, would be to me an unknown dialect. But I should not, therefore, doubt your intelligence and judgment in such matters." A lowering of his head suggested to Joseph that Mr. Blessing requested further confidence in the matter.

"Do I understand you to say, Mr. Blessing, that the call for the fifth installment *can* be met by the sale of a part of my stock?"

A moment of thought passed. "In an ordinary case it might not—under the peculiar circumstances of our operation—be possible. But I trust I do not exaggerate my own influence when I say that it is within *my* power to arrange it. If you will confide it to my hands—you understand, of course—that a slight formality is necessary: a power of attorney?"

Joseph had not considered this ploy, nor any other legal point, as it would have been beyond his pure and gentle nature. "Then, supposing the shares to be worth only their par value, the power need not apply to more than one-tenth of my stock?"

A stranger collided with Mr. Blessing. He uttered a quiet oath and then called out, "Beg pardon!" To Joseph, he said, "Let us turn into the other street. Really, our lives are hardly safe in this crowd." He consulted a polished, golden pocket watch. "It is late and the banks will soon be closed." After rounding the corner, he resumed, "It would be prudent to allow a margin. The money market is very tight, and if a *necessity* were suspected, most capitalists are unprincipled enough to exact according to the urgency of the need. I do not say—nor do I at all anticipate—that it would be so in your case. Still, the future is a sort of dissolving view, and my suggestion is that of the merest prudence. I have no doubt that double the amount—say one-fifth of your stock—would guard us against all contingencies. If you prefer not to intrust the matter to my hands, I will introduce you to Honeyspoon Brothers, the bankers—the elder Honeyspoon being a director—who will be very ready to execute your commission."

Although Joseph had very little trust remaining in his father-in-law, he could not—in all good conscience—say it to his face! The plausible phrases—the import of which he had no power to dispute, yet which seemed at variance with the facts of the case—wearied him. He imagined himself lifted aloft into a dazzling, secure atmosphere, but as often as he turned to look at the wings that upheld him, their plumage shriveled into dust, and he fell—just like the reckless Icarus—an immense distance before his feet touched a bit of reality.

He followed Mr. Blessing back to his office and signed the power of attorney form. Joseph declined the invitation to dine at the Universal Hotel and the offer to stay the night at the Blessing mansion.

On his way back to the train station, he passed the Farmers' Tavern and took a room for the night. Early the next morning, cheered in spirit through the fresh vigor of all his physical functions, he started homeward.

•▼•

At precisely the half-way point on his walk between Oakland Station and home, Joseph encountered a buggy drawn by an aged and irreproachable gray horse. The Reverend Mr. Chaffinch held the reins, and he pulled the cart to a stop in front of Joseph.

The grim-faced Mr. Chaffinch looked down. "Hello, young Mr. Asten."

"Greetings, Reverend."

"Will you turn back as far as that tree?" requested the clergyman, pointing to a tall elm at the roadside about 50 feet behind. "I have a message to deliver." He rode on and stopped in the shade.

When Joseph caught up, Mr. Chaffinch continued, "Now, we can talk without interruption. I will ask you to listen to me with the spiritual—not the carnal—ear. I must not be false to my high calling, and the voice of my own conscience calls me to awaken yours."

After all he had been through with his wife, her father, the Amaranth, and the county bank, Joseph had little patience left for bloviating clergymen. His face flushed in anger, but he said nothing.

"It is hard for a young man, especially one wise in his own conceit, to see how the snares of the Adversary are closing around him. We cannot plead ignorance, however, when the Light is there, and we willfully turn our eyes from it. You are walking on a road, Joseph Asten, it may seem smooth and fair to you, but do you know where it leads?" Joseph looked up blankly; as far as he knew, this road led back to his home. A flame sparked the Reverend's face. "I will tell you: to Death and Hell!"

He reached both trembling clawed hands skyward. Joseph remained silent.

"It is not too late!" The upraised hands returned to Mr. Chaffinch's lap. "Your fault, I fear, is that you attach merit to works, as if works could save you! You look to a cold, barren morality for support and imagine that to do what is called 'right' is enough for the Almighty! You shut your eyes to the blackness of your own sinful heart and are too proud to acknowledge the vileness and depravity of man's nature. But without this acknowledgment, your morality—as you call it— is corrupt. Your good works—as you suppose them to be—will avail you naught. You are outside the pale of Grace, and while you continue there, knowing the door to be open, there is no Mercy for you!" An accusatory finger pointed at Joseph's heart.

The facial flushing faded, and Joseph began to wonder about the impetus for this private sermonette. Was the well-intentioned Reverend speaking out of concern for Joseph? Could he be preaching to his own self-perceived sins with no awareness of his own failings? Or, most likely, might this ti-rade be the result of conversations with Julia, who probably cried and sobbed while imparting her version of their marital conflict.

"I hope," Mr. Chaffinch continued after a brief pause, "that your silence is the beginning of conviction. It only needs an awakening, an opening of the eyes in them that sleep. Do you not recognize your guilt, your miserable conditions of sin?" Two intense eyes stared down at Joseph.

"No!" came the terse reply to the lengthy lecture.

Mr. Chaffinch started, and an ugly, menacing expression came into his face. Just as he opened his mouth once more, Joseph intervened.

"Before you speak again, tell me one thing, Reverend: Am I indebted for this Catechism to the order–perhaps I should say the request–of my wife?"

The Reverend straightened his back, raising up even higher above Joseph. "I do not deny that she has expressed a Christian concern for your state, but I do not wait for a request when I see a soul in peril. If I care for the sheep that willingly obey the shepherd, how much more am I commanded to look after them which stray, and which the wolves and bears are greedy to devour!" In the moment, he appeared more like a wolf or bear than a man of the cloth.

"Have you ever considered, Mr. Chaffinch"–Joseph lifted his head and spoke with measured clarity–"that an intelligent man may possibly be aware that he has an immortal soul– that the health and purity and growth of that soul may possibly be his first concern in life–that no other man can know, as he does, its imperfections, its need, its aspirations which rise directly towards Heaven, and that the attempt of a stranger to examine and criticize–and, perhaps, blacken– this most sacred part of his nature may possibly be a pious impertinence?"

The Reverend waved a hand dismissively. "Ah, the natural depravity of the heart!" he groaned.

Joseph took a deep breath. "It is not the depravity, it is the only pure quality which the hucksters of doctrine, the money-changers in the Holy Temple of Man, cannot touch!

Shall I render a reckoning to *you* on the day when souls are judged? Are *you* the infallible agent of the Divine Mercy?" He stared up at the clergyman with disgust. "What blasphemy!" Joseph turned and resumed his course home.

"I wash my hands of you!" Mr. Chaffinch cried out after the departing Joseph. "I have had to deal with many sinners in my day, but I have found no sin which came so directly from the Devil as pride of the mind. If you were rotten in all your members from sins of the flesh alone, I might have a little hope. Verily, it shall go easier with the murderer and the adulterer on that day than with such as thee!" He gave the horse a more-than-saintly stroke, and his vehicle rattled away.

While to Joseph the tirade seemed full of stock phrases used without a thought of their tremendous character, he could not help feel the sting of outrage in all the sensitive fibers of his soul. The Reverend seemed to apply every word personally. Who could have invoked such passion? Julia! Mr. Chaffinch confessed it.

What false or exaggerated representations had she made? The only measure available to him appeared to be the character of the clergyman's charges. Julia had abused the privilege of Mr. Chaffinch's attention, and now Joseph played the role of black sheep, prodigal son, and Beelzebub all rolled into one.

He sat on a stump by the side of the road to consider what to do next. In his present frame of mind, and sickness at heart, returning home seemed impossible. "Philip!" he said to himself.

Chapter 16: At the Brink

JOSEPH RETRACED HIS STEPS and took the road up the valley, walking rapidly toward the Forge. The tumult in his blood gradually expended its force, but it had carried him along more swiftly than he perceived. When he reached the point where he could look across the narrowed valley, he could see the smoke from the Forge near at hand. He even caught a glimpse of the cottage on the knoll.

He halted, listening to a secret instinct that told him not to submit his trouble to Philip's riper manhood until it became clear and coherent in his own mind. Philip's love and friendship meant more than anything in that moment, and he did not wish to seem a simple creature of merely moods and sentiments. He wanted respect from his friend, not pity.

Joseph crossed a sloping field on the left of the road and found himself on a bank overhanging the stream. Under the wood of oaks and hemlocks the laurel grew in rich, shining clumps. Twenty-five feet below, the water current glimmered through the leaves. The opposite shore appeared level and green, with an herbage that no summer could wither. He leaned against a hemlock bole and tried to think. It became difficult to review the past while his future life overshadowed him like a descending burden that he lacked the strength to lift.

Love betrayed, trust violated, aspirations misinterpreted. These spiritual aspects haunted his whirring emotions. A divided household, entangling obligations, the probability of serious loss. Those material evils accompanied his beleaguered thoughts. With no preparation for such transformation, he could only rebel–not measure or analyze–and cast about for ways of relief.

This miserable strait in which he found himself only seemed to have one unfortunate solution. Other men persisted in finding his better impulses as evil. Such treachery and selfishness felt like a harsh yoke. Life had been to him a hope, an inspiration, a sound, enduring joy. Now it might never be so again! Death, however, might deliver release.

He stepped forward to the edge of the rock. A few pebbles, dislodged by his feet, slid from the brink and plunged with a bubble and a musical tinkle into the dark, sliding waters beneath him. One more step, one foot in front of the other, an additional stride, and the release that seemed so fair might be attained.

A morbid sense of delight arose as he played with the thought in his mind. He bent down and gathered some broken stones, and he let them fall one by one. "So, I hold my fate in my hand," he said to himself and anyone who might be nearby.

In the stream below, he saw a shifting, quivering image of himself projected against the reflected sky. A fancy, almost as clear as a voice, reverberated inside his skull: *This is your present self. What will you do with it beyond the gulf, where only the soul superior to circumstances here receives a nobler destiny?*

As he gazed down at the flickering specter, he heard footsteps behind him upon the dead leaves. He turned and beheld Philip, moving stealthily toward him, pallid, with outstretched hand. They looked at each other for a lingering moment without speaking.

"I guess your thought, Philip, but the things easiest to do are sometimes the most impossible." Joseph forced a smile.

"The bravest man may allow a fancy to pass through his mind, Joseph, which only the coward will carry into effect."

Joseph stood and faced his friend. "I am not a coward!"

Philip took his hand, drew him back from the brink and flung his arms around Joseph, holding him to his own heart. Within moments, lips and tongues intertwined. They sat down, side-by-side, a few feet back from the edge.

"I was up the stream on the other side trolling for trout," Philip explained, "when I saw you in the road. I was welcoming your company in my heart. Then you stopped, stood still, and at last faced away. Something in your movements gave me a sudden, terrible feeling of anxiety. I threw down my rod, came around by the bridge at the Forge, and followed you here." His eyes continued to examine his fragile friend. "Do not blame me for my foolish dread."

Joseph could see seeds of tiny tears forming in Philip's supplicatory eyes, and he explained, "Dear, dear friend. I did not mean to come to you until I seemed stronger and more rational. If that were a vanity, it is gone now. I confess my weakness and ignorance." He smiled. "Tell me, if you can, why this has come upon me? Tell me why nothing that I have been taught, why no atom of the faith which I still cling to, explains, consoles, or remedies any wrong of my life!" He began to choke and tear up.

"Faiths, I suppose, are like laws," Philip opined. "They are adapted to the average character of the human race. You, in the confiding purity of your nature, are not an average man. You are very much above the class, and if virtue were its own reward, you would be most exceptionally happy. Then the puzzle is, what's the particular use of virtue?"

"I don't know, Philip, but I don't like to hear you ask the question." Joseph's mouth tightened. "I find myself so often on the point of doubting all that was my Truth a little while ago, and yet, why should my misfortunes, as an individual, make the truth a lie?" He shook his head gently. "I am only one man among millions who *must* have faith in the efficacy of virtue." He turned and clasped both of Philip's hands in his. "Even if I believed the faith to be false, I think I should still say, 'Let it be preached!'"

Joseph related the whole of his miserable story. He did not spare himself, nor did he conceal his weakness that allowed him to get entangled to such an extent.

Philip's brow grew dark as he listened. At the close of the recital, his face calmed. "Now, put this aside for a little while and give your ear—and your heart, too, Joseph—to *my* story. Do not compare my fortune with yours, but let us apply to both the laws which seem to govern life and see whether justice is possible."

The two looked at each other without speaking. Joseph felt better after baring his entire soul to Philip. The initial embarrassment dissolved away in the freedom to speak his truth knowing that his closest friend would not judge. He smiled at Philip, who closed his eyes and inhaled deeply.

"I, too, realized at an early age how I differed from other boys. It wasn't just the color of my skin or my Race that segregated me—although most of the cruel treatment I received from my colleagues centered around such things. My family had arrived in the Northeast long before The War, and we lived as Free Black Men. My father studied at the Ashmun Institute, founded by one of your Quaker brothers, and just a few years back they renamed it Lincoln University after our slain President. I completed my own degree there as well."

Joseph's heart opened even further as he watched Philip's animated face. Such an admirable gentleman!

"Well… as you now know, my tastes in love run to the male of the species, as does yours"—Joseph smiled at the mention of 'love'—"and I came to the conclusion that I needed to find a woman to marry who could accept me as I was. At first, Miss Clementina Blessing took an interest in me. My family had money, and I believe the mission of the Blessing children is to marry wealthy men." He looked over at Joseph, who rolled his eyes. "When my father's fortune evaporated, so did my courtship with Clementina. While she might have found me fascinating on the surface, her underlying fascination—it appeared—focused more on our accounts." Joseph nodded. "Then—through mutual acquaintances—I was introduced to Emily Marrable—now Hopeton." He glanced in the direction of the Hopeton mansion. "She is the most marvelous young woman I had ever met—with the exception of my dear sister, of course—and I envisioned us ever the happy couple. However, Hopeton came along with his big pockets, large mansion, and healthy investments. Emily found his wealth more appealing than my pauper's pennies." Philip blinked twice.

Joseph had dismissed his wife's suspicion after dinner at the Hopetons. It imparted a bit of shock to hear Philip's confession. How both of them had searched for a female companion, and each of these women had sought only a life of comfort and luxury, not true love. Did Philip know of Emily's romantic intrigue with Lucy Henderson? It did not appear so.

Who are the better angels? Those men who attempt to conceal their inner nature and pretend to love a woman–or the women who pretend to love a man merely for monetary comfort and surety?

"Is there no way out of this labyrinth of wrong?" Philip exclaimed. "Two natures, as far apart as Truth and Falsehood, monstrously held together in the most intimate, the holiest of bonds. Two natures destined for each other monstrously kept apart by the same bonds! Is life to be so sacrificed to habit and prejudice?" He clasped Joseph's hands. "I said that Faith, like Law, was fashioned for the average man. Then there must be a loftier faith, a juster law for the men–and the women–like us who were born with instincts, needs, knowledge and rights–ay, *rights*!–of their own!"

Faith, Law, instincts, needs, knowledge and rights all had their place, but in that moment, Joseph concerned himself only with his devotion to Philip. In his friend, he saw someone who had rescued him–saved his very life!–and stood by him through devastating marital circumstances. And now Joseph had learned that Philip also had attempted to conceal his true nature with marriage, but unsuccessfully. Both men destroyed by women, yet only Joseph had a problematic spouse to contend with.

"But Philip, we were both to blame. You through too little trust, I through too much. We have both been rash and impatient. I cannot forget that, and how are we to know that the punishment, terrible as it seems, is disproportioned to the offense?"

Philip swallowed hard. "We know this, Joseph–and who can know it and be patient?–that the power which controls our lives is pitiless and unrelenting! There is the same punishment for an innocent mistake as for a conscious crime. A certain Nemesis follows ignorance, regardless how good and pure may be the individual nature. Had you even guessed your wife's true character just before marriage, your very integrity, your conscience—and the conscience of the world—would have compelled the union, and Nature would not have mitigated her selfishness to reward you with a tolerable life."

A tempting thought. Joseph wondered if he had known of Julia's insatiable thirst for money, society, and position, would he have withdrawn the offer to marry? He did overhear the sisters discussing the family's financial setback and the concealment of Julia's true age. If only he had addressed his suspicions earlier, perhaps…

"O no!" Philip continued. "You would still have suffered as now. Shall a man with a heart feel this horrible injustice and not rebel? Grant that I am rightly punished for my impatience, my pride, my jealousy. How have *you* been rewarded for your stainless youth, your innocent trust, your almost miraculous goodness? Had you known the world better—even though a part of your knowledge might have been evil—you would have escaped this fatal marriage. Nothing can be more certain, and will you simply groan and bear? What compensating fortune have you, or can you ever expect to find?"

Joseph sat quietly, his trembling hands in Philip's. His breathing accelerated as the profound agitation swelled inside him. "There is something within me which accepts everything you say, and, yet, it alarms me. I feel a mighty temptation in your words. They could lead me to snap my chains, break violently away from my past and present life, and surrender myself to will and appetite." He looked directly into the eyes of his love. "O Philip, if we could make our lives wholly our own! If we could find a spot –"

"I know such a spot!" Philip interrupted. "A great valley, bounded by a hundred miles of snowy peaks, lakes in its bed, enormous hillsides dotted with groves of holly and pine, orchards of orange and olive, a perfect climate where it is bliss enough just to breathe, and freedom from the distorted laws of men. For none are near enough to enforce them! If there is no legal way of escape for you here, at least, there is no force which can drag you back once you are there. I will go with you, and maybe... maybe..."

Philip's face glowed, and the vague alarm in Joseph's heart took a definite form. However, unspoken words loomed like storm clouds behind the hills.

"If we could be sure!" Joseph cried.

"Sure of what? Have I exaggerated the wrong in your case? Say we should be outlaws *there* in our freedom! Here we are fettered outlaws."

"I have been trying, Philip, to discover a law superior to that under which we suffer, and I think I have found it. If it be true that ignorance is equally punished with guilt, if causes and consequences in which there is neither pity nor justice govern our lives, then what keeps our souls from despair but the infinite pity and perfect justice of the Lord? Yes, here is the difference between human and divine law! This makes obedience safer than rebellion. If you and I, Philip, stand above the level of common natures, feeling higher needs and claiming other rights, let us shape them according to the law which is above, not that which is below us!"

An eagle soared above them, screeching. They both raised their eyes to the sky. Joseph smiled, Philip grew pale.

"Then you mean to endure in patience and expect me to do the same?" Philip asked.

"If I can. The old foundations upon which my life rested are broken up, and I am too bewildered to venture on a random path. Give me time. Let us both strive to wait a little. I see nothing clearly but this: There is a Divine government on which I lean now as never before. Yes, I say again, the very wrong that has come upon us makes God necessary!"

Now Philip became restless. Joseph observed the twitches and tension in his friend. Both natures shared the same desire and daring of the dream, but Joseph's deeper conscience prevailed. He looked upon the loveliness of his companion and smiled with all the love he could muster.

"Yes, we will wait," Philip whispered. "You came to me, Joseph, as you said, in weakness and confusion. I have been talking of your innocence and ignorance. Let us not measure ourselves in that way. It is not experience alone which creates manhood. What will become of us I cannot tell, but I will not–I dare not–say you are wrong!"

They took each other's hands. The day fading, the landscape silent. Only the twitter of nesting birds could be heard in the boughs above them. They gave way to the impulse of manly love–rarer alas!–tender and true. Their faces drew nearer and they kissed passionately.

As they walked back and parted on the highway, Joseph felt his life not wholly unkind and happiness not yet impossible.

He returned home to a silent, taciturn Julia. She took one look at the almost imperceptible but indelible smile on her husband's face and quickly strode away to the kitchen.

"Did you not wish to hear of the news?" Joseph asked in a loud voice.

Julia stopped and turned to face him. Instead of saying anything, she merely raised her thinly-plucked eyebrows.

"I met up with your father, and he granted me the right to sell an amount of the stock sufficient to cover the impending fifth installment. He made me sign a power of attorney form so that he could act in my stead."

"I hope you are satisfied that pa will make it easy for you?" she said tentatively.

"He thinks so. However, he depends, I imagine, upon your sister Clementina marrying a Mr. Spelter, whom your father considers 'a man of immense wealth, but I regret to say, no refinement.'" He attempted to speak using Mr. Blessing's manner.

"Please do no imitate my pa so," Julia cringed.

"I am sorry, my dear. I did not intend to offend you."

Julia bit her lip and her eyes assumed that hard, flinty look he knew so well. "If Clementina marries immense wealth, she will become simply insufferable!" A sneer grabbed at her face. "But what difference can that make in pa's business affairs?"

Joseph wanted to say *He probably expects Mr. Spelter to indorse a promissory note*, but he held his tingly tongue and said instead, "What *I* have resolved to do is this. Tomorrow, I shall make a journey to the oil region and satisfy myself where and what the Amaranth is. Your own practical instincts will tell you, Julia, that this intention of mine must be kept secret, even from your father."

She rested her chin upon one fist. After a few moments, she looked up with a cheerful, confiding expression. "I think you are right. If... if things should not happen to be *quite* as they are represented, you can secure yourself against any risk–and pa, too–before the others know of it." She smiled "You will have the inside track. That is, if there is one. On the other hand"–the smile disappeared–"if all is right, pa can easily manage–if some of the others are shaky in their faith–to get their stock at a bargain. I am sure he would have gone out there himself, if his official service were not so important to the government."

And to keeping the coffers of the Wharf-Rat full! Joseph thought to himself.

"Yes. I believe Dennis and I can handle the farm for yet another day or two in your absence." She shot him a side-glance. "And it is in that spirit, I know, you will agree to a plan of mine, which I was going to propose."

Joseph sighed, wondering what new costly scheme his wife had in mind.

"Lucy Henderson's school closes this week, and Mrs. Hopeton tells me the poor girl is a little overworked and ailing. It would hardly help her much to go home, where she could not properly rest, as her father is a hard, avaricious man who can't endure idleness, except, I suppose, in a corpse–so these people tell me." A tight smile appeared on her nearly-closed lips. "I want to ask Lucy to come here. She could take your aunt's old room, and I believe you always liked her." She shot a swift, stealthy glance at Joseph. "She will be an agreeable guest for both of us. She shall just rest and grow strong. You know, while you are absent, I shall not seem quite so lonely. You don't know how long you will be gone, and I shall find the separation very hard to bear, even with her company." She batted her steely eyes.

"Why has Mrs. Hopeton not invited her?" It surprised Joseph that the two women wouldn't want to spend as much time together as possible.

"The Hopetons are going to the sea-shore in a few days. She would take Lucy as a guest, but there is only one difficulty in the way. She thinks Lucy would accept the trip and the stay there as an act of hospitality, but that she cannot–or thinks she cannot–afford the dresses that would enable her to appear in Mrs. Hopeton's circle. But it is just as well. I am sure Lucy would feel more at home *here*."

If Lucy could not go to Mrs. Hopeton, Joseph felt fairly certain that Mrs. Hopeton would eventually come to Lucy. "Then by all means ask her! Miss Lucy Henderson is a noble and virtuous girl."

"Ind-e-e-e-e-d!" Julia drawled.

Perhaps Joseph had spoken too quickly and agreed too easily. "I heartily believe this to be best for everyone. For you and for Lucy."

"And what about you, Joseph? Is this best for you?"

"If Miss Henderson's company staves off the loneliness for you, my darling, I leave the details of the arrangement entirely up to you." He began to climb the stairs. "I believe I shall turn in early as I have an arduous day ahead of me tomorrow. Good night."

"Good night," Julia echoed with whirling eyes.

Chapter 17: Kanuck and the Amaranth

ON HIS WAY TO OAKLAND STATION, Joseph considered the path ahead regarding the wells wedged between the Fluke and Chowder Companies. The situation called for shrewdness, and Joseph knew enough to perceive it better to keep his true identity and his own personal interest in the speculation secret. He would assume the character of a curious traveler and keep his eyes and ears open, learning as much as might be possible to one outside the concentric rings of oil production.

He purchased passage in the train bound for Corry, where he would then catch another rail out to Oil City, the starting-point of his investigation. Other passengers occupied every seat on the train. The fellow seated next to him appeared keen, witty, and red-faced, with an astounding diamond pin and a gold watch-chain heavy enough to lift an anchor. He shuffled constantly, full of "operative" energy, and unable to travel in silence, as is the universal and most dismal American habit. By the third station, he had extracted from Joseph the fabricated story about being a stranger intending to visit the principal wells and that he might be tempted to invest something if the aspects proved propitious.

"You must be sure to take a look at *my* wells," the stranger invited. "Not that any of our stock is in the market. It is never offered to the public—unless accidentally—but they will give you an illustration of the magnitude of the business. All wells, you know, sink after a while to what some people call the normal flowing capacity. We oilers call it 'the everidge run,' and so it was reported of ourn. Since we've begun to torpedo them, it's almost equal to the first tapping, though I don't suppose it'll hold out so long."

"Are the torpedoes generally used?" Joseph asked with some surprise.

"They're generally *tried* anyhow. The cute fellow who first hit upon the idea meant to keep it in the dark, but the oilers, you'll find, have got their teeth skinned, and what they can't find out isn't worth finding out! Lord! I torpedoed my wells at midnight, and it wasn't a week before the Fluke was as it, bustin' and bustin' all their dry anger-holes!"

"The *what*?" Joseph exclaimed.

"Fluke. Queer name, isn't it? But that's nothing. We have the Crinoline, the Pipsissaway, the Mud-Lark, and the Sunburst, between us and the Tideoute.

"What is the name of your company, sir, if I may ask?"

"About as queer as any of 'em," he snickered, "the Chowder."

Joseph started, in spite of himself. "It seems to me I have heard of that company," he said attempting to keep his true identity private.

"Oh, no doubt," replied the stranger. "It isn't often quoted in the papers, but it's *known*. I'm rather proud of it, for I got it up. I was boring–boss, though–at three dollars a day, two years ago, and now I have my forty thousand a year 'free of income tax,' as the Insurance Companies say. But then, where one is lucky like the Chowder, a hundred busts."

"I should very much like to see your wells," Joseph said after reflecting upon the situation. "Will you be there a day or two from now? My name is Asten–not that you have heard of it before."

"Shall be glad to hear it again, though, and to see you." The man offered his hand. "My name is Blenkinsop."

With utter restraint, Joseph took the offered hand and shook it firmly. "Would I be correct in presuming that you are the President of the Chowder?"

"Why, yes," Mr. Blenkinsop answered. "Ever since it's been a company. It was all mine at the start, but I wanted capital, and I had to work 'em."

"Are there other important companies near you?"

"None of any account, except the Fluke and the Depravity. *They* flow tolerable now, after torpedoing. To be sure, there are kites and catches with all sorts o' names: the Pennyroyal, the Ruby, the Wallholler–whatever that is–and the Amaranth–ha, ha!"

"The Amaranth? Perhaps I have heard of that one."

"Lord! Are you *bit* already?" Mr. Blenkinsop exclaimed fixing his small, sharp eyes on Joseph.

"I... I really don't know what you mean."

"No offense. I thought it likely, that's all. The Amaranth is Kanuck's last get-out. He keeps mighty close, but if he don't feather his nest in a hurry–at somebody's expense–*I* ain't no judge o' men!"

Mr. Blenkinsop left the train at Tarr Farm, and Joseph continued on to Oil City. He wandered about the *ad hoc* village, mostly make-shift storefronts and temporary houses, finding nothing profitable there. He then set out up the river, first to seek the Chowder wells.

The peculiar topography of the region seemed remarkable. Soft, rolling hills dissolved away by the sleepy little river bared an assortment of multihued layers. The Chowder property began in a sloping bottom, gradually rising from the river to a range of high hills a quarter of a mile in the rear. Just above this point, the river made a sharp horseshoe bend, washing the foot of the hills for a considerable distance, and then curving back again, with a second tract of bottom-land beyond. Like an all-consuming snake slithering and skulking along, the rippling dark water flowed by.

The Fluke wells sat on that second tract. Joseph reasoned that the Amaranth must be the happy possessor of the lofty section of hills dividing the two. A workman stood inspecting some Chowder equipment, and Joseph approached.

"Do they get oil up there?" Joseph pointed to the ragged, barren heights.

The grease-covered man assessed Joseph for a second before speaking. "They may get skunk oil or rattle-snake oil. Them'll do to peddle, but you can't fill tanks with 'em." He turned a wrench. "I hear they've got a company for that place–th'

Amaranth, they call it–but any place'll do for derned fools. Why look 'ee here! *We've* got seven hundred feet to bore. Now, jest put twelve hundred more atop o' that, and guess whether they can even pump oil, with the Chowder and Fluke both sides of 'em! But it does for green 'uns, as well as any other place."

Joseph laughed feebly in an effort to seem agreeable to the man who provided so much information freely. "I'll walk over that way to the Fluke"–he pointed up the hill between the two drilling sites–"as I should like to see how such things are managed."

"Then be a little on your guard with Kanuck if you meet him." Joseph looked at the fellow with a questioning expression. "Don't ask him too many questions."

Joseph nodded his appreciation for the intelligence. As he climbed up the steep slope, he could see the timber-skeletons on the summit, which appeared to look like gibbets than anything else. Joseph found a dozen or more deserted shafts when he arrived at the top.

He wandered from one to the other, asking himself as he inspected each *Is this the splendid speculation*? Nothing in that miserable, shabby, stony region–a hundred acres of which would hardly pasture a cow–seemed like a source of wealth. Just like the stony and barren natures of men who built their cheating schemes on this wretched basis.

A little farther on, he came to a deep ravine cleaving the hills in twain. He saw another skeleton in its bed, with several shabby individuals gathered about it, the first sign of life or business he had yet discovered.

With the warning of the Chowder workman recurring in his mind, he hastened down the steep declivity. With no clear fixed policy in his mind, he decided to leave everything to chance. As he approached, he saw men laboring. One tall, lean individual, who looked more like an unfortunate clergyman, stood watching. His small, restless, fiery eyes–like those of a black serpent set into a sallow face–turned upon

Joseph as he approached.

"The sooner you leave, the better I shall be satisfied," the fellow hissed.

"This is a rough country for walking," Joseph said to him. "How much farther is it to the Fluke wells?"

One of the workmen looked up. "Just a bit."

Joseph sat on a stone with the air of one who needed rest. "This well, I suppose, belongs to the Amaranth?"

With a quick snap of his head, the lean overseer barked, "Who told you so?"

"They said below, at the Chowder, that the Amaranth was up here."

The men exchanged furtive glances. "Did Blenkinsop send you this way?" the tall one asked.

"Nobody sent me. I am a stranger taking a look at the oil company. I have never before been in this part of the State." Joseph felt uncomfortable presenting this role, but he knew it best to maintain his detachment.

"May I ask your name, sir?"

"Asten," Joseph said before he could stop himself.

"Asten!" the man repeated. "I think I know where that name belongs. Let me see." He pulled a large dirty envelope from his breast-pocket and ran over several papers, unfolded one, and asked, "Joseph Asten?"

"Yes," he responded through gritted teeth, silently cursing himself for want of forethought.

"Proprietor of ten thousand dollars' worth of stock in the Amaranth!" He looked at Joseph accusingly. "Who sent you here?"

Joseph rose, scanned the faces of the workmen, who stared back with a malicious curiosity. He attempted to remain as calm as possible. "No one sent me, and no one, beyond my own family, knows that I am here. I am a farmer, not a speculator. Someone induced me to take the stock from representations which have not been fulfilled. My habit is— when I cannot get the truth from others—to ascertain it for myself." He addressed the tall, lean man. "I presume you are Mr. Kanuck?"

The fellow did not answer immediately, but a quick, intelligent glance from one of the workmen indicated Joseph's surmise correct. They huddled and whispered among themselves. Mr. Kanuck pointed, and the workmen moved away.

"If you are bound for the Fluke, Mr. Asten, I will join you," he said with constrained civility. "I am also going in that direction, and we can talk on the way."

The two walked up the opposite side of the ravine without speaking. When they reached the top and caught their breath, Mr. Kanuck began, "I must infer that you have little faith in anything being realized from the Amaranth. Any man ignorant of boring technicalities might be discouraged by the external appearance of things. I shall, therefore, not endeavor to explain to you my grounds of hope, unless you will agree to join me for a month or two and become practically acquainted with the locality and the modes of labor."

"That is unnecessary," Joseph panted.

"You, being a farmer, of course, I could not expect it. On the other hand, I think I can appreciate your... disappointment, if we must call it so, and I should be willing, under certain conditions, to save you—not from positive loss, because I do not admit the possibility of that—from what, at present, may seem loss to you." He turned to face Joseph. "Do I make myself clear?"

"Entirely," Joseph replied, "except as to the conditions."

Mr. Kanuck visually assessed Joseph once again. "We are dealing on the square, I take it?"

"Of course." They began to walk again.

"Then, I need only intimate to you how important it is that I should develop our prospects. To do this, the faith of the principal stockholders must not be disturbed, otherwise the funds–without which the prospects cannot be developed–may fail me at the critical moment." Mr. Kanuck stared directly ahead. "Your hastily and unintelligent impressions–if expressed in a reckless manner–might do much to bring about such a catastrophe. I must, therefore, stipulate that you keep such information to yourself." He turned to Joseph. "Let me speak to you as man to man and ask you if your expressions, not being founded on knowledge, would be honest? So far from it, you will be bound in all fairness, in consideration of my releasing you and restoring you what you have ventured, to adopt and disseminate the views of an expert, namely, mine."

Joseph responded, "Let me put it into fewer words. You will buy my stock, repaying me what I have disbursed, if–on my return–I say nothing of what I have seen and express my perfect faith–adopting your views–in the success of the Amaranth?"

"You have stated the conditions a little barely, perhaps, but not incorrectly. I only ask for perfect fairness, as between man and man."

"One question first, Mr. Kanuck. Does Mr. Blessing know the *real* prospects of the Amaranth?"

"No man more thoroughly," he answered quickly, "I assure you, Mr. Asten. Indeed, without Mr. Blessing's enthusiastic concurrence in the enterprise, I doubt whether we could have carried the work so far towards success." A smile flashed briefly across his darkened face. "His own stock, I may say to you–since we understand each other–was earned by his efforts. If you know him intimately, you know also that he has no visible means of support. But he has what is much more important to us: a thorough knowledge of men and their means." He rubbed his hands and laughed softly.

They came suddenly upon the farthest crest of the hills, where the ridge fell away to the bottom occupied by the Fluke wells.

"On the square, then!" Mr. Kanuck stopped and offered his hand. The beauty of the hills and glens, rivers and streams sparkled around them. A few birds chirped eagerly. "Tell me where you will be to-morrow morning, and our business can be settled in five minutes. You will carry out your part of the bargain–as man to man–when you find that I carry out mine."

Joseph turned to face Mr. Kanuck with rage and disgust boiling over him. "Do you take me for an infernal scoundrel?"

Mr. Kanuck stepped back several paces. His sallow face became livid and Joseph could see murder in his eyes. When Mr. Kanuck raised his hand to his breast, Joseph involuntarily did the same.

"So! That's your game, is it?" Mr. Kanuck hissed through his teeth. "A spy after all! Or a detective, perhaps?" His eyes whirled frantically. "I was a fool to trust a milk-and-water face, but one thing I tell you: you may get away, but come back again if you dare!"

The two stood gazing steadily into each other's eyes. After a long minute had passed, Mr. Kanuck turned and walked away. Joseph began breathing deeply, relieved the dread of an unknown danger had passed. He swiftly descended the hill toward the Fluke.

That evening, he sat in the bar-room of a horrible shanty–which they had the cheek to call a hotel–farther up the river. He noticed a pair of eyes fixed intently upon him. They belonged to one of the workmen from the Amaranth ravine. He made an almost imperceptible signal and left the room. Joseph followed.

Once outside, the workman whispered, "Hush! Don't come back to the hill, and get away from here to-morrow morning if you can!" He darted off and disappeared into the darkness.

Even with all his inexperience of the world, Joseph found the counsel unnecessary. He saw plainly that his only alternatives were loss or connivance.

As he sifted through the day's events on his way to slumber in his rented room, he realized nothing could be gained by following this vile business any further. He decided to take the train directly to the city and speak with his father-in-law face-to-face, rather than through endless notes full of indecipherable gibberish. The pressure of his recent experience drove him irresistibly in the direction of a man he had no conscious desire to see.

The next afternoon, he stood at the door of the Blessing mansion. He rang the bell, hoping that no one would be home. It came as a bit of a surprise that Mr. Blessing himself answered the summons, and after the first expression of shock, ushered him into the parlor.

"I am quite alone, you see," Mr. Blessing began. "Mrs. Blessing is passing the evening with her sister, Mrs. Woollish, and Clementina is still at Long Branch. I believe it is as good as settled that we are to lose her. At least she has written to inquire the extent of my available funds, which—in her case—is tantamount to... very much more."

Joseph had not traveled for days, nor hiked the oil country hills of western Pennsylvania and faced a potential early and lonely death, to digress from his intended mission. He explained to his father-in-law what he had done, whom he had met, and what he had seen. Joseph observed Mr. Blessing becoming more uneasy and excited as the story advanced.

When Joseph finished, Mr. Blessing sat in thought for a few minutes. "I... I really must look into this," he murmured at last. "It seems incredible, pardon me, but I would doubt the statements did they come from other lips than yours. It is as if I had nursed a dove in my bosom and unexpectedly found it to be a... a basilisk!"

"It can be no serious loss to you since you received your stock in return for your services, at least according to Mr. Kanuck."

"This is true"—he cocked his head—"I was not thinking of myself. The real sting of the cockatrice is that I have innocently misled you."

"Yet I understood you to say you had ventured your all?"

Mr. Blessing cleared his throat. "My all of hope... my all of expectation!" he cried out. "I dreamed I had overtaken the rainbow at last, but this... this is *senna... quassia... aloes*! My nature is so confiding that I accept the possibilities of the future as present realities and build upon them as if they were Quincy granite. And yet, with all my experience, my acknowledged sagacity, my acquaintance with the hidden labyrinths of finance, it seems impossible that I can be so deceived! There must be some hideous misunderstanding. I have calculated all the elements, prognosticated all the planetary aspects, so to speak, and have not found a whisper of failure!"

"You omitted one very important element," Joseph whispered.

"What is that? I might have employed a detective, it is true..."

"No!" Joseph blurted out. "Honesty!"

Mr. Blessing fell back in his chair, weeping bitterly. "I deserve this! I will not resent it. I forgive you in advance of the time when you shall recognize my sincere, my heartfelt wish to serve you. Go! Go!" He pointed to the front door. "Let me not recriminate! I meant to be–and still mean to be–your friend, but spare my too confiding child."

Saying nothing more, Joseph took his hat and hastened from the house. At every step, the abyss of dishonesty seemed to open deeper before his feet. *Spare the too confiding child*, Mr. Blessing had requested. Father and daughter were alike: both mean, both treacherous, both unpardonably false to him.

After another night at the Farmers' Tavern, Joseph headed back to his farm.

Chapter 18: Fate Intervenes

JULIA AND LUCY OCCUPIED ADJOINING CHAIRS in the sitting-room, each working on their own piece of needle-work. A shadow fell through the front window, and heavy steps rang hollow upon the stone pavement of the veranda. Julia gave a little start and shriek, and she seized Lucy's arm. The door opened to reveal Joseph, a halo of afternoon sun creating a bleak silhouette.

When he stepped inside and closed the door behind him, it became noticeable that his face appeared stern and haggard. Julia sprang forward, threw her arms around him, and kissed him repeatedly. He stood still, passively enduring the caress without returning it. Stepping away from his wife, Joseph offered his cold, moist hand to Lucy. Her eyes revealed her inability to repress any quick sympathy.

Julia stood paralyzed, observing the more tender greeting Joseph had given their guest. She approached her husband and stammered, "Oh, Joseph. It is good that you have returned. Your friends, the Helds are invited for dinner. But I'm afraid. I don't dare ask you what... what news you bring. You didn't write... I've been so uneasy, and now I see from your face... that something is wrong."

Joseph stared at his wife, with only the sound of his exhausted, agitated breathing. He noticed how pale her face had become in the few days since he had last observed it.

"Don't tell me all at once if it's very bad!" Julia cried. "But, no! It's my duty to hear it, my duty to bear it. Lucy taught me that. Tell me all. Tell me *all* this moment!"

He continued to stare intensely. He spoke slowly and deliberately, "You and your father have ruined me. That is all."

"Joseph!" pronounced Julia with the essence of tender protest, of heart-breaking reproach.

Lucy rose and walked away.

"Don't leave me, Lucy!" Julia appealed.

"It is better that I should go," Lucy answered in a faint voice as she left the room.

"But Joseph, why did you say such terrible things?" Julia spoke with a wild, distracted air. "I really do not know what you mean. What have you learned? What have you seen?" She kept her eyes fully-open and alert.

"I have seen the Amaranth!"

"Well!" Julia expostulated. "Is there no oil?"

Joseph stepped away from Julia and stood looking out the window at the lawn. "Oh, yes. Plenty of oil!" he laughed. "Skunk oil and rattle-snake oil! It is one of the vilest cheats that the Devil ever put into the minds of bad men."

"Oh, poor, pa!" she cried, walking toward Joseph. "What a terrible blow to him!"

"'*Poor pa*'! Yes, my discovery of the cheat *is* a terrible blow to '*poor pa*.' He did not calculate on its being found out so soon." He turned to face Julia. "When I learned from Kanuck that all the stock your father holds was given to him for services—that is, getting the money out of the pockets of innocents like myself—you may judge how much pity I feel for '*poor pa*'! I told him the fact to his face last night, and he admitted it."

Julia turned away from his accusing glare. "Then, if the others know nothing, he may be able to sell his stock at the first opportunity—his and yours—and we may not lose much after all."

"I should have sent *you* to the oil region instead of going myself." He grabbed Julia's wrist with force slightly more than necessary. "You and Kanuck would soon have come to terms. He offered to take the stock off my hands provided I would go back to the city and make such a report of the speculation as he would dictate."

"*And you didn't do it*?" She twisted her arm out of her husband's tight grasp. He stared at her with incredulity, the color rising quickly. "It is *perfectly* legitimate in business.

Every investment in the Amaranth was a venture. Every stockholder knew that he risked losing his money. There is not one that wouldn't save himself in that way, if he had the chance. But you pride yourself on being so much better than other men!" She pointed at him. "Mr. Chaffinch is right! You have what he calls a 'moral pride!' You —"

"Stop!" Joseph screamed. "Who was it that professed such concern about my faith? Who sent Mr. Chaffinch to insult me?" His nostrils flared and sweat rolled down from his hairline.

"Faith and business are two different things. All the churches know that. There was Mr. Sanctus in the city. He subscribed ten thousand dollars to the Church of the Acceptance. When he couldn't pay it, they levied on his property and sold him out of house and home! Really, Joseph Asten, you are as ig-norant of the world as a baby!" She spun away.

"God keep me so, then!" he exclaimed.

Julia paused a few moments before continuing. "However, since you insist on our bearing the loss, I shall expect of your moral pride that you bear it patiently, if not cheerfully. It is far from being ruin to us. The rise in property will very likely balance it, and you will still be worth what you were." Tears began to flow.

"That is not all," he said calmly, with restraint. "I will not mention my greatest loss, for you are incapable of under-standing it, but how much else have you saddled me with? Let me have a look at it!"

He crossed the hall and entered the new apartment. Joseph inspected the ceiling, the elaborate and overladen cornices, the marble chimney-piece. He peered into the boxes and packages, not trusting himself to speak while the extent of the absurd splendor that his wife had committed him grew upon his mind.

Julia followed, keeping a few paces distant. Joseph turned, noticeably trembling but striving to make his voice calm, "Since you were so free to make all these purchases, perhaps you will tell me how they are to be paid for?"

Her eyes circled in their orbits "Let me manage it, then," Julia said at last. "There is no hurry. These country merchants are always impatient. *I* should call them impertinent, and I should like to teach them a lesson. Sellers are under obligations to the buyers, and they are bound to be accommodating. They have so many bills which are never paid, that an extension of time is the least they can do. Why, they will always wait a year, two years, three years, rather than lose." A smug little smile crossed her tight lips.

"I suppose so."

"Then"–she pressed on as her husband began to boil slowly– "their profits are so enormous that it would only be fair to reduce the bills. I am sure that if I were to mention that you were embarrassed by heavy losses–and press them hard– they would compromise with me on a moderate amount. You know they allow what is called a margin for losses–pa told me, but I forget how much. They always expect to lose a certain percentage, and, of course, it can make no difference by whom they lose it. You understand, don't you?"

"Yes. It is very plain." The lid on the boiling pot began to rattle a bit.

"Pa could help me get both a reduction and an extension of time. The bills have not all been sent, and it will be better to wait two or three months after they have come in. If the dealers are a little uneasy in advance, they will be all the readier to compromise afterwards." Again, she smiled grimly.

Joseph walked up and down the hollow room with his hands clasped behind his back and his eyes fixed upon the floor. Suddenly, he stopped before her and said, still attempting to maintain calm, "There is another way."

"Not a better one, I am certain."

"The furniture has not yet been unpacked, and can be returned to them uninjured. Then the bills need not be paid at all."

"And we should be the laughing-stock of the neighborhood!" she cried, her eyes flashing. "I *never* heard of anything so ridiculous!"

"Perhaps you have forgotten that I warned you of such premature gratification just before this whole episode began. I suggested we wait until the return from the speculation were certain before expending such large sums to avoid public humiliation should we need to return purchases."

"If the worst comes to the worst"—Julia pressed on as if she had not heard her husband's response—"you can sell Old Bishop those fifty acres over the hill, which he stands ready to take, any day. But you'd rather have a dilapidated house, no parlor, guests received in the dining-room and the kitchen, the Hopetons and your friends, the Helds, sneering at us behind our backs! And what would your credit be worth? We shall not even get trusted for groceries at the village store if you leave things as they are!"

Joseph groaned and spoke to himself rather than answering his wife's charges. "Is there no way out of this? What is done is done. Shall I submit to it, and try to begin anew? Or..."

Julia stood facing the marble chimney-piece, her arms folded tightly across her chest. When she turned to face Joseph again, she raised her chin, drew in a full breath and left the room, closing the door behind her.

Feeling the need for fresher, less-ornate air, Joseph stepped outside and stood on the lawn. He looked about for a moment with a heavy, bewildered countenance, and then slowly turned toward the garden. After a few minutes of calming down, he sat in the semicircular enclosure where he could look over the valley.

He could hear footsteps approaching, and he turned to see Lucy. She held a few plucked sprays of amaranth from the garden in her hands.

"Sit down, Lucy. I am a grim host to-day," he said with a melancholy attempt at a smile. His eyelids appeared reddened and his lips compressed with an expression of intense pain.

Lucy gazed upon Joseph, who now appeared so much older than the young man she had grown up with. Tears started in her eyes, and she did not speak as she sat.

"I shall not talk of my ignorance any more as I once did," Joseph attempted to reassure her. "If there is a chance in the school of the world, graded according to experience of human meanness and treachery and falsehood, I ought to stand at the head."

Lucy stretched out her hand in protest. "Do not speak so bitterly, Joseph. It pains me to hear you."

"How would you have me speak?"

Before answering the question, Lucy studied her friend for a few moments. "As a man who will not see ruin before him because a part of his property happens to slip from him, even if all were lost." He turned to face her. "I always took you to be liberal, Joseph, never careful of money for money's sake, and I cannot understand how your nature should be changed now, even though you have been the victim of some dishonesty."

"'*Some dishonesty*'! You are thinking only of money. What term would you give to the betrayal of a heart, the ruin of a life?"

"Surely, Joseph, you cannot mean –"

"My wife, of course. It needed no guessing." He faced away.

"Joseph!" Lucy cried. "Indeed you do her wrong! I know what anxiety she has suffered during your absence. She blamed herself for having advised you to risk so much in an uncertain speculation, dreaded your disappointment, resolved to atone for it. If she could! She may have been rash and thoughtless, but she never meant to deceive you. If you are disappointed in some qualities, you should not shut your eyes and refuse to see others. I know, now, that I have myself not been fair in my judgment of Julia. A nearer acquaintance has led me to conceive what disadvantages of education, for which she is not responsible, she is obliged to overcome. She sees, she admits them, and she *will* overcome them. You, as her husband, are bound to show her a patient kindness –"

"Enough!" Joseph stood as he screamed. "I see that you have touched pitch, also, Lucy. Your first instinct was right. The woman whom I am now bound to look upon as my wife is false and selfish in every fiber of her nature. How false and selfish *I* only can know, for to *me* she takes off her mask!"

"Do you believe *me*, then?" Lucy spoke with a slight defiance.

"I begin to fear that Philip was right. Life is relentless. Ignorance or crime, it is all the same. And if the Good Lord cares less about our individual wrongs than we flatter ourselves He does, what do we gain by further endurance?" He reached his hand out. "Here is Lucy Henderson, satisfied that my wife is a suffering angel, and she thinks *my* nature is changed, that *I* am cold-hearted and cruel, while I know Lucy to be true and noble, but deceived by the very goodness of her own heart!"

Joseph looked into Lucy's unyielding face for a moment.

"I am sick of masks," he continued. "We all wear them. Do you want to know the truth, Lucy? When I look back I can see it very clearly now. A little more than a year ago the one girl who began to live in my thoughts was *you*!" She opened her mouth to respond. "Don't interrupt me!" he barked. "I am only speaking of what *was*. When I went to Warriner's, it was in the hope of meeting you, not Julia Blessing. I believed you and I shared something in common, which I now know to be true. We could have had a convenient marriage if I had not been led away by the cunningest arts ever a woman devised. I will not speculate on what might have been, but this I say: I honor and esteem you, Lucy Henderson, and the loss of your friendship, if I now lose it, is another evil service which my wife has done to me."

Lucy's face drained of color, and she began to tremble. "Joseph, you should not, must not, speak so to me."

"I suppose not," he answered, letting his head sink wearily. "It is certainly not conventional, but it is true for all that. I could tell you the whole story, for I can read it backwards, from now to the beginning, without misunderstanding a word. It would make no difference. She is simple, natural, artless, amiable, for all the rest of the world, while to me..." he trailed off despondently.

"You mistake me, Joseph," Lucy spoke after a pause. "If you think you have lost my friendship, my sincerest sympathy. I can see that your disappointment is a bitter one, and my prayer is that you will not make it bitterer by thrusting from you the hopeful and cheerful spirit you once showed. We all have our sore trials."

Joseph remained still, stooping, with his elbows on his knees and his forehead resting on his palms.

"If I am deceived in Julia," Lucy began again, "it is better to judge too kindly than too harshly. I know you cannot change your sentence against her now, nor, perhaps, very soon, but you are bound to her for life, and you must labor—it is your sacred duty—to make that life smoother and brighter for both. I do not know how, and I have no right to condemn you if you fail. But, Joseph, make the attempt now, when the most fortunate experience that is likely to come to you is over. Make it, and it may chance that, little by little, the old confidence will return, and you will love her again."

He sprang to his feet. "Love her!" he exclaimed with suppressed passion, arms flailing. "Love *her*? I *hate* her!"

Both their heads turned in the direction of a hissing, rattling sound, like that of some fierce animal at bay. The thick foliage of two of the tall boxwood-trees violently parted. Branches snapped and gave way. Julia burst through and stood looking from one to the other.

A Gorgon's face suddenly glared upon them. The ringlets wedged behind her ears, and the narrowness of the brow entirely revealed. Her eyes full of cold, steely light. The nostrils violently drawn in, and the lips contracted, as if in a spasm so that the teeth lay bare. Her hands clenched, and a movement in her throat suggested imprisoned words or cries, but no utterances came.

Lucy started to her feet at the first sound, went pallid and fell, rather than sank, upon the seat again.

Julia's scheme hardly surprised Joseph, as her eavesdropping behavior amounted to nothing worse than he already knew. Indeed, he felt comforted in perceiving that he had not overestimated her capacity for treachery. All limits vanished; anything was possible.

"There is *one* law, after all," Joseph said at last. "The law that punishes listeners. You have heard the truth, for once. You have snared and trapped me, but I don't take to my captor more kindly than any other animal." He faced the over-excited Julia directly. "From this moment, I choose my own path, and if you still wish to appear as my wife, you must adapt your life to mine!"

"You mean to brazen it out, do you!" Julia cried in a strange, hoarse, unnatural voice. "That's not so easy! I have not listened to no purpose. I have a hold upon your precious 'moral pride' at last!" Joseph smiled and laughed scornfully. "Yes, laugh, but it is in my hands to make or break you! There is enough decent sentiment in this neighborhood to crush a married man who dares to make love to an unmarried girl!" She pointed at Lucy. "As to the girl who sits still and listens to it, I say nothing. Her reputation is no concern of mine!"

Lucy uttered a faint cry of horror.

Joseph paused to take a full breath before continuing. "If you choose to be so despicable, you will force me to set my truth against your falsehood. Wherever you tell your story, I shall follow with mine. It will be a wretched, a degrading business, but for the sake of Lucy's good name, I have no alternative. I have borne suspicion, misrepresentation, loss of credit—all brought upon by you—patiently because they affected only myself, but since I am partly responsible in bringing this house a guest for your arts to play upon and entrap, I am doubly bound to protect her against you. But I tell you, Julia, beware! I am desperate, and it is ill meddling with a desperate man! You may sneer at my moral pride, but you dare not forget that I have another quality, manly self-respect, which it will be dangerous to offend."

The three looked at each other in turn with no words.

Julia broke the silence. "So, *this* is the man who was all truth and trust and honor! With you the proverb seems to be reversed: It's off with the new love and on with the old. You can insult and threaten me in *her* presence! Well... go on. Play out your little love-scene. I shall not interrupt you. I have heard enough to darken my life from this day!"

She stomped off up the avenue of boxwood-trees with her dress torn, her hair tousled, her arms scratched and bleeding. Joseph and Lucy mechanically followed her with their eyes. He could see Julia's knees wobble as she walked away toward the house.

Then Joseph and Lucy turned and gazed at each other without speaking. The expression of horror had not yet left her pale face.

"She told me to come to you," Lucy stammered. "She begged me, with tears, to try and soften your anger against her, and then... oh, it is monstrous!"

"Now I see the plan!" Joseph exclaimed. "And I, in my selfish recklessness, saying what there was no need to utter, have almost done as she calculated. I have exposed you to this outrage. Why should I have recalled the past at all? I was not taking off a mask, I was only showing a scar—no, not even a scar but a bruise—which I ought to have forgotten. Forget it, too, Lucy, and, if you can, forgive me."

"It is easy to forgive—everything but my own blindness," Lucy answered with a tiny smile. "But there is one thing which I must do immediately. I must leave this house!"

"I see that," Joseph responded sadly. He then murmured, as if speaking to himself, "Who knows what friends will come in the future? Well, I will bear what *can* be borne, and afterwards... there is Philip's valley. A free outlaw is better than a fettered outlaw!" He straightened himself to his full height, drew a deep breath and exclaimed, "Action is a sedative in such cases, isn't it?" He gazed toward the stable. "It appears that Dennis has gone. I will get the other horse from the field and drive you home. Have the Hopetons returned yet from the sea-shore?" Lucy shook her head. "Or stay! Will you not go to Philip Held's cottage for a day or two? I think his sister asked you to come."

"No, no!" she cried. "You must not go. I will wait for Dennis."

Philip leaned closer to Lucy. "No one must suspect what has happened here this afternoon unless Julia compels me to make it known, and I don't think she will. It is, therefore, better that I should take you. It will put me, I hope, in a more rational frame of mind. Go quietly to your room and make your preparations. I will see to Julia, and if there is no further scene now, there will be none of the kind henceforth. She is cunning when she is calm."

Joseph walked into the house and up the stairs to the bedroom. When he opened the door, Julia sat at her bureau bending over an open drawer, and she started with a little cry of alarm. After closing the drawer hastily, she began to arrange her hair at the mirror. The reflection of her face seemed flushed, but its expression appeared sullen and defiant.

"Julia," he started as coolly as possible, "I am going to take Lucy home. Of course you understand that she cannot stay here an hour longer. You overheard my words to her, and you know just how much they were worth. I expect now, that—for *your* sake as much as mine or hers—you will behave towards her at parting in such a way that the neighbors may find no suggestions of gossip or slander."

She continued to primp her hair. "And if I don't choose to obey you?"

"I am not commanding. I propose a course which your own

mind must find sensible. You have 'a deuced sharp intellect,' as your father said on our wedding-day." Joseph took a chance quoting his father-in-law, but so unaccustomed to victory, he could not guess how thoroughly he had already conquered.

"Pa loved me, nevertheless," she burst into tears. The emotion seemed real, but Joseph refused to accept it. "What can I do?" she sobbed. "I will try. I thought I was your wife, but I am not much more than your slave."

Such foolish pity stole into Joseph's heart, but he set his teeth and clenched his hands against it. "I am going for the horse. When I come back from this drive, I hope I shall find you willing to discuss our situation dispassionately, as I mean to do. We have not known each other fairly before to-day, and our plan of life must be rearranged."

He felt relief to walk forth, across the silent, grassy fields. Joseph had learned to accept a slight relief as a substitute for happiness. The feeling that the inevitable crisis might be over gave him, for the first time in months, a sense of liberation. A dreary and painful task remained before him, and he hardly knew why he should be so cheerful, but the bright, sweet currents of his blood returned to flow, and the weight upon his heart lifted from some impatient, joyous energy.

The tempting vision of Philip's valley that haunted him from time to time faded away. The angry tumult through which he had passed appeared to him like a fever, and he rejoiced consciously in the beginning of his spiritual convalescence. Would he willingly return to his boyish innocence of the world if that year could be erased from his life? His nature had not yet lost the basis of that innocent time, and he felt that he must still build his future years upon it.

While in the midst of this meditation, he caught up with the obedient horse and harnessed him to the light carriage that Julia customarily used. The anxiety concerning her probable demeanor returned as he entered the house. He had feared that some of the workmen might prove to be very inconvenient witnesses, but they had finished for the day.

Lucy Henderson sat by the door dressed for the journey. "I think I will go to Madeline Held for a day or two. I made a half-promise to visit her after your return."

"Where is Julia?"

"In the bed-room. I have not seen her. I knocked at the door, but there was no answer."

Joseph sighed audibly. "I will see her myself," he said sternly. "She forgets what is due to a guest."

"No, I will go again," Lucy urged, rising hastily. "Perhaps she did not hear me."

They went to the stairs together, but scarcely had he set his foot upon the first step when the bed-room door above suddenly burst open and Julia, with a shriek of mortal terror, tottered down to the landing. Her face looked ashy, and the dark-blue rings around her sunken eyes made them seem almost like the large sockets of a skull. She leaned against the rickety railing, breathing short and hard.

Joseph sprang up the steps, but as he approached her, she put out her right hand and pushed against his breast with what little force remained, crying out, "Go away! You have killed me!"

The next moment, she fell senseless upon the landing.

Chapter 19: Hope and Despair

JOSEPH KNELT AND TRIED TO LIFT HIS UNCONSCIOUS WIFE. "Good God! She is dead!" he exclaimed. Tears rolled down his cheek. While he may have wished her dead in thoughts for ruining his life, he truly did not wish her to die.

"No," said Lucy, after taking Julia's wrist. "It is only a fainting fit. Bring some water."

Joseph went to the kitchen and returned with a pitcher and glass.

"But she must be very ill," Lucy presumed. "This is not an ordinary swoon. Perhaps the violent excitement has brought about some internal injury. You must send for a physician as soon as possible."

"And Dennis not here! I ought not to leave her. What shall I do?"

"Go yourself, and instantly! The carriage is ready. I will stay and do all that can be done during your absence."

He waited until Julia displayed signs of recovery. The air and water seemed to help. Lucy then shot him a glare, which he understood to mean he should withdraw before Julia could recognize him.

Joseph did not spare the horse, but the hilly road tried his patience. The nearest physician, Dr. Worrall, lived between two and three miles away, and he arrived anxious and breathless only to find the doctor had been called away to attend another patient. Joseph retraced part of the road and drove some distance in the opposite direction in order to summon the second physician, Dr. Hartman. The doctor had just sat down to an early dinner, and he listened to Joseph's description of his wife's symptoms as he ate.

The doctor mumbled through his food, "It is probably a nervous attack, a modified form of hysteria." He continued to eat, but at an accelerated pace, violating his own theory of digestion.

To Joseph, the seconds ticked by hastily, and the minutes seemed intolerably long. At last the doctor concluded his repast and began filling his bag with a few doses of valerian, belladonna, and a few other palliatives that he thought might be needed. Once they harnessed up the physician's sulky the two headed back to the Asten farm. The doctor followed about a minute behind with Joseph racing ahead. As he pulled up to the farmhouse, Lucy ran out to meet him.

"No better... worse, I fear," Lucy murmured, answering Joseph's look.

"Dr. Hartman thinks it is probably a nervous attack. In that case it can soon be relieved."

"Dr. Hartman?" Lucy asked. "Doesn't he live quite a distance?"

"Yes, but Dr. Worrall had already been called away from home."

"I hope he arrives soon. I fancy there is danger."

The doctor pulled his sulky to a halt, hopped out and grabbed his satchel.

"Dr. Hartman, this is Miss Lucy Henderson. She has been attending Mrs. Asten," Joseph made the introduction.

"And how is Mrs. Asten at the moment?" the physician inquired.

"Well, I got her into her bed and applied a few damp compresses, but that did not seem to help. She appeared to be conscious, but she just shook her head whenever I tried to speak to her. She refused tea as well as the lavender and ginger. Plain water she drank in long, greedy draughts. After that, she started up with clutchings and incoherent cries, and then she sank back again into an insensible unconsciousness."

Dr. Hartman pulled at his chin a few times. "It is not an ordinary case of hysteria. Let me see her at once."

Lucy led the doctor up to the bed-room, and Joseph

followed, not wanting to make the situation worse. When they entered the room, Julia opened her eyes languidly, and she slowly lifted her hand to her head. "What has happened to me?" she whispered in a hardly audible tone.

"You had a fainting fit," Lucy answered, "and we have brought the doctor. He will help you. Tell him how you feel, Julia."

"Cold!" she blurted. "Cold! Sinking down somewhere! *Will* he lift me up?" Her eyes glazed over and her mouth hung open.

The physician made a close examination, but he seemed more perplexed as he advanced. He administered only a slight stimulant and then withdrew from the bedside. Dr. Hartman handed Lucy a bottle and asked her to prepare an application.

Once Lucy had left, the doctor whispered to Joseph, "There is something unusual here. She has been sinking rapidly since the first attack. The vital force is very low. It is in conflict with some secret enemy, and it cannot resist much longer, unless we discover that enemy at once. I will do my best to save her, but I do not yet see how." He grimaced.

Julia began making vain attempts to rise, her eyes wide and glaring. "No, no! I will not die!" she stammered. "I heard you." Her utterings became faint and indistinct. "Joseph, I will try... to be different... but... I must live... for that!" She relapsed into unconsciousness.

Dr. Hartman re-examined her with a grave, troubled face. "She need not be conscious for the next thing I do. I will not interrupt this syncope at once. It may, at least, prolong the struggle. What have they been giving her?"

The doctor went to her bureau and lifted up, one-by-one, the bottles of the household pharmacy. Last of all, he found an empty glass shoved behind one of the mirror supports. He looked into it, held it against the light, and was about to set it down again when he seemed to notice something, a misty appearance on the bottom, as if from some delicate sediment. Dr. Hartman stepped to the window and looked at the film again. He collected a few of the minute granulations on the tip of his forefinger, touched them to his tongue, and, turning quickly to Joseph, whispered, "She is poisoned!"

"It is impossible!" Joseph exclaimed. "She could not have been so mad!"

"It is as I tell you! This form of the operation of arsenic is very unusual and I did not suspect it, but now I remember that it is noted in the books. Repeated syncopes, utter nervous prostration, absence of the ordinary burning and vomiting, and signs of rapid dissolution. It fits the case exactly! If I had some oxy-hydrate of iron, there might still be a possibility, but I greatly fear –"

"Do all you can!" Joseph interrupted. "She must have been insane! Do not tell me that you have *no* antidote!"

"We must try an emetic, though it will now be very dangerous." The doctor listed off ingredients as he hastened down to the kitchen. "Oil... white of egg..."

Joseph walked up and down the room, wringing his hands. This reality represented a horror beyond anything he had imagined. His only thought about saving her life, which she must have resolved to take in the madness of passion. She must not, *must not*, die now. Yet she already seemed in some region on the very verge of darkness, some region where it might be scarcely possible to reach and pull her back. What could be done? The case baffled human science. Would his God, who afflicted him through her, now answer his prayer to continue that affliction? Indeed, the word "affliction" did not even occur to him, only *Life! Life!*

Joseph stood by the bedside and gazed upon her livid skin, her sunken features. She seemed already dead. Then, sinking upon his knees, he tried to pray, if the single intense appeal of all his confused feelings could be called a prayer.

He heard a faint sigh. She moved slightly. Perhaps her consciousness returned. She looked at him with half-opened eyes, her gaze unfocused. The faintest broken whisper escaped her lips, "I did love you... I *did*... and *do*... love you! But... you... you hate me!"

A pang sharper than a knife went through Joseph's heart. He cried through his tears, "I did not know what I said! Give me your forgiveness, Julia! Pardon me, not because I ask it, but freely, from your heart, and I will bless you! Please!"

Her eyes softened and a phantom smile hovered upon her lips. Joseph bent over and kissed her.

"Oh, Julia, why did you do it? Why did you not wait until I could speak with you? Did you think you would take a burden off yourself or me?"

As he lifted her head, the lips moved but no voice came. He bent his ear to her mouth, and in the faintest breath, like the dream of a voice, she began, "I... did... not... mean..."

She stopped. The doctor entered the room, followed by Lucy.

"First the emetic," ordered Dr. Hartman.

"For God's sake, be silent!" Joseph cried out, with his ear still at Julia's lips. The doctor stepped forward and looked at her. He sat on the bed beside Joseph and laid his hand upon her heart. The silence lasted for several minutes.

Dr. Hartman removed his hand, took Julia's head out of Joseph's arms and laid it softly upon its pillow.

She had died.

"It cannot be!" cried Joseph, looking at the doctor with an agonized face. "It is too dreadful!"

"There is no room for doubt in relation to the cause. I suspect that her nervous system has been subjected to a steady and severe tension, probably for years past. This may have induced a condition, or at least a temporary paroxysm, during which she was—you understand me—not wholly responsible for her actions. You must have noticed whether such a condition preceded this catastrophe."

Lucy looked from one to the other, then back to the livid face on the pillow, unable to ask a question.

Joseph arose at the doctor's words. "That is my guilt. I was excited and angry, for I had been bitterly deceived. I warned her that her life must henceforth conform to mine. My words were harsh and violent. I told her that we had at last ascertained each other's true natures and proposed a serious discussion for the purpose of arranging our common future. Can she have misunderstood my meaning? It was not separation, not divorce. I only meant to avoid the miserable strife of the last few weeks. Who could imagine that this would follow?"

Even as he spoke the words, Joseph remembered the tempting fancy that had passed through his own mind–and the fear of Philip–as he stood on the brink of the rock, above the dark, sliding water. He covered his face with his hands and sat down. What right had he to condemn her, to pronounce her mad? Grant that she had been blinded by her own unbalanced, excitable nature rather than consciously false. Grant that she had really loved him, that the love survived under all her vain and masterful ambition. And how could he doubt it after the dying words and looks? He easily guessed how sorely he had wounded her, how despair should follow her fierce excitement!

The words *Go away! You have killed me!* now seemed explicable. He groaned in the bitterness of his self-accusation. What trials had he endured? How light seemed the burden from which he had freed himself. How gladly would he bear it if the day's words and deeds could be unsaid and undone!

"For the present," the doctor advised, "let us say nothing about the suicide." He addressed Lucy and Joseph together. "There is no necessity for a *post-mortem* examination. The symptoms and the presence of arsenic in the glass are quite sufficient to establish the cause of death. You know what a foolish idea of disgrace is attached to families here in the country when such a thing happens, and Mr. Asten is not now in a state to bear much more. At least we must save him from painful questions until after the funeral is over."

"What shall I do?" cried Lucy. "Will you not stay until the

man Dennis returns? Mr. Asten's aunt must be fetched immediately."

The doctor and Joseph attended to Julia's body while Lucy sat quietly outside the front door. Fifteen minutes later, Dennis arrived, followed by Philip and Madeline Held.

Lucy approached Dennis. "Take the buggy and fetch Joseph's Aunt from Magnolia. Tell her Miss Julia has died." He hopped to the other rig and rode off. She then escorted Philip and Madeline into the sitting-room.

"Julia died about a half hour ago," Lucy began. A brief smile appeared on Philip's face, but it quickly disappeared.

"You cannot stay here alone," Philip advised. "Madeline must keep you company. I will go to up and take care of Joseph. We must think of both the living and the dead."

No face could have been half so comforting in the chamber of death as Philip's. The physician started at the sight of a Colored Man in the Asten bedroom, but Joseph made the introduction. "Dr. Hartman, this is my closest and dearest friend, Mr. Philip Held. He knows everything." The two strangers shook hands tentatively.

"Dr. Hartman, a pleasure sir, under the circumstances," Philip began. "You may rest assured that I shall see to all further arrangements. On your way back to your home, could you stop by the neighbor's and summon Mrs. Bishop to call? Thank you."

The physician turned to Joseph, who observed a look of shocked surprise upon the good doctor's face. Joseph nodded his complicit agreement, if only to mollify the fellow.

Once the doctor left the room, Philip glanced down at the cold body of Julia. He took Joseph by the arm. "Now, come with me. We will leave this room awhile to Lucy and Madeline. You must not be alone. If I am saying anything to you, Joseph, now is the time when my presence should be some slight comfort. We need not speak, but we will keep together."

Joseph clung the closer to his friend's arm. Without speaking they passed out of the house. Philip led him mechanically toward the garden, but as they drew near the avenue of box-wood-trees, with the recent angry scars, Joseph cried out, "Not there! O, not there!"

Philip turned in silence and conducted him past the barn into the grass-field and mounted the hill toward the pin-oak on its summit. From this point, the house could scarcely be seen behind the fir-trees and the huge weeping-willow, but the fair hills around seemed happy under the tender sky, and the melting, vapory distance, seen through the southern opening of the valley, hinted of still happier landscapes beyond.

As Joseph contemplated the scene, the long strain upon his nerves relaxed. He leaned upon Philip's shoulder and wept passionately.

After a few minutes had passed, Joseph murmured, "If she had not died!"

Philip did not answer.

"Perhaps it is better for me to talk," Joseph continued. "You do not know the whole truth, Philip. You have heard of her madness, but not of my guilt. What was it I said when we last met? I cannot recall it now, but I know that I feared to call my punishment unjust. Since then, I have deserved it all, and more. If I am a child, why should I dare to handle fire? If I do not understand life, why should I dare to set death in motion?"

Joseph related everything that had passed since they parted on the banks of the stream. He repeated the words spoken in the house and in the garden and the last broken sentences that came from Julia's lips. Philip listened with breathless surprise and attention.

When Joseph finished, Philip stared off into the distance for a few minutes. "There is no guilt in accident. It was a crisis which must have come, and you took the only course possible to a man. If she felt that she was defeated, and her mad act was the consequence, think of your fate had she felt herself victorious!"

"It could have been no worse than it was," Joseph answered. "And she might have changed. I did not give her time. I have accused my own mistaken education, but I had no charity, no pity for hers!"

They descended the hill to discover that Mrs. Bishop had arrived, and the startled household got reduced to a kind of dreary order. Dennis arrived with Rachel Miller around dusk. Philip and Madeline departed, taking Lucy Henderson with them.

Rachel cried but remained composed. She said little to her nephew, but her quiet, considerate, and tender manner soothed him more than any words.

The reaction from so much fatigue and excitement almost prostrated Joseph. When he went to sleep in the new guest-room, he felt like a stranger in a strange house. He lay for a long time between sleep and waking, haunted by all the scenes and personages of his past life. His mother's face, so faded in memory, came clear and fresh from the shadows. A boy whom he had loved in his school-days floated with fair, pale features just before he closed his eyes. It had been years since he had last climbed up into the hayloft with Paul. They would kiss and hug, imitating what they had seen the adults do. One day, Paul did not show up for class, and the teacher said that Paul would no longer be coming to school. Joseph never understood why his friend had been taken away.

Around and between them, a web of twilights and moon-lights, and sweet sunny days, each linked to some grief or pleasure of the buried years. It became keen, bitter joy, a fascinating torment, from which he could not escape. The phantoms caught and helplessly ensnared him until late in the night. The strong claim of nature drove them away and left him in a dead, motionless, dreamless slumber.

Philip returned in the morning and devoted the day to assisting with the funeral arrangements, but more importantly standing between Joseph and the awkward, inquisitive sympathy of the neighbors. Joseph's continued weariness favored Philip's exertions, while at the same time it blunted the edge of his own feelings and helped him over that cold, bewildering, dismal period during which a corpse remains lord of the mansion, controlling the lives of its inmates.

Dennis took a message to the telegraph office to inform Julia's parents of the events. They arrived late the next day. Clementina did not accompany them.

Both Blessings dressed in mourning. Mrs. Blessing appeared grave and rigid, while Mr. Blessing seemed flushed and lachrymose. Philip greeted them upon their arrival, and both parents turned their noses upon seeing him. He led them up to the bed-room, where their dead daughter lay.

A while later, they descended the stairs and found Joseph and Philip sitting in the guest-room. "It is so sudden, so shocking!" Mrs. Blessing sobbed. "And Julia always seemed so healthy! What have you done to her, Mr. Asten, that she should be cut off in the bloom of her youth?"

"Eliza!" exclaimed her husband, a handkerchief to his eyes. "Do not say anything which might sound like a reproach to our heart-broken son! There are many foes in the citadel of life. They may be undermining our... our foundations at this very moment!"

"No. You, her father and mother, must hear the truth," Joseph spoke softly. "I would give all I have in the world if I were not obliged to tell it."

Once again, Joseph narrated the sad tale, a painful task at best. The Blessings interrupted many times with their exclamations, questions, and intimations.

At the tale's conclusion, Mrs. Blessing asked with a tone of alarm, "How many persons know of this?"

"Only the physician and three of my friends," Joseph answered.

"They must be silent! It might ruin Clementina's prospects if it were generally known. To lose one daughter and to have the life of another blasted would be too much."

"Eliza," Mr. Blessing cautioned, "we must try to accept whatever is inevitable. Let us not forget that he has lost more than we have." Mrs. Blessing cast her eyes downward, but Joseph sensed her simmering umbrage.

He then attempted to turn the conversation. "Where is –"

"Clementina?" Mr. Blessing predicted. "I knew you would find her absence unaccountable. We instantly forwarded a telegram to Long Branch. Her reply said, 'My grief is great, but it is quite impossible to come.' She did not particularize why it was impossible, and we can only conjecture." He turned to Joseph. "There was a similar case among the De Belsains during the Huguenot times, but we never mention it. For your sake, silence is rigidly imposed upon us, as the preliminary–what shall I call it?... dis-harmony of views?–would probably become a part of the narrative."

"Pray do not speak of that now!" Joseph groaned.

"Pardon me, I will not do so again. Our minds naturally become discursive under the pressure of grief. It is easier for me to talk at such times than to be silent and think. My power of recuperation seems to be spiritual as well as physical. It is congenital, and therefore exposes me to misconception. But we can close over the great abyss of our sorrow and hide it from view in the depth of our natures without dancing on the platform which covers it."

Philip turned his unexpectedly smiling face aside as Mrs. Blessing cautioned, "Really, Benjamin, you are talking heartlessly! Our Julia is dead!"

"I do not mean it so," he said, melting into tears, "but so much has come upon me all at once! If I lose my buoyancy, I shall go to the bottom like a foundered ship! I was never out for the tragic parts of life, but there are characters who smile on the stage and weep behind the scenes. And, you know, the Lord loveth a cheerful giver." He leaned his head upon his arms and wept bitterly.

"O, don't take on so, Benjamin!" Mrs. Blessing managed through her own tears.

"Perhaps we should give Joseph some time to reflect," Philip advised. "I should be happy to give you a tour of the garden. It was one of Julia's favorite places."

Later on, Mr. Blessing visited Joseph. "When you called the other evening, I was worn out, and not competent to grapple with such an unexpected revelation of villainy. I had been as ignorant of Kanuck's real character as you were. Your early information, however, enabled me—through third parties—to secure a partial sale of the stock held by yourself and me at something of a sacrifice. I prefer not to dissociate myself entirely from the enterprise. And while I do not pretend to be more than the merest gyro in geology, I lay awake last night—being, of course, unable to sleep after the shock of the telegram—I sought relief in random scientific fancies." Joseph turned to look at his father-in-law through misty tears. "It occurred to me that since the main Chowder wells are 'spouting,' their source or reservoir must be considerably higher than the surface. Why might not that source be found under the hills of the Amaranth? If so, the Chowder would be tapped at the fountain-head, and the flow of Pactolean grease would be ours!" He produced his infectious grin. "When I return to the city I shall need instantly—after the fearful revelations of to-day—some violently absorbing occupation, and what could be more appropriate? If anything could give repose to Julia's unhappy shade, it would be the knowledge that her faith in the Amaranth was at last justified!" Mr. Blessing rested a hand on Joseph's shoulder. "I do not presume to awaken your confidence. It has been too deeply shaken. All I ask is that I may have the charge of your shares. In this way I would not need to call upon you for the expenditure of another cent—you understand—to rig a jury-mast on the wreck, and, *Deo Volente*, float safely into port!"

Joseph looked up to his father-in-law, his eyes ringed with red. "Why should I refuse to trust you with what is already worthless?" He pulled the papers from his coat pocket and handed them to his father-in-law.

"I will admit even *that*, if you desire. '*Exitus acta probat*,' was Washington's motto, but I don't consider that we have yet reached the *exitus*! Thank you, Joseph. Your question has hardly the air of returning confidence, but I will force myself to consider it as such, and my labor will be to deserve it."

He wrung Joseph's hand, shed a few more tears, placed the stock certificates into his jacket, and left Joseph to his thoughts.

•¶•

The weariest and dreariest day dawned. They would throw the house open to the world. The corpse must be displayed for solemn stares and whispered comments. Below, the preparation of the funeral meats absorbed the interest of half a dozen busy women. The relatives sat together hungering only for the consolations of loneliness and silence. All the talk under their voice uncomfortably fulfilled their presumed solemn duty. Even Nature changed to all eyes, and the mysterious gloom of an eclipse fell from the most unclouded sun.

Neighbors gathered from far and near. Philip substantiated the impression that Julia had died in consequence of a violent convulsive spasm. People later attributed the cause to one whimsical thing or another.

It only seemed fitting to use the remodeled parlor to lay out Julia. The room had been her scheme, and construction had proceeded under her watchful eyes.

The Reverend Mr. Chaffinch made his way, as by right, to the chamber of the mourners. Rachel Miller sought his attention. Mr. and Mrs. Blessing seemed sadly courteous. Joseph strengthened himself to endure with patience what might follow.

After a few introductory words, and a long prayer, the clergyman addressed himself to each, in turn, with questions or remarks that indicated a fierce necessity of resignation.

239

He bent over Joseph. "I feel for you, brother. It is an inscrutable visitation, but I trust you submit in all obedience?"

Joseph bowed silently.

"He has many ways of searching the heart," Mr. Chaffinch continued. "Your one precious comfort must be that *she* believed and that she is now in glory. O, if you would but resolve to follow in her footsteps!" Joseph looked up in surprise. "He shows His love in that He chastens you. It is a stretching out of His hand, a visible offer of acceptance. This on one side, and the lesson of our perishing mortality on the other! Do you not feel your heart awfully and tenderly moved to approach Him?"

Joseph sat, with bowed head, listening to the smooth, unctuous, dismal voice at his ear until tension of his nerves became a positive physical pain. He longed to cry aloud, to spring up and rush away. His heart moved, but not awfully and tenderly. It had been yearning toward the pure Divine Light in which all confusions of the soul are disentangled. Now some opaque foreign substance intervened and drove him back upon himself. He spoke no word nor made no further sign.

Philip took hold of him and guided Joseph for the last conventional look at the stony, sunken face. Aunt Rachel followed directly behind. Joseph felt barely conscious, but he sensed a crowd and murmurs and steadfast faces. Someone whispered, "How dreadfully pale he looks!"

Finally outside, he preferred the welcome air and sunshine. Dennis helped him into the cart, and they followed some gloomy vehicle in which *something*, surely not the Julia whom he knew, rested.

He recalled the last time he felt this numb, during the performance of the marriage ceremony.

The longest day wore out at last, and when night came only Philip sat beside him.

Chapter 20: The Accusation

FOR THE NEXT FEW DAYS, it almost seemed to Joseph that the old order of his existence had been suddenly restored, and the year of his betrothal and marriage had somehow been intercalated into his life simply as a test and trial.

Rachel Miller had returned to her old capacity, but he could not yet see—what might have been plain to any other eyes—that her manner toward him seemed far more respectful and considerate than formerly. The delicate boy that she had raised had become the strengthened man and widower she now observed.

The true knowledge of Julia's demise—taking of her own life—remained a secret known only to Dr. Hartman, Aunt Rachel, Philip, Lucy, and the Blessings. Neighbors had begun to ask questions and make remarks that only made Joseph's task more and more difficult.

Had people taken offense at his reticence? It seemed so. Their manner toward him had certainly changed. Something in the look and voice, an indefinable uneasiness in meeting others, an awkward haste, and lame excuses for his changes. All these things forced themselves upon Joseph's mind.

Only Elwood Withers met him as of old with even a tenderer, though a more delicately veiled, affection. Yet, even in Elwood's face Joseph detected the signs of a grave trouble. Could it be that Elwood had heard some surmise or distorted echo of his words to Lucy in the garden? Could there have been another listener besides Julia?

Joseph realized he could ascribe these doubts to his own disturbed mind, and he decided to banish them from his memory. His new resolutions included staying quietly at home, avoiding the society of men, and growing into a healthier mood.

With his new outlook, he sought Philip, but on reaching the Forge, he found him absent. Madeline received Joseph with a subdued kindness in which he felt her sympathy.

"You do not see much of your neighbors, I think, Mr. Asten?" she asked with a tone indicating a slight embarrassment.

"No. I have no wish to see any but my friends."

"Lucy Henderson has just left us. Philip took her to her father's and was intending to call at your place on his way home. I hope you will not miss him." She smiled, faced a bit downward, and then added, "That is, I want you to see him to-day. I beg you won't take my words as intended for a dismissal."

"Not now, certainly," Joseph responded as he rose from his seat.

Madeline looked both confused and pained. "I know that I spoke awkwardly, but, indeed, I was very anxious. It was also Lucy's wish. We have been talking about you this morning."

"You are very kind, and, yet, I ought to wish you a more cheerful subject." Joseph attempted a smile.

On his ride home, Joseph considered Madeline. Something in her face haunted him. The lightsome spirit had gone from her eyes, and they seemed troubled as if by the pressure of tears, held back by a strong effort. Her assumed calmness at parting appeared to cover a secret anxiety. He had never before seen her bright, free nature so clouded.

Upon returning to his home, Joseph found Philip in conversation with Aunt Rachel, and he observed a worrisome expression on both faces.

After a hearty hug, Philip began, "Joseph, please be seated. Your aunt and I have discovered a situation which you must be informed of immediately."

As Joseph sat, he considered what possible horrible things could befall his broken life now. He glanced at Aunt Rachel, who turned her gaze to Philip.

"Now, please keep in mind that we both want to help you, and some of the things I am about to tell you may be distressing, but do let me complete what I need to say before you interrupt with questions." Joseph nodded tentatively. "There has been outrageous slander circulating around the village. People have been suggesting that you had a hand in Julia's death, and they want to bring a criminal charge against you. I had Elwood conduct some business and ask a few exploratory questions. He confirmed the existence of such rumors."

Joseph wanted to speak out, but he held his tongue, trusting that his friend would address his concerns. He looked over at Aunt Rachel, who sat still and gray like a stone.

"It appears that Julia's words have somehow become known to others. Did she cry out, 'Go away, you have killed me!'?"

Joseph nodded solemnly. Had Lucy Henderson revealed some of the day's events to someone who divulged the private matter into public ears? Had there been another person in the house that day? A lingering workman? How did his dead wife's angry words become common knowledge? No matter the cause, he must deal with the accusation.

"In addition, Dr. Hartman has filed his official statement as to the cause of Julia's death. People now know that she died as the result of poisoning by arsenic."

Again, Joseph nodded. "I believe it better to meet those suspicions before they come to us in a legal form," Philip continued. "One course is clear. If it is possible, we must try to discover not only the cause of Julia's suicide but the place where she procured the poison, and her design in procuring it." He looked to Joseph who sat motionless. "She must have had it already. Miss Rachel"–he turned to Joseph's aunt– "was there any arsenic in the house when Julia came?"

"Not a speck!" she responded. "I never keep it, even for rats."

"Then, if I may ask, I need you to perform a very careful examination of her clothing and effects, even to the merest scrap of paper. A man's good name–a man's life, sometimes–hangs upon a thread, in the most literal sense." He smiled at the wordplay. "There is no doubt that Julia meant to keep a secret, and she must have had a strong reason. However, we have a stronger one now: to discover it."

Joseph and Aunt Rachel nodded their heads.

"There is no alternative," Joseph spoke. "It was a mistake to conceal the cause of her death from the public. It is easy to misunderstand her exclamation, and make my crime out of her madness. I see the whole connection! This suspicion will not stop where it is. I must demand a legal inquiry before the law forces one upon me. If it is not my only method of defense, it is certainly my best!"

"You are right!" Philip exclaimed. "I knew this would be your decision. I said so to Madeline this morning."

Upon hearing this bit of information, Joseph better understood her confused manner. "Did she question it?"

"Neither she nor Lucy Henderson. If you do this, I cannot see how it will terminate without a trial. Lucy may then happen to be an important witness."

Joseph started, "*Must* that be? Has not Lucy been already forced to endure enough for my sake? Is there any other way than that I have proposed? Advise me, Phillip!"

"I see no other." Philip's head shook slightly. "But your necessity is far greater than that for Lucy's endurance. She is a friend, and there can be no sacrifice in so serving you. What are we all good for, if not to serve you in such a strait?"

Joseph smiled at Philip. He realized he could not pursue this course without his friend's assistance. "I would like to spare her, nevertheless. I meant so well towards all my friends, and my friendship seems to bring only disgrace and sorrow."

"Joseph!" Philip exclaimed. "You have saved one friend from more than disgrace and sorrow! I do not know what might have come, but you called me back from the brink of an awful, doubtful eternity! You have given me an infinite loss and an infinite gain. I only ask you, in return, to obey your first true, proud instinct of innocence, and let me, and Lucy, and Elwood, and your good, kind aunt be glad to take its consequences for your sake!"

The two men hugged as Aunt Rachel looked on with curiosity. When they released each other after nearly a minute, Rachel's eyes had grown to the size of dinner platters.

"I cannot help myself," Joseph declared. "My rash impatience and injustice will come to light, and that may be the atonement I owe. If Lucy will spare herself and report me truly, as I must have appeared to her, she will serve me best."

"Leave that now! The first step is what most concerns us. When will you be ready to demand a legal investigation?"

Joseph looked to his aunt, whose face still retained its look of surprise. "At once! To-morrow!"

"Then we will go together to Magnolia. I fear we cannot change the ordinary forms of procedure, and there must be bail for your appearance at the proper time."

Joseph's head dropped. "Already on the footing of a criminal?" he murmured with a sinking heart.

He saw Philip out and returned to find Aunt Rachel still sitting at the table with a pained expression. "Is there something bothering you, aunt?"

Rachel looked up, eyes reddened. "Joseph, please sit down. There is something I must ask of you."

"Of course, dearest Aunt Rachel. I owe my life to you." He sat beside her.

"I believe I saw something to-day that I never witnessed before. There are words, I know, for such things, but I have not wanted to think of them." She looked over at Joseph. "What is the exact nature of your relationship with Mr. Philip Held?"

Joseph swallowed, the lump getting caught inconveniently. "He is my closest friend. He saved my life, and I owe him mine. And now, with this investi–"

"No"–Rachel held up a hand in interruption–"I can see things. Women see things, Joseph. I can tell you are more than friends with Mr. Held. And while he is a dear and wonderful companion, who—as you have said—once saved your life, I am not certain I truly understand the nature of your interactions." Joseph looked at his aunt with an expression of surprise. "Men do not usually hug in the manner I just witnessed. There is something more than friendship between the two of you, something stronger. I can see it, Joseph." Tears began to form in her eyes. "Tell me, please, the true nature of your relationship with Mr. Held."

Joseph found it difficult to hold back his own tears. He had lived for so long with so many secrets, and he made the instant decision to end that practice immediately. "I love Philip," he whispered. Joseph got down on his knees before his aunt and clasped his hands as if in prayer. "Philip gives me the love I need, and I can only hope I have returned such love as he needs."

Both aunt and nephew began crying openly, and Joseph rested his head upon Rachel's lap. With some hesitation, she placed her hand on his back in comfort. "I am a Christian woman, Joseph, and there are some severe words written in the Bible that speak against such love." She patted him slowly.

He looked up with teary eyes. "But attempting to live a lie with Julia was no better. Did not Reverend Chaffinch quote from the same Bible, 'Lying lips are an abomination to the Lord, but those who deal faithfully are His delight'?"

"You would prefer to be faithful to the desire to live your life with a man rather than with a woman?"

"Living my life with a woman was a lie! And I would have lived that lie every day for the rest of my life, if hers had not ended when it did." He began to weep. "I well know that my nature is contrary to most, and I had attempted to keep it to myself, but someone died as a result of my falseness. Therefore, I am resolved to live my life as it is, not as others would have it." He buried his face in his aunt's lap once more.

Several silent moments passed before Rachel spoke again.

"As a Christian, we are instilled with verses from ancient writings selected by our particular clergy to support their particular points of view at one particular point in time for a particular need. However, as a Quaker, we are also instilled with a spirit of independence and encouraged to question our beliefs when new situations arise." She patted him on the back again. "I raised you as best I could in the manner your mother would have wanted, but my love could never be a substitute for a mother's love." She began to well up with tears. "I do believe that you have never judged my love for you, and if you have found such strong and enduring affection with another man–rather than with a woman–that I have no right to judge your love for him."

Joseph looked up with puffy eyes. Rachel smiled down on him.

"This is difficult for me to say, but I truly believe that Philip will be a better person for you than Julia could have ever hoped to have been."

They hugged for a good, long time.

●▼●

Philip arrived the following morning to retrieve Joseph.

"I have taken the liberty of stopping by the Hopetons on my way," Philip informed Joseph.

"I take it they have returned from the sea-shore," Joseph asked.

"Yes! Hale and hearty I found them." Philip smiled. "I explained to Mr. Hopeton–by the vaguest means possible–your predicament, and he offered to post your bail, should that become necessary."

"Thank you, Philip. A truer friend a man never had." Joseph considered describing the interview about their relationship he had with Aunt Rachel the previous evening, but he decided to keep that between himself and his aunt for the time being.

They proceeded to the Constable's office in the county town. The clerk advised that a warrant had already been drafted, and the Constable had intended to serve it to Joseph upon its completion.

Joseph remained at the Constable's office while Philip revisited the Hopetons to retrieve the bail money. Upon his return, they arranged the matter as privately as possible. Philip stated his serious concerns that some people might manifest curiosity or even ill-will toward Joseph should this become public. A fair and unprejudiced judgment could not then be expected.

In a country where the press is so entirely free, and where, owing to the lazy, indifferent habit of thought—or, rather, habit of *no* thought—of the people, the editorial views are accepted without scrutiny, a man's good name or life may depend on the coloring given to his acts by a few individual minds, it is especially necessary to keep the balance even, to offset one statement by another, and prevent a partial presentation of the case from turning the scales in advance. The same phenomena were as likely to present themselves there, before a small public, as in the large cities, where the whole population of the country becomes a more-or-less interested public. The result might hinge, not upon Joseph's personal character as his friends knew it, but upon the political party with which he was affiliated, the church to which he belonged—nay, even upon the accordance of his personal sentiments with the public sentiment of the community in which he lived. If he had dared to defy the latter, asserting the sacred right of his own mind to the largest liberty, he would already be a marked man.

On the ride back to the farm, Joseph said, "I almost wish that no bail had been granted. Since the court doesn't meet for some time, a bit of seclusion would do me no harm. Now I am a suspected person to nearly all whom I may meet."

"It is not agreeable," Philip remarked, "but the discipline

may be useful. The bail terminates when the trial commences, you understand, and you will have a few nights alone, as it is, quite enough, I imagine, to make you satisfied with liberty under suspicion. However, I have one demand to make, Joseph!" He turned to look at his friend. "I have thought over all possibilities of defense. I would like to secure legal assistance for you."

"Why? I have nothing to fear."

Philip put his thoughts in order before speaking. "There are ways and means of a legal proceeding of which you have no knowledge. In the same way, an attorney would have little or no understanding of how to run a farm as well or efficiently as you. I believe, Joseph, it would be in your best interest—and I am suggesting this as your one, true friend—to have the assistance of one trained in the convoluted manners of the quagmire of our court system."

Joseph considered the point and answered, "I shall give it some thought."

As they pulled up to the farmhouse, Aunt Rachel met them at the front. "Come in! Come in, quickly! I have found something that I think might be important."

The three made their way to the sitting-room. Rachel Miller held a neatly-folded piece of paper in her hand. "It took a mighty search, and I thought I never *should* come upon the least bit that we could make anything of, but *this* was in the upper part of a box where she kept her rings and chains and such likes! Take it! It makes me uncomfortable to hold it in my fingers!"

She thrust the paper into Philip's hand.

He examined it and turned up an apothecary's label on the back. It read, "Ziba Linthicum's Drug Store, 77 Main Street, Magnolia." Beneath the name and address someone had written in large letters the word, "Arsenic." Philip's eyebrows jumped at the sight. He unfolded the paper extremely cautiously. A few bits of white dust remained in the creases. "Arsenic!" Philip blurted, "I know it on sight!"

Joseph and Aunt Rachel exchanged glances, and then both turned to look at Philip.

"I shall go back to-morrow. Thank Heaven we have got one clue to the mystery!" He folded the paper and put it in a coat pocket and turned to Rachel Miller. "Please make another and more thorough search. Leave no corner unexplored! I am sure we shall find something more."

"I'd rip up her dresses!" Aunt Rachel stated enthusiastically. "That is, if it would do any good." She nodded. "But perhaps feeling of the lining and the hems might be enough. I'll take every drawer out and move the furniture! But I plan to halt all these activities at night. I'm not generally a-feared, but there is some things, you know, which a body would as gladly not do by dark, with cracks and creaks all around you, which you don't seem to hear at other times."

•▼•

Philip returned late the next afternoon with Lucy Henderson and his sister. Joseph, his aunt, the Helds, and Lucy gathered around the dining table to hear the day's news.

"I found the Linthicum Drug Store on Main Street with no difficulty," Philip started. "I showed Mr. Linthicum the folded paper Miss Rachel found. He took one look and said that it certainly came from his shop and that the word 'Arsenic' had been written in his very hand."

The others looked to each other with surprise.

"When I asked if he might be able to identify the purchaser, Mr. Linthicum brought a volume to the counter and began looking over the names, starting with the most recent entries. He had to go back a few weeks before he came across the word, 'Arsenic.' Imagine my surprise when he spoke the name associated with the purchase, 'Miss Henderson.'"

All eyes turned to Lucy, who sat wide-eyed and pale-faced.

"Did you visit the drug-store?" Philip inquired.

Lucy raised her eyes in thought. "I remember accompanying Julia to Magnolia during Joseph's absence from home. Did Mr. Linthicum provide a day and date?"

Philip rustled in a pocket and provided a scrap of paper. He handed it to Lucy, who looked at what he had written: A date, a time, her name, and "Arsenic."

"Yes, I recall that afternoon. While we traveled to the town together, I paid two or three visits to acquaintances while she did her shopping, as she told me."

"I did ask Mr. Lithicum to recall the appearance of the woman who made the purchase. As he sees so many clients, it was difficult for him to recall anyone specific, but he looked at the date and time again to strengthen his memories. After a moment, he recalled the person claiming to be Miss Henderson wore a veil. He then stated all his other poison customers are known to him. Other specifics were vague, but he remembered the woman dressed all in black with a soft, agreeable voice."

"Julia did wear a black gown with a veil that day. I can see it in my mind!" Lucy cried.

"Just as well. When I pressed Mr. Linthicum further, as to whether there might have been anyone else present who might be able to identify the veiled lady, he recalled an agent from a wholesale city firm—a travelling agent—who had tried to persuade him to order from his house. The memory came to the surface because he remembered the agent stepping aside as the unknown woman approached the counter. He might have seen her face more distinctly because he laughed and said something about a handsome girl putting her lovers out of their misery."

"If that is the case, I am certainly not the mysterious woman—as it were—because my looks could not evoke such a statement," Lucy said with a slight humor.

"Now, Lucy," Madeline confided, "you are a very handsome woman. Isn't she?" The rest of the table nodded in agreement.

"At any rate, Lucy," Philip continued, "I might suggest writing to each of your acquaintances and ask them to refresh their memories as to the exact times of your visits. Such information is tantamount to an alibi as the poison was purchased in your name!"

"Impossible!" Lucy exclaimed.

"Yes, I say, 'impossible!' too," Philip answered. "There is only one explanation. Julia Asten gave your name instead of her own when she purchased it."

"Oh!" Lucy's voice sounded like a hopeless personal protest against the collective falsehood and wickedness of the world.

"I have another chance to reach the truth," Philip acknowledged "I shall find the stranger, the travelling agent, if it obliges me to summon every such agent of every wholesale drug-house in the region! It is at least a positive fortune that we have made this discovery now." He looked at his watch. "There is just time to catch Elwood Withers before he departs for home. I should like to impart a message to him before it is too late." He stood. "If you will excuse me. Madeline?"

She stood and addressed each of the others individually. "It was so nice to see you all again, and I hope the next time will be under happier circumstances. Good-night."

The Helds boarded their cart and rode off. Aunt Rachel went up to the bedroom to search further.

"Joseph," Lucy broke the gray silence that had fallen after Philip and Madeline had departed. "Do you think that it might have been Julia's plan all along to poison *you* and throw the suspicion on *me*?"

Chapter 21: Suspicions & Suppositions

LUCY AND JOSEPH SAT IN STILL SILENCE following the shrewd speculation. They looked at each other, they looked away. The suggestion that Julia might have planned to kill her husband and blame the crime on Lucy hung like a dense, drab fog above the dining table.

"And now by her own death, after all, she accomplishes her chief end!" Lucy speculated.

"It is a hellish tangle"–Joseph concurred–"whichever way I look. But they say the truth will sooner or later put down any amount of lies, and so it must be here. We must get at the truth, the whole truth, and nothing but the truth! Do you not say so, Lucy?"

"Yes!" she answered firmly, looking him in the face.

"And who knows what it may be necessary to say. They may go to work and unravel my life, and yours, and hold up the stuff for everybody to look at." Joseph turned to Lucy. "Well, let them, I say! If there are dark streaks in mine, I guess they'll look tolerably fair beside her black heart that waxed cold." This statement pained him to say–even with its accuracy–and his tears began again.

Lucy stretched out her hand, and Joseph took it.

"I don't know how anyone could mistake you for Mrs. Julia Asten," he said, gazing at Lucy, who cocked her head in reaction to the indictment. "You are at least half a head taller than she was. Your voice is not at all the same. The apothecary will surely notice the difference! Then an alibi can be proved."

"So Philip Held thinks, but if my friends should not remember the exact time... What should I do?" Lucy began to tear up as well.

"Don't ask yourself that question now! It seems to me that the case stands this way: one self-centered woman made a trap, fell into it herself, and took the secret of its making away with her." Joseph squeezed Lucy's hand. "There is nothing more to be invented, and so we hold all that we gain. Who is to lie us out of our truth? I will grant there isn't much to stand on yet, but another step–the least little thing–may give us all the ground we want!"

Joseph's firm and cheery speech made Lucy smile a little. The sound of a carriage approaching broke their silence, and the two went to the door to meet the arriving guests.

Once again, Philip and Madeline Held approached, but this time, they brought Elwood Withers with them. They all sat at the dining table, and Lucy verbalized her speculation of Julia's treacherous plot to murder her husband and throw the suspicion on Lucy herself.

"There is some logic in such a scheme, and–pardon me for saying this, Joseph," Philip stated, "but Miss Julia Blessing Asten had a mind for such schemes."

Joseph nodded. Even though it hurt to hear his friend speak so, he knew the truth of the statement about his deceased wife.

Elwood raised a fist. "Why that connivin' bi–"

"Joseph! Philip!" Aunt Rachel cried out as she descended the stairs holding a scrap of paper. "Look what I found! Mr. Held said every scrap, and it *is* but a scrap, with half a name on it. I found it behind and mostly under the lower drawer in the same jewelry box I found the other paper from the apothecary."

She sat at the table with the others and handed the new clue to Philip. He looked at it, held it up and examined it closer. "There are but a few markings. I can make out an apothecary's symbol and a few letters, most likely the end of the name: '–ers.' Underneath that, I can see 'Sts.'"

"'Behind and mostly under the lower drawer' of her jewel-case," Madeline mused, repeating Rachel Miller's description. "I think I might guess how it came there. She had seen the label, which had probably been forgotten, and then, as she supposed, had snatched it away and destroyed it without noticing that this piece, caught behind the drawer, had been torn off. But there is no evidence–and perhaps none can be had–that the paper contained poison."

"Can you make somethin' outta the letters?" Elwood asked.

Philip handed the piece of paper to his sister, and she looked at it studiously. "The 'Sts.' certainly means 'Streets'–now I see! It is a corner house! This makes the place a little more easy to be identified. If one of us cannot find it, I am sure a detective can." Madeline rose and commenced walking up and down the room, suddenly and unusually excited. "I have a new suspicion. Perhaps I am in too much of a hurry to make conjectures because Philip thinks I have a talent for it– and yet, this grows upon me every minute! I hope... oh, I hope I am right!"

"Yes," Philip said, "let us hope that you are right. If we can simply prove that Julia, and not Lucy, purchased the poison, we shall save both of you!" He smiled at Joseph and Lucy. "But, at the same time, I will try to find this '–ers' who lives in a corner-house."

Aunt Rachel stood. "The hour is late, and I have some victuals that might feed the lot of you. Lucy, Madeline, please assist me in the kitchen."

Joseph, Philip, and Elwood remained at the table. Knowing smiles circulated among them.

·▼·

In the course of the next few days, Joseph returned to the business of working his farm. He and Dennis labored from sunup to sunset in the fields. Aunt Rachel used the time to re-order the house to her ways. Lucy Henderson–who had taken up staying with the Hopetons–and Elwood Withers joined Joseph and his aunt for dinner each evening.

Philip Held had sent a note to explain that he and his sister would be absent as they travelled in search of clues. While

Joseph missed his friend, and longed for the glance of his sympathetic eyes, or even just the touch of his shirt, Philip's absence allowed him to better concentrate on the farm work.

When the neighbors heard that Joseph himself had approached the Constable regarding Julia's death, the general sense of the case changed. Instead of accusing Joseph of complicity in murdering his wife with the assistance of Miss Lucy Henderson and Mr. Philip Held, the concern shifted to Joseph's well-being.

One evening, Madeline and Philip Held appeared at the Asten farm. Joseph ran to greet his friend with a grand hug. He wanted to kiss him, but decided not to do so in the presence of Madeline.

"It is so good to see you, Philip! And you as well, Madeline," he added in afterthought. "What news?"

Philip's beaming face suggested good tidings. "Shall we discuss this with Miss Rachel?"

Joseph looked at Madeline and then back at Philip. "If we postpone the interview until dinner, Lucy and Elwood will be here as well." He escorted the brother and sister to the house. "Aunt Rachel!" he cried out, "there are to be two more guests for dinner."

Rachel Miller met them in the sitting-room. "Philip and Madeline, it is good to have you in our home once more. Well, if you two are going to be joining us for a meal, then, Madeline, may I request your assistance?"

"Of course, Miss Rachel." The two women repaired to the kitchen together.

Philip glanced about nervously. "May we sit, Joseph?"

"Of course. Will you tell me what you have found?"

As they sat in adjacent chairs, Philip smiled and said, "Patience, my friend. I shall reveal all when the entire company is assembled. For now, just know that the intervening time has weighed heavily upon me."

"I am sorry to hear of this, Philip. Is there something I can do to assist in the matter? After all, you have graciously given of your time to assist me in mine." Joseph continued to look upon his handsome friend's glum face.

Philip shifted in the chair. "Here it is, Joseph. I have come to the realization that... well... I'm not certain how to say this..." Joseph observed his friend's uneasiness but did not speak. Philip looked directly at Joseph, his deep green eyes fully open. "Mr. Joseph Asten, I love you. I thought of nothing but you these last few days, and being apart has shown me where my true feelings lie." He looked away, a tear in one eye.

Joseph reached over and placed a hand on Philip's cheek, "And I love you, Mr. Philip Held." They both smiled. "You have saved my life once and again, and, if my sense of the matter is correct, you are about to do so one additional time. My life has truly been in your competent hands, and I do not wish to alter that fact."

They turned to each other and clasped hands just as Aunt Rachel walked into the room. Upon seeing his aunt, Joseph let go of Philip abruptly.

"Joseph Asten! How dare you conduct yourself like that in my presence!" Joseph's face began to flush. "As long as I live, I never want to see this kind of behavior again!" She stared at her nephew with a fiery glare. "You take that man's hands at once!"

Both Joseph and Philip started at this command. They looked at each other, then at Rachel Miller.

"Yes! Take his hands," she ordered. "Mr. Philip Held has been your very best of friends, if not the sole reason you are still among us, and I never want to see you act so disrespectfully towards him again!"

The men stood, walked to Rachel and hugged and kissed her simultaneously.

When Lucy and Elwood arrived, they all sat around the dining table to take the evening meal together.

"Well, Philip," Joseph began, "I have been waiting anxiously to hear what you might have discovered in your absence."

All eyes turned to Philip, and, after a few bites of food for sustenance, he started his narration. "First, I returned to visit with Mr. Linthicum to ask if he knew the travelling agent who had been in the shop the day Miss Julia purchased the poison. He gave me the gentleman's card–a Mr. Case, by the way–and I sought him out to ask if he remembered the day in question. He replied that he retained a very clear memory of all his business transactions, and that day was no exception. Following that, I went to the city to look for an apothecary that matched the bit of paper that Miss Rachel found in Miss Julia's effects. After a bit of searching, I found Wallis & Erkers at the corner of Fifth and Persimmon Streets." He paused to take a sip of tea. "Inside, I showed the scrap of paper to the druggist–Mr. Erkers–who assured me it did, in fact, come from their store. I asked if they happened to dispense arsenic, and he stated their emporium carries all manners of powders and potions germane to the apothecary business." Several people nodded at this. "While he could supply no other information regarding the scrap, Mr. Erkers informed me that they had recently adopted a new masthead for their forms, which meant this scrap is from at least one year ago."

People looked from one to the other, but Rachel asked the question, "So what does that mean for Joseph?"

"Yes"–Elwood joined in–"how does that help our Joseph?"

Philip nodded. "Perhaps I should let Madeline relate this next part of the story as it was her deduction that led to a result." He glanced at his sister.

"Years ago," Madeline began, "while I worked myself through the academy, one of the ladies I attended looked much younger than her husband. She had long, curly blonde hair that framed her pale, pink face." She moved her hands around her own face in imitation. "One day, while cleaning her dressing-table, I saw a jar marked, 'A.' Inside was a fine powder. She walked in just as I picked up the container. 'Put that down, girl!' she screamed, 'That is not for darkies like you!' 'What is it, ma'am?' I asked. She grabbed the jar out of my hands and put it back on her table. 'Arsenic!' she spat, 'and if you don't keep your Black hands off of things that do not belong to you, I might just put some of it your next meal!'"

Again, people around the table looked at each other in surprise.

"The next day," Madeline continued, "I asked a school friend who studied chemistry why the lady would have such a thing, and she told me that some women use small doses of a specific dehydration operation of arsenic to maintain their complexions. However, it only works on blondes."

"But Julia had dark hair!" Joseph interjected.

"Quite correct," Philip remarked. "With that knowledge, I called upon the Blessings to inquire into the practices of the ladies there. Mrs. Blessing did not wish to reveal her secrets at first, but I stressed the importance of the information in dismissing Joseph of the alleged guilt. With much reluctance, she confessed that she had used the powder in the past—purchasing it from none other than Wallis & Erkers—and she had suggested it to Clementina as well. After Julia met Joseph, she asked to begin taking the same treatment, but Mrs. Blessing forbade it because Julia's complexion did not match the suggested profile for its use."

"Are you telling us that certain women will take small bits of rat poison to maintain a younger-looking complexion?" Rachel Miller asked with incredulity.

"It boggles my mind as well, Miss Rachel," Madeline concurred. "But in my limited experience, there are ladies who would risk and sacrifice their own health for the maintenance or improvement of their youthful appearance."

"That might help to explain her pallid and childlike face. But how, then, did Julia obtain arsenic while still living with her parents?" Joseph inquired.

"That is where a bit of conjecture is required," Philip responded. "Miss Clementina is currently on the Continent with her new husband on their honeymoon. However, I am quite confident that she procured some extra powder–from Wallis & Erkers, of course–and gave it to her sister. That explains the scrap Miss Rachel found in the jewelry box."

Lucy spoke up. "And you mean to say that when Julia exhausted what Clementina had given her, she exploited my friendship, travelled to Magnolia in order to purchase her own supply of arsenic–at Mr. Linthicum's apothecary–and gave my name instead of her own."

"That is my current theory," Philip asserted. "Her death came at her own hands from careless use of the Arsenic powder. An accidental self-poisoning, you might say." He turned to Joseph. "Do you have a photograph of Julia that we might use, if necessary?"

"Of course. We have several wedding photographs," Joseph stated.

"But do you have any of her by herself?"

"I believe I might be of assistance here," Aunt Rachel said. "I came across a likeness in one of her boxes. I imagine she had it taken before she ever met my dear, sweet Joseph, but she still looked the same, even years later."

"Then I believe I wish to propose our next step," Philip spoke, and everyone turned to him. "Given the intelligence we have gathered, I would like to approach the Constable and ask for a hearing on the matter. We could present the various witnesses and information that we have, and he might determine that there would be no need for a trial."

Smiles spread around the table.

Joseph stood, holding his glass. "To you, Philip. You have once again saved my life."

"And to my sister Madeline," Philip proposed, "for without her I would never have understood the use of the arsenic powder."

The party toasted to both the Helds, the health of Joseph, and the longevity of Rachel Miller.

As the guests began to leave, Rachel took her nephew aside. "Joseph, I believe it might be best for you to accompany the Helds back to their cottage."

"But Aunt Rachel, there is much to be done around the farm," Joseph protested.

"I'm sure that Dennis and I can take care of things for a day or two." She smiled. "Now, run upstairs and grab your bag. I do not want to see you back here for a while." Joseph stood awestruck. "Git! I told you to go!" she pointed.

Joseph approached Philip. "My aunt just suggested that I spend a few days with you at your cottage. Do you have any objections to an uninvited guest?"

Philip merely closed his eyes and smiled.

•▼•

The morning following, Philip and Joseph drove to Magnolia to consult with the Constable regarding the impending case. As it turned out, the circuit judge scheduled to preside at the trial had already planned to be in town the following week in order to familiarize himself with the facts of the case. Philip requested a preliminary hearing be granted so that he could present the unfolding facts and persuade the judge of Joseph's innocence. The Clerk scheduled a day and time for such a hearing, to be conducted behind closed doors.

From the courthouse, they proceeded to the Magnolia Blossom Hotel to procure rooms for the prospective witnesses. Following that, they visited Linthicum's Apothecary to invite Mr. Linthicum to the hearing and to determine the whereabouts of Mr. Case so that they could invite him as well.

Philip and Joseph rode the train to the city the next day to persuade the Blessings to travel to Magnolia for their highly-significant testimony regarding their daughters' use of arsenic powder as a beauty aid.

Once Joseph and Philip returned home, they approached Dr. Hartman, who readily agreed to assist as needed. Philip instructed Lucy to contact her acquaintances in Magnolia expeditiously so that she could account for her time during that ill-omened day she had travelled with Julia.

When two people have a common interest of vital importance that calls upon their utmost cooperation, deeper feelings of appreciation and devotion develop between them. During the time Philip prepared for the upcoming hearing, he and Joseph grew closer than they had ever been before, and Joseph began to feel that he never wanted to be separated from Philip ever again.

•▼•

Joseph had to decline many offers of support from his neighbors who wished to attend the hearing to testify in his support, providing witness of character. As comforting as the offers might have been, he believed that many of these people had made themselves available more as a way to be present at the spectacle rather than to provide any supportive evidence.

On the appointed day, a party of strangers, friends, and relatives descended upon the courthouse, each to present their individual thread of a tapestry that might grant Joseph his innocence. The sartorial leader, Philip, stepped forward to present his evidence to save the life—once again—of the man he loved.

Chapter 22: The Truth of the Matter

ONCE ALL THE PARTIES HAD BEEN SEATED, the Bailiff strode to the front of the room, stood before the judge's bench and shouted, "Oyez, Oyez, Oyez! All manner of persons having ought to do before the honorable, the judge of the court of common pleas in and for the State of Pennsylvania, here holden this day, will now draw near, their attention give and they shall be heard. God save the commonwealth and this honorable court."

From a door behind the bench, a wiry middle-aged man with a severely-receding hairline appeared. The assembled group stood in deference to the jurist. He wore a black robe and Oxford-style pince-nez spectacles. He climbed the stair and took his seat.

"Honorable Judge Maynard Q. Sterrett, presiding! You may be seated."

"Thank you, Bailiff." The judge spoke with a nasal voice. Perhaps the spectacles pinched his nose too much. After shuffling some papers and glancing at a few of them, he addressed the visitors. "We are here today to hear statements regarding the pending case, *Commonwealth of Pennsylvania v. Asten*. Who speaks for the Defendant?"

"I do, your honor," Philip rose to address the bench. "Mr. Philip Held."

"This was supposed to be a closed hearing, Mr. Held. Are all of these people here to testify?" Judge Sterrett asked.

"Yes, your honor."

"Bailiff, swear in the room as one."

The Bailiff stood before the party and performed the swearing in, admonishing all present to speak the truth, the whole truth, and nothing but the truth.

"Mr. Held," the judge resumed, "are you an attorney before the Bar? I do not see your name on the register."

"No, your honor. I am not learned in the ways of the law, but I am acting on behalf of Mr. Asten as these matters are fairly straightforward, apparent, and obvious."

"I believe that is for me to determine, Mr. Held," the judge stated with a twang. "Do you have pertinent evidence and testimony to present before me?"

"Yes, your honor, I do."

"Pray proceed, Mr. Held." Judge Sterrett relaxed in his high-backed, padded leather chair.

"Dr. Hartman, if you please." The doctor rose. "Could you testify as to the cause of Mrs. Asten's death?"

"Of course." Dr. Hartman retrieved a slip of paper from his jacket pocket. "The day of Mrs. Asten's death, I was summoned from my home by Mr. Asten to attend his wife, who had suffered some sort of hysterical collapse. Upon examining her, I could not immediately determine any cause for the unconscious state or the excitement she had demonstrated. However, after searching her dressing-table, I found a small drinking glass hidden behind the mirror. It had a powdery residue, which I determined to be arsenic. Given the symptoms of the deceased, and the proximity of the empty glass, I found no need for a *post-mortem* examination, and I determined her cause of death to be poisoning by arsenic."

"Dr. Hartman," the judge addressed the physician. "Did you witness the deceased drinking from the glass you found?"

"No, sir."

The judge addressed the audience. "Did anyone here observe Mrs. Asten drinking from the aforementioned glass?" No one responded to the question. "Was anyone in the same room as the deceased with you, doctor?"

The physician searched his memory. "As far as I can recall, the only two people in the room with me were Mr. Asten, of course, and that young lady there." He pointed at Lucy Henderson.

"Thank you, doctor, that will be all." Judge Sterrett pointed at Lucy. "You, young lady, what is your name?"

"Miss Lucy Henderson, your honor." She stood.

"Were you in attendance at the time of Mrs. Asten's demise?"

"Yes, your honor. I had been staying at the Asten home as a guest."

"I see. Could you please tell me, as best as you can—and I remind you that you are under an oath to tell the truth—the order of events?"

"Of course. I had been visiting with Julia—Mrs. Asten—when Joseph—Mr. Asten—returned home. They had some angry words I could hear from my room, and Mr. Asten left the house to go to the garden. I followed soon thereafter—at Mrs. Blessing's instruction. She hid behind some shrubs and overheard our conversation. It upset her very much. She went back to the house, and we followed. When we got to the stairs, she... she..."

"The whole truth, Miss Henderson," the judge prompted. "I have heard the rumors, but I would rather have the pleasure of your eye-witness account."

Lucy nodded and held back some tears. "Mrs. Asten screamed 'Go away! You have killed me!'" She hid her face in her hands and turned away. "I'm sorry, Joseph."

"That's fine, Lucy. The truth will out," Joseph said from his seat.

"And then, Miss Henderson?"

"She collapsed and we took her to the bed. I suggested Mr. Asten seek medical assistance, and he left to fetch the doctor."

The judge's eyebrows moved up. "And, if I understand the situation rightly, you were alone in the house with Mrs. Asten while Mr. Asten went out?"

"Yes, your honor."

"And approximately how long was that period?"

Lucy thought back. Joseph did not return immediately as he had to go to the distant house of Dr. Hartman. "Approximately two hours, your honor."

"Two hours, you say?" Judge Sterrett wrinkled his nose and the pince-nez bounced up and down. "Then you were by yourself with an unconscious woman for a matter of time. If I have read the accompanying documents correctly, it appears that a supply of arsenic had been sold to a 'Miss Henderson' from an apothecary in Magnolia. How can we be sure that you did not poison Mrs. Asten yourself and attempt to blame the death on Mr. Asten?" He pointed to Joseph.

Lucy shrieked. "Oh, no!"

"Your honor," Philip approached the bench. "If I might be able to have a few other people testify, I can establish that Miss Henderson did not purchase the arsenic, and that it was procured by Mrs. Julia Asten herself."

"Well... that complicates matters..." the judge mused. "Pray proceed, Mr. Held."

Philip turned to Lucy and motioned for her to sit down. "Mr. Ziba Linthicum, please." The apothecary stood. "Mr. Linthicum, please explain to the bench the events of the day when the arsenic in question was purchased."

"Of course," Mr. Linthicum began. "Your honor, my apothecary emporium is located here in Magnolia on Main Street, and –"

"Yes, Mr. Linthicum"–the judge interrupted–"I have some familiarity with your establishment as it is where my own wife procures her various powders and potions."

"Very good, sir," the apothecary demurred. "On the day in question, a woman in a black dress and veil purchased a quantity of arsenic from me." He held up his ledger book and opened it to the page he had marked. "I asked the woman her name, and she told me, 'Miss Henderson.' Now, your honor, it is required by the Commonwealth of Pennsylvania that I record any purchase of potentially-dangerous or poisonous substances. Because I have been in business for many years,

I know all of my regular customers personally, but this woman I had never encountered before, and, because of the veil, I could not identify her by sight."

"Thank you, Mr. Linthicum. That does complicate matters." Judge Sterrett turned to Lucy. "Miss Henderson, do you own such an ensemble, a black dress and veil?"

Lucy still wept from the anxiety of having to provide testimony against Joseph. "No, your honor, I do not."

Judge Sterrett turned to Philip. "Mr. Held, while your amateur detective work is rather impressive so far, please explain to me how you knew for certain that Mrs. Blessing patronized Mr. Linthicum's establishment in the first place? Had she told you or anyone of the assembled mass here?" He looked at the faces confronting him.

"No, your honor. It was Mr. Asten's aunt, Miss Rachel Miller, who discovered a slip of paper bearing Mr. Linthicum's shop information among the deceased's belongings while preparing for their disposal." He pulled it from a pocket and handed it to the judge.

"I see. How convenient. A mere slip of paper appears in the hands of the defendant's aunt at a crucial moment." He examined the evidence briefly and then searched the crowd, pausing at Joseph's aunt. "Are you Miss Rachel Miller, aunt of Mr. Joseph Asten?"

"Yes, your honor." She stood and curtseyed the way her mother had taught her.

"Do you make your home with your nephew and his wife?"

"No, sir," she responded, "I left the farm once Mrs. Asten had a complete understanding of the ways. It was long before she and Miss Lucy Henderson made the trip to Magnolia."

"Of course, Miss Miller. I did not meet to impugn you. And where did you take up residence during this time?"

"Magnolia, your honor"–Aunt Rachel spoke softly–"with a cousin."

"Magnolia! Again, a convenience." He turned to the pharmacist. "Mr. Linthicum, have you seen this scrap of paper with your particulars upon it?"

"Yes, your honor. Mr. Held brought it to my shop shortly after the death of Mrs. Asten and asked if it was from my apothecary. The imprint certainly indicated it, and I had written the word 'Arsenic' upon it myself."

"So very convenient, but how do we know that it was not Miss Miller, herself, who donned the black dress and veil?"

"Your honor, the next person may be able to shed some light on this matter," Philip stated. The judge nodded. Mr. Linthicum sat down. "Mr. Augustus Fitzwilliam Case, please stand."

A tall, thin, young man stood. The elegance of his posture matched his elegant suit. "I am Augustus Fitzwilliam Case."

"Mr. Case," Philip continued, "could you please give us your account of the day in question at Mr. Linthicum's store."

"Of course." He turned to the judge. "Your honor." He bowed slightly. "I am employed as a travelling agent for the house of Byle and Glanders, a quality wholesale druggist. From time-to-time, I travel through your beautiful landscape in search of new clients. On the day in question, I happened to be discussing business with Mr. Linthicum when a woman in a dark dress and veil entered his shop. I am impressible to beauty, and I saw at once that the lady had what I call 'style.' I recollect thinking, 'More style than could be expected in these little places.'"

Some of the people laughed, but Judge Sterrett did not seem amused by the opinion. "Keep your thoughts to yourself, Mr. Case. Describe the lady as correctly as you can."

"Yes, your honor." He shot his cuffs and stretched his neck. "Something under the medium size. A little thin, but not bad lines, what I should call jimp, natty or lissome. A well-trained voice, no uncertainty about it. Altogether about as keen and wide-awake a woman as you'll find in a day's travel."

"And you guessed this all from her figure?" the judge inquired.

"Oh, no, your honor. Not entirely. I saw her face. While Mr. Linthicum was weighing the arsenic, she leaned over the counter, and her veil fell forward slightly. I also bent forward–as if to examine the soaps–and I had what a photographer would call a three-quarter view."

"Can you remember her features distinctly, Mr. Case?"

"Quite so. In fact, it is difficult for me to forget a female face. Hers was just verging on the sharp, but still tolerably handsome. Hair quite dark and worn in ringlets. Eyebrows clean and straight. Mouth a little too thin for my fancy, and eyes– well, I couldn't undertake to say exactly what color they were for she seemed to have the trick of letting the lids droop over them."

The judge sat up straight in his chair. "Mr. Case, I must say you have quite a remarkable memory. Is this your standard method of operations?"

"Yes, sir. I am cursed with total recall, your honor. Give me a date and I will tell you what day of the week, the weather, and phase of the moon."

Judge Sterrett shuffled through his desk calendar. "March 31st of this year."

Mr. Case fluttered his eyes and tilted his head. Then he faced the judge directly. "'Twas a Tuesday, the moon was waxing, half-full. As far as the weather, I was in Iowa, and –"

"That is quite sufficient, Mr. Case. You have demonstrated an incredible display of your memory. Were you able to judge the lady's age at all?"

"Tolerably, I should say. There is a certain air of preservation which enables a practiced eye to distinguish an old girl from a young one. She was certainly not to be called young. Somewhere between 28 and 35, I would venture."

"And did you hear the name she gave Mr. Linthicum?"

Mr. Case glanced back at Lucy and then returned to face the judge. "Distinctly. At first, she hesitated to provide a name, but Mr. Linthicum politely stated that it was his custom to register the names of all those to whom he furnished either poisons or prescriptions requiring care in being administered. She said, 'You are *very* particular, sir,' and after a pause she muttered to herself, 'What name then?' She hesitated once more, then stated with certainty, 'Miss Henderson.' She took the packet and went out of the store with a light, brisk step."

"And was the lady in question this Miss Henderson?" The judge indicated Lucy.

"No, your honor. Not at all. This lady here has not the slightest resemblance to the Miss Henderson I saw that day. She is younger, taller, and modelled upon a wholly different style."

"Would you be able to recognize the lady if you saw her again?"

"Quite sure." Mr. Case smiled patronizingly, as if the question were superfluous.

Philip approached Joseph's aunt. "Miss Rachel, may I have the photograph." She reached into her bag and retrieved a small cardboard, which she handed to Philip. He turned to Mr. Case. "Sir, do you recognize the woman in this photograph?"

Mr. Case barely glanced at the picture before blurting out, "Yes! That is the woman. I am quite sure. And she is in three-quarter face, as I saw her."

Philip approached the bench. "Your honor, this is a photograph of Julia Blessing Asten, the deceased." He handed the likeness to the judge.

"Yes, I see that. Mr. Case, you have positively identified the deceased as the person who procured the arsenic from Mr. Linthicum's apothecary shop in Magnolia on the date in question."

"I suppose so, your honor." He bowed slightly.

"Thank you, Mr. Case," Philip acknowledged. "Your honor, Miss Lucy Henderson also has details of her whereabouts that day as she was visiting acquaintances in Magnolia at the same time Mrs. Asten was in the apothecary. Do you wish to see that intelligence?"

Judge Sterrett held up an open hand. "That will not be necessary, Mr. Held. I think we have established, quite well enough, that Mrs. Asten, the deceased, purchased the arsenic herself. However, that still does not explain why she should have taken the very poison she had obtained. Can you describe how a young woman drinks a solution of arsenic and then accuses her husband of killing her?"

"I think I can address that now, your honor." Philip turned to Julia's mother. "Mrs. Eliza Blessing, will you please stand."

"You are the mother of the deceased?" the judge asked.

Mrs. Blessing pulled a handkerchief from a pocket and dabbed at her eyes. "Yes, your honor."

"My condolences, ma'am. I am sorry to have to put you through this questioning, but Mr. Held believes you have pertinent knowledge on this subject."

Mrs. Blessing nodded and sniffled.

"I know this is difficult for you, but can you explain to the judge how the arsenic preparation is used?" Philip prompted.

She dabbed at her eyes a few more times before proceeding. "Your honor, it is a well-kept secret amongst ladies of a certain social circle that a very specific operation of arsenic can be used—in small does, mind you—to maintain one's youthful appearance. It is a small miracle, indeed. Once I attained a certain age, my own mother introduced me to this magic powder, and I myself took recurrent doses until I reached another certain age, when I realized it had done all it could."

She wiped a few more tears away. "When my eldest daughter, Clementina—who could not be here today because she is on her honeymoon abroad—reached that age, I introduced her to Mr. Erkers, of Wallis & Erkers, back in the city, at the corner of Fifth and Persimmon Streets. They provided my daughter with her own supply of the drug. However, when my youngest, Julia," she broke down and cried. Mr. Blessing stood and comforted her. "Thank you, Benjamin. I can go on now." He sat. "Upon meeting Mr. Asten, Julia wished to begin the physic treatment as well, but I told her it would not work for girls of her complexion. It is my belief that her sister, Clementina, supplied Julia with some of the drug, which she then used without proper supervision."

"Your honor," Philip intervened. "We have a scrap of paper from the Wallis & Erkers store that was found among the deceased's belongings." He held it up and the judge nodded.

"That must have been from the supply that Clementina gave her." Mrs. Blessing began tearing up again.

"Thank you, Mrs. Blessing. Please be seated," Philip instructed. He approached the bench. "Your honor, it is my belief that the deceased, Mrs. Julia Asten, purchased the lethal dose of arsenic from Mr. Linthicum using the good name of Miss Lucy Henderson to remove any suspicion of her scheme. As she had no medical training in the proper use of the preparation, it is possible that she might have ingested more of the substance than her body could tolerate. While, at first, we suspected a suicide, we now believe that Mrs. Asten consumed a lethal quantity of arsenic and caused her own death—by her own hand—but as an accident, not intentionally."

The judge leaned back in his chair and held up a few papers from his desk. Only the tick-tick of the clock at the back of the courtroom broke through the hazy silence in the darkly-paneled room. "You have quite adequately demonstrated that Mrs. Asten herself purchased the poison—using the name of an innocent acquaintance—and that her death came from an overdose of arsenic; however, I am not certain that the lethal dose had been delivered by her own hand." He scoured the faces of the party before him. "Can you address this inadequacy of your case, Mr. Held?"

Philip looked down at the floor. "Only the direct testimony of Miss Henderson and Mr. Asten stating they had no prior knowledge of the poison being in the home would accomplish that, your honor."

Judge Sterrett sat in thought a moment. "Mr. Asten, did you have knowledge of the arsenic in possession by your wife? Please remember that you are under an oath to tell the full truth."

"No, your honor, I did not."

"Miss Lucy Henderson," the judge called, "did you have prior knowledge of the use of arsenic as a beauty aid?"

"No, your honor."

"And did you have knowledge of the arsenic in the Asten home prior the doctor's assessment? And may I remind you that you are still under the same oath."

"No, your honor. No, sir, not at all."

Judge Sterrett bolted upright, causing his chair to scrape noisily against the floor. "Dr. Hartman," he called out, and the physician stood. "Does the account that Mr. Held delivered correspond with your findings of this particular case?"

"Yes, your honor. The state of the dead woman's body, and the behavior exhibited shortly before her death clearly indicate the classic symptoms of poisoning by arsenic. That is what I indicated on the certificate of her death, and I stand by my assessments."

"And you found no indications of a fight or rough handling? No bruising, no reddened skin?" the Judge inquired.

"No, your honor."

Once again, the judge shuffled through some of the papers in front of him. The tick-tick from the clock seemed even louder than before. "Mr. Asten, Mr. Held, approach the bench."

Joseph and Philip stepped forward. "As there is no evidence to prove that anyone else knew about the arsenic in the Asten home, and there were no marks on the body indicating foul play, it appears that Mrs. Asten must have administered the lethal dose herself, whether by commission or accidentally, we cannot determine. That being said, I have no reason to hold you over for trial. Bailiff, return the bail money to the defendant. Mr. Asten is free." He stood and stepped down.

"Thank you, your honor," Joseph and Philip said simultaneously. They turned to one another, and Joseph considered whether to kiss him in front of the assembled guests, but he settled for a warm hug. "Thank you, my love," he whispered in Philip's ear.

The group cheered as one, and Mr. Blessing declared, "Dinner for everyone at the hotel on me!" He bowed repeatedly, as if he had just given a virtuoso performance.

Philip led the small throng out into the open air, and the others followed. Soon, the entire party stood in the large parlor of the Magnolia Blossom Hotel.

Mr. Blessing sought out the *maître d'hôtel*, and his hands flew about during a mumbled conversation. Joseph and Philip accepted the greetings and blessings of the others.

"This way, everyone!" Mr. Blessing announced. He waved an arm in the direction of a banquet room, where a table had been set for a reception.

As the assembled guests found seats, two waiters entered the room bearing carts with wine, ice, and other refreshments. After all present had received a beverage, Mr. Blessing lifted his with an air that imposed silence on the company.

"'Out of the abundance of the heart, the mouth speaketh.'" He toasted. "There may be occasions when silence is golden, but to-day we are content with the baser metal." He chuckled at his *bon mot*. "A man whom we all confide, whom we all love, has been rescued from the labyrinth of circumstances. He comes to us as a new Theseus, saved from the Minotaur of the Law! Although Mr. Held, with the assistance of his fair sister Madeline, acted in the place of Ariadne, who found the vital clue, it has been our happy lot to assist in unrolling it. And now we all stand together–or sit, as you may–like our classic models on the free soil of Crete to chant a pæan of deliverance." He turned to his son-in-law. "While I propose the health and happiness and good-fortune of Joseph Asten, I beg him to believe that my words come *ab imo pectore*– from my inmost heart. If any veil of mistrust, engendered by circumstance which I will not now recall, still hangs between him and myself, I entreat him to rend that veil, even as David rent his garments, and believe in my sincerity, if he cannot in my discretion!"

"Spoken like a man!" Philip shouted.

"I have again been unjust," Joseph spoke, "and I thank you for making me feel it. You have done me an infinite service, sacrificing your own feelings, bearing no malice against me for my hasty and unpardonable words, and showing a confidence in my character which–after what has passed between us–puts me to shame. I am both penitent and grateful. Henceforth, I shall know you and esteem you!"

Mr. Blessing stammered through tears that had started from his eyes, "Enough! Bury the past a thousand fathoms deep! I can still say: *Foi de Belsain!*"

The company drank, and the waiters refilled the glasses.

"And while I'm still standing"–Mr. Blessing resumed–"I believe it only fitting to raise our glasses in honor of the departed, our dear daughter, Julia. She was a rosebud–for she surely had her thorns"–he smiled at Joseph–"but a lovelier beauty–with the exception of my wife, her mother, of course–never trod upon this green globe!"

"Here, here!" the party cheered.

"One more toast!" Philip proposed. "Happiness and worldly fortune to the man whom misfortunes have bent but cannot break, who has been often deceived but who never purposely deceived in turn, whose sentiment of honor has been to-day so nobly manifested"–he turned to Mr. Blessing–"Benjamin

Blessing!"

Again the company drank. The waiters returned, but with trays of food. An hour passed as people ate, drank, and put their pasts behind them.

·▼·

In the morning, the guests parted company after a light breakfast. Joseph approached Mr. and Mrs. Blessing to invite them to stay a few days at the farm.

Mr. Blessing answered, "Will you allow me to postpone, not relinquish, the pleasure? Thanks! A grave duty beckons, a task in short, without which the triumph of yesterday would be dramatically incomplete. I must speak in riddles because this is a case with some expectations of financial reward in which a whisper might start the overhanging avalanche, but I am sure you will trust me."

"Of course! After all you have done for me." The two shook hands vigorously.

"*Foi de Belsain!*" Mr. Blessing answered as he and his wife headed to the train station.

Joseph stood looking at the handsome figure of Philip Held, who had brought the horses from the stable. Rachel Miller, wrapped in her great crêpe shawl, stood nearby.

"We must not separate all at once," said Philip. "Miss Miller, will you invite my sister and myself to take tea with you this evening?"

She smiled warmly at him. "You are always a welcome guest, as is your sister. I hope you do not mind if I consider you both part of our family."

A tear appeared in Philip's eye. "Miss Rachel, you are much more than gracious allowing my sister and myself into your heart like this. We are not accustomed to such open treatment by –"

"Hush, now!" Rachel Miller tutted. She took one of his bare hands and patted it. "Family is family." She climbed up onto the cart.

"Good-bye, my love," Joseph whispered into Philip's warm ear. "I look forward to seeing you later."

As they drove out of town, Rachel asked of Joseph, "Do tell me the time o' day. It's three days in one to me, and a deal more like day after to-morrow morning than this afternoon. Now, a telegraph would be a convenience. I could send word and have chickens killed and picked, against we got there."

Joseph answered by driving as rapidly as the rough country roads permitted without endangering horse or vehicle. He could hardly think coherently, impossible to thrust back the single overwhelming prospect of relief and release that had burst upon his life. The future lay before him clear once more, and even the miserable discord of the past year began to recede and form only an indistinct background to the infinite pity of the death-scene. Mr. Blessing's toast enabled him to look back and truly interpret the last appealing looks, the last broken words. His heart banished the remembrance of its accusations and retained only a deep and tender commiseration. As for the danger he had escaped, the slander that he endured, his thoughts lifted above the level of life that they touched. He sensed the true independence of soul that releases a man from the yoke of circumstances.

"Yes!" exclaimed Aunt Rachel after a while, "there's a little of the old currant wine in the cellar-chest! Town's-folk generally like it, and we used to think it good to stay a body's stomach for a late meal, as it'll be apt to be. But I've not asked you how you relished the supper, though Elwood, to be sure, allowed that all was tolerable nice. And I see the Lord's hand in it, as I hope you do, Joseph. For the righteous is never forsaken. We can't help rejoice where we ought to be humbly returning thanks and owning our unworthiness. Philip Held is a friend, if there ever was one, and the white hen's brood, though they are new-fashioned fowls, are plump enough by this time. I disremember whether I asked Elwood to stop —"

"There he is!" Joseph interrupted, "turning the corner of the wood before us. Lucy is with him, and they must both come!"

He drove on rapidly and soon overtook Elwood's lagging team. The horse, indeed, had his own way, and the sound of approaching wheels awoke Elwood from a hypnotic trance.

When they reached the Asten farm, Dennis waited with a glowing face, holding the gate to the lane open. He appeared to want to say something to Joseph, but he just thrust his hand up and shook heartily. Then he turned to care for the harnesses.

In the kitchen, Aunt Rachel found the neighbor, Mrs. Bishop, standing with a stew-pan. "Mr. Bishop returned about an hour ago with the good news. I figured there might be company coming to celebrate, and I thought it would be a help to set things commencing." She put down the pan and gave Rachel a big hug. "You may not feel inclined for victuals, but there's the danger!" They smiled at each other through tears of joy.

After the meal, friends and neighbors sat on the veranda in the still, mild air. Joseph drew his chair next to Philip's, and they touched fingers. Their smiles, which caressed each other, demonstrated the happiness in the tender and perfect man-love that united them.

Madeline sat with Lucy gossiping. No one knew how the time went by or could recall much that had been said. When the moon hung chill and clear above the creeping mists of the valley, the guests departed.

Chapter 23: Concluding Affairs

JOSEPH WOKE THE NEXT MORNING with the desire to depart from the walls where ghosts of his former life dwelled. He wanted to breathe another atmosphere, one free from persistent memories.

After his day's work, he approached Rachel Miller. "Aunt, would you have an objection to me spending a few days with Philip and Madeline up at their cottage?"

Rachel appeared to be stifling a smile. "I believe a few days with the Helds might be beneficial to you, my nephew. Dennis and I can take care of things here for you."

He packed a small bag and headed up to the forge. He found Philip and asked, "I hope you don't mind the imposition, but I needed to see you."

Philip smiled broadly. "You must have been reading my sister's mind, Joseph. Just this morning she instructed me to invite you up here for a few days. For some reason, she believes you need to get away from that old house. A more welcome guest never crossed our threshold."

Madeline, acting with the hospitable observance of a hostess, prepared a meal for the three of them. After clearing the table, she lit the fire and arranged the two easy chairs facing the mantle-piece. "I believe I shall go to my room for the night, gentleman." She held up and patted a thick book. "Pray enjoy yourselves." She smiled at her brother, then at Joseph, and then she retired.

The two sat in the chairs Madeline had positioned, next to each other in the same manner as a married couple might sit.

"Now, Joseph," Philip began, "I'll answer 'Yes!' to the question in your mind."

Joseph faced his friend. "Are you and your sister both mind readers? How ever do you profess to know my thoughts?" Philip merely smiled. "You have been talking with Bishop?"

"No, but I won't mystify you. As I rode up the valley, I saw you two standing on the hill and could easily guess the rest. A large estate in this country is only an imaginary fortune. You are not so much of a farmer, Joseph Asten, that it will cut you to the heart and make you dream of ruin to part with a few fields." He winked at Joseph. "If you were, I should say get that weakness out of you at once! A man should *possess* his property, not be possessed by it."

Joseph nodded. "You are so right. I have been fighting against an inherited feeling."

"The only question is, will the sale of those fifty acres relieve you of all present embarrassments?"

"So far that a new mortgage of about half the amount will cover what remains."

"Bravo!" cried Philip. "This is better than I thought. Mr. Hopeton is looking for sure, steady investments and will furnish whatever you need so there is no danger of foreclosure."

"Things seem to shape themselves almost too easily now," Joseph mused. "I see the old, mechanical routine of my life coming back. It should be enough for me, but it is not." He looked into his friend's deep eyes. "Can you tell me why, Philip?"

Their intimate stare continued for a few moments. "Yes. It was never enough. The most of our neighbors are cases of arrested development. Their intellectual nature only takes so many marks—like a horse's teeth. There is a point early in their lives where its form becomes fixed. There is neither the external influence, nor the inward necessity, to drive them a step farther. They find the inquisitive Sphinx dangerous and keep out of her way. You can say that they all read and write, but I have observed a lack of either. Of course, as soon as they passively begin to accept *what is*, all that was fluent or plastic in them soon hardens into the old molds. Now, I am not very wise..." Joseph went to speak, but Philip held up his hand. "I am not very wise, but this appears to be the truth. Life is a grand centrifugal force, forever growing from a wider circle towards one that is still wider. Your stationary men may be necessary, and even serviceable, but to me–and to you, Joseph–there is neither joy nor peace except in some kind of perpetual growth."

Joseph looked away. "If we could be always sure of the direction!"

"That's the point!" Philip eagerly continued. "If we stop to consider danger in advance, we should never venture a step. A movement is always clear after it has been made, not often before. It is enough to test one's intention, unless we are tolerably bad, something guides us and adjusts the consequences of our acts. Why, we are like spiders in the midst of a million gossamer threads, which we are all the time spinning without knowing it!" He grinned at Joseph. "Who are to measure our lives for us? Not other men with other necessities! And so we come back to the same point again, where I started. Looking back now, can you see no gain in your mistake?"

"Yes, a gain I can never lose. I begin to think that haste and weakness also are vices and deserve to be punished. It was a dainty, vulnerable soul you found, Philip–a moral and spiritual Sybarite, I should say now. I must have expected to lie on rose-leaves, and it was right that I should find thorns."

"Perhaps the world needs a new code of ethics," Philip suggested. "We must cure the unfortunate tendencies of some qualities that seem good and extract the good from others that seem evil. But it would need more than a Luther for such a Reformation." He reached over took Joseph's hand. "I confess I am puzzled when I attempt to study moral causes and consequences in men's lives. It is nothing but a Gordian tangle when I take them collectively. What if each of us were, as I half suspect, as independent as a planet yet all held together in one immense system? Then the central force must be our close dependence on God, as I have learned to feel it through you." He glanced over at his beloved.

"Through me!" Joseph exclaimed.

"Do you suppose we can be so near each other without giving and taking? Let us not try to get upon a common ground of faith or action. It is a thousand times more delightful to discover that we now and then reach the same point by different paths." He smiled. "That reminds me, Joseph, I believe the time has come for you to travel a different path—so to speak—to see something of the world before settling yourself down. For once you plant your roots in this bountiful, fertile soil, you may never get the chance to extricate yourself from it again."

Joseph frowned and pulled his hand away. "You want me to depart from you? Have I said something to offend you? Have your feelings towards me changed all of a sudden? What has brought this unexpected turn?"

Philip stood and stepped between Joseph's legs. He reached down and hugged the man he loved so much followed by a lingering kiss. "I don't believe I said that you need travel alone."

"Ah. You want me to see more of the world before I decide upon the Allegheny Valley as my final resting place."

Philip chuckled. "I don't know if that is how *I* would put it into words... but I do get a sense that the two of us will be spending much more time together in the days ahead, and I believe that it might be best if you experience some other places first."

"I have been to the city... and I have seen the oil fields. What more do I need to see?"

Philip stepped back with an amused smile. "Oh, Joseph, Joseph, Joseph... Perhaps I could show you the valley I spoke of. I do believe you will find peace there that you might never achieve here."

Joseph nodded as he thought. The vision of Philip's valley had given him strength during some of his weaker moments when the Lord had tested him like Job. "That might be a good thing for me to see. When can we leave?"

"Are you in a hurry, now?" Philip asked as he sat once more.

"My work at the forge is nearly finished, and what has yet to be done could easily be taken over by your friend Elwood Withers. He has readily learned the craft faster than anyone I have ever worked with. I should probably return to my apartment in the city to retrieve a few items for the journey."

"And I could call upon the Blessings. I believe they might enjoy that."

"I believe you are right," Philip nodded. "However, tonight we are here–virtually by ourselves–with our hearts' mutual throb. Let us make the most of this precious, ephemeral time, my love."

•▼•

"We were in Europe as children," Madeline contributed over breakfast. "I have very clear and delightful memories of the travel."

"I am not sure I am ready for all of Europe, Madeline," Joseph responded. "Philip wishes me to experience some of the sights he saw in the western territories." He took Philip's hand. "And now, we have a question to ask of you?"

"*We*, is it now?" Madeline asked with a mirthful air.

"Well... me, actually, but it is a decision for all of us. I know that the lease on this cottage will end soon, and I wish to ask if you would mind moving to my farm to live there."

"What? And leave this little piece of paradise?" she joked.

"It is more serious than I make it, I am afraid." He glanced at Philip and then back at Madeline. "What I would ask of you is that you work with my Aunt Rachel to run the farm in our absence. We might be gone for a year or so."

"I see how you are, Joseph Asten. You think you two men can run off to your mountain pleasures and leave me behind to do all the chores with the spinster aunt. Two unmarried ladies. Do you think two such women are even capable to perform the work of one whole man?" One of her eyes glared at Joseph.

He balked, "Well... I... did not..."

Madeline broke up in laughter. "Joseph, do not worry yourself. I was making fun with you. I love your aunt, and I am honored that you would consider me worthy to manage your land in your absence." She smiled. "My only question would be: Can the two of you handle living under my supervision upon your return?"

The three of them burst out in guffaws.

When Joseph explained the situation to his aunt, she had little to say. "I cannot think of anyone more suited to assist me here in your absence, Joseph."

The next morning, Philip and Joseph took the train to the city. Philip went directly to his home while Joseph paid a call on the Blessings.

"Joseph, my boy! Do come in," Mr. Blessing greeted Joseph at the door. "Please sit with me in the parlor."

Upon entering the once-familiar room, Joseph noticed immediately new furniture, a new mantle-piece, a new piano, and new wallpaper.

"Yes, there are some changes here, and I was going to write to explain, but I have not yet had the time. Would you like something to extinguish your thirst?" Joseph shook his head. Mr. Blessing went to the bar and poured some dark fluid from a dark bottle. "Straight! Always straight!" He hoisted the glass, tipped it back and emptied all the liquid in one swallow. "First of all, let me impart a few heretofore, previously-unspoken sentiments of the missus and myself." He took his handkerchief and dabbed at his sweaty forehead. "You can probably understand how we initially blamed you for our daughter's death."

Joseph nodded, thinking how most people had assumed his own hand had delivered the fatal blow.

"Yes, well..." Mr. Blessing seemed to stumble for words. "When Mrs. Blessing discovered the true nature of the situation, and that she had played a part in the drama, well... my dear Eliza became inconsolable. We both agreed that you had done everything possible you could have to make our dear Julia happy—which was no easy task; how well I know!—and you should never have earned nor felt our distrust. I heartily apologize and humbly hope that you can see to forgive us."

It relieved Joseph to hear those words from his father-in-law. He nodded and smiled. "Thank you, sir."

Mr. Blessing poured himself another drink. "Do you remember asking us to spend a few days on your farm following the trial?"

"I do. You mentioned some secret affair."

"Yes. Secret indeed. Now I can spill all." He downed the dark liquid with alacrity. "Instead of returning to the city, I sent the missus home and I traveled on to the Oil Region to get a look at the old Amaranth myself. When I inquired after Mr. Kanuck, I was told he had taken the available remnant of funds and fled. Imagine my surprise!" Joseph shook his head in disbelief. "Although the merest gyro in geology, I used my incipient theory of fluid pressures to determine the approximate spot that might cause the neighboring wells to gush so mightily. I selected a spot back of the river-bluffs, in a hollow of the undulating table-land, sunk a shaft, and... success!" He threw his hands skyward like a gushing oil well. "They called it 'an inspired guess.' I telegraphed instantly a trusted business associate and succeeded in purchasing a moderate portion of the stock before its enriched value could become known. As for the result: *si monumentum quœris, circumspice!*"

"I am happy for you, sir. Your story is quite inspiring."

"But wait! I know that you risked everything you and Julia had... and more... putting your good name and the title of your farm at risk because of my poor judgment."

"All well and good, Mr. Blessing. I have forgiven the –"

"But I have not, dear boy!" his father-in-law interrupted. "I had planned to deliver this to you in person, but as you have saved me the trouble of dragging the mountain to Mohammed, as it were..." He stood and went to a locked cabinet, produced a key from his waistcoat and opened the door. From the darkness, he grabbed a satchel and handed it to Joseph. "Here! It is yours, and my conscience is clean!" He wiped his palms together in a gesture of conclusiveness.

Joseph opened the bag and looked inside. While he could not calculate the value immediately, he saw bundles of one-hundred-dollar bills. With the widest of eyes, he looked up with thousands of interrogatory marks.

Mr. Blessing laughed and smiled. "It is the funds you lost due to my incompetence, the cost of the renovations and furnishings my daughter forced upon you, plus twenty-five thousand dollars of good will. I would say you made a pretty respectable return on your dodgy speculative investment!"

He had never hugged his father-in-law before, but that seemed like a good moment to do so.

From the Blessings, Joseph walked to Philip's apartment whistling airs, swinging the satchel, and smiling. Even though he could have taken a carriage, he wanted to spend time in the outdoors, even with all the unpleasant smells and sounds of the city.

"How was your visit with the Blessings?" Philip asked.

Joseph could not conceal his joy. "I have something to show you." He set the satchel down and opened it for Philip to see.

"Did you rob a bank just now, Mr. Asten?" Philip's eyes bulged in disbelief at the contents of the satchel.

"No, Mr. Held," Philip chuckled. "My dear father-in-law somehow turned his sour oil deal into a gold mine single-handedly. Fortunately, I caught him in his magnanimous condition, and he returned to me all the money I had lost in the Amaranth, plus quite a bit more. I would say that you and

I shall be travelling in style!"

Joseph treated Philip to a sumptuous dinner at a top-drawer restaurant near to the apartment. Over the meal, they discussed how best to use the unexpected money. At the very least it would allow them to take luxury accommodations on their upcoming travels.

That night, they enjoyed each other's company until well after midnight, even though they had to rise early to catch the train to Oakland Station in the morning.

This time, the train performed as promised, with no life-threatening, catastrophic wrecks. However, their progress slowed when a freight-carrying train ahead of them got caught at a switch. The sky had begun to darken by the time they reached the station.

As they rode back to the farm in a hired carriage, the moon hung over the landscape, edging the summits of the trees below them with sparkling silver. The air felt still, sweet, and warm. They smiled at the beauty of the land and the promise of better days ahead.

Over dinner with Aunt Rachel and Madeline, the two men discussed their plans for travel and after their return.

"It seems to me the best arrangement would be for Philip and me to take the upstairs room, after a bit of remodeling, of course. Aunt Rachel, you have your room, and Madeline… well, I believe you have two choices: You can remain in the guest room and fashion it to your wishes, or we can build you a new room. Either way, there shall be some construction."

"I will think upon your offer, Mr. Joseph," Madeline responded. "Your aunt will be educating me upon the finer points of running a farmhouse, and by the time you two return, I am certain I will have arrived at a decision."

Joseph reached into his pocket and retrieved a bank note. "Here, Aunt Rachel. I want you to take this to Magnolia and get yourself—and Madeline here—some new outfits." He handed her the money.

"Oh, my goodness," Rachel hooted. "A real 'C' note, with two big Cs! I have never held such a thing in my life!" She handed the bill to Madeline who smiled and nodded. "We shall travel to Magnolia at our very first opportunity! I know just the shop."

The sound of an approaching carriage halted the conversation. "Put that away for now, Aunt Rachel," Joseph cautioned. "We do not know who that might be."

"Joseph! Joseph!" called Elwood's voice. Joseph ran to the front door and found three unannounced callers: Elwood Withers, Miss Lucy Henderson, and Miss Elizabeth Henderson.

"Well, do come in. How nice to see the three of you. Philip and I have some news to share." He ushered them into the dining-room and found seats for them.

"And we have news, too! And great, great news!" Elwood gushed. "Miss Elizabeth Henderson here has agreed to my proposal of marriage!" He bent over and kissed her forehead.

The assembled guests expressed their joy and gave hugs and kisses all around.

"But what about Lucy?" Aunt Rachel asked.

"Oh, I will live with the Hopetons," she looked at Joseph. "When I am not teaching at the school, I will provide light housekeeping services for them."

"I believe we need to host a grand gathering of our neighbors and friends to announce all the good news!" Joseph stood stretching his arms wide. "We must invite everyone we know: The Hopetons"–he winked at Lucy–"the Warriners, the Hendersons, Elwood's family, the Frosts, the Bishops, the Penns, everyone! Including the Reverend Mr. Chaffinch and his daughter."

"And what about you and Philip?" Elwood queried. "You said you had some news to share with us."

"Yes, yes." Joseph muttered as he sat. "Philip and I are going to travel to the western territories. He once served as a geological scientist, and he wants me to see the beautiful, open country."

"As beautiful as what the Good Lord has divined upon our Allegheny River Valley?" Rachel Miller asked.

"Miss Rachel"–Philip addressed the question–"you cannot believe what lies to the west of our civilized world here. There are such wonders–valleys, canyons, mountains, lakes, rivers–in unending abundance. I will agree that the charm of this particular area"–he waved his arms about–"is perchance some of the most loveliest greenery I have ever seen. However, your nephew must have something to compare it with. When we return, he and I might never want to leave this farm again, but at least he will know why."

Rachel poured tea, enough for everyone present. "A toast, my friends"–she raised her glass–"first, to the happy couples"–she looked at Elwood and Elizabeth, then Philip and Joseph–"and the unmarried ladies," she nodded at Lucy, and finally Madeline. "May they find the happiness they seek wherever they happen to be on God's good earth!"

THE END

WAYNE GOODMAN has lived in the San Francisco Bay Area most of his life (with too many cats). When not writing, he enjoys playing Gilded Age parlor music on the piano, with an emphasis on women, gay, and Black composers.

Other Books by
Wayne Goodman

The Last Great Hope

A retired Secret Service agent, with a secret of his own, is called up for one last mission: find the long-lost child of John and Jacqueline Kennedy, whom he adopted out unknowingly under orders of his power-hungry boss.

Britain's Glory:
Charlotte, the People's Princess

Princess Charlotte was the daughter, and only child, of Princess Caroline of Brunswick and Prince George of Wales, eldest son of King George III. Destined to be Queen of Great Britain, her storybook life ended too soon, leading to a scramble for another, suitable, royal heir to take the throne.

The Seed of Immortality
Mahjong at Changshou Shan

A peasant on his deathbed is given immortality by a less-than-trustworthy Mahjong sharp. They travel around China, learn its secrets, and even meet with the first Emperor of China in his mysterious subterranean palace, complete with rivers of mercury.

Vanya Says, "Go!"
A Retelling of Mikhail Kuzmin's *Wings*

Wings was the first Russian-language novel to deal with same-sex relationships in a positive way. *Vanya Says, "Go!"* presents the story in a modern, more open way with an additional chapter.

Praise for *Better Angels*:

"A lovely story, sumptuous in language and ideas with a rich ambience. For people who love a love story, it is thoroughly rewarding."

—**VINCENT MEIS**, author of *Deluge*

"Goodman has turned the pallid prose of travel writer Bayard Taylor into a scintillating trip through 19th Century America. Those who loved James Baldwin's *Another Country* and *Giovanni's Room* will find something of value in Goodman's latest triumph."

—**KEVIN KILLIAN**, author of *Tony Greene Era*

"*Better Angels* is a great read and a wonderful glimpse into a story of the 19th Century that has rarely been told. It writes queerness back into literary history, with an anti-racist spin."

—**DR. AJUAN MANCE**, author of *Before Harlem*

"A remarkable literary feat of resurrecting the first American gay novel. With meticulous prose and clever dialogue, Goodman offers a fascinating glimpse into love between American men in the 19th Century."

—**ELIZEYA QUATE**, author of *Face of Our Town*

"*Better Angels* takes another obscure, early Gay novel and brings it back to life, updating language, amplifying the story, and presenting love between men and men, and women and women more directly than it could have been presented when the book was first published. Goodman performs a historical service, giving readers a glimpse of Gay life lived 150 years ago."

—**RICHARD MAY**, author of *Inhuman Beings*